RICK LEE

THE
LIES
WILL
HAUNT US

authorHOUSE®

AuthorHouse™ UK
1663 Liberty Drive
Bloomington, IN 47403 USA
www.authorhouse.co.uk
Phone: UK TFN: 0800 0148641 (Toll Free inside the UK)
       UK Local: 02036 956322 (+44 20 3695 6322 from outside the UK)

Published by AuthorHouse 10/21/2020

ISBN: 978-1-6655-8080-9 (sc)
ISBN: 978-1-6655-8081-6 (hc)
ISBN: 978-1-6655-8079-3 (e)

For Audrey

ACKNOWLEDGEMENTS

Thanks once again to my readers
Shura Price, Bruce Paterson and Nadine Venn.

In a time when it was difficult to make things up,
this sequence of initially unconnected
events may feel not so far-fetched.

Richard

JOHN OF GAUNT

This royal throne of kings, this sceptred isle,
…
Is now leased out, I die pronouncing it,
Like to a tenement or pelting farm:
England, bound in with the triumphant sea
Whose rocky shore beats back the envious siege
Of watery Neptune, is now bound in with shame,
With inky blots and rotten parchment bonds:
That England, that was wont to conquer others,
Hath made a shameful conquest of itself.

—William Shakespeare
Richard II, Act II, Scene i

'The essential English leadership secret does not depend on particular intelligence. Rather, it depends on a remarkably stupid thick-headedness. The English follow the principle that when one lies, **one should lie big**, and stick to it. They keep up their lies, even at the risk of looking ridiculous.'

Joseph Goebbels 12th January 1941

JANUARY
2020

CHAPTER 1

Ex-DI Mick Fletcher hates funerals.

It isn't long since he had to go to Irene Garner's and he still hasn't forgiven anyone, particularly Laura, for not telling him she was ill, even if he knew it would have been hard for him to deal with it. He still found it difficult to come to terms with the idea that she would even get ill, let alone die. She'd always been so strong and full of life. He still couldn't bring himself to delete her number from his phone.

He and Laura had come to a silent agreement not to mention it, which he knew they both hated, but now she'd been diagnosed herself he suspects they'll never ever mention it again.

And how could that happen, his closest colleague dead and now his lover losing her marbles? He forgets all sorts of things, but she now has a dreaded black hole slowly dissolving her brain.

He'd been horrified by the scan, which literally showed the blank space where her short-term memory used to be. Now he has to grit his teeth and tell her every five minutes where they are going or what day it is or where so-and-so is. Fortunately Grace takes her off now and again, but then he misses her and worries all the time while she's away.

Grace has also finally convinced him that he should take her with him to the funeral, because she will know people there who she hasn't seen for some time.

Anthony Adversane is someone else he couldn't imagine ever dying, but here they are south of London driving to his funeral.

'Where are we going?' asks Laura for the umpteenth time.

'To Adversane's funeral,' he repeats, trying not to shout.

'Who's he?'

'Good question,' thinks Fletcher. 'Who knows?'

'I don't think you met him very often,' he says. 'He was one of those mysterious people who work in the shadows. Top secret. Nobody really knew who he was working for.'

Laura looks out of the window.

'Will Grace be there?'

'Yes, and Ellie as well, I think.'

'Who's Ellie?'

'Number one granddaughter. You remember her?'

She looks at him.

'Do I?'

He nods and puts his foot down.

Parking is hopeless.

He ends up calling Grace and getting her to collect Laura near the church gates before going off to find somewhere to park.

This means he has to walk miles to get back. He gets lost and finally arrives after most people have gone in, leaving him to apologise to the whole bloody crowd while getting to the front where Grace is, with all the other police connections. Which, one has to say, is a small group of poor church mice.

When he eventually looks around, he can tell most of the rest of the congregation are wearing clothes he wouldn't wear and could never have afforded.

'The Surrey great and good, no doubt,' he whispers to Grace.

'West Sussex,' she murmurs, 'meaning really old Catholic posh.'

'Oh, pardon me,' he whispers back.

'No, really. We're talking the Percys.'

'Who they?'

She grins.

'The castle behind the church.'

'Ah, I see,' he says, recalling a glimpse of a huge facade.

'The Wyndhams still live there in the south wing,' she adds.

He looks at her.

'She's genuinely nice. Went to school with Louisa.'

Fletcher rolls his eyes.

'Of course she did. And where is the old witch?'

'Front row,' nods Grace, indicating a black-laced head leaning forward to the man next to her.

'Oops. Should have realised,' he whispers.

At that moment the organ begins to wheeze, and so Fletcher keeps his head down and his eyes averted for the duration.

Afterwards the inevitable meeting occurs.

Grace and Ellie have taken Laura off to wander round the gravestones when a hand links through his arm. He turns to meet the stern blue gaze.

Louisa Cunninghame never seems to age. Lauren Bacall blonde without any wrinkles. Possibly the figure is slimmer, the hand is cool, but the eyes still shine with that penetrating knowingness, which he still finds unsettling.

'Michael,' she says. The tone, as always, manages to be both patronising and alluring.

He gives her the slight peck on the cheek, which he knows is a rarely awarded permission. It has taken him half a lifetime to achieve such an honour.

'How is Laura?'

This is a question he is tired of being asked, but he knows this one is genuine.

He sighs.

'Good days and bad,' he answers, with a shrug.

'Walk with me,' she says.

They go out into the sunshine. He can't remember ever going to a funeral when it rained.

Outside people are talking in twos and threes, although many of them are heading to their cars, no doubt looking forward to the 'baked meats'.

He is surprised to find that he can talk about it, as there aren't many people he finds that easy to do with, especially as their awkwardness is more than he can bear.

Louisa listens and he ends up crying.

She holds him close, her signature perfume filling his head.

Later her car arrives, and they go to the wake.

As he expected, it is a grand affair in a huge hotel. He recognises quite a few of the people: politicians, and business grandees. Mostly people heavily embroiled in the nasty goings-on at Westminster … or not going on there at all. What else should he have expected?

He can't see Laura, so assumes Grace has taken her somewhere more pleasant.

Louisa is soon taken away and he feels abandoned, so he takes out his phone and is about to call Grace when another person's arm links into his.

He turns to find he's been storked. DCI, retired, Violet Constance Cranthorne, aka the Stork, is giving him her serious face. She has a thin face on a thin body, and is given to unnerving stillness in meetings and other situations.

'I'm so sorry, Michael,' she says.

He still hasn't managed to deal with this, so he does his usual shrug and mumbles some words that he hopes sound positive.

She lets him say his bit and then smiles, saying,

'I can't imagine how you manage. I'd be hopeless.'

Again, he shrugs.

'"Love conquers all" might sound a bit trite,' she adds, 'but I can't think of anything else that might sustain you.'

He nods. She is right.

She indicates the church doorway and they walk back into the cool interior.

4

He knows then that being asked to break his promise is something he has been dreading.

Violet checks that they won't be overheard.

'I promise this is all I'm going to ask of you.'

He frowns. He can't imagine that someone, even her, would ask for his involvement in anything at all in the current febrile climate.

She puts a finger to her lips.

'Just listen,' she says, her eyes searching his.

He frowns.

'I can't...' he begins.

Again, she holds his hand.

'Five minutes?'

He sighs and gives her the slightest of nods.

She takes a deep breath.

'A month ago, I went to see Anthony... He was drugged up to his eyeballs, but he'd sent a message that he had something to tell me.'

Again, she looks round.

'It was brief. He only opened his eyes for a few seconds at a time. I imagine he was in terrible pain.'

Despite himself, Fletcher is intrigued. For a man like Anthony Adversane to share any knowledge was unheard of. You were lucky if he gave you a cryptic clue.

'Have you heard of Cambridge Analytica ... AIQ?'

Fletcher knows that they were something to do with rigging the referendum, and were the same gang playing in different shirts at work in the election, but beyond that...

He shrugs.

'They're supposed to be defunct, no longer operating,' she says, 'but, of course, the reasons for their existence haven't gone away. It's become more open ... and yet also even more deeply hidden.'

He can't imagine how he can help. Flickering about behind

a bank of screens sounds more like his son Christian's line of work,.

He waits. She stares into his eyes.

'Bottom line?'

He flinches.

'You can do this at home. I can fix it all up. I value your gut instincts. Your nose.'

He stares at her.

'What?'

She storks: looks carefully left and right.

'I'm assembling a team. People you know, mostly. We don't have much time. A young woman's life is at risk. We're surrounded by bright-eyed vultures. We're trying to ameliorate the worst events that are going to happen in our lifetime.'

He waits. He'd given up on the whole thing months ago. There is nothing he can do. He hates politics. Part of him thinks that people should suffer the consequences of their gullibility. Civil war seems the likely outcome.

He waits.

'All I'm going to do is ask you occasionally what you think we should do, who you think is lying, where we should go, what questions we should ask.'

She looks away. She is shaking.

'What exactly did Adversane say?'

She jerks back at him.

'You see, that's what you're like. Straight to the heart of the matter.'

'Seems obvious to me,' he thinks.

He waits.

She comes close.

'He didn't "say" anything. He had throat cancer. He communicated via text.'

Fletcher thinks how rubbish he would be at that.

She produces a phone, presses a few buttons, and shows him a screen.

At first it doesn't make much sense, until he realises he is looking at a maze. In the centre is a symbol, a circle with two horns, and around the top edge are three words: *filum scissa est*, and, along the bottom, *hoc isle valida fulcis*.

He looks at her.

'Literally, is says, "the thread is torn", but more likely, and yet surprisingly, given Anthony's distaste for any music composed after Elgar, it's a quote from Leonard Cohen's song "Dance me to the end of love.": "every thread is torn."'

Now he nearly laughs. What a devious, awkward old bugger Adversane was. What the hell is he on about?

'And the rest?'

'This sceptred isle.'

He frowns. His old English teacher's smile pins him to his chair.

'John of Gaunt?'

She nods and smiles at him.

'I know. Typical of him, I'm afraid.'

'So what does it all mean?'

She hesitates.

'OK,' he says, despite the voice telling him to step back from the edge. 'Thread, maze, bull ... must be Theseus and the Minotaur.'

Her smile becomes bigger.

'I think he's got it.' She nearly giggles at the ridiculousness of it all. They are at a funeral, for heaven's sake.

'No, I haven't,' he says. 'Who is Theseus? Where is the maze? Who is the minotaur?'

He pauses and looks at Violet's face with a questioning raised eyebrow. Then nods.

'Who is Ariadne? Where's the string?' he murmurs with a frown.

She shakes her head.

'Not sure. There are various evil, self-seeking bastards everywhere. But here's the clincher. He often used to say,

7

"Puzzles are distractions. Look for who wants you to be distracted … and we have a few leads."'

He looks at it again, closes his eyes and breathes out the words long-lost till now.

'… is now bound in with shame,

With inky blots and rotten parchment bonds.'

Her eyes widen.

'My, my,' she whispers.

He shakes his head.

'Can't remember much more, but I know what the whole speech means … and how appropriate it is today.'

She sighs.

He stares at her. His eyes are full of that questioning intelligence.

'So,' he breathes. 'Bushy, Bagot and Green.'

Again she can't offer more than a shrug of uncertainty.

Fletcher looks away, turns and walks towards the door. Holding her breath, she watches him go.

He disappears.

She waits.

Two minutes.

'Oh well, I don't blame you,' she says under her breath and walks to the doorway.

She looks out at the trees. The sun is glaring off the car windscreens. There is no one in sight. She shrugs her shoulders and takes out her phone to call Calum.

'Who else have you got?' says a voice.

***

Janet Becket is no longer a police officer.

She is more than happy with this new situation after everything that has happened. No longer she have to work the ridiculous overtime, nor does she have to pretend to be a security guard or deal with testosterone-heavy lightweight-brained Geordies. Life is good.

Or so it was until a week ago.

Now she's staring out of the window.

Mountains. In every direction. The theory is that no one can get anywhere near you without you seeing them at least two miles away.

She'd pointed out that helicopters, drones and planes can fly.

'Not without us knowing,' said the men in suits.

'So why me?' she asked.

They didn't even smirk, merely stared at her.

Eventually the old guy in the corner who'd not said anything so far shifted in his seat. He didn't look in her direction.

'Because you're real difficult to kill.'

'Yeah, he said that... Bastard.'

'Who says?' he said. Then he turned to look at her.

One of his eyes was white, dead.

'Quite a few people, although there are many others who can't say anything any longer.'

She glared at him, a kaleidoscope running in her head. Bodies falling, crumpling. The same ones she saw every night, unless she drank or doped herself to sleep.

She folded her arms.

'How much did you say?'

'Twenty thousand.'

She leant forward.

'Double it,' she whispered.

None of them as much as blinked.

Now she wishes she'd asked for the boredom excess.

She shifts in the office wheelie chair to consider the western peaks.

She'd climbed some of them, way back before she made the

biggest mistake of her life. If only she'd stuck to climbing. Now she might be coining it as a lead instructor, like her friend Chaz.

She's even considered pretending she or the Geekess were ill. She would get the helicopter to land, take out the crew and disappear over the Minch, never to be seen again.

This would have been possible, except the bastards know she is capable of this and made damn certain they didn't touch down.

Speaking of her charge, she hasn't heard her moving about for a bit.

It's impossible to get off the chair without it squeaking. She saunters to the doorway into the study.

No change, as usual.

A shaved dark ginger head is in front of the screen. Her fingers are only still for a second before fluttering across the tiles.

She doesn't turn round.

Becket walks over and looks at her screen, which is a mosaic of different-sized rectangles of text and images.

Impossible.

How can anyone look at that all day?

'Cup of tea, madam?' she asks.

Slight stiffening in the neck.

'Fine,' comes the response.

'Fine,' thinks Becket. Nothing was fine at all... It was incredibly boring.

'Chocolate biscuit, pint of brandy, cyanide cocktail?'

'Whatever.'

Becket sighs and saunters through the room and into the kitchen.

Is this really worth it? No, she isn't going to go through her spending list again. If she's honest, she doesn't really think they'll stick to their side of the bargain anyway.

She's not been told more than she needs to know, except that there are a lot of people, worried and determined people, who are trying their damnedest to find this woman.

The kettle boils.

Back in the room she puts the mug on the desk, but then goes over to the window at the other side of the desk and surveys the view.

'Do you know where we are?' she asks.

The tapping pauses for a few seconds.

'Roughly ... north-west Scotland, six miles to the nearest habitation, so someone said.'

Becket turns to look at her.

'Not your usual habitat?'

The fingers flutter to a stop.

'Obviously not ... but I assume you're comfortable with it.'

'Climbing was my first love... Now I'm thinking I should have stuck at it. Falling off crags is less dangerous than this ... and a damn sight more exciting.'

The woman reaches out for her tea and leans back in the chair.

The air between them simmers.

'This is not my idea, I can assure you,' she says.

Becket shrugs.

'Mine neither. In fact I suggested you'd be better off in a busy city.'

'And you don't know why they want me hidden away?'

'Nope. And I couldn't care, unless it would help me keep us both alive.'

There is a long silence. The woman looks past her at the mountains. She takes a sip of the tea.

Eventually she puts her hand up to feel her shaven head.

'You don't even know my name.'

Becket stares at her. She doesn't.

And that's fine.

A raven lands on a rock about twenty feet away.

'What about her?'

Becket looks at the bird.

'Why do you think it's a she?'

She shrugs.

'How about Freya?'

'Not your real name?'

She gives a shy smile.

'Doesn't matter, does it?'

Becket turns away. This is pissing her off.

She hears the chair shifting and turns back in time to see 'Freya' heading for the door.

She doesn't look back.

Becket lets her go. She'll hear any door or window if she tries to go out. And, in any case, they're all locked, the keys are in her pocket, and she'd be still in view for hundreds of yards.

She steps over to the laptop. There's only a screen saver. A photograph of the mountains outside the window, which is surprisingly eerie. Why do that?

She reaches out and touches a key and almost has a heart attack. The screen explodes into a huge black bird flying at her. Its beak opens wide and the sound of its rage makes her clap her hands to her ears. She staggers back but sees that the screen is completely filled by the raven's eyes, cruelly glaring at her. There is another fearsome croak before the screen fades to black.

Bloody woman.

***

The mobile that Violet has given Fletcher squirks.

He fumbles it into an upright position and presses what he hopes is the right button. The screen goes dark, and then, thankfully, it clears to reveal a message.

Even if she hadn't been using textspeak, Violet would have been as brief.

Wednesday, 9 30. Helton Arms.

Fletcher finds his own mobile and contacts Grace.

She can do it. He is worried that she doesn't question him about it. He's told her nothing, except it's too secret to even hint at anything... But she isn't stupid. She knows that the meeting at the funeral hadn't been a coincidence, and he detected a certain amount of relief that she could look after her mother for a while. He knows she's seen him lose it a couple of times but doesn't dare criticise him. No, not dare. Maybe she understands how difficult it is.

Violet still hasn't given him any clues about who else will be there, but he is pretty certain that Calum McNeil will be at her shoulder. It won't be old George Humberstone, because he passed away months ago.

'It's only funerals nowadays,' he mutters to himself.

'What's that?'

He looks up to see Laura in the doorway. She's wearing three tops again, but the rest of what she is wearing is fine.

'Cup of tea?' he asks.

She follows him into the kitchen.

'Are you going somewhere?' she says.

He puts the kettle under the tap and turns it on.

'No. I think Grace wants you to go round next Wednesday.'

'Why?'

'Does she need a reason? She's your daughter.'

Laura looks at him suspiciously.

'So what will you be doing?'

He shrugs.

'Nothing much.'

He doesn't want another row. It is difficult. It's his own fault. He's not been the most faithful of partners ... with her or anyone else. He wishes Irene were still alive. Maybe he'll go and have a talk with her. The Helton Arms is only a few miles from Haweswater, where he scattered her ashes. It would do him good to get out in the fresh air.

Laura gives him one last stare and sits down in front of the television.

He finds the tennis repeats and brings her some tea and a biscuit.

Upstairs he stares out of the window. It's the endless hopelessness of it that gets to him. Tears have never come easy for him, but they do now.

A few minutes later he finds himself sitting on the bed.

'Pull yourself together,' he growls.

As he looks out of the window he recalls the last time he saw Irene. They were at the Snow White Killer's burial ground. She'd been cross with herself because she'd assumed there was nothing there any longer. And then there were the most recent burials … men, instead of women … not their bodies but the trophies.

She must have been ill already, maybe feeling a bit under the weather, unaware of what was to come. He still couldn't believe how quickly she succumbed, how someone so full of life could fade away in a few weeks.

'Better than what Laura's going through,' he says out loud.

Later, as she lies snoring quietly beside him, he ponders again whether he should get involved in this latest trouble.

He is tired of all the lies and ridiculous charades.

Unless, of course, Adversane was on to something.

He's never known anyone as close to real power as him and yet he has never been sure whose side he was on. Certainly not the plebs, but he knows he'd been his protector more than once, if not visibly.

He turns off the reading lamp. He's not read a word.

Soon he is asleep.

And too far gone to hear the engine growl into life across the road and the car quietly creeping down the lane and away.

FEBRUARY

CHAPTER 2

Twenty-four colour photographs, although the last six are blurred, unclear, are arranged on the whiteboard.

The first sixteen all feature the same woman in a green dress with red hair, sometimes with other people in the background. One is of her and a man. He is turned towards her, his hat shadowing his face. Holiday snaps? Somewhere abroad? Cafes, a big church, street views and distant shots of the countryside. Another is of her standing at a balustrade staring into the distance. One is of her and the man, who is looking away to his right.

But then the last two are different. The woman is tied to a chair. She's sagging forwards with her hair covering her face. In the last one she's on the floor with her hand over her face. Is that blood creeping through her fingers?

I look at Ziggy. His eyes are bright. Is that curiosity, or something he's taken?

The man in front of us is waiting. Not impatiently, more like nervously. Keeps looking towards the door. He's not the man in the photographs.

We both look at him.

I guess you'd call him one those anonymous people who isn't easy to describe. Neither tall not short. Late forties, probably. Sad, lined face, pale blue eyes, thin hair cut short. He's wearing a grey outdoor jacket, jeans and trainers. In the street you'd forget him before he reached the next turning, even if you'd noticed him at all in the first place.

'They came in the post a week ago.'

He produces a not very clean handkerchief from his trouser pocket and blows his nose. I have to tell my impatient self not to urge him to,

'Pull yourself together, man.'

Ziggy is intrigued, and is still looking at the photos with a frown on his face.

He looks away towards the window.

We wait. I risk a glance at Ziggy. His eyes might be bright, but his face is still. Frozen. Attentive.

The man clears his throat.

Again, Ziggy gives him a slight smile and nods. I'm trying hard not to give him a good shake.

'So this woman is your wife?'

'Yes, but I didn't take them.'

Ziggy nods slowly.

'So...'

The man shakes his head.

'I've no idea,' he says. 'She disappeared last October.'

I stare at him.

He shrugs, blows his nose again.

'I don't know who the man is or where they were taken, although I'm guessing abroad. She's wearing clothes I never saw her wear before … and she's smiling…'

He stops and looks down at his hands then gets up and walks to the window, where he stands to one side to look out.

Ziggy gets up and crosses to one of the mirrored sliding cabinets built into the wall, and returns with a rectangular magnifying glass.

He places it above one of the photographs and studies it through the lens.

'France, I think,' he says. 'There's a menu in French on this wall.'

He offers it to me, but I don't know why. He knows I don't speak French, but I recognise plat du jour.

'Aha,' he grins, 'Limoges. La gare. And I think that's the cathedral,' he adds, holding it up to show the man, who, like me, looks at it mystified.

But then he isolates three of the photos and frowns.

All I can see is the woman sitting in a bar in and the other two she's standing outside a huge building. A chateau?

The man comes back from the window and studies the other photos.

'So Limoges is in France?' he asks.

'Yes. Bang in the middle,' says Ziggy, switching to his laptop.

His fingers patter away and then he's showing us a whole array of photos, swishing through them until he finds an image, which he compares with the man's photos. He's spot on. It's definitely the place, with a huge cathedral.

He goes back to the remaining pictures and taps each one.

'I think they were all taken on the same day and so I imagine the last two are from there as well, although the light's different in these three. Might not be in the same place, but still in France.'

The man looks puzzled.

'She never talked about going to France.'

Ziggy looks at him.

'What's puzzling me is why you've only received them now.'

Again, the man's face is blank. He shakes his head.

The three of us are silent. This is surprising for Ziggy, as he carefully straightens the images again, but not for me, because I can't think of how we can help, and the man is perhaps beginning to think the same.

He is about to ask something when Ziggy stands up.

'We could track the route they took,' he says. 'As I said, I'm fairly certain that all the outdoor ones are the same day. The light's the same…' He mutters to himself and starts fingering his phone.

'When do you think this film was taken?'

The man is startled.

'Er… Well … I've no idea.'

I point out that the leaves are autumnal. Ziggy gives me

a pout and a raised eyebrow. Am I thinking I'm the detective now? I make a face. He hasn't said anything about the trees, but he ignores it.

'So we can check her passport and—'

The man shakes his head.

'She didn't have one. Neither do I.'

Ziggy frowns.

'She must have had. She wouldn't have got there without one, would she?'

The man stares at him.

It's only now I realise, as I came in after he arrived, that I don't even know his name, so I ask him.

He looks at me with his red-rimmed eyes.

'Jimmy Sparrow,' he says, and then looks away.

Ziggy and I exchange glances. Really? He's not a pirate, is he?

***

I've only got two or three photographs of my younger self.

My 'mother' was a strict chapelgoer who thought photographs were 'an affront to God', and 'an indication of inappropriate self-regard'. It turned out that she wasn't my real mother, although that wasn't such a terrible revelation.

So the few photos I do have are those terrible school prints, which seemed to be designed to make everyone look like gawky fledglings forced to wear someone else's hair. Nowadays kids seem to do this to themselves on their phones, so it's maybe true that we are all gawks when we're growing up.

As a gawk, I thought I was Rachel Henderson, but it turned out my real name is Ursula White. My mother Fern is – or was – a Robinson … and she is suspected of killing at least five women and three men. She was known as the Snow White Killer.

I know…

It's possible I saw her briefly at the top of a burning tower, but the police and other people seem reluctant to accept she is definitely dead, as she seems to have had a charmed life. She'd be nearly eighty now, but they're still looking.

I found all this out by going to a private detective, who, unbelievably, I now work with … or for?

Ziggy Hook is a strange 'man' half my age, who took us a on a bizarre trip trying to find her, my mother, which ended with us arriving at this broch, an old tower in the west of Scotland, just in time to see it burst into flames. Inside the other building nearby there were three, maybe four, dead bodies and some survivors, including two police officers, Fletcher and Becket.

I shouldn't be telling you this, because we were all whisked away by a group of hard-faced military-looking men and other men in suits who told us to forget everything we'd seen … and who came back later to insist we sign some official secrets documents.

Until then my life had been fairly humdrum, so even now I am still coming to terms with the revelation that I was adopted and my real mother was this lifelong serial killer, which was a bit of a shock for a Chorley girl brought up in a Methodist gulag.

And now I'm girl Friday to this bisexual weirdo called Sigismund Hook, who makes money in ways I don't understand, who plays keyboard in a band who make loud music I don't recognise and who occasionally operates as a private detective.

Sparrow is back at the window.

I look at Ziggy, but he's filling his screen with hundreds of overlapping pages and images.

'Have you told the police?' I ask, trying to bring some realism into this stand-off.

Sparrow sighs and turns to look at me with what might have been a wry smile if he could have managed it.

'You're joking, aren't you?' he says. 'They're convinced I've done away with her.'

I point to the photos.

He shakes his head and gestures through the window.

'There's probably someone out there waiting till I come out, and then they'll be up here in a flash, turning your stuff upside down and inside out.'

I glance round the empty space that Ziggy says he has to have. There are four walls, one of which is a whiteboard covered with graffiti. One is a huge screen, which is switched off at the moment. One is currently an enormous picture of the Northern Lights over the Arctic ice cap. And the other is all windows and doors, of which only two of each are real. The table and the chair are only there on my insistence because I can't work sitting on the floor or walking about like Ziggy does.

'Good luck with that,' I think.

Ziggy tuts and then looks at Sparrow.

'Do you want to come with us?'

Sparrow glances at me.

'To Limoges?' he asks.

Ziggy nods.

'But … I still haven't got a passport.'

'Not a problem,' says Ziggy.

Sparrow looks at me. I shrug my shoulders. I'm used to Ziggy thinking and doing things that most people would regard as problematic or downright impossible.

'OK,' says the man, looking back towards the window, 'but they follow me wherever I go.'

Ziggy laughs and shakes his head.

'Not if I make you disappear, they won't.'

Again, the poor man looks to me for reassurance. All can do is shake my head and make a face that I hope says,

'Go with the flow.' I can't say I've become comfortable with Ziggy's 'Hook or by crook' approach, but it's worked so far.

Sparrow looks like those poor sods on that advert with

that American actor, whose name I can't remember, assuring random people they'll be perfectly all right if they're signed up for his insurance company.

'OK,' he says doubtfully, like the people in the advert.

'Right,' says Ziggy. 'Go and stand against that wall.'

He points at the blank screen.

Sparrow hesitantly walks over. Ziggy goes after him and, after adjusting his collar and getting him to put up his chin, takes a few photos of his face with his phone.

The poor man looks at me.

Again I shrug my shoulders.

'Yes,' I think, 'that does mean that this weird guy is going to manufacture a false passport for you. And yes, that's an offence punishable by being sent to prison.'

I don't say this out loud, but I've come to accept that for Ziggy anything is possible, legal or not. He whizzes off a few messages while nodding in the direction of the coffee machine.

Sparrow and I wait until the messaging is all done and then all three of us stand, mugs in hand, until Ziggy's face breaks out into his most mischievous grin.

'And for my next trick, we'll now all disappear... Shazam!'

Before either of us can question or doubt this, we can hear sirens wailing in the distance. More than one. Ziggy puts his mug on the desk and nods towards a door, which I thought was false. We obediently follow. I manage to pluck my bag from the chair and we set off downstairs.

We go down a spiral staircase to the cellar and through a door in the back of an innocent-looking cupboard. Yes, really. Ziggy comes last and, after closing the door behind him, presses some buttons on the wall. This instantly produces a heavy slithering noise, followed by a sullen clunk.

'Steel plate now,' he grunts, and sets off though a tunnel that could be straight out of Harry Potter.

We follow.

The sirens are at first increasingly loud, but soon we're out of earshot and following a warren of tunnels. We eventually exit through a door in another cellar and walk upstairs and out on to a street.

In a taxi Ziggy expands at length about the underground mazes that burrow underneath virtually all European cities, he says.

Later we're in a hotel room waiting for the 'passport woman', who turns out to be someone's East European granny, who Ziggy communicates with in Czech, he tells us.

Unbelievably, by the next morning we're on the train heading south. Ziggy is fast asleep on the floor, while Sparrow and I try to practise our French as instructed, although both of us know we're too old for that.

We agree to give up, and instead I regale him with my recent adventures as a serial killer's daughter. And he reluctantly tells me of the four months of suspicion and isolation he's survived as a suspected wife-murderer.

*** *

Fletcher is early.

The pub looks closed. There are no cars in the car park.

He parks and strolls over to the door. It is open, but the bar is empty. No one is in sight. He leans on the counter and calls out.

He hears a bit of scuffle, a girlish giggle, and a grunt.

A young woman appears, blushing and straightening her blouse.

Fletcher suppresses a laugh. He is jealous of this after all.

'What can I get you?' she asks.

'Some of that action with you,' he thinks. She's perkily attractive, with a short blonde bob, lively eyes and a slight figure.

24

'I was beginning to think you were closed,' he says, 'or too busy.'

She gives him a frown, which turns into a lustful smirk.

'No, not really. Just putting someone back in their box.'

Before Fletcher can make his mind up about either some more repartee or which ale he might like, a recognisable voice can be heard commenting on the sunshine.

He turns to look towards the door to see Violet enter the room, Calum McNeil at her heel, looking a bit more careworn than usual, closely followed by another man he doesn't know.

'Ah, Michael, there you are. Ahead of me for once.'

Fletcher manages a sheepish grin and forgives her.

'This is Graham Prentice, techie extraordinaire and almost as difficult as you.'

Both men pretend to be affronted by this and neither manage it, so they both laugh.

'Well, there's a dubious introduction,' says Prentice.

'I wouldn't say I was difficult,' says Fletcher. 'Maybe a bit impatient occasionally.'

Both Violet and Calum burst out laughing, as the two other men give each other rueful looks and a handshake.

Five minutes later they're sitting out in the sunshine, chatting like any ordinary group of tourists planning their holiday walks. But when they are joined by another person, they look more like the huddle of conspirators they are about to become.

The final arrival is another woman.

Bianca Kennedy has the slightest of Irish accents and a voice so soft that Fletcher has to lean in to catch her words, which, given her dark hair and blue eyes, is not a problem. He catches Violet giving him the arched eyebrows and responds with a 'What, me?' look.

Once the young barmaid has brought all the drinks and sandwiches, Violet asks them to briefly introduce themselves.

Fletcher listens to her and Calum giving their thumbnail sketches, which tell little about their actual power or expertise. He mutters a few words about being the over-the-hill sad bastard who can't escape the constant resurrections of his erstwhile troublesome career failing to put any of the real bastards away where they belonged.

Prentice merely confirms that he is only here to press the relevant buttons when he finds out what on earth he is getting himself into.

Which leaves Bianca.

She takes a sip of her beer and wipes the back of her hand across her face.

'I help people to disappear.'

Violet meets Fletcher's eyes with a look that says,

'You weren't expecting that, were you?'

He looks back at the woman. She's looking at him with a blank face.

'I see,' he says.

She smiles.

'Only people who deserve it,' she adds.

Violet holds up her hand.

'When we receive a message that it's clear, we'll go somewhere more … accommodating…'

This proves to be less country mansion than Fletcher was expecting. All five of them climb into a battered old VW camper van and set off.

He knows that Calum has the highest-level police driver qualifications, but he drives this old vehicle like someone the same age as him, barely getting it into third gear.

'Not as daft as it's stupid-looking,' murmurs Prentice as he catches Fletcher's eye. Fletcher nods back with a half-smile. It would have been impossible for a tailing vehicle to disguise its intention.

Fletcher knows the lanes near Helton round towards

Ullswater well, and that soon they'll be beneath the fells where he scattered Irene's ashes.

Calum slows to a standstill to let some old biddy come out of a side entrance halfway into the journey and follows her at the pace of a funeral march to the Pooley Bridge turning, after which he powers away down the lakeside.

At the point where it seems they might be going all the way to the dead end at Howtown, Calum takes a steep left up a farm track for about two hundred shuddering yards before bringing the vehicle up short in a creaking cough next to an old farmhouse.

Violet climbs out like the Queen arriving at Balmoral to lead her entourage along a broken-down old terrace towards the front door, where an outdoor pursuits guy is on guard, pretending to look like someone cleaning his boots.

Inside the abandoned look is maintained, but the cellar door takes them down to a vision Fletcher thinks is straight out of a sci-fi movie. It has more hi-tech equipment than he's ever seen in a such a small space. Just three people are waiting there, all glued to a bank of screens.

Violet says something to one of them, who pauses a few seconds before nodding.

The door to the cellar has closed silently behind them.

Violet indicates the five waiting chairs and sits at the head of the table.

The three technicians are all wearing headphones and go back to their screens without a word.

The only sound Fletcher can hear apart from the low hum of the machines and the occasional click is the ringing sensation in his ears.

He shakes his head and realises he isn't the only one doing that.

He looks at Violet.

'We're only here for an hour,' she says. 'That's the longest time, I'm told, that they can guarantee that we will definitely not be overheard by anyone or our conversation recorded.'

No one says a word for a few heartbeats.

'Wow,' whispers Bianca. 'Will there be replicants?'

Violet gives her a stare over the top of her glasses.

'Certainly not.'

***

Becket is watching some figures high up on An Teallach through the powerful bins she'd insisted she should have.

They look reasonably experienced as they progress carefully up the last ridge, which she knows has a few iffy moves to deal with.

As they near the summit, she becomes aware that 'Freya' has sidled into the room.

'You shouldn't do that to people like me, you know,' Becket says.

The woman comes alongside and looks out.

'Why? Are you going to attack me?'

'Offence is the best self-defence,' says Becket, turning to look at her.

'I can't say I'm keen on mountains,' she says. 'Don't know what the buzz is.'

Becket knows how she feels about that, but also remembers from previous attempts that it's pointless to try and share her passion.

Neither of them says any more for a quite a long time. The silence gathers like snow beginning to fall.

'Do you know why they've put us out here?'

'No ... apart from the fact that there must be a lot of people wanting you to disappear ... or you know stuff they don't want ordinary people to know about ... or you have special powers ... like turning yourself into a raven.'

'Ah, yes, I can do that.'

A thin smile and another long silence. The invisible snow settles softly.

'No, it's something more worrying … for some people.'

Becket stays still. She can smell the dusty confessional box.

'I can't forget stuff … well, things written down, mainly … I'm not so good with the spoken word.'

Becket's head clouds with dark childhood memories, which aren't things she ever wants to revisit.

'You mean you've an exceptional memory?'

'Photographic, but also if I retype a page and insert headings, that sticks even better.'

Becket tries to think what that might be like. She's heard of it but can't imagine it, can't believe it.

'How...?'

'Doctors tell me... Apparently anyone's brain is capable of it, but most people don't use it, don't need it, and … to be honest, it's a pain.'

'So when you're on the computer just now, you were remembering stuff?'

'No, I was looking at pictures. They're not so memorable and I find them soothing.'

Becket puts the bins down and goes to stand next to her.

'What about the real world?' she asks, pointing at the hills and the clouds.

The woman shakes her head.

'Not really.'

There is another silence. Becket is trying to get her head around this.

'So do some of the people, the people who've put you here... Are they...?'

'Using me? Yeah, but I can't do anything about it, can I? It's not as if I can make a run for it. You're here to stop that as much as to protect me.'

Becket nods. They've said she might try and escape, but

it wouldn't be safe for her. They've also said there are other people, maybe even that little group up on the ridge, who would try to find her.

'But what stuff have they asked you to remember?'

'All manner of things. Technical jargon I don't understand. Scientific papers full of words I don't know. Political papers, policy documents, emails, transcripts … all sorts.'

Becket shakes her head.

'But that's crazy … why?'

There is a shrug of shoulders and a sigh.

Becket paces back and forth. Part of her head is angry that she hasn't been told about this, and the rest is worrying about how dangerous this situation she's walked into now seems to be.

'Bloody twats,' she mutters. 'No, it's me. Daft tosser. Should have known.'

She swings round and stares at the woman. How can she have fallen for this? The money. How gullible can she be? They've agreed because they know they probably won't ever have to pay her. They can't let her walk away knowing what this woman, this 'asset', as the Americans call them, can do.

She stares at the back of the shaven head. Whose idea was that?

'What's that light?'

Becket steps towards her.

'Where?'

'Over there on that little hill.'

Becket realises that the clouds have now covered the summits and the sun is lower in the sky.

'There it is again.'

Becket's heart stops, while her instinct tells her,

'That's not a light. That's a reflection'.

Her body reacts before she tells it to.

She knocks the woman to one side as the window shatters

and a whump thuds into the wall behind where she's been standing.

They lie in a heap on the floor, where the look of total astonishment on the woman's face gives way to a mask of fear.

Becket holds her close. So close she can hear both their hearts racing and feel their bodies shaking.

'I think we just both became surplus to requirements. Do you want to run or die?'

The woman stares into her eyes.

Becket thinks the woman is going to cry, but no tears come… In fact her eyes harden.

'That's not much of an option…'

'I think that's all there is.'

***

We are in Limoges in time for lunch the next day.

Ziggy's organised a taxi from the airport into the city.

He twitters on in rapid French to the driver all the way to a hotel he's booked, and by half twelve we're sitting in a restaurant.

I'm starving, but a bit suspicious of the food.

Ziggy suggests we all have the menu du jour and advises us that the joue de porc is wonderful, and it is.

By now I'm feeling a bit sleepy and Ziggy says that's fine as it'll be quicker if he zizzies around, checking out possible places in the photos. Sparrow insists on going with him.

I think he'll soon learn.

A couple of hours later they return.

They've found all the places where the photos were taken, but haven't found anyone who remembers the people.

Ziggy says he's going to revisit some of the sites and see if he can find someone who was living or working there last October.

Sparrow and I sit outside and watch the world go by.

Suddenly I realise he's speaking to me.

'I couldn't say we were happy together,' he murmurs.

I nod. Been there, done that.

'But I thought she was OK… She had friends… We weren't poor.'

I am thinking of Edward's father … selfish bastard. Sparrow didn't seem like that, but there was no way of knowing.

'So tell me about her disappearance,' I say softly. I'm thinking, 'We haven't done that, have we, Captain?'

Sparrow looks at me and then towards the passing strangers out on the street.

'It was a Saturday. I was having a lie-in. She shouted up that she was off to the hairdresser's and then having lunch with a friend. I went back to sleep.'

He pauses as though he's letting himself slip back into that moment.

'Eventually I got up, had some breakfast, read the paper, probably… It was just another ordinary Saturday… Well, given what was going on at the time.'

The waiter comes to fetch our glasses, and I nod when I think he asks if we want some more. Sparrow waits till he's out of earshot.

'I'd agreed to meet some friends at the pub before going to the match in the afternoon. They confirmed to the police I was there, but I got into a row with one of the other guys. He was making sexist comments about some women on the other side of the bar, saying he wouldn't let his wife go out like that.'

He looks at me again. I raise my eyebrows as if as to say that I know the type.

'So then he says that at least his wife isn't playing away, like mine.'

I must have frowned.

He shrugs.

'I couldn't believe he said that, so I told him to shut his lying mouth … or something like that.'

The waiter returns with our drinks.

'There was a fight… Well, not really. I threw a punch. He decked me. My mates pulled him away … but then…'

He stops, gazes into the past.

'But then?'

'I can't remember. I suppose I was a bit concussed, but mostly I was confused. I'd never thought she might look elsewhere. We had our ups and downs, but…'

I nod. I know.

'Anyway, I didn't go to the match and went home. Walked all the way…'

Again he stops. His eyes are searching something long gone.

'She wasn't there… I never saw her again.'

I sort of expect him to cry at this point, but he doesn't, only sits staring into space.

Eventually he recovers and takes a big gulp of his beer.

'At first I thought she must have told me where she was going, and I hadn't paid any attention. But when I started ringing around it became obvious that she'd planned it. She hadn't been to the hairdresser's and none her friends had agreed to meet her for lunch. Eventually, when the police got involved, many of her friends said that she'd been behaving a bit strangely lately. Not meeting them when she said she'd be there, when I thought she was out with them.'

I tell him it was like that with my husband, who'd been seeing someone else until it all came out, so I know how he must have felt.

'But no one could or would tell me or the police about who she might have been seeing,' he mumbles.

It suddenly feels strange, sitting here in the shade outside a French bar in a place neither of us has ever visited before, sharing our sense of loss and betrayal. The sun is bouncing off the pavements and people are walking about without anoraks or woolly jumpers.

'So eventually the police came back. There were different questions. Accusations. They searched the house, lifted the floorboards, dug up the garden, emptied the attic… And now these photos, which I didn't dare show to them.'

He is on his feet. I reach out to hold his arm. The cars on the street aren't going slowly or carefully. There are quite a few horns and a lot of beeping.

He shrugs himself clear.

'Where has she gone?'

He shakes his head. Stalks one way then another. But eventually he just slumps back in his seat and stares at the passing strangers.

It's at this moment that Ziggy reappears, accompanied by a young woman.

We must look odd, because he stops and looks from one of us to the other.

'What?' he asks.

I tell him.

He nods.

'Of course they looked. But I don't think they searched that hard, because I've found a young lady who can possibly tell us something. She's called Marie and she's worked at the bar down the road for over ten years.'

Sparrow looks at the table. Maybe finding out wasn't going to be as much of a relief as he might have thought it would be.

'And she remembers your wife,' he says to Sparrow. 'She knew her as Anna and she was with a guy called Max. They seemed to be in love, very happy.'

Sparrow is as still as a statue.

Ziggy orders a bottle of wine.

No one speaks for what seems a long time.

Without looking at Sparrow, Ziggy asks,

'What did your wife do?'

I look at him. He still hasn't moved.

After what seems like an age, he looks up at Ziggy

'She worked in an office.'

'Where?' I ask.

Sparrow looks uncomfortable.

'I'm not really sure. She never talked about work, except once or twice to say it was boring, the other women weren't nice, her boss was a bully. Things like that.'

'So you don't know whether she was a typist or something else.'

Sparrow shakes his head.

I can't bear it.

'You mean you never asked? Really?'

He gives me an embarrassed look.

'No, I didn't… Look, when I met her, she seemed the most glamorous woman who'd ever even looked at me.'

I must have frowned.

He laughs, a sad laugh.

'No, I was just a nerd working in a repair shop, mending people's knackered old TVs and computers. In the winter I hardly saw daylight. I was a mole.'

'So how?'

'She came in one day with a kettle. It only took me a few minutes. It was merely a loose connection.'

'And then she asked you out?' I ask, trying not to giggle.

He looks at his hands.

'Well, yes… I couldn't believe it.'

I look at Ziggy. He gives me an intense stare, which I understand to mean to go on.

When I look back at Sparrow he is crying quietly. Tears are running uninterruptedly down his face.

I wait.

He wipes his cheek and looks away down the busy street.

'It wasn't real, was it?' he says softly.

Ziggy puts his hand on my arm.

'No, I'm afraid not, Jimmy,' he says. 'You've been used. You've been what operational undercover people call a shop front. That's a cover for someone who needs to look ordinary but who is probably involved in top-secret activities.'

No one speaks for some time.

I sip at the wine. Cold. A faint taste of pears.

'Secret activities?' I think to myself. 'In Chorley? The munitions factory was long gone. How on earth can she have been involved in secret anything? Chorley folk were not exactly known as tight-lipped. I can't help but think of my mother. Couldn't keep a secret if you paid her. Except, of course, she didn't tell me, or anyone else as far as I know, that I was adopted.'

Ziggy as usual is on his phone, murmuring to himself.

'James, how long do you think it took her to get to work?'

Sparrow looks at me and then back at Ziggy, who is concentrating on the flashing images.

He shrugs.

'Well, not far. She didn't set off until about a quarter to nine most mornings and was always home before me.'

I'm still trying to get my head around the fact that he didn't know where she worked.

'So on foot or in a car?' says Ziggy.

'Car.'

I assume that Ziggy is now on a map.

'Um,' he says. 'In uniform?'

'Uniform?'

Ziggy nods.

'No,' says Sparrow, mystified.

'From your house there are three military establishments within twenty minutes.'

'Of course,' I say. 'Fulwood, Weeton, and where's the other one?'

36

'Lisieux.'

'No, that's a care home.'

'You're right,' says Ziggy. 'I've been there.'

Ziggy flicks a few more times.

'What do you mean, you've been there?'

His face is serious. Is he kidding me?

'There are more things in heaven and earth, Horatio,' he murmurs.

'What?'

He gives a me a stern look.

'You'll see.'

We are both looking at him in bewilderment.

'You mean she worked for the military?' asks Sparrow.

Ziggy stands up.

'Let's go and see Marie.'

***

Violet's gaze lingers a few more seconds in Bianca's direction before looking from one to the next of the remaining people round the table.

The only sound left is the hum and mumble of the machines surrounding them.

She sighs.

'To be clear … I'll explain the purpose of this group in a few moments, but you probably already realise that your presence here is at the threshold of seditious behaviour.'

It's difficult for anyone not to glance at anyone else. A mixture of uncertainty and bravado fills the space in between, but no one speaks.

'So I'll outline what I'm about to invite you to collude in.'

Again, there are only looks and glances, a bit of shuffling of feet and some readjusting of seats.

'Even those of you who have given up watching the drama unfold will be aware that things are looking worse every day.

The Brexit talks are deadlocked and with Boris "on leave" the rest are looking more like headless chickens with every minute that passes.'

Fletcher finds himself looking at his hands. A lifetime of unsuccessfully trying to avoid political matters crawls into his mind like a miasma of dead ends and frustrated effort. Adversane's ghost is here, hovering over the gathering like a pinstriped avatar.

Violet probably hasn't expected any response at this point, but gives them the space they might want.

No one speaks.

'To be brief,' she continues, 'we will be operating at the sharpest edge of this ... current episode. Our powers are extremely limited and our efforts are likely to be unsuccessful and dismissed. But I, for one, am not going to let this happen without some attempt to ameliorate the coming disasters.'

Again, there is no attempt at a question or even a raised eyebrow.

'I can only guess at the intentions of the praetorian guard while the emperor is indisposed, but you can see already that they're only expendable front men.'

She looks again directly at Bianca, whose expression now is a mask of neutrality. She doesn't move a muscle and Violet nearly smiles.

'Our mission...' she begins, and then shakes her head. 'Sorry, it's difficult not to descend into melodrama when the absurdity of what is happening is beyond parody.'

'Are assassinations an option?' offers Bianca, now smiling.

'They'd only make things worse, I suspect,' replies Violet.

Bianca sighs. 'I suppose you're right... Pity, though. I've two or three delightfully appropriate finales in mind.'

This produces more smiles and a relaxation of the tension in the room. One of the operators even turns round to wink at her.

'So what are we going to do?' asks Prentice.

'We're going on a bear hunt.'

'You mean "the" bear?' asks Bianca.

Violet shakes her head.

'No. We all know he's only the fall guy, the stooge, Harpo rather than Groucho.'

'Not the *nisti*?'

Violet shakes her head again.

'No, not them, either, although I'm sure they've got their fingers in the same pie.'

Fletcher frowns.

'What or who is a *nisti*?'

'The Russian "bear",' murmurs Calum.

Fletcher looks away, feeling a bit stupid.

'There are other "bears" out there,' adds Prentice, covering Fletcher's embarrassment, 'who've already started making their next lot of millions.'

Violet nods.

'Yes, you're all right, but this bear is a rogue animal and a shape-shifter, so doesn't even look like a bear. More like a shifty mongoose.'

Fletcher is getting irritated with this wordplay.

'Well, who the hell is he?' he rasps.

Violet looks at him sternly.

'You'd be well advised not to know their names or utter them unwisely, but they are already planning a high-octane path of destruction … one which will possibly sideline Parliament and lead to another civil war.'

Fletcher stares at her.

'Are you serious?' he asks.

'Never more so,' she breathes.

'What can we do?' is all he can think of to say.

'Not much, but there is someone who has the wherewithal to expose their real intentions.'

'Who? Where are they?'

'Aye, there's the rub. She's been disappeared.'

'By who?' asks Bianca, now urgent to get on with the chase.

'Not sure. I'm not even sure whose side they're on, but what she knows is dynamite.'

The room falls silent.

'Any leads?' asks Fletcher.

Violet turned her gaze on him.

'Only two… Her code name seems to be "Ariadne".'

He stares. She nods and then continues.

'And she's been put under the protection of someone, codename "Tommy", who will only communicate with one other person.'

'Who?'

'You.'

***

'Where are you?'

Becket waits for the reply. He's probably driving, but she knows he has hands-free.

She looks at 'Freya' huddled in the corner, her eyes staring back at her. It's the first time she realises they are a vivid green. Creepy.

Her phone vibrates. It's John.

'Hi,' she says.

'I'm at the hotel.'

'We need you now.'

There is a slight pause.

'On my way.'

'There's someone outside. A sniper.'

There is a longer pause … a slight sigh.

'Twenty minutes.'

Becket thinks that is way too ambitious, but says nothing. She reckons a good half hour.

She looks back at 'Freya'.

'Is that your real name?'

The green eyes hold hers.

'I like it. It'll do.'

Becket nods. It's not as if she hasn't had a few monikers herself.

'That's John. He'll be here soon.'

The eyes close briefly, and her body shudders slightly.

'John?'

'A friend of mine.'

'On his own?'

Becket nods.

'Aye, but well-armed,' she says.

It is nearly forty minutes before they hear the sound of the Land Rover.

Becket scuttles through to the kitchen door and unlocks it.

The sound of the engine grows louder, and as she peeps out the car appears over the last ridge.

After a short pause it grumbles the last hundred yards or so and pulls up as near to the door as he can get.

She can see his dark curly hair and can't stop herself from giving a sigh of relief.

She watches as he takes his time getting out. He is still a big man, but not heavy, and she knows that a hard-muscled body is inside the flak jacket and army trousers. He has one bag over his shoulder and another in his hand.

Five steps and she opens the door.

No shots follow, which would seem to indicate that the sniper is still in the same position on the other side of the building.

He follows her through into the back room, where Freya is still in the same corner. He nods at her and gives Becket a peremptory kiss.

'Do you think he's still there?' he asks.

'Don't know,' she murmurs, wondering about the kiss.

'Maybe he's alone,' he says, unslinging the gun bag from his shoulder.

Becket nods again.

'John Shepherd,' he says reaching out a hand towards the woman.

She gives him a slight smile.

'She's decided to respond to "Freya",' says Becket.

He looks from one to the other.

'This'll be good,' says Becket, 'hiding out with a couple of mutes.'

John gives her a hard stare.

'Any ideas?'

Becket grins.

'I guess the best option would be to sit tight. We've plenty of supplies, but … patience is not my strong point.'

John looks at the other woman, who stares back at him. He recognises that look. He's seen it in men before a battle. Terror behind a mask of bravado.

'Well,' he says. 'I'm not doing that track in the dark, so it's now or…'

***

Ref:TD/HO/0213201538.

'Have you found that woman yet?'

'Completely disappeared.'

'How come? We're supposed to be the people who make other people disappear.'

'We've got the best people on it.'

'So tell them to get their damn fingers out.'

CHAPTER 3

I've become used to Ziggy's changes of mind, but this was off the wall.

One minute we are going to go and see this woman called Marie, who had recognised Sparrow's wife in the photo. The next we're in a taxi going to the station.

I ask him repeatedly what's going on but he just mumbles stuff about a change of plan, how stupid he could be and other half-finished head-shakings and mutterings.

In the end I realise that it's poor Sparrow who is completely baffled.

To cap it all we have to run from the taxi to catch the train.

Running was never my favourite activity, but at my age I wasn't even sure I could remember how to do it.

The station looks like a church, it's so grand, and all the platforms are downstairs.

But we make it.

I'm trying to catch my breath. Sparrow is leaning with his back to the wall, gasping like a stranded fish.

It is only then I see that Ziggy has put the window down is and taking photos with his phone.

'What for?'

Which is what I say to him when I get my breath back.

'Two guys, at least,' he says, his eyes wild.

'But why? What?' I stammer.

He indicates the carriage and it's only then that I clock that everyone, absolutely everyone, in the carriage is staring at us. Some look bewildered, others curious and a lot fearful.

Ziggy bursts out laughing.

He rattles off something in French.

There is audible relief. A few people give us a round of applause and we slink though to the next carriage.

'What did you say?' I ask.

He laughs again.

'I said we were escaping from your husband.'

I glare at him.

'No, that we had a terminally slow Moroccan taxi driver.'

I frowned. Really? But maybe true.

'I don't suppose you found time to get any tickets,' I say, pretty certain that's a no.

'Oh, Urse, you are so fifties sometimes.'

'Fifties? You cheeky sod. And don't call me that.'

We find some seats and flop down, although he's straight onto his iPad.

I look at Sparrow. He's recovered somewhat, but now staring at Ziggy as if he's a strange being from another world … which he is.

He turns to look at me. I shrug my shoulders at his questioning gaze.

'Where … what?'

I've no answer for either, so I get up and ask them what they'd like to drink or eat.

A few minutes later I'm standing in the queue.

Where are we going? I can't ask someone where the train is going without looking a complete fool, and my French isn't good enough anyway.

The woman in front of smiles at me. I smile back.

'That seems like an exciting life you're living,' she says, in a Home Counties accent.

I grin stupidly.

'Not really…'

'No?' she grins back. 'I've been trying to figure out what sort of people you were fleeing from.'

I shake my head.

'Taxi got stuck in the traffic.'

She pulls a face.

'Oh, but I'd have invented much more dangerous stuff than that.'

I laugh, but am relieved when my interlocutor reaches the front of the queue.

Five minutes later I get back to the other two with coffee and croissants.

Sparrow declines the croissant, but Ziggy wolfs down two in a trice.

'So,' he says, leaning back against the seat.

We wait. He stares out of the window.

'We'll get off at the next stop. I've figured out how to get back without being followed.'

'Get back? I thought we were following a lead.'

'No. Herring, rouge, or as the French would say, we need to brouiller les pistes.

'You mean the girl, Marie?'

He nods.

'Too good to be true. She was clever. Had me fooled for a while.'

'How did you find out?'

Ziggy looks at Sparrow.

'I asked her about the cathedral.'

'What?'

'Richard, Duc d'Aquitaine.'

'Who?'

'She was flustered and then guessed.'

'And?'

'She'd no idea.'

I look at Sparrow who shakes his head.'

'The Lionheart, you English ignoramuses. He was crowned there in 1172.'

We both frown, although Sparrow has looked away.

'OK.' I look out of the window. 'So now where?'

'Back to the scene of the crime. They didn't want us there, so that's where the answers must be.'

With that he closes his eyes. He can do that. Annoying … and I don't even know what the questions might be.

Sparrow looks at me.

Yet again, I can only I shrug my shoulders.

The journey back is complicated, exhausting and definitely illegal.

I'd no idea, considering Brexit and everything, that it would be remotely possible to gain re-entry to the UK without using a legal route.

It involves going to some dark and dangerous creepy places on the docks in Rotterdam, spending the sailing across the Channel deep inside a huge ship that smells only of fish, followed by scrambling about an enormous dockyard, although I am not convinced we are back in the UK until we pass a sign saying Grimsby. I have never been there before, and anyway we are soon on the A1 in a car that Ziggy had arranged to be waiting for us in a multistorey car park at five o'clock in the morning.

We don't stop until we pull up on the drive of a big house on a private housing estate.

The last sign I see through droopy eyes is Thirsk. Don't know it. Never been there before either.

Again, there is no one there, but Ziggy finds the key round the back somewhere and we're inside.

He waltzes around, demonstrating he's been there before, and suggests which bedrooms we should use.

'So whose house is this?' Sparrow asks.

'A friend's. She's in Singapore at the moment.'

I don't remember much more. I am so tired I collapse on

the bed. My last thought is wondering how unlike Ziggy's place this house is.

***

Becket recognises the look as well. Not the fear in the woman's eyes, but the scary steel in John Shepherd's brown eyes.

She's not seen it for some time, but recognises it at once and is immediately fearful.

She stares at him.

'I'm not sure that's a good idea, John,' she manages to whisper.

'But it's the right one,' he mutters back at her and goes towards the door. It isn't a goodbye on his face, but she knows his service record, so also knows it is no point arguing with him. He doesn't wear his medals. Probably couldn't quickly find them, and doesn't value them as much as she thinks he should.

There one minute, gone the second. Why did this always happen to her? She's no trouble finding the bad and even the ugly guys, but why can't she hold on to the good ones?

She creeps up to the window, giving 'Freya' a stern 'Stay where you are or you'll die' look. 'Freya' doesn't look convinced, but she huddles further into the corner, her eyes fixed on the closed door.

It is probably only thirty minutes or so, and getting dark, when they hear the door open again.

Becket is flattened against the wall, gun in hand, giving the woman a 'Don't move' stare.

But it's John.

Hi eyes are dead. No sign of battle apart from that.

'Come on,' he says.

The two women follow him out to the Land Rover.

He doesn't speak until they're back on the main road heading north.

'We're better heading to the Isles,' he mutters. 'I know a woman in Ullapool who'll hide us for a while, until I can get us some different wheels.'

Neither of the two women even acknowledge this suggestion... Becket because she knows it is the best idea and is wondering who the woman is, while 'Freya' is reciting the meaningless content of some document under her breath, which has decided to spool through her memory – like you do.

*****

It hasn't happened that often since I met Ziggy, but since we got back he's been impossible. Bad-tempered. Not sleeping. Almost certainly taking drugs. God knows what. I've no idea about drugs.

Sparrow follows him about like a dog who knows he's done something wrong but doesn't know what it is.

I don't know what to do either. If I ask Ziggy if there's anything he wants, he either looks at me as if he doesn't know me or as if it's obvious what I should be doing. He spends a lot of time on a variety of screens, but despite an occasional 'Whoop,' most of the time he's cursing and swearing, and on two occasions the machine he's on gets wrecked. One of them just misses Sparrow as it flies across the room towards a splintering death against the wall.

So it's getting to the point when I'm thinking of buggering off ... when there's a shout of,

'Kereten!'

I know that he speaks maybe nine or ten languages, but I've no idea which one this is.

Before I can ask, he's grabbed Sparrow and is almost shaking him. Then he controls himself, holds him by his shoulders and looks him in the face.

'Sorry, Jimmy ... but ... have you got some other photos of your wife?'

Sparrow is at first shaken into a trance but slowly reaches into his jacket pocket and produces a wallet, from which he extracts a photo … and then another.

Ziggy snatches them and takes them to one of the surviving laptops, and compares them to various images before putting one of them on the scanner.

We all wait as the machine slithers to itself and his fingers blur over the keys.

After a tense few minutes we all wait for what seems to me like a eureka possibility.

Indeed, it does seem to be this, as Ziggy nods his head and sighs.

Sparrow looks at me and I can only shrug.

Ziggy gets up and walks round in circles muttering to himself in what I guess is something Eastern European, which he lapses into when he's stressed or excited. I think it's Croatian or Czech.

Eventually he stops and his face breaks into a beatific smile.

'Well?' I say in exasperation.

'It was obvious,' he sighs. 'The torture photos are mock-ups: they're good – professional – but I should have thought of it earlier.'

'Mock-ups?' I ask.

'As in not real, not her … not Jimmy's wife.'

I look at Sparrow. He can't work out whether to be pleased, relieved or frightened.

Ziggy figures this out and goes over to him and puts his arm round him.

'I can't tell you this means she's still alive, but it's not her in those photos.'

Sparrow can only stare at him.

'But…' he manages.

'Here, look at this. I can show you how easy it is, if you have the right program.'

I watch as he bamboozles Sparrow by covering the screen

with one image after another as he warps one famous person's face into another. I know it can be done but have never seen it effected so rapidly.

Eventually he stops.

We all stare at the last screen.

'So now what?' I say, trying not to sound irritated.

Ziggy looks at me and nods.

'Um … I think we have no choice.'

I frown at him.

'We'll have to go back to the start.'

'So where the hell is that?' I nearly shout.

Ziggy just grins and starts to sing.

'Let's start at the very beginning … a very good place to start…'

I chase him round the room with him continuing to sing and me screaming at him to stop, while Sparrow stands in the middle, utterly bewildered, until he starts to slowly weep.

We stop.

I put my arm around his shoulders and hold him, as he cries like a baby. Eventually he stops.

Ziggy is sitting cross-legged on the floor, staring at the images of Sparrow's wife that he's had in his wallet, not the false ones.

'So how tall is she?' he asks.

Sparrow looks at him.

'An inch or two taller than me… We used to joke about it… So five feet ten.'

'Weight?'

'About seven and half stone. I worried about her.'

'And is the dark auburn hair natural?'

Sparrow nods, but his eyes are filling up again. He turns away.

I give Ziggy a glare. He pulls a face.

'OK. Let's see,' he says, and turns to his machinery.

I look at Sparrow, who is hunched up against the wall, head down.

'Come on, Jimmy, let's go for a walk. He won't miss us, and we can get out of the war zone for a while.'

He looks up at me and then at Ziggy.

Ten minutes later we're in the cafe at the park.

I remember when you wouldn't want to wander around here on your own. The grass wasn't cut often enough, dogs roamed in packs, and kids hid in the bushes. Night-time was worse: druggies and doggers. Not a place to go.

Now, as part of the council's drive to make the place somewhere better than a run-down mill town, it has been spruced up.

Sparrow looks out at the women and the prams.

'No kids, then?'

He doesn't seem to have heard me, so I wait.

'No… I wouldn't have minded, but I never asked.'

I nod. I don't regret having a child, even though his bastard father left me as soon as I gave birth. No, that's not true. I kicked him out.

'We didn't talk much. She said she wasn't allowed to talk about what she did to anyone, but that it was boring as hell anyway.'

'So what did you do together?'

Again, he hesitates.

'Not much, now I think about it.'

'Neither did you,' I thought about the bastard, recalling long evenings sitting watching the telly. No interests, looking after Edward, worrying about the bastard when he was out with his mates. What a boring life … and all the time I had a serial killer for a mother rampaging about all over the place.

'She didn't like having her photo taken. Said she couldn't bear how miserable she looked,' he says.

'Was she?'
'Not to me. I thought she was beautiful.'
I can't think of what to say to that, so I don't say anything.
The sun is shining.
We continue to sit there.

***

Fletcher is sitting in his car.

He's staring straight ahead, but not seeing anything.

He's managed to drive out of the care home and round a few corners, but then pulls in and turns off the engine ... eventually.

What has he done?

Everyone says it's the right thing to do.

But there's nothing 'right' about it at all.

Presumably they think he'll just drive home and carry on with his life, as though putting the person you love in the 'care' of a bunch of strangers is 'the right thing to do'?

Especially when he'd said to Laura over and over that he'd never do it.

And now he has.

'No tears for us,' he mumbles out loud, as the forbidden streaks course down his cheeks.

He's no idea how long he's been there.

Is it getting dark?

When did he leave the care home?

With no real determination he starts the car and drives off.

Where?

The thought of 'home' is unbearable. 'Their' home? No longer. He now regards it as just an old pub facing a blackened church on the side of a valley.

Grace has urged him to come to her, but he can't imagine

that, and the thought of his eldest granddaughter's eyes burning into his is beyond bearing.

So he keeps driving.
North.

It's only when he's going past the sign for Scotch Corner that he realises where he's going.

He cuts in dangerously onto the slipway, ignoring the blaring horns of outrage, and pulls up in the hotel car park.

Sits there for an age.

Takes out his phone. Finds the name and presses the button.

The conversation is brief.

The answer is,

'Yes, of course.'

He declines the idea of having a coffee. The thought of people gathered together in a loud and brightly lit room is too much to even contemplate.

He doesn't need the satnav. He knows the way.

He starts the engine.

'What a traitor you are, Mick Fletcher,' he growls, and re-joins the bright lights streaming north.

Two and half hours later he pulls into the drive. The long avenue of Scots pines opening out onto the gravelled forecourt.

Unusually, the main door opens almost immediately, and a tall figure stands framed in the bright light of the entrance hall.

It's only then that he realises he's brought no bags, no change of clothes. Not even a toothbrush.

He turns off the engine and gets out of the car.

It's raining slightly and he reaches back into the car to find his coat.

A hand appears on his arm as he straightens up. The stern face beneath the umbrella, boring into his.

Despite the rain, the umbrella to one side, she holds him close. The familiar scent and the wave of her hair falling on his face.

He can't stop the tears.

She holds him tight. Both get wet in the increasing rain.

Inside the umbrella is taken from her by the inevitable 'young man', who then backs away, as she shepherds her guest into the warmth of the huge sitting room basking in the roar of the open fire.

With a nod the man is dismissed, having already been told what to prepare.

Fletcher is posted into a big wingback chair a few steps from the heat.

A large brandy is offered and taken in hand.

No words are spoken.

The young man returns with platters of food.

Fletcher shakes his head, but they're deposited on the sideboard, in case.

Without further ado the couple are left alone.

A silence rests.

There is a history here.

Unspoken. Sometimes troubled. Always combative. Knowing. But, they both realise, in their different ways, that it's a solid understanding and with no need for debate or reassurance.

It's a good five minutes before a word is spoken.

Fletcher hasn't drunk any of the brandy and now puts it on the side table.

'She doesn't know me any longer,' are the first words he utters.

Louisa says nothing, but her eyes meet his and then she looks away.

'I can't … imagine…' she begins to say, but then stands up, walks to the sideboard and pours herself another drink.

Despite themselves the next few minutes are as awkward as any they've ever experienced in each other's company.

But eventually Fletcher smiles at her and, after frowning first, she smiles back.

'You know this is the worst possible betrayal, don't you?' he whispers, his voice hoarse with guilt.

She smiles.

'It isn't a betrayal to seek solace.'

He shakes his head.

Louisa leans back in her chair.

'You've no idea what Laura and I talked about, do you?'

He frowns again. He doesn't. Neither of them have ever said a word to him about their tête-à-têtes.

'In any case, mostly it wasn't about you,' she says with her wicked smile.

He shakes his head and smiles back.

'We came to an agreement way back, which was easy enough for me … to explain that as far as I was concerned, she was welcome to you … and worthy of my admiration for such a brave, even foolhardy, trust in you.'

He stares at her in disbelief, thinking of all those threats – those killer stares – he'd endured.

And then she laughs.

An astonishing girlish laugh, which is so incongruous he is lost for words.

When she stops laughing and he has recovered, they both sit, staring at each other.

The smiles disappear.

'You can stay as long as you want,' she says.

He shakes his head.

'Thank you, but I'll go back in the morning.'

Louisa nods.

'But now you must eat something. I bet you've not had anything at all.'

He allows himself to be shepherded into the 'small' dining room and forces down some food.

But afterwards he realises he is so tired, that he allows her to take him to a bedroom, where he falls on the bed and goes to sleep fully clothed.

CHAPTER 4

Becket comes awake with a start.

Without looking, she knows he isn't there.

The duvet has been carefully folded over on his side. It seems that he has left her.

She listens.

This huge empty old mansion creaks and groans with all sorts of morbid tales and grumblings.

He's probably gone into the nearby town for supplies.

She snuggles down into the warmth, but continues to stare at the window as the red slowly mutates into orange and then from yellow to white.

Tears dribble down her cheek onto the pillow.

Why did people have to make things so bad when the world was so beautiful?

She sits up and wipes her cheek with the back of her hand and finds herself giggling.

Five minutes later she's downstairs, dressed in one of John's big shirts. They've decided not to go back to their own houses, especially as they've agreed to continue looking after 'Freya'. She still hasn't told them her real name yet, and in fact seems to have retreated into a solo lockdown. In another situation Becket would have called a doctor, but the woman still communicates, albeit with a nod or a shrug. John has seen this sort of escaping from terrible experiences before and says they just need to be patient.

This mansion is on the edge of Selkirk, somewhere she's never been before. John did a training course there a few years ago and knew that it was out of bounds for the locals, although he doesn't think that would definitely include the teenagers and the druggies. Whatever the case, he thinks it's worth the risk.

The signs about unexploded bombs have been up for years, but again he doesn't think there are any. It's just a scare tactic.

The good thing is that the army has not fully decommissioned it and so the gas cookers still work, once a new cylinder is fixed, although oddly the lights and sockets don't – which is OK, he says, because that means they won't accidentally turn them on and give themselves away.

The time spent in the wilds of Sutherland kept them safe, but you can only take so many short days – no sun, cold and wet weather – before Freya's constitution began to become a problem. There was still no sign of ending her protection. Becket was beginning to think maybe they'd forgotten all about them, but then they'd get another message to keep lying low. Although there's been nothing for over a week.

She makes a mug of tea, puts on his big coat, and goes outside.

It is cold, but unbelievably bright. So bright she has to squint to make out anything.

The lake shimmers in the early morning fog.

A heron makes its elegant way across her eyeline, followed by a couple of moorhens busily motoring along. A company of rooks are doing their early morning name-calling to check they're all present and correct.

She goes to stand next to one of the life-size statues on the edge of the crumbling terrace. She thinks the one she's standing next to might be Athena, because she's got a strange-looking wand. The only thing 'Freya' has said of any length was to go from one to the other and name them all.

As the cawing dies she can hear the unmistakeable grumble of John's Land Rover, and then it appears from behind the stand of oak trees down the valley.

She watches for a few moments and feels her crotch betraying her desire, before standing up and waving.

His lights flash a reply. She turns to go back inside, puts the kettle on and stands waiting for him, with memories of the tempestuous lovemaking last night … and the one before … and before flashing through her mind.

His arms are around her and they kiss. Gently. They are both sore.

He kicks off his boots, and they sit on the doorstep and listen in silence to the birds and the wind.

'I didn't get a paper,' he says.

She says nothing.

'Has she got up yet?'

She shrugs.

'Not sure… Don't think so.'

So they both continue to sit there as the sun climbs resolutely into the cloudless sky.

Later they check on Freya, but she is facing the wall and doesn't answer.

John goes and finds a stash of logs and Becket cooks them something to eat. Freya does come to join them, but says nothing, other than a mumbled 'Thank you,' before going back upstairs, leaving the two of them together in front of the fire. His head is in her lap and she is leaning back against an old sofa.

'So what do you think we should do about "Freya"?' she murmurs.

He doesn't reply for a few moments.

'Dunno,' he says finally. 'Maybe in all the election bollocks and then now the virus coming they've forgotten about her.'

She nods.

'I bet there aren't any documents she's read about surviving a pandemic.'

'You mean "herd immunity"?' he mutters.

They both turn to see Freya standing leaning on the door frame, the firelight giving her a flickering presence.

'Only to say it doesn't work…' she says.

They wait. Is that all?

'The scientific evidence is contradictory about what's the best response, but herd immunity is what eventually happens whatever you do … although not fighting it hard from the beginning will make things far worse.'

She comes slowly over to them and sits cross-legged on the frayed carpet.

'To be honest, I've no idea, only what I remember reading.'

None of them speak for a while, although Becket and John share glances.

'By the way,' she adds quietly, 'thank you … for keeping me safe.'

They both smile, but say nothing.

'What are we going to do next?' she asks.

'We're doing it,' says John. 'Keeping our heads down, waiting for the storm to pass.'

She nods.

'You do realise that thousands are going to die, don't you?'

John nods back.

'More than most people think, probably.'

Freya looks up.

'I never thought I would get away.'

They both frown at her.

'Away from what … who?

'The job … keeping secrets … not being able to say anything.'

She turns to look at the fire, they wait.

'I was told to get myself a husband.'

Becket snorts.

'Like from a shop?'

Freya almost grins, but then shakes her head.

'Jimmy's a good guy, a shy, gentle man… He was kind to me.'

She stares back the fire, wipes away a tear. Becket glances at John. Is this the truth?

He shrugs.

'Anyway, it didn't last. They took me away. First to somewhere down south, but then on a boat to France. Ended up in a run-down hotel in a town on hill. Don't know where it was.'

She shakes her head, eyes now springing with tears.

Becket puts out her hand but she shakes her head, grits her teeth.

'Some other men arrived, started asking me questions. Over and over. I told them everything they wanted to know, often things I don't understand. Dates. People. Meetings. Everything...'

Her face is contorted with fear and anger.

She looks up at the two staring faces.

'You don't believe me, do you?' she rasps.

They're both staring at her.

She stands up, pulls her jumper over her head, undoes her shirt, and pulls that off too. Turns round. Her chest and back are covered in old bruises and healed cuts.

Even this hard-faced couple have to wince and look away.

'You want to see the rest?' she demands, starting to unzip her jeans.

'No,' says Becket, reaching out and taking her arm.

She helps her put her clothes back on.

They sit looking at each other.

'Did they ever tell you what they wanted to know?' asks Becket.

Freya shakes her head.

'No ... I'm not sure they knew either.'

Becket frowns.

'So ... how did you...? When did you...?'

Freya almost laughs.

'I was drugged. Woke up in the back of a van. Didn't know where we were. It was a long journey. But occasionally, when we were going through a town or somewhere, I could hear voices, so I knew we were back in England. I must have slept again, but then there were the last few miles along a rough track and we arrived at a hut. In the middle of the night. No other houses. No lights. Mountains. You.'

She stares at Becket.

She doesn't cry. Merely sighs like a balloon slowly deflating.

Becket hugs her. Not something she does often. To anyone.

Not one of them speaks for what seems like a long time.

But eventually John stands up and goes to fetch the wine he bought earlier. Freya declines.

They sip at the glasses but no words are spoken. The three of them staring at the fire as the green wood splutters and coughs.

Eventually, she gets to her feet and goes towards the door.

Becket turns to look.

'My name really is Freya,' she says with a half-smile. 'Double bluff.'

When she's gone, Becket looks back at John, who is shaking his head.

'Did you know that?' she asks accusingly.

He shakes his head.

'I don't like games,' he murmurs.

'So what do we do now?'

Again, there is a pause and then gives her a weak smile. So they do the only thing which makes them feel better … but gently.

***

When we get back to the office Ziggy is still glued to the laptop, but almost immediately stops and looks at us.

'Hi… You OK?'

I nod.

'You're certain your wife's name was Paula? Maiden name Lisle?'

Sparrow nods but looks puzzled.

'Why?'

'Well … I've tracked her via a traffic camera turning into the Lisieux grounds on more than one occasion shortly after she left for work, so she was definitely going there.'

Sparrow looks at me.

'That could mean she was working in the nursing home, either as a nurse or in an office job,' I suggest.

Ziggy shakes his head.

'She's not on the employee list at the nursing home.'

Again, Sparrow is looking at me, probably wondering how Ziggy is able to do this.

I can only raise my eyebrows and shake my head at him.

Ziggy stands up and paces about.

'So here's the plan,' he murmurs, as much to himself as at us, but then looks inquiringly at us both.

'When was the last time either of you had a mental breakdown?'

We both look at each other.

In the event neither of us have troubled the health service for quite some time, so Ziggy decides that I will be best. Although I realise later that any 'records' about my mental health are likely to be what he's made up rather than the admittedly odd truth.

On the way there in the car I find Sparrow's hand in mine.

I smile at him, knowing full well how scared I am.

Ziggy, of course, is looking oddly dapper in a suit I'd never have thought of seeing him in.

At the entrance we're waved through and park in the car park.

Ziggy says he's memorised the ground plan and, when we've been shown around inside, he'll ask if we can stroll around the grounds.

So it's over an hour later that the two of us are sitting in the car as Ziggy sneaks one last look round. By now it's getting dark and, given the odd behaviour of one or two of the inmates we've seen, I'm getting a bit twitchy.

Suddenly, Ziggy reappears from behind some bushes and gets hurriedly into the car.

'Drive,' he shouts.

I fumble with key, stall the car, and then get it jumping forward, only to slam on the brakes as a figure lunges itself onto the bonnet. Before any of us can do anything, there's another face gurning behind him. There's a struggle. I look across at Ziggy. It's the first time I've ever seen him worried.

But then the inmates are off, scuttling into the undergrowth.

I manage to find first gear and drive slowly back to the main gate.

Back at the office, Ziggy is straight online. There is no mention of the incident that the two of us are still recovering from.

Sparrow sits down beside me on the floor.

'What's he doing now?'

I shake my head.

Ziggy claps his hands.

'Ta-dah!'

We both go over to see what he's found.

It's a high-resolution map showing the grounds where we'd been earlier.

'Here,' he says, pointing at the roofs of a small complex away from the main hospital buildings that is surrounded by lots of trees, with a car park for about twenty cars.

'That's where I think she was working.'

Sparrow can only give him a blank look.

'So now I expect you're going to want to get in there, aren't you?'

Ziggy shakes his head.

'No chance, and in any case that would give us away.'

I wait. I know he's 'Hooked' into this now… He'll find a way. For once he's still.

I look at Sparrow. He's slumped by the wall, looking down at his hands.

I become aware of the rain rattling on the window. It feels like a moment. You know when things are going to change. Something in the air, as the song goes.

On cue Ziggy begins to sing. It's not in English, but I think I recognise the tune.

He stops mid line and clicks his fingers.

'Simples.'

He stands up.

'We only need to clock a few cars in and out. Check their plates, find out where they live, until we get a stooge.'

'A stooge?'

'Uh-huh.'

He looks at his iPhone.

'When did Paula get home from work?' he asks Sparrow.

'About five thirty, I think. She was generally home before me.'

***

You have to laugh. Well, grin at least. The ridiculousness of it.

It's later that day. At going-home time.

I'm the driver. I'm hardly Faye Dunaway, and I've never worn a beret in my life.

Although I have to admit that Ziggy's doing a good enough Clyde. He even has the fedora. I can't think of anyone else who could get away with that.

And Sparrow's doing a good take on C. W. Moss, the squint-eyed guy, but he's probably no idea who or what I'm talking about. Bonnie and Clyde. Way before my time as well, but I've watched it more times than I can remember. Why? Forward planning?

Ziggy looks at his watch.

A car slows to a stop at the gates and then pulls out in front of us.

I look at him, but he continues to stare at the entrance.

How will he know who best to follow?

I can't let myself think of how wrong this can go. Hijacking a government employee?

So, when he nods at me after the sixth or seventh car, it's a bit of a relief.

We follow the car, a VW Beetle – the new sort, the one with the engine in the front. No, I don't think that's right either. She negotiates the busy junctions carefully, so she is easy to follow. Soon we're out on the motorway.

I'm beginning to worry about her realising she's being followed when she indicates left at the south Lancaster junction. I know Lancaster well, and at this time of day the traffic will be impossible. But Ziggy's luck wins out again. She turns right in Galgate and parks on the drive of a modern bungalow.

I park beyond it, in the next turning.

Ziggy turns to look back at the woman. I watch in the mirror as she opens her front door and disappears.

Ziggy produces two police warrant cards. Like a bloody magician. Without another word he gets out of the car and, with a glance at 'C. W.' in the back, who is doing his best goldfish impression, I follow him.

We cross the road.

There is no one in sight.

We knock on the door.

Ziggy checks the street again.

The door opens.

He shows his card, mutters the words, and we're in.

Neat and tidy. Home alone, I surmise.

She doesn't seem surprised, and invites us to take a seat in one of those front rooms you see in adverts. How do people manage to be so tidy?

Ziggy chooses to stand looking out of the window. He's watched too many American cop movies.

The woman looks at me. I try to show the blankest face I can manage, but inside I'm giggling like a silly teenager.

'Whatever you tell us won't leave this room,' says Ziggy, in a ridiculous American accent.

The woman glances at me with a look of disbelief almost quivering into a guffaw.

I can't help but shake my head at her.

'But you know that's not true, don't you?' says Ziggy in his real voice, as he turns round to look at her.

She stares at him and then glances at me.

'Are you two for real?' she mutters.

'We are,' he says, 'and we realise we're putting you and ourselves in serious danger.'

As if I didn't already know.

'However, it's a matter of national security, so it's important that you help us if you can.'

She crosses her legs and leans back in the chair.

'How do you know I haven't alerted the police already?'

Ziggy stares at her. She looks away.

That'll be a no, then… I hope.

'The woman in your office who's disappeared, went AWOL … five months ago?'

She stares at him.

'Fiona Sparrow?' he adds, quietly.

She frowns. Shakes her head.

'Paula Lisle?'

Again she shakes her head. Looks at me.

Ziggy sighs.

'No, of course not, she isn't called that either… But you know who I mean, don't you?'

Again the frown.

Ziggy walks towards her. She backs into the chair.

He produces one of the photos, like a croupier, clicking the edge with his finger.

She takes it. Stares at it. Looks up at him. Still with a frown.

'She didn't disappear... She was transferred.'

'Where?'

She shakes her head.

'Don't think we were told.'

'Is that normal?'

'It happens.'

Ziggy goes to sit on the arm of the settee.

'What do you do there?'

'Typing.'

'What?'

'Letters, minutes of meetings, emails.'

He stands up, walks back to the window.

'Is there anything "different" about her?'

She looks at me again.

'How do you mean, different?'

'Any special powers?'

The woman laughs.

'What? Like Wonder Woman, you mean?'

Ziggy stays at the window.

She stares at him, glances at me.

'Well, now I think about it, she was a bit strange...'

Ziggy turns round, silhouetted against the light.

'How "strange"?'

'Her memory. She can retype something she'd already done. Word perfect ... even if it was weeks ago.'

Ziggy sighs. I look from one of them to the other. The woman does the same at us.

'Anything?'

The woman shrugs.

'Don't know... She was a bit embarrassed when anyone asked her about it... Said it wasn't such a good thing.'

'Why?' *I ask.*

Again, the woman makes a face.

'Well … I suppose, a lot of the stuff we type is either incomprehensible or as boring as hell. You know: "He says this", and "She says that". None of us would want to have to remember it as well as type it … and in any case we've signed papers saying we wouldn't do that or take anything out of the office.'

Ziggy walks towards the door.

'I'm sorry if we've caused you any distress,' he says.

I get up to follow him. I manage a 'Sorry about this' smile.

Ziggy turns and stares at her.

'By the way, what was her name?'

The woman stands up.

'Joyce … Joyce Denham.'

*** *

I suppose we shouldn't have been surprised.

The car is empty.

No sign of the Sparrow. The bird has flown.

We sit in the car. Ziggy is still, staring way beyond the view.

It isn't immediately apparent, but I begin to realise how quiet it is in this little estate. I suppose everyone's still at work… No, that can't be right. I look at my watch. Half past five.

Ziggy's hand appears on my arm.

'Don't move.' His storytelling voice, soft but firm.

Nothing happens.

I glance at him. Is that a smile or a grimace?

'I think we've been sussed," he whispers.

'Sussed?'

He nods. A black Mercedes appears round the corner and comes towards us, pulling up in front of us, nose to nose.

Two men.

The passenger opens his door and steps out. Leather jacket and jeans, but definitely a policeman. How do I know that?

He walks towards us.
Ziggy opens the window.
The man leans down.
'Mr Hook?'
Ziggy nods.
'Can you take the key out of the ignition, sir?'
Ziggy complies.

Ten minutes later I am in another car with other 'police officers', speeding down the M6. Ziggy is a passenger in our car behind us.

There are no flashing lights or sirens, but we are driving terrifyingly fast in the outside lane. Other drivers instinctively get out of our way.

There are no questions, no conversation at all.

But now I know James Sparrow is not who he seemed to be… So what on earth is going on?

We eventually arrive at a large anonymous building in Manchester.

Everyone is eerily polite and calm, but I know that making a run for it is out of the question.

I am taken to a room containing nothing but a table and three chairs, one of which is offered to me by the man from the car.

Another man appears and the man from the car leaves without a word. I know that his replacement is there by the door, even though there is not a sound.

I turn to look at him.
'Should I be asking for a lawyer?' I ask.
He gives me a blank look.
I smile at him.
Nothing.
I turn away.
What is going on?

If Ziggy thinks we've been used, then who by? Why? Was everything Sparrow said untrue? Is the whole story about his wife a pack of lies? Why come to us?

In the end it is probably about half an hour before anyone else comes to see me.

It's a tall man in an expensive-looking suit. He has blonde hair and is good-looking in a posh sort of way. With him is a woman who is older. She is also well dressed, with dark hair pulled back in a tight bun.

They dismiss the silent man and the woman sits on one the chairs facing me, while the man goes to the window to look out. Like Ziggy did earlier, but this isn't funny.

The woman puts down the thick dossier she is carrying and opens it.

I wait. I'm trying not to worry what might be in such a set of documents, given my history.

The man by the window turns and clears his throat.

'Ursula White? Robinson?'

I nod. Are we going to play games?

The woman looks at me through the glasses she's now put on, which don't make her look threatening. More schoolmarm-like.

'What were you doing following Miss Johnson?'

I look at one, then the other.

'Who are you?' I ask.

The woman doesn't look at the man.

'We're police officers.'

I try a nervous laugh.

'Well, I hope so … but where's your identification?'

The woman gives me an even sterner look.

'I don't think that's necessary, do you?' she says.

I look her in the eyes. Dark brown.

'Well, actually, I do,' I say as quietly as I can.

'And, actually, we can arrest you now under the Official Secrets Act and you'll go straight to prison.'

I look at her. She doesn't waver.

I don't know why, but I have to laugh. Not a belly laugh, more a 'Can you believe this?' laugh.

The woman's face hardens.

The man comes and sits down on the other chair.

'I don't think that would be a good idea, Helen,' he says without looking at her. She doesn't look best pleased, but she doesn't say anything, although if she purses her lips any harder, they'll give her a mouth hernia.

I look at him, wondering what I can usefully tell him.

He's still smiling, so I give in.

'We were trying to find out what happened to our client's wife.'

The smile stays, but he doesn't speak.

'But the problem now is that I'm not sure if he was for real or that the woman we were looking for is his wife, or what her real name is either.'

The smile remains, but the pursed lips crinkle into a frown.

'Client?'

I can't help but sigh.

'Look, if you really are spooks, then I think you're missing a trick here,' I begin.

The man laughs softly. The woman gives him the stare before refocusing on me.

'We're not spooks,' she says, in a spookish manner.

'In what way is he a client?' the man asks again.

I sigh again, wondering what Ziggy is likely to be confusing some other spooks with somewhere else.

'Ziggy – Mr Hook – is a private detective. Well, when he's not doing other things. And, I don't know quite why, I'm his … girl Friday, secretary, driver, accountant, et cetera.'

They both look at each other.

'That doesn't explain why you were interrogating Miss Johnson.'

'Well, in the first place we didn't know her name. We just

followed her from her place of work because we thought she was a colleague of Jimmy's wife.'

'Jimmy?'

'Sparrow … although I'm now not sure that's his real name.'

I can see this is confusing for the topknot.

'Perhaps if I tell you what I know?'

He nods. She repurses the lips.

I tell them the story.

When I'm finished they're looking at me with the blankest of faces. Do they get trained to do that?

The woman stands up, clutching her heavy file.

'I think we'll leave this for now,' she says.

The man gives me a wink and they both leave the room.

I turn to watch them go. The other man steps back inside and resumes the trademark blank stare.

I wonder how Ziggy's getting on. Knowing him, he'll be telling them all sorts of fairy tales.

And I'm now wondering if anything 'James Sparrow' told us was true, including his name. And has a woman really gone missing?

I realise I'm speaking out loud.

'What the fuck is going on here?'

The strong, silent type behind me doesn't even blink.

*****

So? 'James Sparrow'?

That didn't work, did it?

I thought we were getting somewhere. That weird Hook guy and his kooky sidekick. Like some fifties noir set-up. Off the wall, but they were obviously getting close to waking those spooks up. Anyway, can't complain. Only hope at least it means that Freya's safe.

Anyway, it'll be good not having to remember I'm a

Sparrow, although maybe it'll be just as hard remembering I'm a Kemball.

What else have I got, other than despair? Faced with such ignorant and blinkered self-harming determination, what else is there to do or say?

I'm sitting in a cafe watching the world go by, with its mentality of 'Get on and it'll be all right... Please don't bring up politics again. It's Sunday... Keep your head in the sand...' What can you do?

Even the threat of this virus isn't stopping the party going on or the summer hotel bookings.

And even when it eventually begins to dawn on them that their ostrich approach isn't quite working, which will be constantly denied by the press anyway, they'll be easily coerced and bullied into finding someone else to blame. It will still be Tommy Foreigner not playing ball and the Communist traitors back-stabbing their own compatriots who will need to be exposed and silenced. After all, Hitler and Goebbels provided an evidently successful blueprint.

Who will make up the heroic resistance? Who would take such a risk?

Soon the doom-mongers and the climate activists will be put back in their cardboard boxes and life, and death, will be able to go on.

Unless.

Unless, even if it risks an explosion of violence, bringing death and destruction to 'ordinary people'... What else can someone do?

But ... where does an ordinary person get a gun from? It's not going to be America.

FEBRUARY 29

'an ephemeral ghost.'
Vera Nazarian

CHAPTER 5

Dawn is crisp.

No birds sing.

Carole Morgan lies in bed until a red glow creeps through her window.

The cat remains on her bed. Doesn't even look up as she slips out of the bedroom door.

She stands briefly at the front door, sipping her black tea, until she's shivering so much she's spilling half of it.

Back inside she lights a fire. Sits and watches it grow.

Memories come of other places she's been alone. Often hidden.

'A life in the shadows,' she smirks to herself.

The smirk creases the tight skin on her face. She reaches up to feel the still roughened flesh, which will never soften.

It has not been soft for most of her life.

The memory of it happening is still vivid after all these years. The grin on his face. One hand gripping her neck, the other holding her arm up her back. His body heavy on top of her. His hard cock against her thigh. The smell of her burning flesh. The slow, burning pain gradually increasing, until the blackness swallowed her. The awakening to feel the agony over again, and again, for the rest of her life. Her beauty ravaged. The faces turning away. The gasps of horror and the whispering … always the whispering.

She felt the eyes watching her as she returned from the hospital yesterday. She has been expecting a visit, but not until this morning.

So it was a long night without much sleep.

The specialist hasn't told her the whole truth. But she's no fool.

Maybe a couple of months, she guesses.

Is that a shadow across the window?

She goes to the door.

The sun is now behind the skeletal ash tree, sitting in the crux of its branches like a lost balloon.

She watches as it slowly frees itself from the tree's clutches and hangs free in the still air.

A subtle warmth to her right tells her she's there.

She hardly dares to look, but can hear her breath in the frozen silence.

She turns.

Thinner than ever.

Almost a skeleton in rags.

But the pale eyes pierce her through.

Even, for once, an almost smile.

Fern Robinson.

No words are spoken.

The figure is there for only a few moments. Not moving. The grey dog-wolf at her side is just as still.

She beckons them in, but the smile fades and the eyes slowly shut and then open again. The faintest of a shake of the head.

And as she watches, the two of them fade into the trees as if she's only imagined them.

She stands there a long time, wondering if they'll reappear, but the wind starts to blow and she's shivering again.

Back inside the fire has nearly gone out, but she's incapable of helping it and can only lie down on the floor and stare at the glowing embers as one by one they wink and die.

It's not long before she hears the cat purring near her face and then the strange roughness of its tongue on her cheek.

She opens her eyes as he nuzzles her hand.

Slowly she gets to her knees and finds some sticks.

Gradually the fire revives and she kneels there until she can find the strength to get to her feet and stagger to the settee.

Did she see her?

She recalls the night on the boat as they escaped the fire and the killings.

The weeks spent hiding in the old croft.

Eating rabbit and drinking black water.

Eventually being found by old Robbie, who took them back to his croft and brought them back to life. No questions. No judgement.

And then one morning she was gone.

No goodbye. She never said goodbye.

Is that goodbye? Just now?

Who can say?

But it is the right day.

The extra day.

February 29 2020.

Fern's twentieth birthday. Eighty years old.

Her last?

Who knows?

It's only later, when she goes out to collect some more wood, that she sees the stick on the doorstep. A glint of something.

She stoops to pick it up.

There's a band of silver.

She pulls it from the stick.

Silver thorns holding one stone. Pale yellow.

She looks up. There's a slight breeze now, from the south, from the sun still only low in the sky.

She pulls the ring from the stick and puts it on her own finger.

Looks again to see if she's there.

But nothing.
Not a breath of wind.
Silence.

***

Jeanie Tait is dog-tired. She'd agreed to stay on overnight when that bloody idle Sassenach, Joyce Harburn, phoned in sick again at the last minute yesterday evening.

In the event the inmates have been good, apart from auld Jessie wandering about all hours of the night, but that was par for the course. And she would always be singing, so easily found, and not difficult to coax back into bed with a chocolate biscuit or five.

It's only at breakfast that the nightmare begins.

She's struggling to get Henry Salmond into his trousers when Eva comes running.

At first she can't manage English, and is gabbling away in her sing-song Jamaican patois.

Jeanie pulls up Henry's zip at last and takes hold of the big woman's arms.

'I can't understand a word, Eva. Calm down.'

Eva stops, gulps and points along the corridor.

'Eedith … Missus MacDonald … she 'as gone!'

Jeanie stares at her.

'Gone?'

Eva nods furiously.

'But… I just looked in on her. She was still in bed.'

'No,' gasps Eva, shaking her head. 'It's only her … her hair, her vig.'

Jeanie frowns and then realises what she's saying.

'Oh, my God,' she whispers, dreading the barrage of possibilities popping up in her head.

'Here, you take Henry down to breakfast. I'll deal with this.'

80

She wags her finger at the old man, whose eyes are glistening.

'You behave, Henry Salmond, or I'll have your guts for garters.'

She knows damn well he'll take a chance, but Eva is a big girl. She can look after herself.

Edith's room is downstairs. Jeanie hurtles down, cursing her bad luck. She shouldn't even have been there.

Sure enough Edith's bed is empty, but the sheets have been pulled back to reveal her revolting ginger wig resting snugly on the cold pillow.

Jeanie presses the alarm bell and tries the garden window. It's open.

How can that have happened?

That's not her job.

Who was on security last night?

It wasn't her, and Mrs Parkinson would never have given that job to Joyce Harburn. Would she?

She goes into the garden.

It hasn't rained, but the lawn is wet and the trees are all drooping. It's freezing cold. She looks right and then left. No one in sight.

Back inside she hurries along to the main office, and meets Mrs Parkinson as she's setting off to look for the person who had pressed the alarm bell.

'It was me,' says Jeanie. 'Edith's done a runner.'

***

Standing in the doorway of what once would have been a drawing room, but which is now designated the day room, DS Riccardo Gatti questions his uncomfortableness, what his *nonna* would call *scomodo*, especially as she doesn't recognise him any more either … like lots of these folk.

His gaze takes in the drooping heads and the glazed expressions of those who do look his way. If any of them have witnessed anything it is unlikely they'll be able to give any useful information. The only person who seems at all helpful is one of the night nurses, Miss Tait, but she has also admitted she is dog-tired after doing a double shift last night.

No one saw anything.

The woman in charge is understandably defensive, particularly about the unlocked door.

'It was checked at six thirty by the security man,' she tells him, but her lips are thin and her eyes won't hold his.

He questions the man.

'Definitely,' he growls. 'Absolutely certain.'

Well, he would say that, wouldn't he? And his eye contact was as brittle as anyone's at pub-kicking-out time.

The black girl just cries, but he doesn't think she's lying. So where can Edith have gone?

He looks over towards DC Jamie Armstrong, who is watching the SOCO woman dusting the guilty door frame … it's probably more to do with her blonde ponytail than any interest in her expertise.

This isn't going well.

He's phoned in and suggested a search party, but no response back yet. After all, she isn't a teenager or a young mum, which upsets him a bit. Makes him think of his *nonna* again, wandering about in the dark in her nightdress and slippers, which seem to be the only things missing. This woman has not even taken the cardigan still hanging on the bedpost.

He catches Jamie's eye and beckons him over.

'So come on, local guy, where should we be looking?'

Jamie shrugs his shoulders. The sergeant with the funny name was born and brought up in Glasgow after all.

'Your guess is as good as mine.'

Gatti frowns at him.

'Not good enough. She can't have gone far. Seventy-eight, uses a stick, nothing on, just wearing slippers?'

Jamie produces a well-used local map and opens it up on the hall table.

He points to the home and then at the two major roads that border it on two adjacent sides, east and north.

'If she's set off in either of these directions someone would have seen her. Even at night there's pretty well constant traffic, and that's if she could climb over the deer fences.'

Gatti nods his understanding, but points to the other two directions.

'If she's gone to the river, we'll find her on the bank here. That's where the jumpers end up,' says Jamie, full of local knowledge on that one at least.

'Jumpers?' asks Gatti.

Jamie points to the narrow line across the river a couple of centimetres away.

'That's the old railway viaduct, where people go to end it all, although not many of them manage to hit the river ... which is always messy,' he adds, with evident distaste.

'So what about this way?' asks Gatti, pointing at the only alternative direction west of the care home, although he immediately notices the crowded contour lines.

Jamie shakes his head.

'No chance. I'd struggle to get up there even in me hiking boots. This time of year, muddy as hell from the dafter sheep clambering about ... and some of them end up in the river as well.'

Gatti stares at the map.

'Unless, of course...'

He looks over at the 'local man', whose straight face breaks into a grin.

'Unless?'

'She's away with the fairies.'

Gatti frowns at him.

Jamie affects disappointment.

'Even you must have heard about Thomas the Rhymer.'

Gatti frowns again and then nods his head.

'Yeah, right. So are you suggesting I tell the local press that's our considered opinion? Or shall I offer your suggestion to Inspector Steil?'

Jamie's eyes go big.

Gatti takes that as a no.

'So you think our best bet is to wait for the river to give her up?'

Jamie frowns, but to be honest he has no better idea.

***

The answer is in the following day's newspaper:

'Captain Tomasz Steil and two other soldiers were arrested on the Greek island of Hydra, after being involved in a fight in a bar, which resulted in five local men ending up in hospital, some with serious injuries. The three soldiers have been sent back to the UK to await disciplinary proceedings.'

But it's what it says about Steil later in the article that draws my attention. He's a highly decorated marksman credited with over two hundred kills.

It also tells me that he's been allowed to return to his family, who live in the Borders.

I'm sitting there reading this on Saturday afternoon in the empty snug bar of my local pub. All the rest of the gang are away at the match.

Except for Sam Finch, who's now asking me if I want another. I stare at him, remembering he's an ex-squaddie.

'You all right?' he asks.

I nod and say yes, and then it's relatively easy to coax a story or two out of him.

'Scots Guards,' he says. 'All nutters.'

I show him the article and the piece about Steil. He nods and says he's heard about him.

'Yer glad yer've got weird bastards like him on yer side, but I wouldn't go drinking with him.'

I give him a questioning frown.

He shakes his head.

'They're not human. Weird eyes.'

I do a lot more research.

Not the first trouble he's been involved in. Been busted back to the ranks twice before. But his father was a brigadier and his grandfather was killed at the Somme.

So I find out where he lives.

In the Scottish Borders, not far from Galashiels.

A huge mansion on the top of a hill.

My head says,

'No way,' but my instinct says otherwise.

I find a cottage on the Net and book myself in.

***

As expected, DI Magdalena L Steil is not impressed. Not that anyone calls her by her first name or knows what the *L* stands for. Her mother is from the far eastern forests of Poland and her father's family still farms the high tops between the Gala and the Tweed. She has her mother's soft voice and her father's preferred communication skills of saying nothing much with an air of disdain.

She's now standing in the front porch of the care home, looking up at the hills.

DS Gatti has learnt to be patient.

It's still cold, and although there's a blustery breeze the weather forecast is for a bright, calm day but another cold night.

'If she's managed to get up there, we need to find her in the next few hours,' she mutters.

Gatti pulls out his phone.

She nods.

He walks away to make the call.

When he's done, he looks back to find she's disappeared.

He finds her in the garden, following the boundary, which is mainly a well-maintained high stone wall that would be impossible to climb without a ladder.

He tells her he's organised a search party. She gives him a slight nod, but something's bothering her.

She stops by one of the well-established rhododendrons and looks back at the house.

'Why now?' she asks quietly.

Gatti can only shrug.

'Is that care worker still here, the one who did the double shift?' she asks.

He nods.

They make their way back to the front door.

Jeanie Tait has come back in to work only a few hours after being sent home and is now helping to serve cups of tea and toast.

Gatti has a quick word, and she comes over to where Steil is staring out of the entrance hall door.

'I understand you've known Edith for a long time,' she asks, with her best encouraging smile.

Jeanie frowns and then nods.

'Yes. She's older than me, but we went to the same schools.'

Steil smiles again.

'So you grew up here. You know the countryside?'

Jeanie nods again.

'Aye. In those days you had to make your own entertainment.

And if you'd done your jobs, you'd be outside afore you were found another one.'

Steil smiles again.

'But if she was older than you, you've not come across each other that often?'

Jeanie shakes her head, but Steil knows there's something she wants to say.

She waits. Jeanie's eyes flicker back to the house and then back to the laird's daughter.

Steil glances at Gatti.

'Sergeant, will you go and check if the SOCOs have any more information?'

Gatti suppresses a smile as he turns away.

Steil looks back at Jeanie, who can't face the pale eyes.

How can she say it without it being an accusation?

Steil waits.

'Childhood memories can be extraordinarily clear,' she eventually murmurs, looking up at the hills.

'I'm not accusing anyone,' says Jeanie.

Steil nods.

Jeanie points towards the big house on the hillside above them.

'Edith's mother worked up there, in the kitchens, most of her life. Edith would go with her if it was the school holidays. She and the other workers' kids.'

Steil continues to stare at the house. She doesn't know the family, although her father probably does.

'Once … I was playing out, with my friend Jenny… We saw Edith walking out with the laird's son … Randolph… He's now the laird.'

She stops and looks back at the inspector, who is looking at her.

'They didn't know we were there… We were very still and quiet.'

Steil stands very still herself, like a heron.

Jeanie looks away again.

'They were kissing … and then … they…'

Steil doesn't move or speak.

'Or rather he … you know … had his way with her'.

No, she didn't say that. Well, not the sex bit.

None of it. She never has.

Nor the sequel when she went through the same ordeal.

He regarded it as his right, while probably thinking that the privilege was all theirs. Could even be still at it, although he probably has to pay for it nowadays. Even foreigners like Eva wouldn't put up with that now.

She watches as the inspector walks away.

What if she did go up to the big house?

He probably wouldn't recognise her … and he wouldn't be answering the door anyway.

Maybe she could just go up and have a look round.

DI Steil knows when a person, even a person who isn't a suspect, isn't telling the whole story. So what can a fifty-something woman have to hide about the big house?

She isn't yet thinking of talking to her father. It always begins cordially, but generally degenerates into a 'Why on earth are you doing this job?' row.

After all, she could drive up to the big house and ask to search the grounds.

Yes, that's what to do.

She calls over to DS Gatti, who is questioning someone who looks like a gardener.

'Do we know the owner?' she asks, nodding up the hillside.

'Now why has that made Gatti twitchy?' she wonders.

'Why yes, of course,' he says. 'Shall I give him a call?'

In the event, Lord 'Randy' Ballantyne isn't at home.

Left for Aviemore yesterday evening. Is that suspicious?

Miss Lewthwaite, the housekeeper, obviously understands that, but is quick to say that if the snow beckons, he does drop everything and go.

She's a trifle dubious about allowing the grounds and buildings to be searched, and suggests they wait until His Lordship can be contacted. But, under Steil's steady gaze, she makes the call.

After returning from the other room she indicated it was necessary to retreat to, she comes back with a pasted-on 'warm' smile and nods her head.

'His Lordship thinks you're wasting your time, but is more than happy to aid the authorities in tracking down the poor woman. He recalls that he does know her from his childhood, but had no idea she was unwell and hasn't knowingly seen her for years.'

Steil gives her back the 'warm' smile and puts her mouth to her phone to give the go-ahead.

Given this response, she is pretty certain that even if the woman is found in the grounds she'll probably be dead by now from exposure, and so any link to any past misdemeanours would be impossible to unearth.

Having assured herself that Gatti is more than capable of overseeing the exercise, she walks back to her car.

Ten minutes later she is still sitting there, staring out at the mist-covered hills.

'Maybe just once?' she whispers to herself, and starts the engine.

***

So I set off up north. Memories of being snowed in and wintry walks, although there's no sign of that sort of weather at the moment. Even so, I've filled the boot with

walking gear and warm clothing, even the tent, although it's some time since I last went camping.

The journey up the motorways in the dark passes without incident, apart from a quick detour into Darlington, where I park the car I stole in Preston and put my stuff into the one I find in the next street. Shame the owner couldn't take it in part exchange. He'd get the better deal.

I decide to cut through on the Wooler Road from Alnwick and arrive in Kelso in time for breakfast.

I always thought that this town thinks too highly of itself and so I'm not surprised it's gone even further upmarket, cafe-wise at least. 'Bijou' is probably their word, meaning overpriced 'home-made' cakes, but not a bacon sarnie in sight.

I find the least updated-looking one and settle for tea and toast.

The Guardian is struggling to point out the lack of urgency, but Johnson is still pretty well AWOL and Parliament is now neutered. And behind it all, pulling the strings like some monstrous fairy tale gargoyle, is the puppet master, shambling about in his techno-guru dressing-up clothes.

I look round the gathering of the less well-off old folks quietly carrying on with their daily routines. A smattering of *Sun*s, *Mail*s and *Express*es indicate the ongoing Brexit delusions of these people, although they don't look so victorious now and are not in the majority here.

Outside the passing figures are more vigorously doing their early morning shopping, then no doubt returning to their restored farm cottages and grand mansions after a quick chat with their smug compatriots, who are all wearing tartan skirts or jackets.

I pay the bill and walk back to the car.

Then find myself sitting there fighting the anger and

sense of helplessness. So I give myself a shake and start the car.

The mission proceeds.

***

Ref:TD/HO/022922219.

'Where's ▓▓▓▓▓▓▓▓ now?'

'Heading north.'

'North? Where, for heaven's sake?'

'He's booked himself in to a cottage in the ▓▓▓▓▓▓▓ ▓▓▓▓▓▓▓▓'

'Where?'

'Not far from ▓▓▓▓▓'

'Why?'

'Not sure.'

'Well, don't lose him.'

CHAPTER 6

DI Steil is struggling to remember the last time she's been home.

Last month?

Yes, her mother's birthday.

The usual false greetings. Three kisses and hugs.

It hadn't lasted more than a couple of hours.

They'd managed to keep away from all the flashpoints: her lack of a relationship, her clothes, her hairstyle … her job.

But then it exploded. Her father was still ranting on about 'that stupid Greenpeace activist woman' interrupting someone's dinner. It was last June, for heaven's sake, she tried to tell him.

She didn't even finish her meal. Left the table, gathered her things, and walked out. Mother was in tears. She drove down the hill far too fast and nearly collided with a caravan trundling along the main road.

So why try again?

Well, she knows Tommy is going to be there. He's 'home from the war'. She'd received a typically outlandish card informing her that her 'doting brother' was hanging out in Hydra finding his inner Cohen and thinking of chucking it all in and going AWOL … but needing to top up his funds before disappearing.

This was his usual hyped-up screwball self, hiding the contorted screwed-up Peter Pan he's never escaped, who always needs his Wendy-sister to come home to.

Well, she's his sister but she has never been his Wendy.

But she does miss him.

Life is a lot more ordinary without him.

Getting 'home' is always a slight dilemma, as in which way to get there from Galashiels. Either way it was a long journey:

north and then the slow crawl up and over, or the long way west and up the steeper climb north.

She went the latter way, along by the Tweed. She knew exactly when the steep hillside on her right became her father's demesne, although the house is completely invisible from far above. Only people driving along the narrow lane the other side of the valley would have any chance of spotting the house, and then only in winter when the trees have shed their leaves.

She imagined people looking across and wondering how on earth such a huge mansion could have been built so high up with no apparent access.

She slows down to take the sharp turn through the village and then the long slow drag up the hillside. The house only comes into view once for a few seconds near the top of the climb.

Sure enough, Tommy's Alfa is slewed across the yard, its red gloss displaying yet another war wound, that is in the war he single-handedly wages with 'plebs driving like sloths,' as he puts it in such a public school boy way. He isn't like that about anything else. It's the single hangover from an experience he thoroughly detested.

The boy himself appears at the stable yard gate, riding boots on, a sulky-looking Cleo glistening and steaming like a small train behind him.

'Hi, Zsa-Zsa. You missed a fine gallop.'

She grins at him.

'So I see, poor lamb. She won't have done that for a long time.'

Tommy laughs.

'Cleopatra's no lamb, and she always reminds me how strong she can be.'

They embrace and then put each other at arm's length in their traditional sizing-up procedure, which they invented during their school holiday reunions.

'You've got your tired eyes on, Sis,' he says.

She hesitates, knowing that it's true, but what she sees in his face is more worrying.

She holds him close and feels the shudder.

He lets her hold him.

'Do you want to tell me?' she whispers.

He pulls away and looks at her with those piercing blue eyes.

'Not now,' he growls. 'Probably never.'

They hold each other again, slowly rocking back and forth.

'Oh, Magda, you should have said you were coming,' comes their mother's voice from the kitchen steps.

They grin and raise their eyebrows at each other.

'Later?' he whispers.

She nods, knowing that will have to be somewhere else.

She leads him over and the three of them embrace. Their mother is unable to stop her tears.

Later, gathered in the drawing room in front of the unnecessarily roaring fire, Magda is trying to avoid even meeting her father's eyes, but knows they are fiercely directed her way most of the time.

'Well, we can't get a word out of your brother, Magda,' he says.

Tommy shakes his head.

'There's nothing to tell. War isn't exciting at all. Just bloody … day in, day out. Nothing to see there.'

He gets up and pours himself another large gin.

'Can't get used to this daft idea, mixing it with all sorts of other tosh,' he murmurs as he goes to sit again, one leg over the arm of the chair.

His mother sighs.

His father ignores it as a childish tantrum, which it is.

'So, Magda, what brings you here, other than to see your brother, of course?'

Now she looks him in the eye. At least she knows where both her anger and her stubbornness come from.

'Actually, the case I'm on involves one of our neighbours, Father.'

He glares at her, assuming it will mean an attack on their class, whatever the issue is.

'Randolph Ballantyne,' she announces. 'What do we know about him?'

Her father makes a face. This at least isn't going to cause an argument.

'Jackanapes,' he announces, with a grunt. 'A wastrel, a liar and a womanising wretch.'

Tommy laughs out loud.

'Steady on, Papa.'

His father gets up now, strides over to the drinks sideboard and pours himself another Glenlivet.

'What's he done now?'

'Nothing, as far as I know, so far,' says Magda.

'Does it involve a woman?' he asks.

'Well, yes, although she's over eighty years old and has gone walkabout from the care home near the river below his estate.'

He looks at her and frowns.

'Are you serious?'

'There may have been "contact" when they were much younger,' she offers.

'Aye, well, they did say no woman was safe when he was younger, but now? He's not much younger than me.'

'This woman has dementia. She may be recalling something from the past,' she adds.

Her father shakes his head and looks at their mother.

'Have you heard anything, Helena?' he asks.

She, startled, shakes her head.

'Me? No? Why would I know anything about him? I've only met him once or twice. As you say, not pleasant at all.'

The three of them look from one to the other.

'He sounds interesting,' laughs Tommy. 'Where does he live?'

All three shake their heads at him.

The room goes quiet.

'On the slopes of the Eildons.'

'Oh, well, that solves it, then. The fairies will have taken her,' says Tommy.

Again they all shake their heads.

Later, over lunch, which both Tommy and Magda have failed to avoid, despite Magda's claims to be needed back at the case, the conversation returns to the woman's disappearance – although, as Magda has had no communication, she can only assume there's been no news about it.

'When did she go missing, this old lady?' asks Tommy.

Magda shakes her head.

'Not sure. Any time after ten o'clock last night.'

Tommy frowns.

'Aren't there nurses, care assistants checking all night?'

'Yes, there were, but this old lady left her wig behind, so they thought she was there in the bed … until this morning when they went to wake her up for breakfast.'

Helena shakes her head.

'Poor woman … and are you saying she was outside? During the night? It must have been below freezing most of the time.'

Magda thinks about this and checks her watch.

'I've got to get back. My sergeant is very efficient, but not given to quick decisions.'

Tommy accompanies her out to her car.

They embrace again.

'What are you doing tonight?' he asks.

She shrugs.

'It depends.'

He nods.

'I'll book that restaurant in Melrose,' he says.

'OK, but I can't guarantee to be there.'

They hug again. This time it's not family. There's something wrong. She looks him in the eyes. He looks away.

'I'll be all right. Shit happens. I'm dealing with it.'

She stares at him.

'I'm here, you know.'

He nods.

'I know. Now bugger off.'

He pushes her towards the car and walks away.

She watches him go. He doesn't look back. His shoulders are hunched. He's carrying some terrible burden, she's sure.

She's halfway down the lane when she realises she can't see properly, pulls in and wipes her eyes.

Her phone bleeps.

It's Gatti.

'Ma'am, there's been a development. We've found her shoes and a necklace.'

'Where?'

'The shoes were in the woods in the grounds of Ballantyne House... The necklace was hanging from a branch above them.'

'I'm on my way. Ten minutes.'

She did what she always did when things like this happened in a case. What DI Tranter had taught her.

'Jump to conclusions if you want, but beware the obvious, the logical... They may be convincing, but keep your mind open. Unintended events and coincidences can be both bizarre and true ... and, also, there are criminals out there who are both clever and devious and downright bonkers.'

She waits. No quirky ideas float to the surface.

But as she starts the engine it occurs to her that they haven't asked exactly when Ballantyne decided to go skiing and how he got there.

'He could even have his own plane,' she adds out loud.

***

Randolph Ballantyne doesn't have his own plane, but he is rich enough to get on any plane that will take him to the snow … and by all accounts the housekeeper is correct in saying that he does just go, if the snow is good.

But ten thirty at night? On a plane? No, but the car he's taken is more than capable of doing the distance in no time at all.

The housekeeper gives Steil the phone number of the hotel he's staying at, but, looking at her watch, suggests that it's likely he'll be skiing right now.

This is correct.

She leaves a message asking him to contact her urgently.

Now outside, she watches as the team search the grounds in widening arcs from where the two items were found, which have now been taken away for analysis.

If there had been snow here there would have been footprints, but there may be some in the dead leaves and fallen twigs, even though there hasn't been a drop of rain for a week or so.

She walks over to Gatti, who is talking to one of the SOCO team.

His look tells her,

'Nothing yet.'

'How far is this from the care home?' she asks.

He shrugs his shoulders.

'Depends on the route, ma'am.'

She sighs.

'So can we hazard a guess or search the possibilities?'

Again he makes a face.

'We've only got twenty men so far, ma'am. Ten here, and the others are slowly making their way up, but it's half a mile at least … mostly uphill.'

She looks off towards the direction she thinks is the way down and glances back at Gatti, who points her slightly to the right.

'There are two paths that go about halfway. But then it's much steeper and there's a fence, although it's not been maintained that well. Lots of gaps.'

She nods, knowing she'll only get glared at by the SOCOs if she starts wandering about.

'I'm going back inside to talk to the housekeeper again,' she says.

Gatti nods and watches her walk away.

'Where has she been the last couple of hours?' he wonders.

Back in the house she wanders about, pretending to look for the housekeeper, but in reality is more curious to see what sort of lair this suspected womaniser inhabits.

However, it's eerily similar to her parents' house.

There is ornate furniture in the main rooms, old family portraits, lots of flowers, Persian carpets, and all the other *objets* collected, probably stolen, from the long-dead empire.

In the absence of the world-weary woman, who said she had work to do (what would that be?) she quickly ascends to the next floor.

Here is a more mundane environment. More boys' club than downstairs. Fitness bikes and a punch ball? The pictures were more appropriate to the world traveller and the bon viveur.

But the main bedroom is a surprise. It contains some of the same elegant furniture seen elsewhere in the house, but nothing commensurate with Ballantyne's reputation as a roué. No pornography in sight, and she doesn't think his sudden disappearance merits rifling through his drawers and cupboards yet.

Just one portrait of a woman. Not an old master. More recent. Very beautiful, but a sad face. No, distracted.

While shaking her head she backs out, almost bumping into a young woman carrying a Hoover.

The two of them stare at each other.

'I'm sorry, madam,' the girl mutters, perplexed by this stranger.

Steil produces her warrant card.

The girl nods her understanding and glances towards the master bedroom, but then shrugs her shoulders and continues on along the corridor.

Steil follows her.

'Excuse me,' she says, catching up with the girl, who turns to look at her. 'Can I ask you a few questions?'

The girl shrugs and puts the Hoover down, rubs her arm, and looks towards the window.

But what on earth can she ask?

The girl looks back at her.

'He's all right,' she mutters. 'I know what people say, but he's never tried anything with me.'

Steil frowns. The girl's accent is instantly recognisable to her. Is it cruel to think that this young woman, with her dark hair falling loosely out of an untidy chignon and her farmer's daughter's rough, reddened cheeks, wouldn't be attractive to the gentleman of the house? Not a handicap, according to the rumours, but she seems fairly relaxed about him.

'What do people say?'

The girl nearly grins.

'Oh, you know … dragging you off to bed, and all that.'

'But he doesn't do that?'

She shrugs again.

'Not with me he hasn't.'

She holds Steil's gaze with a steady confidence.

'Thank you for being frank about that,' says Steil.

The girl makes a face.

'It's not as if I'd say no,' she murmurs, a slight grin lighting up her face. 'If it meant becoming Lady Ballantyne, I wouldn't say no to that.'

She laughs, in a slightly hollow way. But then she frowns again, perhaps worried by the detective's steady gaze.

'Come on… He's older than my father.'

Steil manages a smile, but still waits. There's something the woman's not saying.

'Bit surprising him going off like that, though, so … abruptly.'

Steil frowns, but the girl is glancing down the corridor.

'Why abruptly?'

The girl doesn't turn immediately. Her shoulders hunch up.

'He was supposed to be going to the theatre last night, in Edinburgh. Two tickets. I saw them on the sideboard yesterday afternoon.'

Now she turns.

'They were still there when I arrived this morning, but they've disappeared since then.'

Steil holds her gaze.

'I don't know who with. Obviously, he doesn't tell me who he's going out with.'

Their eye contact is interrupted by the arrival of the housekeeper through the door at the end of the corridor.

She gives the young woman a cold look.

'The downstairs front room needs doing, Nadia,' she says, a tad sharply.

The girl shrugs her shoulders and sets off towards the head of the stairs.

Steil watches her descend. She sees her look back at her and raise her eyebrows.

She turns to look at the housekeeper, whose lips are now a straight line of disapproval.

'I shouldn't give much credence to servants' gossip if I were you, Inspector,' she says, and continues past her towards the other end of the corridor, where she doesn't look back before disappearing through the doorway.

Steil stands looking out of the window.

So does it look like a hasty change of mind after all?

She makes her way after the woman, wondering how she can wheedle the truth out of her, while telling herself not to feel annoyed about the woman's obvious racism or pointing out that she has Polish blood herself.

Her thoughts are interrupted by DS Gatti, who calls up to her from the entrance hall.

'Ma'am, I think we've found further evidence of the woman coming up the hillside.'

Steil descends quickly and follows him to the path leading down towards the river.

They arrive as one of the search officers is putting a multicoloured woollen hat into an evidence bag.

She hands it to Steil.

'Where did you find it?'

The WPC points down towards the hillside.

'Caught on a bush, ma'am, below the bottom fence.'

Steil goes down and looks at the scene and then at the steep drop down towards the river, which she can't see, but she can hear the distant sound of rushing water. She remembers that for a short stretch it goes through a deep gorge, before joining the bigger flow of the Tweed.

How on earth could a frail old woman with dementia get up there?

She looks at Gatti, who is staring downwards, shaking his head.

'Like you asked me before, I'd say it was impossible, ma'am,' he says quietly.

They both watch as the search team continue on down, holding on to branches and taking care. They're dressed in outdoor gear and walking boots. The staff at the home insist that only her slippers are missing, along with a thin cardigan, a nightdress, and underwear.

The two officers look at each other.

It doesn't look possible.

Steil nods Gatti back up the hillside to the house, but stops him by the front steps.

'One of the maids told me she saw a couple of tickets for the theatre last night, which have now disappeared.'

Gatti frowns.

'Did she say which theatre or show?' he asks.

Steil shakes her head.

'I'll go and ask the housekeeper. I think she's keeping one or two things to herself.'

Gatti nods again.

'Shall I find the old lady's doctor, ma'am? I can't believe she could have got up that hill on her own.'

Steil nods her agreement and sets off in pursuit of the housekeeper.

***

Jennifer Lewthwaite has been Ballantyne's housekeeper for the last five years, which she knows is by far the longest anyone has managed to do that. But then she made it clear from the beginning, having worked with similar 'gentlemen' before. No funny business, everything above board and, in her head at least, she'd protect him from the nosy parkers who were always sniffing around for trouble or, more likely, were attracted by the scent of money.

She's no idea why he suddenly upped and left last night.

She has removed the theatre tickets, although she can't be sure who the other one was for. Lots of potential 'partners'. He often goes to Edinburgh and other places to the theatre or concerts. Occasionally he'd mention who he was going with or who he was going to meet there, but not always. She's obviously met quite a lot of his 'friends', who do include quite a few 'young ladies', some of whom were … what her mother would have called unsuitable.

She's also recognised DI Magda Steil, but can't remember where or on what occasion. This nags at her all the morning.

And now the woman's coming down the stairs towards her.

She's only then struck by the thought that the tied-back blonde hair and the blue eyes are exactly the sort of woman Randolph goes for and has to control her inner smirk as she waits for the inspector to reach the landing … which instantly gives her the venue of the previous sighting of her. The Christmas event at Abbotsford.

The detective smiles at her.

'Just a few more questions, madam,' she says. 'Miss Lewthwaite, is it?'

Steil sees the woman's eyes hardening, but pretends otherwise.

'I was wondering if you know what happened to the two theatre tickets, which were seen earlier this morning on the sideboard there,' and to be clear, she points at the flower arrangement on the level above.

The housekeeper doesn't look where she's pointing, but gives her a thin smile.

'I removed them. He obviously doesn't need them now he's gone skiing.'

Steil smiles again.

'Have you still got them?'

She watches as the woman weighs up the odds of lying … and decides not to.

'Yes, they're in the bin in the kitchen.'

Steil continues to smile at her.

'I'll go and get them … if you think they're important.'

Steil nods.

'I'm more interested in who the other person would have been.'

The housekeeper shakes her head.

'I've no idea.'

Again Steil smiles.

'Educated guess?'

A returning smile.

'Sir Randolph has so many friends…'

Steil nods.

'I imagine.'

The two of them stand still for longer than is comfortable.

'An old lady is missing, possibly lying somewhere nearby, slowly dying from exposure. I need all the help I can get,' says Steil in her coldest voice.

The housekeeper frowns.

'I hardly think he was taking someone from an old people's home,' she says.

'Ah, well,' says Steil. 'Maybe you don't know that they knew each other.'

This completely mystifies the woman, so Steil thinks that avenue isn't worth exploring any further with her at least.

But she does step past her and sets off downstairs to the kitchen.

Steil follows and watches her find the tickets.

Two circle seats for *The Lion King*?

She looks at the woman.

'Maybe his granddaughter,' she offers.

Steil nods and waits.

The woman frowns.

'Do you want me to give you her mother's contact number?'

Steil smiles again.

'If you have it, yes, please.'

Blood out of a stone or what?

And, what's happened to his daughter's mother?

The following conversation with the girl's mother isn't any more helpful. The woman is clearly annoyed with her father, but says it's not the first time he's let them down. At least she's able to confirm the name of the hotel he's gone to near Balmoral.

Steil rings it again.

Yes, he has spent a night there, but has received some distressing news and is on his way back down south.

Weary with all this toing and froing, Steil goes back out to check on the search.

There is nothing more.

And that's how it stays.

She does get to interview Ballantyne the next day, who isn't the roué she was expecting, and surprisingly she finds him rather charming, in an old-fashioned sort of way. He asks after her parents and insists that his gardeners continue the search, even though the SOCOs have declared no likelihood that Edith even reached the house.

The only odd moment occurs when she asks him about having a relationship with Edith when he was younger.

He looks at her and frowns.

'What?'

'We've a witness who says she remembers seeing you with Edith in the woods … when you and she were in your teens, probably.'

He stares at her.

'Are you serious?'

Waiting to bring out her trump card, Steil nods.

He leans back in his chair and affects to be searching his memory.

'What did you say her surname was?'

'MacDonald.'

'Um… the name does ring a bell, but I can't put a face to it. And there's still plenty o' MacDonalds around, as they say,' he murmurs, and then gives her a sly look. 'Bit of a bad lad when I was young, I'm afraid. A tad forward with the ladies … but nothing serious, honestly, m' lady.'

Steil doesn't rise to that, although it infuriates her. Typical of her father's class and generation.

'Perhaps if I found an old photograph?'

'Possibly,' he admits, but is now looking a bit shamefaced. 'Anything I can do to help.'

She smiles.

'The portrait in your bedroom?'

His eyes harden. Is there anger there?

'My wife.'

Magda feels awkward.

He stares at her.

'She died. Eight years ago.'

Magda frowns but feels awful.

'I'm sorry. I didn't know that,' she manages to say.

He shrugs his shoulders and looks away.

Outside in the winter sunshine, but stiffened by a bitter wind, she stands looking up towards the Eildon Hills again. One of the three tops pokes up above the trees.

Apart from her irreverent brother, no one else has yet mentioned that, given the well-known local mythology, one or two older folk must have already muttered Edith that is away with the fairies, as in literally dancing with them inside those hills.

She shakes her head and sets off to find that care worker, who may well know even more than she's already admitted.

***

It turns out that Edith MacDonald has a local relative. Her sister's daughter Cathy, who is accompanied by her son Kenneth.

Steil quickly decides that this is one for DS Gatti. The thin mouth and the large handbag clutched firmly to the woman's lap tell her that his gentle approach will be best. She suspects that the woman will be defensive, like many relatives are, when they've been complicit in the putting of loved ones in a home.

She takes herself off to forensics.

When she has occasionally watched detective shows on the television, she's always irritated by the way they always make the pathologists quirky or rude, as if they need to be made more interesting. Or, even worse, that some nauseating love interest for the detective is involved. In her experience they're generally quiet, down-to-earth sorts, who wouldn't dream of cracking jokes or be short-tempered.

This is definitely the case with Philip Carstairs. He is matter-of-fact and explains scientific terms if he feels the need to, but is always specific and clear.

However, the frown he greets her with implies a problem.

'Go on, tell me the worst,' she says.

Carstairs glances at her quizzically.

'Not sure what you mean by the worst.'

Steil shakes her head.

'Well, anything at all would be good.'

'How about an abandoned woolly hat?'

Steil frowns. He's never been sarcastic before, but then she realises he isn't smiling.

'No footprints, either in the grounds of the care home or

on any of the suggested routes up the hillside. No fingerprints anywhere, even in the room.'

Seeing Steil's look, he nods.

'It was cleaned by one of the staff before they realised she wasn't coming back to the bed. Routine practice, apparently. I asked straight away.'

Steil stares at him, but he shrugs his shoulders and continues.

'One wig, which was cold when the nurse found it. I'm assuming it was hers, but we're testing it for DNA.'

'We only have the hat, the necklace and the shoes, and, until you find me the woman dead or alive, I can't even confirm that any of them are hers. You have to admit that the home is clean. No sign of the woman's prints anywhere, apparently. It's like she's never been there. The SOCOs couldn't believe it either, so they double-checked.'

Steil waits. Was there going to be anything at all?

'Sorry,' he says, with now a shy smile.

'No … if there's nothing, that's how it is,' she manages, but can't stop the frown again.

'I know,' he says quietly. 'Unheard of, really, although there are … shall we say, occurrences, unexplained disappearances historically. I even went and looked them up.'

He offers her a book.

She takes it and glances at the cover.

'Are you joking?' she asks.

He shakes his head.

'I've nothing else.'

She stares at him. The man is a scientist. Can he be even considering this? Fairy tales? Thomas the Rhymer?

She doesn't know what to say.

'Bring me a body, another article of clothing. Explain how a woman who apparently fell over recently walking to the dining room ten steps away could climb that hillside, in below freezing temperatures, dressed in her nightie,' he adds, his voice cold.

All she can do is say,
'Thank you.'

Five minutes later she is back in her office.

And is still sitting there, the book unopened in front of her, when Gatti appears in the doorway.

She looks up.

His face tells the story.

'I did my best, ma'am,' he offers.

She frowns.

'Mrs Braeburn, ma'am, thinks we haven't tried hard enough. Says we should have had the dogs out and the mountain rescue team.'

'You did tell her we did do that, didn't you?'

He shrugs.

'I did, ma'am.'

'Did you get anything out of her about her aunt?'

'Only that she was difficult, argumentative, but still wouldn't have been put in "that home" if it weren't for her rheumatism.'

'She was rheumatic?'

'No. Mrs Braeburn is.'

'What about the necklace and the shoes?'

'Doesn't recognise them at all … or the woolly hat, either.'

'What?'

Again he looks shifty.

'You do remember that the people at the home said they didn't recognise the necklace, although the shoes and hat might have been the ones she was wearing, don't you? They have a huge collection of unclaimed clothes and jewellery. The old folk lose them all the time, apparently.'

She doesn't remember that. When did they say that?

'I left a message on your phone, ma'am,' he says, looking a bit peeved.

'Ah … anything else?'

Gatti looks away.

'Come on,' says Steil, getting impatient.

Gatti looks sheepish.

'She said she's probably been taken away by the fairies … ma'am.'

Steil stares at him and then indicates the book on her desk.

'She's not the only one.'

Gatti stares back at her.

She shakes her head.

'Of course, I don't,' she mutters, and then they both break out laughing.

It's only later that she realises she still doesn't know what happened to Ballantyne's wife.

***

Tommy stares out at the waves.

Can't remember the drive.

It would have almost certainly been caught on camera.

He always comes here when everything gets too much, which was often when he was a teenager, even before he had a licence, although he had been driving tractors and Land Rovers since he could reach the pedals.

It's trying to rain, but he's walked down to where the noise and the fret go some way to dousing his anger and despair.

He's oblivious to the final surges soaking his shoes until he sees that his trouser bottoms are soaked as well. Ignoring the cold seeping up his legs, he walks through it for a few yards, before bending down and taking his shoes off, and his socks, and throwing them into the surf.

He watches as they bob about. One shoe is taken off by the rip tide, and the other is left high and dry.

He waits, transfixed by its survival, until the seventh wave comes to collect it and take it off to join its brother. His feet are tingling, but he laughs. An echo comes back from the nearby cliff.

He walks towards the rocks. Their sharp edges and the barnacles bite his soles and toes but he manages to get to the grass at the top of the beach.

He stands watching the coming and going, the foam frothing up in the gullies.

His left foot is stinging like hell.

He looks down to see the blood.

Stares at it.

He is instantly back in the moment.

Freddie's face is smashed to bits. He is still trying to scream, but then the blood fills his throat and he gurgles into a spasm and is still.

Tears come, but he furiously wipes them away.

He's aware of barking.

Before he can turn, a black Lab comes snuffling round him and licks at his bloody foot. He pushes it away.

A middle-aged woman calls the dog.

'Dasher! Come away.'

The dog copies its name and gallops towards her. She stops and looks at the stranger.

He stares back in her direction, but his eyes are looking somewhere else.

She frowns. Sees he doesn't have any shoes. Jumps to a conclusion. Her face goes white.

'Er … are you all right?' she asks, taking a couple of steps towards him, while glancing off to see where the dog has gone. He's dashed off, of course.

The man isn't moving, just staring … beyond her, not anywhere here. She hesitates, sees the dog coming back. The man focuses on her. Looks confused. She steps towards him.

Half an hour later he's sitting in her kitchen with his foot bandaged, drinking tea.

He hasn't said much.

The woman, Nina, who is a retired teacher, has done her first aid, but has not asked any questions as yet. She can hear her father's calm voice telling her to be careful:

'You don't know where he's been,' et cetera.

Now he seems to be coming round. Starting to take in his surroundings, wiping his tear-stained face. Looking at the grandad slippers on his feet. The bandage. The red stain.

He looks up at her. Who is she? Where is he? His eyes meet hers.

'You might need some stitches in that foot,' she says.

He nods, but shrugs.

'Yeah, maybe.'

'Where … how did you get to the beach?' she asks.

He stares at her. Good question? The car?

'My car … parked it near the gate … I think.'

She nods.

'Red?' she asks.

He nods.

''Fraid so,' he says, with a sad laugh. 'I know. Boy's toy. Pathetic.'

She makes a face.

'If you've got the money, your choice.'

He stares again.

'Sorry.'

She smiles.

He looks at his foot.

Later, in a pair of her husband's old walking boots, fortunately a size bigger, he manages to hobble from her car to his own.

Wincing, he manages to start the engine and reassures the woman he'll be all right, as it's an automatic and he only needs his good foot. He promises to give her a call when he gets home and will go to a doctor as soon as possible. She's not convinced, but what else can she do?

It's only as she's washing up that she finds herself crying, her face creasing into an angry scream. When it's gone, she finds the card on the table. Goes into the study. Her husband's room. Everything is as neat and tidy as he left it.

The silence is dead.

She shakes herself and finds the right map and takes it back into the kitchen. Opens it up and spreads it wide. They drove that route many times, generally heading for Dawyck Gardens, on the other side of Peebles, but his address isn't that far.

He said it was before Walkerburn, didn't he?

Ah, there it is. High on the hillside, looking south.

She sits and looks out of the window.

What's that word?

Serendipity.

'Don't be so daft,' she snorts and folds the map up … but doesn't take it back to its place on the shelf.

MARCH

CHAPTER 7

I haven't seen Ziggy for nearly four weeks now.

We were released from the anonymous building eventually. Ziggy wouldn't say anything sensible about what had happened to him and I couldn't tell him very much either, because I was only interviewed once more. More routine questions about my life.

They know everything.

My mother.

The incident at the hobbit house … all that mayhem coming back into my head.

They didn't ask me any more questions about Ziggy, and when we talked afterwards he said they were a bunch of tossers.

So now I don't know what's going on.

Nor does anyone else, I suppose.

Parliament's been shut up, although the leaked documents are starting to worry people. Johnson's still AWOL.

Going to the shops or sitting in a cafe is a bit surreal. No one talks about it.

I listen to the old biddies talking about their grandchildren … how tall they are … how they are always on their phones.

Out in the street everyone's going here and there. Some of them are busy but most look a bit listless.

The newspapers tell different sorts of lies.

The TV news is much the same.

I hear men talking about the cricket or the football, but maybe they are not as animated as they usually would be. What will they talk about if it all stops?

I try texting Ziggy, but he doesn't often reply. And, when he does, he only tells me not to worry.

But I do wonder what he's up to.

The last time I saw him there was a faraway look in his eyes … like he was planning something.

But what can he do?

What can any of us do?

The news is full of the oncoming virus, but the government don't seem to know what they're doing. Herd immunity? Well, a lot of people are like sheep, but I don't know whether that protects the wolves as well.

I watched a programme last night about Neolithic Man. An archaeologist working for the Nazis before the war was told to stop because of what he found … which didn't fit with their fairy tale superior race beliefs. The woman presenter then meets an old Finnish guy, a shaman, who talked about becoming a wolf.

The presenter asked if he could show her that … and he did.

It was terrifying.

I wish Ziggy would tell me what he's up to.

***

I find the perfect place to spy on the Steil residence from the other side of the Tweed. In reality it's the only place, as it's so carefully shielded from view from any other vantage point. I've parked my car down in a walkers' car park half a mile away and found a position behind an old ruin. So I'm hidden from the road, which has little traffic anyway.

And I'm in luck, the third time I'm there.

The building is huge, with lots of outhouses and a small cottage to one side. No one seems to be living down there at the moment. No smoke comes from it in the evening, but it does come from the big house.

But then I spy a figure leading a horse. It must be him. Not tall, fair hair, but the right age.

Then a car arrives and a woman gets out. They embrace,

stand looking at each other like a strange dance move, except it's stationary. Brother and sister?

Another figure appears and the three of them go indoors.

Maybe she's his wife. Can't remember that in the papers. Or a sister?

I wait, pondering the possibilities.

I spend the time waiting looking on the Internet, which would have not been possible if I had not found that Captain Hook guy. He fixed me up with some no doubt illegal way of accessing other people's connections. The current victim is a solitary house about half a mile away.

So I examine the Steil family story, and oh dear. His sister is a policewoman. A detective inspector, no less. Not much more online apart from the odd involvement in local investigations. Further back in time she was head girl at a private school in Edinburgh.

So is this a problem? Or an opportunity?

I access another dodgy site I saw Hook using, which allows me to find her home address. A flat in Selkirk in a 'prestigious new development', it says on the site.

I'm still looking at photographs of what 'prestigious' looks like when I glance up to see her car racing down the long slope.

Lunch is over. I wait to see which direction she takes. It's east. Back to work? I run back to the car and set off, thinking she'll be going to Galashiels.

As it happens she isn't, but my luck holds and I catch up with her on the Melrose bypass, after I thought I'd lost her.

At the next roundabout she turns left and then right, then up into the grounds of another grand house.

I pull into a parking space the other side of the road,

signed to some local viewpoint, which affords quite a good view of the big house and gardens.

I check it out online. It belongs to another local grandee called Ballantyne.

What's she doing there? She's had lunch. Can't be another social call, surely.

I go on the local news.

Aha.

'Local woman goes missing from care home. Police still searching banks of the Tweed. Hope fading of finding her alive.'

She doesn't stay long at the Ballantyne residence. Goes back briefly to the police station in Galashiels and then to her own place in Selkirk.

By now it's early evening, so I think she's home for the night. But, just as I decide that's it for the day she reappears, carrying two suitcases. Puts them in her car and returns for her briefcase and a box.

We convoy back to the family home and voila. She parks and takes all her gear into the little cottage.

So she's not exactly going home to Mum and Dad. Maybe lockdown *en famille* would be a bit fraught? But she is obviously moving in for the duration.

Is this the opportunity?

The plan I was thinking about becomes much more possible with her on-site.

***

It was only much later that Ziggy calls me and confesses that he went to the Lake District after we were released from interrogation.

He rented a cottage in Ennerdale, went for long solitary walks and didn't look at any news. Although of course he declares he always knew what would happen after the election … and if I wanted to know how they'd rigged the results.

I don't. I hate politics. Don't trust any of them.

So now he says that's the problem: people like me only want good news rather than the cold hard truth.

I don't continue with that, which he says is typical.

Anyway, I ask if he has any further ideas about Jimmy 'Sparrow' and the mystery woman.

He snorts.

'All a fiction, dearie,' he laughs.

I hate that word, so I say nothing. I don't want a long diatribe that I'll lose interest in within two sentences.

'Anyway, I've a new game. You interested?' he says.

I wait.

'Is that a yes?'

'A maybe,' say I.

'You do realise what's happening with the virus, don't you?'

I nod, thinking,

'What can we do about that?'

'So you think you'll be OK on your own for six months?'

I can't think of an answer to that. What does he think I'm going to do? Ignore all the instructions?

Long pause. What's he thinking?

'So I'm going to gather a stack of supplies and hibernate till the summer, when hopefully it will all be over.'

That sounds a bit extreme, I think. Although staying at home alone doesn't sound great.

'So do you want to come?'

Now this is a surprise. Why? Ah, dogsbody duty. Who's he kidding?

'I don't think so,' I say.

'I'll pay you double,' he says.

He can't see me, but I'm shaking my head.

'OK,' he continues. 'I'll send you the directions, and when

you see the tsunami coming you can get yourself there. You won't regret it. Lovely old cottage by the Tweed, not far from Peebles.'

I've only been over the border once before and remember how that went. Death and mayhem and exploding buildings … my only fleeting sighting of my notorious mother.

He waits.

I'm now a bit worried. What if he's right? He often bloody well is.

'OK,' I mutter. 'I'll give it some thought.'

Again, only his breathing.

'I'm taking all my gear, so you can contact me as usual … and I've sent you some moolah to be getting on with.'

Again, I can't think of anything to say, wondering what 'moolah' is? Money?

Before I can say anything else, he's gone.

I sit looking out at the spring sunshine. The garden needs a good seeing to.

I look up 'moolah'.

I check my bank.

Bloody hell.

Good as his word.

Double salary. Six months' worth.

This takes time to sink in.

He's also sent me the directions to get to White Cottage.

I look up the coordinates on Google map.

Halfway between Peebles and Selkirk. I've heard the names, but have no idea what they're like. Are the Borders hilly? I spot the river. The Tweed? Doesn't that go through Berwick? It does, but many miles to the east. I switch to an OS map. Mr Ogilvie, my O level geography teacher, is looking over my shoulder. Yes, there are lots of close contours above White Cottage.

Is he for real? Asking me to go to a cottage with my name? Creepy? Or just one of his jokes?

I make myself a milky coffee and go to sit in the garden in my big coat.

I reflect on how things have changed in my life since I met Ziggy. Gone are the dreary days spent correcting peoples' adding up. OK, I never know what's going to happen next, but isn't that more exciting? More alive?

By the time I come back in, I've decided. I'll spend some of that money on a gardener … and know immediately who that will be… And Mrs Kenworthy over the road has being dying to see round my house ever since I moved in and would jump at the chance to have another venue for her nosy cleaning obsession.

I think of getting straight back to Ziggy, but then decide to keep him hanging on for a bit. Doesn't pay to seem to be too eager. Be better to play the 'Well, somebody needs to look after you' card in a day or so's time.

My final thought before I set out is to make a list of outdoor winter clothing. It snows in Scotland, Mr Ogilvie said, and he was definitely a Scot. Couldn't understand half of what he said, especially when he got excited about glaciation.

As I get in the car, my phone pings again.

'Don't go out. Parcel arriving in five minutes.'

I stare at this message and then look out to see the looming shape of a transit van pulling up in front of me.

I watch as the man jumps out and goes to the side door of the van.

I slowly get out of the car.

He appears with a medium-sized box and sets off towards my front door.

I follow him. He turns to look at me. Suspiciously.

'I think it's for me,' I say cheerfully.

He doesn't smile.

'Gotta have ID, madam,' he grunts.

I give him my best 'Don't be so silly' look, but it cuts no ice.

'Bloody hell,' I mutter, searching my bag.

'Two pieces,' he adds, looking at his phone, 'preferably a car licence and a Yorkshire Bank card.'

I give him another look of disbelief. He makes a stony face.

'You're enjoying this, aren't you?' I smirk.

'Not really, madam, but it's obviously something important, I guess.'

I find the two items he's asked for, which he spends some time studying.

He gives me another look and pulls out his phone.

I'm standing there holding out my hand, thinking it's like being in the police interview room again.

He walks back to the gate and so I don't hear the conversation, which is however, curt.

He turns round.

'Can you open your front door, madam?' he asks.

I stare at him. Now with a mixture of disbelief and some fearfulness.

He manages a wincing smile.

'Sorry,' he mutters.

I fumble in my handbag. Where the bloody hell are my keys? I look up at him. He's looking worried now. They're in the car. Of course. I walk back, retrieve the keys, come back and open the door.

He's speaking on the phone again. Looks back at me and grimaces.

'OK,' he says, 'I need to take and send a photo of you.'

Before I can manage a protest, it's done. He waits, staring steadfastly at the phone.

It's only a few seconds but it seems for ever.

His phone beeps. He looks up at me and gives me a smile of relief.

I am me.

He passes me the box, which isn't as light as I was expecting, and backs off, apologising, but then rushes back to his van and drives off at speed.

I'm starting to worry it's a bomb. Surely it's far too big and heavy for a phone?

I go back inside and put it on the kitchen table.

My phone chirps up.

Got it? It's not a bomb. Open sesame and play. They're all numbered, so start with number one and follow the instructions in the letter.

It turns out Ziggy's sent me not one but ten phones.

All brand new.

I open up the first one as directed and find it's all set up for me with my addresses and apps.

Creepy. I know Ziggy's a techie wonder, but this?

I send him a message, as directed.

He sends me a picture of White Cottage, which is indeed white and looks wonderful in the spring sunshine.

I have to sit down and have another strong cup of tea.

What is going on?

***

At first Tommy doesn't know where he's going.

Getting through the central belt going north will be risky, especially getting Wallace over the motorway at night.

He needed somewhere no one knows about.

The sea beckons.

How will she react?

The house is on the edge of the cliffs, and in the dark he is sure he could get to it from the cliff path. She's said that a couple of the fields belong to her as well, so plenty of room for Wallace.

But what the hell is her name?

Total blank.

He's never been good at that. The men he commanded quickly got used to it and accepted whatever nickname he gave them, which was rarely anything to do with their actual name, but more likely some attribute which he identified them with.

This makes him think of Boxer and Trout. At least he's managed to save them from being discharged … by telling the brass they were only defending him.

Anyway, decision made, he turns east and considers the route he'll need to take. Straightforward to begin with – over the hill to Lauder then the Southern Upland Way to beyond Duns. He knows the difficult bit will be avoiding Berwick, but also decides the Honey Chain Bridge will have to be the crossing as the Tweed will be too strong and deep to cross even on a charger like Wallace.

Cheered up by this challenge, he spurs his steed up the last few fields to see Stow lighting up in the valley below.

And it is then that her name comes back to him.

Nina.

MARCH 21

CHAPTER 8

Randolph Ballantyne is feeling sorry for himself.

Not used to looking after himself is the main problem. Although he realises that he's not that disappointed to see the back of Miss Lewthwaite. She was beginning to get on his nerves with her pursed lips and the even more irritating habit of repositioning his possessions according to some pernickety, arcane world view of her own.

Unfortunately Nadia has gone as well – didn't turn up one day – so here he is, camping out in his own kitchen. He hasn't cooked for himself since he was at university.

So he is pleasantly surprised two days before lockdown to find Jeanie Tait at his door.

She smiles awkwardly as he invites her in. What can she want?

He indicates the kitchen, where he finds himself embarrassed by the chaos he's caused.

'Would you take a cup of tea, Miss Tait?' he asks.

She nods. And then they're sitting there in the gathering silence, only measured by the increasingly louder kitchen clock.

Then there is the classic 'Both trying to speak at the same time' moment and the following 'You first' altercation, until they're both laughing.

Silence descends again.

He's thinking,

'More tea?' when she blurts it out.

'I hear Miss Lewthwaite has left you.'

Surprised, he can only nod.

'The thing is,' she continues in a rush of explanation. 'I can't go back to the home, because I'm taking immunosuppressant pills for my arthritis, and I can't imagine rattling around in my little house on my own, so...'

She runs out of steam and gets to her feet.

'I'm sorry, it's really ... forward of me... I'm sure you can manage yourself.'

He's staring at her.

She makes for the door.

'No ... no, I'd ... be delighted. Completely hopeless on my own,' he gushes.

She looks at him doubtfully.

'Are you sure?'

'Absolutely.'

They stand looking at each other, then both break out laughing again.

So it is agreed.

He takes her down to her 'little house' in the Gala estate he's only ever seen from the other side of the valley and she collects her things. People stare at his car as he waits outside.

They're back within the hour and she sets to in the kitchen.

Randolph goes to his study and settles down with the crossword. How fortunate can a man be?

She stands at the kitchen window, looking out at the trees.

Her plan is going to work. She will find out the truth.

***

Despite all the team's efforts, the search for Edith MacDonald was eventually closed down, without finding any more traces of her other than a few muddy footprints and the woolly hat.

Ballantyne said he intended taking his granddaughter to accompany him to the theatre, but then the snow beckoned and he forgot all about her.

DI Steil didn't believe that. But, as Gatti wearily stated, they'd no way of disproving his statement.

And all this was overtaken by the gathering storm of the virus lockdown.

***

Gatti was put in charge of a small squad of officers making sure the local town centres were closed down and kept that way, while Steil was put on office duties managing the area's coordination procedures, which she could do from her computer at home. She regarded this as the worst type of incarceration, but buckled down as best she could. At least she could take the dogs for a walk and the horses for rides without leaving her father's estate. And she then realised that she could take over the abandoned gillie's house. Her mother couldn't hide her disappointment, but at least Magda was in sight and could be force-fed.

Tommy was a different problem.

He couldn't bear being cooped up anywhere at the best of times, and was twice caught driving on the main road. The second time was after a high-speed chase when he thought he'd lost the police cars, only to find them parked on the drive when he got back.

It was only thanks to his father's position within the local hierarchy that the car wasn't towed away, although Tommy was forced to give up the keys.

There then followed an increasingly acrimonious and fraught couple of days before he disappeared altogether.

Magda flops down on the chair in the hall.

Her mother appears in the doorway of the dining room.

The look she receives from her daughter confirms her worst fears.

'He's gone, *Mamusia*.'

Her mother turns away and disappears back into the room.

Magda knows it won't help to go after her … and her father is even more difficult to deal with. He has buried himself in his genealogical research.

She sits there.

Where has he gone?

The car is still there and all the others as well. It's two miles to the nearest main road.

Thinking the worst, she goes out to the stables.

He's taken Wallace, inevitably.

She knows what she ought to do … but she doesn't.

It's more than an hour later when she realises that Hengist has gone as well.

Where can he have gone with them? A man on a horse with a hound at his hooves, like some romantic warrior. Daft sod.

She's no doubt he can look after himself and the animals. A quick check in the pantry suggests that a full pair of saddlebags' worth of supplies have gone with him.

So where?

He knows the local hills as well as anyone and has spent many summer holidays camping rough.

'And he's a battle-hardened soldier as well,' she says to the chickens, who are as usual only focused on the next scrap or insect, but who give her a wide berth, just in case.

'If he travels the hills by day and crosses the main roads at night, he could go virtually anywhere in any direction,' she says to herself.

She stares out at the opposite hillside.

And has memories of waving to her best friend Amelia on evenings when they weren't allowed to meet. Is she at home?

Her phone buzzes.

She looks at the message. Sighs. Goes back to the computer.

***

Fletcher is watching two swans making their way upstream and idly wondering how much strength that must take, with the river so full and charging along.

It's only the wetness on his cheeks that breaks his gaze. He wipes the tears away and blows his nose.

He can't stop thinking about the phone call yesterday, in which he tried to persuade the woman at the home that he has the right to go and see Laura and her telling him he won't let him in.

Of course, he understands her reasons, but feels such a traitor. He also knows Laura no longer recognises him on the weird Skype calls, but it still feels so wrong.

A dog barks.

It's running along the opposite bank, way ahead of its owner, who is scrambling over a rocky section under the cliff. A minute later he's waving at the figure, who's looking a bit forlorn and who gives no sign of seeing him. He knows that the other bank is owned by Louisa Cunninghame and so the elderly chap must be a guest of hers, but he doesn't seem to be enjoying his stay too much.

Not wanting an encounter even thirty yards away, Fletcher chooses to ignore him.

He waits until the man has disappeared up the cliff towards the bridge before turning to walk back to the house.

Louisa has been watching him all this time. It's not often she's felt so powerless. Not only can she not help the man, but she knows they're both racked by the guilt of their relationship.

'Oh, for heaven's sake, woman,' she says out loud. 'It's not as if you've ever bedded him. You're only looking after the poor sap.'

She makes her way through into the library and turns on her laptop, intending to look occupied at least.

She listens out for him getting back in through the conservatory, knowing he'll struggle shutting the door. And hears the gruff argument between man and warped frame, which the wood invariably wins.

He makes it through without too many expletives and stands in her doorway.

Trying to sense his temper, she pretends not to have heard him.

He snorts quietly like an apologetic bull and walks away, which makes her smile. The man she knows is still there.

After he's spoken to the home again and been reassured that Laura's doing 'fine', he wanders back to see if Louisa is still in the library. Then he has to trundle about the ground floor until he realises she will be in the conservatory and so makes his way there.

They sit in silence.

Her with a book.

Him gazing into space.

This seemingly lasts for an eternity, but probably only a couple of minutes in reality.

'How is she?'

'Fine.'

Louisa lowers her book.

'You know...'

He nods.

'I know,' he growls.

She shuts the book and stands up.

'Come on, we'll go for a drive.'

He frowns at her.

'We shouldn't.'

'I can,' she asserts. *'Droit de seigneurse.'*

He shakes his head.

'No such word, and in any case that would only apply to sexual matters.'

She laughs.

'Listen to you.' She shakes her head. 'Grammar school boy.'

But she does take him for drive. To the sea.

They walk along a deserted beach.

If he were here with Laura, she would be looking for shells and he would be trying to beat his skimming record. But Louisa has her binoculars and is intent on spotting gannets, fulmars, or dolphins.

Still, they get some air and it doesn't rain.

They only meet one other person. A woman walking with her dog. A smiley bustling, tail-wagging Labrador, who comes over to see if this couple know about sticks, but they don't. How boring.

The humans smile and say good morning, but then carry on in their different directions.

Louisa and Fletcher walk back to the car park and away. The woman returns to her empty house on the cliff.

***

As I said, I have been to Scotland before, but not the Borders.

The Borders? Why is it still called that?

I found a book my not-father must have had, although I don't recall us ever going there.

I get a brief introduction to the history. Blood feuds, burning and pillage. Wonderful.

The geography, meanwhile, is all about the rivers, although mainly about the big one. The Tweed. I hadn't realised it was so long. Anyway, White Cottage sits a few hundred yards from it, so I'll get a front-seat view.

The satnav suggests two routes. One via the M6 and then up through Hawick, or the other, which takes me further up the M74 and then across on a higher, smaller road. I decide on the latter. Looks a bit more interesting.

And it is. If you like an empty road.

There are a few sections where there's not a car in sight. Maybe in the summer it'll be busier. Looks like a bikers' route to me and, sure enough, I'm passed by a couple at speed.

Soon it's down to a place called Innerleithen, which is a prime contender for one-horse town status. Then I turn off the main road and across the Tweed onto a riverside single-track lane, which brings me to White Cottage.

It's true! Not one of Ziggy's pranks. Wyrd!

I pull off the road onto a grass parking area and get out. Not a soul. No welcoming party.

I walk up to the door and knock.

No response.

I try the door. It's locked. Go round the back. No back door?

Peep through the windows. Lots of net curtains.

I try Ziggy's number. No signal. Nothing at all.

I go back and sit in the car and wait.

And wait.

After about half an hour I get out and wander down a lane I think will take me to the river.

It does … and it is big and wide.

I can see cars on the other side trundling along.

No bridges in sight.

No Ziggy.

I look up the other side of the valley, which is steep, with enclosed fields and no roads, but is that a big house up at the top? Must be a road somewhere.

I walk back.

Still no Ziggy.

I sit in the car and read my guidebook. Look at the OS map.

I figure out that the big house I saw is right on the top of the ridge and there is a lane from the road over the other side. Who would live there in such a remote place?

I go back to the book and fall asleep.

I come to. Dreaming of horses, for some reason. Never been on a horse in my life. Which is a bit of a weird coincidence because, as if out of my dream, comes Ziggy … riding on a white horse. No way!

He gives me a wave and I get out of the car.

The sun has gone and it's cold.

He 'parks' the horse by the wall and ties it to a post.

'I'll see to her when I've opened up for you,' he says.

I keep well away from the horse, which is looking at me like it fancies its chances.

I carry my case in through the door, noticing that Ziggy has to duck his head, while I fit easily underneath.

He shows me to another door and a small bedroom. I dump my stuff and look for a kettle. He's off out to put the horse in its 'garage', I suppose.

My phone bleeps a signal and riffs a few messages. I'm not expecting any, so I'll look later.

By the time Ziggy gets back I'm onto my second cuppa and deleting all the unnecessary dross that fills up your phone if you don't talk to it for a bit.

Apart from a message from Janet Becket wondering where we are.

Indeed?

I look up as the door opens.

That's a smile on Ziggy's face.

Is that a good thing? Or trouble afoot?

***

It's difficult to find a place to get a close-up of the cottage, and this lay-by is well over a quarter of mile away. Even with the binoculars, all I can see is probably half of the south-facing facade of the big house, and the cottage is screened by a high hedge of privet.

I decide not to stay long there and find somewhere to wait

for darkness. No doubt there will be dogs and presumably a certain number of staff. So any attempt to approach secretively is out of the question. I've been weighing up how convincing it would seem for an investigative reporter wanting some meat on the 'fighting squaddies' story to be still on the case in the current situation. Now it's more and more unlikely. So the 'exhausted lost walker' seems to be the only viable option.

I decide to go back down and along to the car park. I make my way over and come out above the house to watch from above and to gauge the number of bodies on-site.

Part of me thinks that I should forget it and go home, but now I'm here, it's intriguing ... and with the news of my first-choice target's latest arrogant announcements, the anger wells up again.

***

The thought of being incarcerated with her parents doesn't bear thinking about, although Magda worries for her mother not having the choice of escaping such an imprisonment. Still, Maggie Fraser has agreed to look in on them, as her own family live in Glasgow and won't be visiting any time soon.

So staying in what used to be the gamekeeper's cottage is not the worst sentence in the world. Quite the opposite, in fact. Kenny MacKay now lives down in the valley and has taken most of his vast collection of vehicle parts and other junk with him. It's quite the eyesore in the village, all that rusting metal overrun by his equally weird collection of cats, dogs, chickens, geese, even swans.

And, given her father's devotion to him, the cottage is extremely well equipped with technical gizmos that enable her to still do her work, although some of them are neither necessary nor understandable to her anyway ... and there is the view over the valley, which is as good as from her father's cluttered front room.

The coordinating and tracking duties she's been told to do aren't onerous, merely time-consuming check-ups and information-gathering. They are not too difficult for someone with a lifelong belief in her organising strengths.

The family farm over the hill is still operating and she's seen young Gavin zooming about on his four-wheel bike feeding the new lambs, who by now have stopped frolicking about and who are instead getting down to some serious hoovering of the spring grass.

She's also aware of the increasing number of wildlife species getting more and more comfortable with the absence of worrying humans. She's been thoughtful enough to include birdseed in her supermarket drop and saves all her leftovers for the variety of other creatures that she knows are about. There was even a pine marten in the wood the other day. And two pied wagtails on the lawn a few minutes ago, doing that funny head-jerking Egyptian dance move.

She's also pleased to find that Amelia has come back to her parents' house on the other side of the valley and they've had one group wave already. Her three older girls managed to make whoops loud enough for her to hear them, which stirs a strangely dormant sensitivity in her abdomen.

It's as she's reflecting on this that she notices the car parked in the little lay-by on the long straight drop towards the village. It's not that unusual, someone trying to catch a closer glimpse of the house, which is difficult to do from anywhere else. Probably someone out for a drive to escape the four walls. She looks back at the wagtails and, when they fly away, she sees the car has gone as well. So she goes back to the report she was reading.

***

Tommy feels free.

The sun is in his eyes as he sets off for the second day.

Wallace is well rested and up for a gallop, but the ground is too uneven to risk that. Hengist is running here and there, following whatever.

He figures that he can probably make it to the beach by late afternoon. He's no phone number for her, nor a phone to ring from, and anyway thinks she'd most likely say no.

Why on earth should she take him in?

He shakes his head and concentrates on the way through the tufted tumps.

Mid-morning he takes a rest by a stream that his instinct tells him, and the map confirms, is the way down to the bridge.

He knows the family who run the honey farm, but has no intention of calling on them. They'd be welcoming, but then there'd be lots of questions and they'd feel compelled to let his mother know.

So he checks out the best way round and then takes the lane towards the A1. He's remembered that there's a farmer's cattle bridge that goes over the dual carriageway a bit further south than where he's heading, but it will be better than trying to cross the two lanes on a horse with a dog, even in daylight. Nutters like himself driving way over the limit make that a no-no.

Smiling to himself, he drops Wallace to a walk.

His thoughts go back to the beach encounter.

She's a vague image in his memory.

Blonde hair, blue eyes, like him. Sad face. Whatever her story is, it almost certainly includes trouble with men.

'So why make it any worse?' he says out loud.

Both the horse and the dog cock their ears at him, but, used to his solitary outbursts, they don't worry too much.

It takes quite a lot longer than he anticipated to get across the main road by the diversion. Meeting a slow moving herd of cattle on the road takes up over half an hour, and he is worried that the young farmer has a good long look at him. Still, if he's anything like Gavin up at the estate farm, he'll not be watching any news programmes later on.

So it's after six when he turns up the lane to the woman's house, which, given dusk is gathering in, isn't such a bad idea.

He stops a few yards down, where there's a wide verge and a handy gatepost to tie Wallace to. The horse immediately sets to, munching the unmown grass, and Hengist lies down patiently to wait.

He gives up trying to slow his breathing and walks up to the gate.

There are no lights on as far as he can see, but her car is in the driveway.

He knocks on the door.

No answer.

But also no dog barking.

So is she down on the beach? He knows that her garden has a little gate out onto the cliff path, so he makes his way round to the back and stands looking down at the beach.

Sure enough, there she is coming back along the tideline, her dog way ahead, chasing some indolent seagulls.

Not sure whether to set off down or stand waiting, he decides to go back into the garden. He even tries the back door, which is surprisingly not locked.

What a temptation.

Despite himself he resists it, and goes back to the front gate. This is awkward. By the time she's got up the cliff, it will be nearly dark. Looming out of the gloaming isn't a good idea, and any gun dog worth its salt will smell the horse and another dog so near.

This isn't going well.

In the end he takes himself and his retinue back along the lane and down to the beach. Hengist can't resist the open empty space and gallops off. Wallace is less interested, and quite happy with the nearest bit of grass.

In the end, having given up whistling for the dog, he sits down and waits.

The sea and the sun do that beautiful violet evening scene, where the breakers hush and the birds go quiet. The dying of the day. Mauve death.

He sits absolutely still, like a giant gnome on his tuft of grass.

Only a big daft lump like Hengist can break such a magical moment … which he does by slavering all over his hands as if he wants to share his latest adventure.

The plan isn't working out, because now he'll be turning up in the dark.

With no better idea coming to mind, and with the reappearance of a now filthy wet dog of his own, he retraces his steps, thinking the worst.

And it is difficult.

She eventually opens the door, long moments after he knocked the second time. He has his back towards it, and is pretty certain that she's peering out of the side window and through the glass pane in the door.

But only a few inches.

And she doesn't speak.

He turns round.

Even then he can't think of anything to say. Just stares.

'What are you doing here?' she asks quietly.

He looks at his shoes.

The silence deepens.

'Not sure.'

She almost laughs.

'Is this a joke?'

He looks up.

'I'm afraid not.'

She stares at him.

He looks away.

'Are you serious?' she says, trying not to think of John McEnroe, which only makes her give a snort of a laugh.

Again he doesn't speak.

'Well, what do you want?'

He risks a glance. She's opened the door a bit further.

'A cup of tea would be nice,' he manages.

She stares at him in disbelief.

Shakes her head.

But she does let him in.

Her dog sniffs at him and wags its tail, but she tells him to settle down, which he does obediently.

Tommy follows her through into the breakfast room. She goes to the kitchen and puts on the kettle.

He stands looking out at the sea. Just enough light to see the breakers, soundlessly collapsing into a dark purple sea.

She comes back to the doorway.

'Where have you come from?'

'Over the hills and far away,' he mutters.

She shakes her head.

The kettle burbles.

She goes back into the kitchen. Returns with two cups, ushers him to sit down at the table and goes to sit in a chair near the window.

She sips her tea. He puts his cup down on the table and stares at it.

'It's taken me two days,' he says.

She stares at him.
'Why?'
He looks up at her.
'It's a long story.'
She shakes her head again.
'In your car?'
He nearly smiles.
'No … on my horse.'
Her eyes go even wider.
'What? Why?'
He shrugs.
'If you'd met my father, you'd understand straight away.'
She frowns, thinking,
'How old is this man?' And then thinking "on a horse?"'
'So where is it?'
'On the verge … with Hengist.'
'Hengist?'
'Sorry, my dog. Lurcher. Embarrassingly friendly.'
She shakes her head again, feeling it'll fall off next time.
'So you've come across country – what, thirty miles or so – with a dog and a horse, and are now expecting … a bed, a field, a three-course meal?'
He tries a boyish grin, which fades in the face of the glare it produces.
'I could take you out for a meal.'
She stands up, not knowing whether to slap his stupid face, scream or hustle him straight out onto the lane.

Somehow or other, and neither of them can believe it afterwards, she does none of those things or accept his ridiculous offer of taking her for meal, when all the restaurants are shut anyway. Neither of them mention the lockdown. Him because he's naturally against doing as he's told, her because … well, the thought of being entirely alone is – has been – unbearable.
Instead, she allows him to put the huge horse in her field,

the big daft dog into the hall with her own – they greet each other like long-lost friends – and makes him, if not a three-course meal, something damn close to that ... and then takes him to her bed.

It's only when she's lying awake, listening to his steady breathing, that she remembers she shooed away that silly word.

'Look at you now,' she whispers.

**

The one advantage they had in this coming lockdown situation was being with John Shepherd.

Both Becket and Freya are used to living on their own, but not out in the middle of nowhere in an abandoned mansion. John bought his cottage near Hadrian's Wall when he left the army, but although it was where he wanted to be, the only property available was a long-abandoned farmhouse and the surrounding untended fields. So he knows what they need to do to survive there.

The basic essentials of food, warmth and sleeping arrangements were quickly sorted, but organising an Internet connection proved a little trickier until he found a socket in one of the stable cottages, which looked like it had been an artist's studio. However, it was Freya who had the technical know-how to be able to appropriate a link. She'd noticed the telecom tower on the hilltop across the lake.

So, feeling a bit of a passenger through all this, Becket decided to become chief cook and bottle-washer.

None of them talked about how long the isolation was going to last. But then, of course, it turned out they were ahead of the game, because soon everyone else had to stay home too.

John continued to visit the local supermarket and made a friend of the woman in the small veggie shop next door. When Freya asked him how he could manage that, he said he had an army document that did the trick, but he didn't go into any detail about how he acquired it or where he kept it. She gave him a suspicious look, but didn't pursue it.

He also acquired some torches and a couple of storm lamps and the fuel. The main problem, however, was keeping warm, because a fire in the daytime would betray their occupation, so could only be lit after dusk.

Freya kept on at the Internet until she established links to various password-protected government sites, so she was able to keep them informed about what was happening ... which wasn't much. Especially, after 'the Johnson', as she called him, contracted the virus.

Becket begged John to find her something to read, so he sighed and took her upstairs where she hadn't ventured, to show her a whole room full of books stacked in piles on the floor, which she diligently put back on the shelves. She hadn't realised her repressed Virgoan tendencies until the other two stood shaking their heads at the alphabetical stricture she'd applied.

So they were well set for the duration.

Throughout all this they didn't interrogate Freya about her involvement in whatever skulduggery the government was up to, and became used to her eye-rolling at the flickering images on John's laptop.

The only sad thing for him was that he had left old Cadger back at home with his neighbour, but this situation was ameliorated when he was befriended by a thin mongrel in the woods, who he decided to call Cuff.

Cuff had some greyhound in him and could disappear in a trice, but they couldn't have had a better warning system than his ever-flickering ears.

***

Ref:TD/SB/03222022018.

'What now?'

'█████████ He's checking out a place not far from █████████.'

'And?'

'Belongs to a family called █████████.'

'So?'

'███'

'Presumably in his dotage now?'

'Yes, but his son is █████████████████████ grounded for ██████████████████████████████'

'And?'

'He's one of the ████████████████████'

'Ah. I see.'

'What do you want us to do?'

'I'll be in touch.'

CHAPTER 9

Freya hates dogs. Not all of them, but a pack of them barking and howling is a childhood memory that has scarred her subconscious deeply. Even that moment in *The Hundred and One Dalmatians* when the other dogs all send each other signals would have her hiding behind the settee.

And these dogs are baying.

The sound of hunting.

And she knows they'll scent her fear.

She's out on the terrace so she has to get around the side, away from the direction they're coming from.

She daren't run too fast in case she stumbles and falls, cuts her leg. She knows they go crazy for blood.

She gets to the corner and peers round. In the logical part of her brain, which is now only a tiny voice against the mounting miasma of terror, she knows it's only a few yards to the front door.

But there are bushes, so she has to venture out beyond them, where she can be seen. Then there are the steps up to the front door, which is always difficult to push open. Its old hinges and the warping of the heavy wood are not conducive to a quick entry...

And now they're getting nearer she can hear their bodies thrashing through the undergrowth, and their barking and yelping fill her head.

She stumbles on the first step but manages to right herself before she tumbles onto the stone.

She gets to the door, twists the big handle, and pushes and ... nothing.

It's locked.

She can't believe it. Why? Who?

She looks frantically to her right. The noise is blurring her vision. She stumbles past the far pillar and down into the bush the other side, then struggles through to the wall. The corner.

The side door is five yards away … and it's open.

But she can hear the dogs coming through the old stables, only fifty yards away.

She stumbles across the uneven flags. Trips. Falls. Screams. Is vaguely aware of strong arms grabbing her.

The noise of the dogs is deafening. She can hear the scrabbling of their claws on the flags and the thrashing of the bushes as they force their way through.

But then she's inside.

The door is forced shut.

Just before their bodies thunder against it. Scrabbling. Howling. Baying. Snarling. Fighting. Yelps and growls and then snuffling. Searching for a way in. Silence.

They've gone?

But then she can hear them in the distance, as she's helped around a few corners into the front room.

She realises it's Becket holding her, virtually carrying her, to one of the big old chairs.

But it's not over.

The dogs have found their way round on to the terrace and are now jumping at the windows. Maybe twenty of them.

Becket goes over and pulls the curtains.

Isn't she even frightened a bit?

She comes back to Freya.

'It's OK. They can't get in,' she says, and leans over to hold her.

Freya realises she's shaking so much she can't see straight.

John appears at the door looking serious.

'You'd better go upstairs,' he says.

Becket helps her up and the two of them go out into the hall and climb the stairs.

There's little furniture up on the first floor and they've had to make beds with some of the cushions from the big settees.

Becket helps her to one of them and covers her with blankets.

'I'll get you a drink,' she says, but goes to the window first.

The dogs are quieter now, although there is the occasional howl and outburst of barking.

Freya tries to control her breathing while nodding to Becket that she's OK for the moment.

Becket smiles and disappears.

The barks are now in the distance. Maybe the dogs are going elsewhere.

She lies there feeling her heart thumping and her pulse racing.

She almost laughs, but instead starts to weep helplessly.

It seems a long time, but Becket reappears with a couple of mugs and a packet of biscuits.

She grins.

'Look at me, with my Girl Guide first aid badge,' she laughs. 'Tea and sugar for the patient.'

Freya can't help but smile back. She never got further than the Brownies. All those group activities were unnerving for her and, of course, memorising all the written down stuff straight off was one of the first times she realised that she had an embarrassing talent.

They can still hear howls and barking, but it is all getting more distant by the minute.

The two of them sit listening, sipping tea. Becket is glancing at Freya, who is still being attacked by bouts of shivering.

Her own experience of dogs during childhood hadn't been brilliant. She didn't particularly like them. Preferred cats, who were less trouble and generally self-sufficient.

'OK now?' she says.

Freya nods.

'Sorry. Childhood experience,' she offers.

Becket waits to see if she's going to tell that story, but realises that it's not going to come out just now.

It's a good half hour before John reappears.

Becket goes to make him a brew.

He sits down with his back to the wall. A sheen of sweat on his face. Sleeves rolled up. He looks at Freya and smiles.

'You OK?'

She nods.

'Nothing to be ashamed of,' he says. 'Bad experience when you were young, I expect.'

She nods again.

'My dad bred whippets and lurchers, so they treated me like I was one of their puppies. My face was never dirty,' he says, and laughs.

She shivers at the thought of that, only once having been licked by a sloppy-mouthed spaniel … which was more than enough.

'I knew they were coming before I heard them,' he said. 'Cuff. He growled at first and then whimpered. Maybe he knows them. Didn't want to meet them, that's for sure.'

Freya has lots of sympathy for that.

On cue, Cuff sidles into the room, comes over to snuffle her hand and to settle down beside her. She's all right with him.

Becket comes back with a brew for John.

'So who were they? What are they up to?' she asks.

'Gang of lads. Not gypsies, as I thought at first, which is a relief. They would have probably tried to get inside.'

Freya shudders at that.

'They're probably rabbiting. There are lots of burrows on the far side of the lake. Only young kids, I think.'

Later, when Freya has recovered enough, they go over to the studio and tune into the latest news. Johnson definitely has the virus.

'There is a God,' mutters Becket.

'I don't know,' says John. 'The gang of shysters and yes-men he's surrounded himself with won't have a clue what to do, especially as Cummings is out as well.'

The two women nod their understanding, but neither of them are smiling.

They go back to the main building. Freya goes to lie down. Becket picks up her book and settles in one of the old armchairs. It seems a good time to reread *Animal Farm*, but she soon tires of its clunky prose and turns to a Donna Leon. At least her light-fingered touch rings true in its weary acceptance of human nature.

She's five pages in when John comes into the room.

He looks serious as he comes to sit beside her.

'They weren't kids,' he whispers, and gives her a look.

She frowns.

'Security guards giving their dogs a bit of exercise. Not sure where they were from. Certainly not guarding this old ruin, which is why they didn't try to get in.'

Becket waits to see if there's anything else, but he just looks thoughtful.

'Maybe we'd better look for somewhere else,' she suggests.

He nods, but he's still frowning.

'That'll be hard. They're stopping people walking about, and are asking what they're doing. We'll have to wait till dark. I'll do a recce tonight. No point in going together until I've found somewhere.'

They're both quiet for some time, but end up in each other's arms. There's no better succour for fear.

***

Jeanie lied to the care home that she's been invited to go to the big house, which made most of them give her a knowing look or two. Randolph seems to accept her lie about her arthritis condition, which isn't true, but he probably wouldn't care about it anyway. He's good on the laptop, though, getting them deliveries. Not sure what strings he's pulling there, but she doesn't care.

They soon settle into their own routines, although quite different ones.

He is, surprisingly, a crossword addict, and she gets used to finding the abandoned papers folded open at them. Nearly always completed. She's never bothered with them. Doesn't think any woman would find the time. When he's not doing that he watches history programmes on obscure channels she didn't know existed. Plus, of course, as a rich man with an extensive, ancient garden tended by a platoon of on-site crusty old retainers, he wanders about checking on their progress. She hears him occasionally having muttered and incomprehensible conversations with the old men, which she assumes are both knowledgeable and polite. She doesn't see them making signs at his back as he walks away, at any rate.

It's some time before she realises where the two oldest fellows live. Two sturdy gatehouses for two solitary gentlemen. Neither of them says much to her, other than a slight touch to their hats and a solemn comment on the weather, which never seems to differ from a resigned acceptance.

She's only met them when she's putting out some washing, thinking there will be little to find in their vegetable beds, until she finds potatoes, onions, and the odd cabbage on the kitchen table. This always happens when she's not there, like they're gnomes hiding from human contact. She hasn't asked or been told their names, so decides they're Dum and Dee, as they're not easy to tell apart anyway.

Occasionally, when she finds herself singing under her

breath or gazing out of the window, she has to remind herself why she's there.

So how can she find out what happened to Edith? It's not something she can mention as she serves a meal or meets him on the stairs, although he has insisted that she joins him for dinner.

'Can't exactly invite anyone else over, can I?' he says,' although most of my contemporaries are either dead or doddering old fools anyway.'

He does have the occasional phone call and spends quite a bit of time on the Internet, so maybe he is communicating that way or watching some smutty porn sites.

Even if she could take a look when he was out, she's no computer whizz. Google and the NHS site are about the extent of her 'hacker' status. But she does gradually get a sense of the layout of the house. Rooms and rooms lying empty or full of dust-sheeted ghosts. What must it have been like in its heyday? Different guests week in, week out. Children running along the corridors and chasing each other up and down the staircases. The hustle and bustle of servants hither and thither.

So where did they all live? Where did they all go to bed?

It is quite some time until she finds the door. Its locked anyway, but she knows where the keys are kept and returns with a handful she's not used so far.

Eventually one works, but it's a struggle. Probably not been used for some time.

Whatever she was expecting, it's largely a disappointment. Lots of small bedrooms, some still with beds lying empty. No sign of bedding, until she finds the cupboard, which by the smell she can tell the moths have taken over. She shudders and quickly closes the door. The thought of them in her hair is a long-dead childhood nightmare, but all the more vivid in its sudden resurrection. She scuttles back down to the next landing and stands looking out of the window at the trees slowly beginning to green, until her breathing returns to normal.

'So what if there isn't a mystery here?' she says to herself. What if there is a simple explanation for Edith's disappearance? Her body may be rotting somewhere the dogs didn't go. Or caught underwater by some barrage of logs in the river, more like. The meeting of the Lauder and the Tweed is a well-known cemetery for dismembered branches.

She goes back downstairs, stopping only to look at the light softly falling on the entrance hall. A stillness mourning the lost comings and goings of its previous busy high life.

***

The pictures don't have any sound.

But someone is screaming. Like one of those monkeys? Long tails.

Who is that?

Dust and sun. Can't see. Something wet in my eyes. Someone tugging my shoulder.

'Don't look. Don't look. Don't look.'

Fighting.

'Get off.'

'Got to run. Go.'

He opens his eyes.

'Who's that?

'What's she doing here?

'No place for a woman.

'Get down, you stupid bitch. You'll get shot.

'Now.'

He's sweating, fighting with this bloody woman who doesn't understand.

She's screaming now.

Then the black hole. Falling. Can't stop. Going to die.

Tommy opens his eyes. Sun coming through a curtain. Where's his gun?

He sits up, puzzled by the room. Blue curtains, slightly shifting in the breeze. Where is he? What's that noise? Sobbing?

He blinks and realises he's on the floor. There's a woman. Think it's a woman, sobbing somewhere.

He sits up. Where is he? Who's sobbing?

He looks over the side of the bed. The woman is curled up, her body shuddering with each sob.

He gets up, tries to help her up, but she pushes him away.

He tries again, manages to fend her off and get her sitting up.

She looks at him, terrified.

'Leave me alone,' she croaks. He backs off, trying to remember who she is? Where they are?

Gradually he remembers. Riding the horse, Wallace. Where is he?

The woman is now sitting up, staring at him fearfully. Who is she?

Nina?

He backs off. Realises he's had one of his nightmares, but is still fighting to figure out who this woman is.

She seems a bit calmer now.

'Sorry,' he says. 'Nightmares. Can't stop them.'

She stares at him.

He doesn't know what to do.

She struggles to her feet. It's only then he realises she's naked … and so is he. So?

He doesn't know whether to laugh or cry. But now she's going towards the door, picking up a dressing gown from the floor. With one more frightened look she opens the door and slips out of the room.

He's not sure what to do. Looks round for some clothes.

156

Sees them on the chair. Gets up and puts on trousers and a shirt. No shoes in sight.

He opens the door.

He's on a landing, can see the stairs going down. He slowly descends not knowing what downstairs looks like. Follows his nose to an open door at the end of the corridor.

She's standing at the sink. The kettle is beginning to whistle. She turns off the gas and pours the water into a teapot. Turns to look at him.

Blue eyes. Blonde hair. Still frightened. He stays where he is. Tries a smile. What can he say?

'Why the nightmare?' she asks, quietly.

He stares at her.

'Seen terrible things,' he says. 'PTSD is the official name for it, but we call it a lot of other names.'

She nods her understanding, but rubs her arm and looks at it. There's a purple and black bruise already.

He shakes his head.

'Did I do that?'

''Fraid so,' she says, but almost smiles.

He knows that 'Sorry,' won't cut it, but mouths it anyway.

She pours the tea and they sit down at either side of the little table. Looking at each other.

'It's not as if I'm not used to it,' she mumbles and looks away, wiping her cheek and then glaring back at him. 'I put up with worse, until he left me... How stupid could anyone be?'

He looks down at his cup. What can he say?

Her dog? A black Lab appears and nuzzles into her lap.

'Does someone want his morning walk?' she smiles, fondling his ear.

Tommy looks round.

'You put him in the garden,' she says, indicating the window.

He gets up and looks out of the window, where sure enough is a sad-looking Hengist, balefully staring at him. His tail wags hopefully.

Ten minutes later they're all on the path going down to the beach, the two dogs racing ahead.

The tide is in, bringing bigger rollers than yesterday, crashing at the limit of their reach, which leaves only a thin strand of pebbles being pushed farther up with every crash.

They crunch along the edge of the grass, and occasionally have to get up on to the grass itself. The dogs aren't bothered about getting wet and are now fighting over a branch, which is too big for either of them to carry anyway. Nina points to the rocks at end of the bay and they climb up to the headland, where there's a bench. It's too wet to sit on this morning, so they stand looking out at the roaring waves.

'I thought I'd got past it,' he says.

She looks at him.

'I can't imagine it.'

He nods.

She can't think of anything to say that doesn't sound either crass or insensitive, so she doesn't.

There's silence between them, but conducted in the midst of the thundering crashing and sucking back down in the gullies.

'Not the same as this noise,' he mutters. 'More staccato, with constant chattering in the background and the occasional ear-blasting thumps. Static in your ears. You learn to block it out, concentrate on what you can see. Tiny movements in the distance. It's not like you imagine. Hardly any of the hand-to-hand combat that we spent all that time training to do. Mostly we kill people we can't see except through the scope, and men around you die without hearing the bullet or the shell.'

They stand there not speaking, until the new buddies come slavering up to them to check out why they aren't throwing sticks or stones.

They turn back down to the beach, where now there's a fine line of sand. The tide has turned and the sucking of the gravel is stronger than the surge.

They play with the dogs for a bit, but their hearts aren't in it, so soon they go back up the lane and along to the village shop. Nina has explained that it's still open despite the imminent lockdown, because it's also the post office and the newsagent's. But only locals can go in, so he has to stand outside with the dogs.

She comes out carrying a couple of bags.

He takes them from her and they walk back along the clifftop to her house.

Inside she prepares a proper breakfast, while he reads the paper she's bought.

'My father thinks this is a Communist rag,' he says.

She laughs.

'He's a Torygrapher,' I suppose.'

''Fraid so, although I never read any of them.'

'Well, it could be *The Mail* or *The Express*, or even *The Sun*, I suppose.'

'Hardly, old gal. Them's for the plebs, y' know,' he replies in his best old fogey voice.

They both laugh, but it doesn't last.

Tommy reads a few pages and then puts it down.

'Bunch of liars,' he grumbles.

She puts a plate of eggs and bacon in front of him.

'I thought you would be for Queen and Country.'

'Bollocks,' he mumbles through his first mouthful.

She sits down across from him with her own plate.

They eat in silence, only occasionally making eye contact.

Afterwards he washes up, while she manages a more thorough reading of the news, but neither of them make any further comments.

He makes a pot of coffee and they go into the conservatory.

She sits in a high-backed chair, blowing on the hot drink. He stands looking out at the sea.

What can either of them say?

She's thinking of her bastard husband, unbelievably now shacked up with that old tart. How long will that last? He's thinking about Magda. Will she be out on the street stopping idiots breaking the lockdown? Idiots like him, for example? No, of course she's been sent home.

Perhaps he ought to let her know.

'Can I use your phone?' he says.

She frowns.

'Of course. Haven't you got a mobile?'

He shakes his head.

'You can't disappear with one of them,' he replies.

She stares at him.

'If you're a bad boy trying not to be found,' he adds.

'It's in the kitchen,' she says.

He grins and goes through.

She hears a quiet but brief conversation, but he doesn't reappear straight away after putting the receiver down.

She waits.

He comes back in looking glum.

'My sister. Police detective, for her sins.'

'Is she OK?' she asks.

He slumps down on the settee.

'Yeah, but put on organising duties from home. She has a rare blood condition, which makes her high-risk.'

'Sorry about that,' she says.

'Um … could be worse. She's not locked up with our parents, fortunately. She's requisitioned the gillie's house as her command post. Couldn't do her job with the old bastard looking over her shoulder.'

'Difficult?'

'Old school Border reiver bastard, my father. Owns half of Peeblesshire, or used to, and still thinks he's the laird of all he surveys.'

She stares at him.

'Yes, I'm afraid so. I'm not some Tommy from the Gala cattle sheds. I'm Fettes, St Andrews and the Scots Guards, ma'am.'

She tries hard not to laugh.

'And don't think that's not a bastard of an upbringing, because it was. Only joined up because it meant I'd learn how to kill people efficiently ... and I can and do.'

She looks away, frightened by the sudden anger in his face and his voice.

'Total count, so far? Officially? Two hundred and thirty-three.'

She does now turn round.

He is standing, as if at attention, looking out the window again.

What can she say?

She waits.

Eventually he turns to look at her. His eyes are also blue. But somehow dead.

***

Somehow or other Ziggy has managed to get priority service with the supermarkets.

He won't say how he's done this, just annoyingly taps the side of his nose.

I tell him I think it's not right to bypass the system if he shouldn't.

'Why do you think I've done that illegally?' he demands.

I stare at him. He's not angry or even annoyed. Merely has a slight smile on his lips. Exasperating.

So this morning a van arrives and we receive six boxes of groceries, some gizmos I don't recognise, and loads of sweets.

I offer to put them away and he accepts, after picking up the gizmos. And most of the sweets.

We seem to be back on the usual footing, which is uneven at the best of times. I try to sustain some normality, while he delights in disappearing or sending me 'curve balls', as he calls them, to 'keep me on my toes'.

Today, however, he's visible, but unreachable, as he's wired up to his numerous machines with that blank expression on his face, which could mean he's playing some complicated game or gaining access to inaccessible sites. Or both. At the same time.

I make him a coffee and give him some biscuits, which he doesn't acknowledge, so I take myself out to explore. I've been to the river, so now I wander along the road until I see a path heading up through the huge dense conifers. I'm wearing my walking boots, so think I'll see if I can get above the treeline.

The slope isn't steep, but it is relentless. I realise that I am not as fit as I thought, and have to stop four or five times before I come out above the wood.

A few more yards and then I can see out over the trees.

I can see right across the valley to the hillside opposite, which looks higher than where I'm standing. I can see the big house I saw yesterday, although only its roof and chimneys. One of them is issuing a thin trail of lazy smoke, so someone must be in residence. There also seems to be a smaller building lower down, also with smoke. So there are servants there as well, I think.

I turn to look further up the slope I'm on and see what looks like a ruined building above me.

I'm thinking that I might go up and explore it when it starts to rain. By the time I'm back down into the trees I'm drenched. I trudge down through the dripping trees. This is hardly a holiday. More like a school trip. It always rained on my school trips.

I get back. Ziggy doesn't even acknowledge the drowned rat coming through the door.

I divest myself of all my clothes and lie in a hot bath for ages. At least he's got this right, which means I'm up for making him a good dinner, which of course he gobbles down and then returns to his screens. It's a bit like holidaying with a screen persona rather than a real person. And we're here for the duration. Two days and I'm ready to kill.

Still, the forecast for tomorrow is sunshine, with a cold wind. So I go for the early bed. And am asleep as my head hits the pillow.

***

Fletcher hates not having something to do.

He goes out for a walk every morning. But although striding along the Tweed may be invigorating, you can only count so many herons before breakfast before it becomes tedious.

Louisa spends a lot of time on the phone, listening more than talking. When asked she says,

'Care in the community,' or, 'There are lot of elderly folk around here, you know.'

Finding him wandering about on another morning, she says in exasperation,

'Why don't you go and write your memoirs?'

He stares at her.

'Memoirs?'

'You know, all your seedy exploits. A list of collared rogues. A catalogue of villains sent down. Whatever.'

He's lost for words.

'Well?' she demands.

He shakes his head.

'Don't be daft,' he mutters.

'Have you forgotten everything?' she teases him.

'Certainly not. Remember every one of the nefarious bastards,' he splutters.

She stands glaring at him.

'So what's stopping you, then?'

He frowns.

'Why bother? Many of them got away with it ... some of them are dead.'

Again she harrumphs.

'Can't harm you, then.'

He looks away.

'Hopeless at writing. Typing … no patience with it,' he mumbles.

She folds her arms.

'That's not a problem.'

He looks at her, puzzled.

'Follow me,' she commands, and sets off towards the front door.

He follows, feeling like a poodle needing a bow in his hair, wondering where they're going.

Instead of going to the front door and driving him off somewhere, she turns abruptly left at the entrance hall and into the study cum library.

A startled young man looks up from his laptop, knocking over his coffee cup as he tries to get to his feet. Fortunately it is nearly empty, but he's looking oddly guilty.

Louisa ignores all that and introduces Fletcher.

'William, this is my friend Michael. He's a retired detective who needs an amanuensis to write his memoirs. He had a long and distinguished career, in which he put many violent and despicable people behind bars.'

Both William and Fletcher stare at each other. The young man because he's seen this shambling figure wandering about for the last few days and Fletcher because he is wondering whether he's ever heard the word 'amanuensis' being spoken out loud before.

'Er, certainly, madam. When should we start?'

Louisa turns to look at Fletcher.

'Right now, I think, Michael.'

Fletcher stares at her.

There's a slow-motion moment in which the young man looks from the woman he works for and adores to the dishevelled old gentleman, who doesn't look as if he could put anyone behind bars... And then Fletcher begins to shake his head, but then realises he's on the end of Louisa's famous death stare.

And so it is that every morning, Fletcher does the walk along the Tweed, reminding himself of a particularly spicy tale, before returning to the young man's den and regaling him with an exaggerated version of the events – including as much blood and guts as he can remember or invent.

The young man laps it up – or more exactly, 'laptops' it up.

Two hours is enough for both of them, but the first draft appears by teatime. One copy for him and one for Louisa.

He doesn't think of himself as a pernickety person regarding punctuation and grammar, but he finds the odd gripe here and there, which William politely accepts. Louisa is more punctilious, but the young man wouldn't have acquired the position without impeccable references, so the editing is minimal.

Sometimes, if Louisa has been a party to a particular exploit, and she is surprised to see that she was more times than she would have said, this leads onto further discussion before dinner, but not afterwards, because that's when they play bridge.

Various people are bussed in to make up these foursomes. Illegally, of course, in the lockdown, but they are also the source of much hilarity as they sit at the long table in the salon, which is easily ten feet long and five feet wide, wearing pairs of gloves provided by the hostess, which she says she had specially made for some event forty years ago.

Fletcher is also amused by the variety of these miscreants. Most of them are elderly, but not all. There is one young couple who come on Tuesdays, who are in their late twenties, exceedingly glamorous and excellent players, although the young woman, Charlotte, is viciously competitive and glares at her husband for his occasional mistakes.

Louisa maliciously says that he does it for sex.

'How do you mean?' asks Fletcher.

She smirks at him. An unusual look for her.

'He does it deliberately. He's playing for pleasure,' she says, her eyes glittering.

Fletcher looks away.

Memories of playing with Laura. Foursomes with Roger Aughton.

He covers his tears by going for another drink.

When he comes back Louisa is looking at the fire.

'I'm sorry,' she says. 'Thoughtless of me.'

Once this routine is established it becomes set in stone. Although occasionally people can't make it for cards and no other short-notice participants can be found.

Fletcher dreads those evenings, because neither he nor Louisa can bear the drivel on the television. She compensates by reading, but he's more restless.

On occasions he ends up on the riverbank in the gloaming, which he knows he won't be able to do when the weather warms up because he'll be harassed by the 'midgies'.

It's on one of these nights that he is surprised to see someone coming towards him. Although this part of the bank is within Louisa's property, he knows that plenty of locals and others have her permission to walk it.

The man comes up to him smiling.

'Evening, squire,' he says, which always irritates Fletcher, people trying to do a mockney accent, so he only nods and looks back at the heron on the other bank.

But he man stops and looks over at it as well.

'Beautiful birds,' he says. 'I can watch them for hours.'

Fletcher nods.

'How is her ladyship?' he asks.

Fletcher stiffens even further.

'Fine,' he answers.

'Aye, well,' says the man. 'Tell her young Angus asked after her.'

Fletcher nods, puzzled as to whether he means himself, because he looks well over sixty, or someone else.

The man grunts, probably disappointed to find such a silent Sassenach, and strides on.

Back at the house, he tells Louisa the tale.

She laughs.

'Aye, he is still "young Angus", even though his father's been dead these last twenty years.'

Fletcher smiles.

'Knows the river like the back of his hand ... been incarcerated more times than I can remember ... professional salmon-stealer.'

'Incarcerated?'

'Aye. It's the biggest crime you can commit on the Tweed,' she says, with a hard face.

Fletcher nods.

'He is also the man who spotted James Ferris's body.'

Fletcher stares at her.

'Have you told William that contorted little tale yet?' she asks.

He shakes his head, which is spinning all the way back to his first case up north. Rochdale. The young woman and her baby found dead at the bottom of a tower block. The milkman didn't do it, but Fletcher put him through the wringer before he found out where he'd been.

He looks at Louisa, who is trying hard to give him her most enigmatic look.

But it doesn't work.

They both shake their heads, stifling guilty laughs.

'You in that ridiculous hat,' he says.

'You in that disgusting leather coat,' she counters.

They are both silent for a moment.

'But I did find Laura,' he says. The moment he first saw her across a crowded pub comes blazing back to him and his eyes prick with tears.

Louisa looks away. He's no idea how she feels about that young man now. Or what she put men through in those days.

'He's still living in Alnmouth,' she murmurs, 'with the Dark Lady.'

Now Fletcher looks away.

'You don't go to see them, do you?' he can't stop himself from asking.

'No, I wouldn't do that, Michael.'

They're both silent, reliving past indiscretions and dalliances. And they're both feeling a trifle lost, but neither one of them is ever likely to tell anyone, and least of all each other.

CHAPTER 10

I leave the car in the forestry car park. There are a couple of others there, so nobody will pay it attention for some time. People will just think the owner's gone on a long trek, and I can think of it as a possible backstop in an emergency.

When I look at the map I can see that I can get most of the way there on the forest tracks, so even though I am carrying a heavy sack and a tent, it doesn't look too bad.

But I'm not feeling as good about it a mile up the hillside. I really am not as fit as I thought.

I come out at the top and can see the trees hiding the big house over the other side of the road. I rest for a while and think this through. The bag and the tent are a good excuse, but a cumbersome burden for a quick spying out of the land. I park the tent and some of the kit under a fallen tree and scramble over to the road.

The house driveway leads into the trees from the summit of the ridge, the one-track road going north all the way up to Stow, which now has a station, so it might be useful as a getaway option.

I follow the drive until I can see the house, then cut to the left and stay in the trees all along the back fence, which I'm hoping is far enough away for any dogs to hear or scent me. The 'lost walker' is the story I'm ready to proffer either way. I want to get round behind so I can drop down to the cottage. I figure that the woman is less likely to have dogs.

By now it's even getting light.

The house is huge. Maybe twenty rooms, which could explain the errant son's lack of punishment.

'Not what you know … et cetera.'

Soon I reach the fence at the other side, climb over to the easier walking on the grass and come out above the cottage.

Now I can see the cottage garden, looking a bit overgrown, so maybe the cottage is not regularly occupied, although smoke is still rising from the chimney.

I watch for a good ten minutes.

No sign of any movement. No dogs visible or audible. I climb the fence and make my way to a side window.

Quick peep. Kitchen. Bowl and spoon in the sink. Cornflakes box on the table.

I creep to the next window. Bedroom. Bedcovers thrown back. Door open, revealing passage to outside door. I figure that the sitting room is likely to be facing the valley and the sunshine, so continuing round the back will bring me to either to a back door or all the way round to the door I've just seen.

My assumption is correct.

I can see part of the big house beyond some big bushes, but don't think I'll be visible going up to the door.

Still no sign of a dog, but it's an easy job pulling out the Internet connection.

So, adopting a convincing limp, I knock on the door and get ready to tell my tale of woe.

***

Magda has had a bad night.

Rowing with her father always does this. He is such an arrogant old bastard, saying no one was going to stop him going to his bloody daft meeting in Edinburgh next Tuesday, even though she tried to tell him there'd be no one else there anyway.

Her mother didn't help, telling them abruptly not to quarrel.

She left without having dessert, which she knew was going to be her mother's *szarlotka*, and stormed out into the rain, getting soaking wet as she walked off the anger.

Now she's trying to catch up on what she was supposed to do yesterday and is not getting any help from HQ.

She is wondering if a good scream would help when there's a knock at the door.

Who the hell could that be? No one in the family or from the farm would knock.

She takes a look through the side window.

It's a skinny-looking man with a rucksack, holding his leg.

God, that's all she needs. A bloody injured walker.

She goes to the door.

Five minutes later the man is sitting at the kitchen table with a mug of tea in his hand while she's putting bacon in a pan.

Short version, he says, was getting completely lost on the moors above the forest while bivvying for the night. Fell over his feet coming over some big tussocks and sprained his ankle. Couldn't get a signal and, feeling fearful of ringing up, considering the lockdown rules, anyway, managed to struggle to my door.

She's only half-listening to this, wondering whether she should be arresting the bloody man, but also recognises that he's a welcome distraction.

A quarter of an hour later they're both sitting in the front room, he with his leg on a chair, talking about the crisis and what can anyone do? She hasn't divulged that she's a police officer and that's she should have cautioned him. Yet.

After a slight pause he nods over in the direction of the main house.

'You work for them, do you?'

She manages a reluctant smile.

'Not bloody likely. I'm the errant daughter.'

'Oh, sorry. I'm not being nosey,' he laughs.

'Ah, well, you might ask. They do have employees. The farm is still a working operation. But that's over the other side of the summit, down in the next valley. Most of our remaining land is that way now.'

He nods.

'For now, my parents are having a visiting housekeeper for the duration. Most of the house is closed down nowadays, anyway. They're too old to entertain any more … and my father is … barely polite.'

She laughs.

He smiles.

'So you camp out here?' he asks.

'Only for now. I've got my own house in Selkirk, but I'm working from home here, as it were.'

'Ah, right.'

There is an awkward silence.

'On your own?' he says quietly.

She frowns. Not sure what he's thinking.

'Hardly,' she says. 'Work are onto me most of the time.'

She's now worrying about the lost signal.

'Yeah, I suppose a lot of folk are doing that now,' he agrees.

Another pause.

'So what do you do?'

Again, she has the chance to tell him, but something tells her not to.

'Oh, organisational stuff. I do most of it online anyway.'

She glances at the laptop, which is fortunately half-buried under her papers.

He nods and then looks out of the window.

'I'm afraid I've not been entirely honest with you,' he says.

She freezes.

He looks surprised, then embarrassed.

'No, no. Nothing like that. I was hoping to find someone here. Your brother, I think. Tomasz?'

She stares at him and then laughs. More in relief than understanding.

'Well, he's not here. He rarely is. He's a soldier, generally far away in terrible places trying not to get killed.'

He smiles again.

'That's what I read … but not just now.'

She frowns again. This is no accidental meeting.

'I understand from the newspapers that he's been in a bit of trouble? Been stood down. Back in the UK. Here probably?'

She stands up.

'What do you want?'

If it were a film, it would be a freeze frame.

I can't tell her the whole story. My full intentions.

I pull out the gun from my pocket. It's only a replica, but I doubt that she's the sort of police officer who uses one.

She stares at me in disbelief.

I stand up, giving away my bad leg ploy, but I've no choice now.

Magda has had only one previous incident with someone pointing a gun at her. In Dundee.

They were chasing some dealers. She was only a young uniformed WPC. He was a desperate young black guy. Red-ringed eyes. Face full of fear.

She stood stock still. Told him not to do anything he'd regret. Like she was his mother. Hadn't a clue what to do. But fortunately there was an older armed officer, who took charge, calmly talked the guy into dropping his gun, then ruthlessly bashed him against the wall and cuffed him. He didn't even speak to her afterwards, just winked at her later at the station.

She sits down. Don't frighten him. Eye contact and all the other things she's subsequently been taught, but inside her heart is thudding.

'He isn't so confident himself,' she thinks, but she knows that's more dangerous. She know she needs to engage him in talking.

'What do you want?' she asks quietly.

'I only want to speak to him, ask his help. That's all. I don't want to harm you or him. There's something I need to do and I need someone who can use a gun.'

'Well,' she's thinking, 'Tommy's probably your man,' but knows he wouldn't shoot anyone in a civilian situation ... would he?'

'I'm sorry,' she says. 'I can't help you. He's not here. Not sure where he is. He doesn't carry a mobile. Never has.'

That's confused him. Is that good or not?

'But you've got one,' he says, pointing at her mobile on the table.

In seconds she knows she's given herself away.

He leans over and picks it up. Flicks through the calls with one finger. Too far away for her to lunge at him. She curses herself for her compulsion to namecheck every caller, so knows he'll see Tommy's name against the call yesterday.

He smiles up at her.

'How efficient. Impressive.'

She bites her tongue.

'So...' he says, standing up. 'All I need now is for you not to warn him. I'll take your phone. I doubt you've remembered the number. We don't do that any longer, do we?'

'You won't get anywhere with this, you know,' she says, instantly regretting it.

He shakes his head again.

'I'm constantly surprised by my own resourcefulness,' he replies. 'So don't worry. I don't want to harm you. After all, you've been most helpful.'

She looks up at him. What on earth is he going to do?

'Get on the floor,' he says, now in a menacingly cold voice. 'On your front, hands behind your back.'

She does as she's told.

He's scrabbling in his rucksack.

One of those plastic ties is expertly pulled round her wrists and then another is attached around her ankles.

'I don't think you'll need the gag. No one to hear you, is there?'

She's immediately thinking, hopefully, that her mother will be down at some point with last night's dessert.

There's a moment of silence. What is he doing?

Can't see him, but he's not moved.

She tries to turn her head to look, but can't do it.

She closes her eyes in frustration, but then realises she can see him in the mirror she bought over a week ago, which is still resting against the wall where she put it.

He's tapping and fingering softly on her laptop. What's he doing? Doesn't need her password, obviously, as she was already on it. Is that a USB stick? Oh, God. She closes her eyes. When she opens them again he's standing up. The laptop's still there, but then suddenly everything goes black. A cloth? Her coat?

He doesn't say anything else. There's a bit of shuffling and other noises. Clink of keys? Hers? But then she feels the draught from the door and then it's shut.

Silence descends.

She can't do anything but weep.

***

Next day I'm up early and determined to explore the ruin up the hill.

Breakfast alone. No sign of Ziggy. But then he is a nightbird.

Forewarned by yesterday's downpour, I take my rucksack and my newly bought waterproofs. I hate wearing in new clothes, but going up the hill there's not likely to be anyone else around. There are multiple bike routes further along the valley, but this slope is too steep for even the most extreme of the nutters.

It turns out to be a ruined castle, not a house.

I realise it's marked on the map.

None of the first floor is left, but the chimney stack is still there.

And what a view.

Looking both ways, up and down the Tweed, you can see why it was built there. The main route the other side of the river means that in the old days you'd need a bridge and the only ones indicated now are two or three miles in both directions, so it's well off the beaten track.

I sit there taking in the view. It's a fine morning, and the dew is still wet on the grass. Or maybe it rained in the night.

I train the binoculars on the opposite side. There's a huge forest, and I can see from the map that's its riddled with tracks. Mainly bikes nowadays. Bloody maniacs taking over everywhere. There's a small car park marked. Ah, there it is. Two or three cars parked there.

Nearby, there's a small hamlet next to the road. Only eleven houses, although one of them has a weird collection of outhouses, lots of broken-down cars, and are they swans? In the backyard?

Anyway, more interesting to me is the sloping road going up to the big house.

I follow it up.

The house is surrounded by a massive garden, most of which is densely planted fir trees. The people who own the house definitely don't want to be seen.

However, I'm probably in the best place to spy on them, and the binoculars Ziggy has bought me are army issue.

'You'll be able to see the zits on a boy's nose at half a mile away,' he said.

So I peer through them and scan the facade and count the

windows. Twelve on the second floor. Eight on the first. The ground floor has only five, but they're much bigger. There's a huge entrance doorway with pillars and an arched roof.

At the front there's a terrace with three lots of steps down to the drive, which comes from the road to the left. Gardens down the slope to a long hedge.

Over to the right is another building. Much smaller. A gamekeeper's residence, no doubt. It's all shooting and fishing up here. There's already smoke coming from the big house, but nothing from the smaller one. He's maybe out already, seeing to the birds. Although they're probably not shooting while the lockdown's on, and I think it's the wrong time of the year anyway.

As I watch I see someone come out of the cottage and turn to lock the door.

He's carrying a rucksack and what looks like a laptop in his other hand. Off to work probably. No … going round the back.

I pan up to look for any cars. None in sight.

Back to the cottage, the person comes back into view … but without the laptop. What on earth has 'he' done with it?

Is it a 'he'?

Think so.

Now he's making his way along the bottom of the garden towards the road. Maybe the cars are somewhere in the trees. Sure enough, he climbs up to the terrace on the grass, instead of on the wide steps. As if he's avoiding the front door.

At the top he turns round and stops. Is he looking my way? Like he can see me? Shouldn't think so, and in any case … unless the sun's catching my bins.

I lower them for a moment, but can still see him not moving.

The sun goes behind a cloud.

I look again. Focus more finely.

No.

Impossible.

It can't be.

I fiddle with the focus again.

Difficult to be sure. Bobble hat. Glasses?

He sets off to the left. Walking quickly. Disappears into the trees. Where is he going?

I keep scanning back and forth, until, yes, there's a car coming out onto the sloping road. Not fast. Black Audi, I think. Can't get the number. He's down at the hamlet. Comes out onto the main road and turns right, heading for Peebles.

No. He immediately takes the first turning into the forestry car park. Parks next to another vehicle. Transfers from one to the other, sets off, turns left and heads along downstream. Could be going anywhere east. Galashiels, Melrose, Kelso and on. Only an hour to the A1. An hour to Edinburgh. Anywhere.

What would he be doing here? There?

I gather up my sack and set off back down the hill.

It's impossible, although I've plenty of recent examples from anything to do with Ziggy. He seems to be a magnet for weird connections.

Just when you think you're having a break from all that hoo-ha.

Sheesh.

***

John says he's found another place.

One of his mates does some work up here when it's the shooting season. But now they're breeding the little buggers until the end of August, so he's not there.

We all pile into the Land Rover and set off. It's only six o'clock. John thinks there are not likely to be many people about and they're going a roundabout route of minor roads, so it shouldn't be a problem.

He uses a big pair of cutters on the thick chain on the gate and we're onto the main road for half a mile and then back on a minor road signed to Bowhill and St Mary's Loch.

John nods at the turning to Bowhill.

'Worked there when I was a kid,' he says.

We both look to see if there's more history.

'Don't ask,' he says, with a grim smile.

We don't.

We're soon out of the trees and the hills loom up on both sides. Bare tops and slopes. Sheep country. Leaves Becket cold.

Now she's is staring sightlessly, thinking of a beach in Spain. They come to a crossroads with a pub. Who on earth comes here? Bikers? They turn off again to the right and head up into more bleakness.

It's probably only five miles or so, but it is a route of such emptiness that she thinks she might be getting whatever is the opposite of claustrophobia.

But now they're descending into another valley.

A little church and a few houses, a small hamlet calling itself Traquair. A castle signed to the left a couple of miles further on. Then, as they seem to be approaching a small town, John turns off right again on to smaller road and we're trundling along by a big river.

'The Tweed,' John intones. 'Not far now.'

Becket looks across at the town, thinking of a glass of beer, but knowing that's not possible and not knowing how long it will be.

It's only a few miles and then they pull off onto a dirt track and come to halt outside a wooden building next to a little stream. There is a huge stack of logs against one of the walls. In better weather this might have been pleasurable. However, there is a smokestack, so at least they'll be warm.

They go in. It's surprisingly well furnished. All mod cons.

'OK,' says Becket, trying not to grin.

John flops down.

'Breakfast in ten, skivvies,' he growls. Becket disabuses him.

Freya watches sadly, like she's wishing she had a demanding lover.

***

Jeanie is out on her 'exercise walk'. She's considered going up the Eildons, but it's a bit cold at ground level, so knows it'll be a damn sight colder up there.

Having been born here, she knows lots of the lanes and tracks, so sets off on what she expects to be a more leisurely route.

Spring has been trying hard to arrive for some time now and the easterly winds aren't helping.

But she enjoys this time of year, when you can see the new growth and the early flowers. The snowdrops are over already, but the daffodils are hanging in there, fluttering gaudy flags in the breeze.

She's expecting to meet a few people on the way, as the farm track is wide enough to observe the distancing rules.

She's smiled and chatted with a young couple and nodded at a runner as he puffed past. Never understood the desire herself. Cross-country was one of her pet hates at school. Getting cold, wet, and splattered with mud not her idea of fun.

It's on the long straight lane that she sees a woman standing looking out at the view towards the Cheviots.

Not someone she knows.

Black hair hanging loose. Long dark blue coat like they wear in western movies. Black boots. Wide-brimmed hat.

Jeanie comes level, says,

'Hello'.

The woman raises her head and Jeanie has to swallow a gasp. The right side of the woman's face is covered by a silvery mask, with blue jewels winking in the sun.

Despite this the woman smiles.

'Beautiful morning,' she says in a husky voice.

Jeanie nods.

'It is, but a bit fresh.'

The woman stops and holds out her hand, which is encased in a black leather glove, but then realises that's wrong and smiles. Her smile is made weirdly crooked by the mask.

'Are you just visiting?' asks Jeanie, then also realises that no one should be doing that either.

The woman crookedly smiles again.

'No, I've been renting the cottage for the last few weeks or so, along here, for the time being, somewhere to stay until this madness ends,' she says. Not Scottish. North of England somewhere. Yorkshire?

Jeanie guesses which of the estate houses that might be.

The woman nods.

'Well,' says Jeanie, 'I'm camping out at the big house down by the river, looking after one of the local bigwigs.'

The woman nods as though that's perfectly normal. Then Jeanie realises at the same moment that it isn't.

They both hesitate.

'My name is Carole,' says the woman, and fingers in her bag for a card.

As the woman's wearing gloves, Jeanie thinks it's all right to accept it, but then feels embarrassed because she's left her bag at the house. She only has a card because the home had them done for all the staff.

The woman's card says she's a 'Life Force Enhancer'. The picture is of a face behind what looks like a briar. With one green staring eye

Jeanie doesn't have a clue what that might mean, but it's a far cry from 'Care Assistant'.

She looks back at the woman, who is still smiling crookedly. With one green eye.

'It sounds pretentious, I know, but it is what I do.'

Jeanie can only nod.

'I've come to see the Eildon Tree,' she says. 'Where is it?'

Jeanie smiles. How many times has she been asked that?

'Oh, it's not far away, but you'll need to go down to Eildon Village and take the road on the left. It's about a quarter of a mile to the top, where there's the stone and the tree.'

The woman nods.

'I know it's not the real thing,' she says.

'Aye, my grandad was alive when it was put there. He and his mates used to frighten folk with daft pranks.'

The woman smiles, but then shakes her head.

'Some people tell stories about me, but the truth is far more unpleasant.'

Jeanie frowns. Is she going to tell her about some terrible torture? But she just smiles again and looks away.

'Well, it was nice meeting you. Perhaps I'll see you again,' she says, and tries to set off.

'Stay safe,' says the woman, although the crooked smile has been replaced with a look of genuine concern.

Jeanie is puzzled and can only say the same.

The woman smiles again and walks on.

Jeanie shakes her head. What a strange encounter. She turns to look back at the woman … but she's disappeared. Where has she gone? The lane is bordered on both sides by straggly fir trees and hawthorn bushes that are not easy to get past, and the next turning is a good fifty yards away.

She stands there both confused and a bit frightened. After all, she did look like a witch. Her weird, crooked smile. The odd card.

She shakes her head. Don't be daft. But she does decide to go back a different way, even if it takes a lot longer.

Back at the house she is surprised to see a car on the drive. Not one she's seen before. Not the sort of expensive car that many of his friends arrive in, although she can't remember ever seeing an old-style black VW Beetle before. They were generally orange or blue.

She doesn't think they are expecting any visitors or deliveries this morning, so she's a little apprehensive. It's only when she looks back the way she came that she sees either Dee or Dum – she can't tell which one when they're not together – standing in the driveway, staring in that dour way they do, before he turns and stomps slowly away.

She shakes her head and goes in through the side door, takes her hat and coat off in the kitchen and then goes to listen in the hall.

Not a sound.

Where could they be?

She goes back into the kitchen and makes herself a cup of tea and a small cheese sandwich.

She can't stop thinking about the strange woman and her disappearing act.

Then she finds the card she was given and studies it. Carole Morgan. Was that her real name? Morgan? As in Morgana, the witch in the Arthurian tales. She remembers reading them as a child and being rather frightened. She shivers. Shakes herself.

'Don't be so daft,' she says to herself.

It's at that moment that she hears a noise.

What was that? Someone calling? More like a shriek.

She goes out into the hall.

Is that someone talking or is it laughter? It's coming from upstairs.

She slowly climbs up to the first landing. There is a voice. Another laugh. Definitely female. Coming from the main bedroom.

Is he?

Well … it is his house. His bedroom. He doesn't have to ask her permission. Although he does normally tell her if he's expecting a visitor. Didn't say anything this morning at breakfast. Looked a bit pasty, now she thinks about it.

She stands and listens.

Only a few murmurings, and then, as she turns to go back down, there's a shriek. Of pleasure ... or pain?

She sets off downstairs, goes back into the kitchen. Absent-mindedly washes up the dishes, but then goes and opens the kitchen door again.

What's that noise? Was that groan or a snarl? Is there a dog upstairs?

Randolph told her he was not going to get another dog after the last one, Rufus, a red setter, died of old age a couple of months ago.

No, that was definitely human.

What can she do?

Nothing.

Then there is another shriek.

She goes back into the kitchen and gets her coat.

And goes out through the back door and into her car and drives away, not sure where she's going or whether she'll be coming back.

***

Fletcher has been informed that he's to be ready for cards by three o'clock.

'Is this allowed?' he thinks, but the look on Louisa's face tells him it's non-negotiable.

'They're not my favourite people ... well, he's definitely not, although the wife is deserving of all the support she can get,' says Louisa. 'Can't abide the husband. A bully and a bad loser.'

Fletcher is taken aback by the casual vehemence of this tirade, but is too busy struggling not to laugh to question any of it.

Louisa gives him one more glare and stalks off.

He glances at the clock on the mantelpiece. One o'clock already. But time for a quick stroll down to the river. Check up on the heron. He's been entranced by the female sitting on her nest. Hasn't told or asked anyone about it. Doesn't want to expose himself to birdwatcher chat or wisdom. Just wants her to himself.

He can't help but laugh as he strides through the garden. Is this him? Wanting to keep a secret about a damn bird?

'Well, it's better than feeling guilty about Laura,' he says in his defence, and refuses to let any tears drop. A hopeless endeavour, and he has to wipe his face before he can focus on the heron.

It's not exactly exciting, because she doesn't move much at all. Only to receive the occasionally delivery of a fish from her mate. He may be a languid big bird, but there's no doubting his loyalty.

Refreshed by this display of courtship, he strides back at pace for the afternoon games.

The old couple arrive in a vintage Mercedes.

The man gets out first and slams the car door shut before walking towards the front door.

Fletcher is watching from the side window and is beginning to think the wife hasn't made the trip, when the passenger door slowly opens and a surprisingly tall angular woman climbs out onto the gravel.

She stands still for a moment, gathering her breath. More likely waiting for the pain going off, judging by the wincing face she's making. Even without Louisa's comment about the man, Fletcher is outraged at this behaviour and gets himself out into the hall and manages to open the front door in time to help the woman up the steps and inside.

She is all smiles and thank yous as they continue along to the drawing room. He's forgotten all about distancing and so gets a worried glance from Louisa and a glare from the man.

'I'd take it kindly, sir, if you would unhand my wife. We're not supposed to be touching each other. Don't know you from Adam, and doubt you have the lineage to have the honour.'

Fletcher stares at him, all his hatred for the rich and entitled rising in his throat.

But it is stifled and assuaged by three interventions.

Firstly, by the woman he's helped into the room, who smiles at him and claps his hand more firmly to her arm.

'Ignore him, dear man. My husband can't abide a show of chivalry from another man. Still jealous after all these years.'

Secondly, by Louisa smiling and announcing the couple.

'Can I introduce the two of you? George Steil, Laird of Steil and Order of the Thistle and, Helena, who you seem to have already become acquainted with, but need to be told formally, is his wife, and the daughter of Count Stefan Tarnowski ... and Michael Fletcher, Detective Inspector, retired.'

And thirdly, by now grinning from ear to ear as he finishes his first gulp of his first drink, the old man, who laughs and beams at Fletcher.

'Take the old witch away with you, if you want,' he declares and pulls a face at her, 'but only after we've trounced the pair of you at cards.'

Fletcher stands speechless.

'I can't think of a better plan,' the woman says with a harsh laugh. 'If Louisa is up to challenge.'

So five minutes later, they're sitting at the huge table. Fletcher and Helena across the width and Louisa and George at either end lengthways. All wearing gloves, but none of those ridiculous masks.

This arrangement is apparently traditional for this trio and whoever is 'fortunate' to make up the fourth hand. The cards have to be kept by the players rather than stacked in the middle. Winning tricks vertical and losing horizontal for each pair.

Fletcher is relieved to realise that as long as Helena is

in charge, and she is fastidious in this, he's absolved of full responsibility for being correct with this arrangement.

Once they're playing there's little small talk, and Fletcher realises that although this couple are old and George's hands are arthritic, there's nothing wrong with their memories or their combativeness.

So two hours pass quickly. They take only one short break, although George has frequent visits to the bottles, which don't seem to affect his attention or skill either.

In the end Fletcher and Helena win, but only by a few hundred points.

They retire to the conservatory, where none of them talk about politics or the lockdown. Fletcher is questioned as thoroughly as any defence counsel he's ever faced by Helena, who is particularly intrigued by his part in the demise of James Ferris a few miles down the river.

'A blackguard of the worst order,' comments George when he realises who they're talking about.

'He's dead, George,' says Helena, 'and no heirs.'

'Damn lawyers, making a bloody fortune out it. There'll be nothing left by the time those leeches have taken their cuts off the carcase. Owes me thousands. Never see a sou.'

They're saved by any further tirades by the gong for dinner, which is served in the grand dining room, with all the accoutrements and again plenty of space in between them. Louisa's young girl is serving with her gloves on and an awkward-looking mask.

It's nearly eight o'clock when George declares he must take the young lady home.

She shakes her head, but agrees.

Handshakes and embraces are gestured and the laird does manage to accompany his wife to the car with a gruff,

'Keep your hands to yourself, young man,' to Fletcher.

As they stop waving as the car disappears down the drive, Louisa sighs.

'Excellent, Michael, getting civilised in your old age.'

He ignores this and shakes his head.

'Bloody rich people. What have I done to deserve any of this?'

She laughs.

'You may well ask.'

Back in the conservatory, with a brandy each, he listens to the wind buffeting the windows.

'So how could a daughter of that couple end up being a detective?' he asks.

'The opposite reason from her brother. Women have choice in that sort of a family. The men don't.'

Fletcher looks across at her.

'He's a soldier. Scots Guards. Last seen in action in the hills of Afghanistan.'

'He's dead?'

There's a pause.

'No. Sent home in disgrace.'

'Cowardice?'

'Far worse than that. Brawling in a Greek bar, most recently, as well as long list of other misdemeanours.'

Fletcher frowns.

'Really?'

'I'm afraid so,' she adds.

There's another long pause.

'He's not unlike you,' she says.

He looks across at her. She's smiling.

'How d'you mean?'

'A bad penny, with a short fuse … who is also damn good at his job.'

He snorts.

'Bad penny?'

'Um… As in doesn't take orders at all well, has a low opinion of most of his superiors and is given to bouts of extreme violence.'

Fletcher grins.

'So how is he "damn good"?'

She gets up and goes for more brandy.

'He's a marksman. A sniper. Held the record for the longest shot to kill for a short while a couple of years ago, I think.'

Fletcher stares up at her as she hands him his glass. He's thinking of that man back in Barrow who had planned to shoot someone a few hundred yards away, which he was told wasn't that far for a marksman, even then.

'How far exactly?'

She swirls the brandy in her glass.

'Nearly one and a half miles.'

He stares at her in disbelief.

She nods.

'It's further than that now. Check it out.'

Fletcher shakes his head, but now he knows which story he is going to tell the young man tomorrow.

Barrow-in-Furness.

'Longest cul-de-sac in the UK.' A runaway girl and a ghost. The tide coming up over the mud.

He shivers.

***

It is only because her attacker didn't realise that the hall light was on that Magda's mother comes down to see her after they returned from the outing to Louisa's.

She is immediately worried when she sees the plastic container with the dessert in it still on the shelf by the front door.

She tries the door, but it's locked.

It's getting dark by now, so she has to take care going round to the front window. Kenny's obsession with hydrangeas makes that difficult.

She peers in through the window, but there's nothing to see.

She goes back to the front door and knocks again. No reply … or was that a noise?

She goes round to the kitchen window.

Peers in. It's too dark. Only a couple of red lights.

She's really confused now. Where is Magda?

It's only then that she realises that there is something moving on the floor. A spark of light in a face. It's Magda. What's she doing on the floor, wriggling about?

Helena goes back to the front door and finds the spare key under the mat, opens the door, and goes in. She finds the light switch and hurries through to the kitchen.

By now Magda is weeping with relief.

Helena quickly realises the problem, finds the big kitchen scissors and cuts through the ties on Magda's hands and ankles. She holds her tight while she sobs though gritted teeth, like she used to do when she was young and Tomasz had tricked her in some way.

Helena puts the kettle on and finds a clean cloth to wipe the blood from her daughter's wrists and ankles. There are some deeper cuts, which she thinks might need a stitch or two, but she quickly finds Magda's first aid kit and applies soothing cream and a couple of bandages for the two worst limbs.

All this takes some time, and it's only when she's sure she's done as much first aid as possible and Magda has stopped crying that she demands to know what happened.

Magda shakes her head.

'How could I be so naive?' she cries.

Helena stares at her.

Magda controls herself, blows her nose and tells her the whole sorry story.

Her mother doesn't interrupt until she's finished.

'So now we must call the police,' she says.

'No,' rasps Magda, with a glare of anger. 'The only things he's taken are my phone and my laptop, and by now he's probably dumped them both.'

Helena shakes her head.

'No, the most important thing is that we have to warn Tomasz.'

Helena stares at her.

'Why? What has he to do with this?'

'I don't know, Mother, but it was the reason the man came here. I told him he wasn't here, but then he took my phone and found the call Tomasz sent me yesterday.'

'So where is your brother?'

Magda shakes her head.

'I don't know, only that he called to say he was all right and not to worry.'

Helena looks at her doubtfully, not trusting either of them to tell the whole truth when it came to her son's behaviour. Magda has always protected him.

'It's true, *Mamusia*. I've no idea where he is.'

They both sit staring at each other, both wondering what to do next, but then Magda bangs her head with her fist, which hurts both her head and her wrist.

'Ow,' she cries. 'Stupid woman.'

Helena stares at her, worrying about concussion.

'Have you got your mobile with you?' Magda demands, pointing at her mother's handbag.

Helena nods at it and produces the machine that her daughter has made her adopt, but that she still doesn't feel confident with.

Magda finds it, wakes it up, and, closing her eyes, remembers Gatti's personal number.

He answers on the fifth ring.

'Hello,' he says, in his puzzled voice.

'Hi. It's me, on my mother's phone. Look, I need you to do something for me, on the quiet, OK?'

'Right,' he says.

'It's extremely embarrassing and I'll kill you if you tell anyone, but I've been robbed. My phone and my laptop.'

She hears the intake of breath, but he only says,

'Oh...'

'So here's what I want you to do. Check my phone record and tell me the last few numbers. I think it's a landline, somewhere locally, sometime this morning, probably the last call. This is really urgent. He may be trying to find my brother. Don't know why, but he's not likely to be an old friend wanting a night out.'

'Understood. I'm onto to it, ma'am.'

There's a short pause.

'Are you all right?' he asks.

'I'm fine, just want to get the bastard.'

'Ah,' he says. 'I'll get back to you soon as possible.'

'Rico? Not a word to anyone. You understand?'

'Yes ma'am. *La bocca cucita.*'

She's not sure what that means, but ends the call anyway. She realises she's standing by the window and was probably shouting at the poor man.

She turns to look back at her mother, who is trying hard not to cry. She can't deal with that, so tells her it'll be all right.

'It's OK, *Mamusia*, it's only some men stuff. He probably owes him money or has been seeing his wife.'

That's so not the thing to say, and she immediately regrets it. Her mother bursts into tears. Could she make the whole thing any worse?

She stalks round the room, but then realises she's starving, rummages in the kitchen cupboard and wolfs down half a packet of biscuits while opening a can of baked beans and putting them in a pan.

Her mother stops crying, shakes herself and sets to, making breakfast.

'*Mamusia*, it's ten o'clock at night.'

'You need food, Magda.'

Magda gives in. What an idiot she is. And now she's going to cry again.

She angrily goes through to the front room, puts the light on and stands at the window. Where the hell is Tomasz?

Gatti is true to his word. Ten minutes.

'It's a house in a small place south of Berwick, ma'am.'

'Bastard,' she says.

There's a silence at the other end. Gatti knows the problem. It's over the border. Outside their jurisdiction.

'Give me the number,' she says.

Gatti tells her.

'You've not told anyone?'

'No, ma'am.'

'Can you come and get me?'

'Now, ma'am?.'

'Yes, now.'

Again a short pause.

The face of Gatti's feisty wife surges into Magda's brain like a mad-eyed Lady Macbeth.

'OK, first thing in the morning. I mean six o'clock, right?'

'Yes, ma'am.'

'And, Rico, not a word.'

'No ma'am,' he softly replies, with both relief and worry in his voice.

Magda refocuses on her mother, who is diligently poking three bacon slices round a couple of eggs in the frying pan.

'I'll have to borrow your phone again, please.'

Helena nods. She only has it because her daughter has insisted on it.

'Of course, but...'

Magda sighs.

'I don't like you to use those words.'

Magda shakes her head and goes back into the front room.

No laptop. God, how awful this is. She starts to imagine the dressing-down she's going to get. The embarrassment when the rank and file get to hear about it. The whispering behind her back. All the old resentment about the laird's daughter getting the post above the local hard man.

'Jesus,' she cries and rings Gatti again, who answers straight away, fear in his voice.

'Yes, ma'am.'

'Can you give me Frank's number?'

'Yes, ma'am.'

There's a short pause, then he tells her the number. She thanks him and stops the call. Rings Frank, who, being the worst sort of techie – never known to need any sleep – answers immediately.

'Hi, Rico, how is your beautiful wife? Dumped you yet?'

'Frank, it's me, Magda.'

'*Dobry-den*,' he says, happily, switching to his surprisingly good Polish.

'Disaster, I'm afraid.'

'Pregnant?' he asks, in that blithely cruel way he has.

'Far worse, Frank. Someone stole my phone and my laptop.'

She doesn't yet want to talk about the USB stick, and is not even sure now that she saw it or dreamt it. If the man tries to infiltrate the police system, she's pretty certain that Frank and his colleagues will able to deal with that.

'Oooh,' he whispers. 'Very naughty.'

'Not naughty, Frank. More like job-threatening.'

'Um, see what you mean.'

'Can you block it?'

'Hey, Mags, who you talking to, sister?'

'Yeah, cut the bad accent. Can you do that?'

'Can I do that?'

'That's a yes?'

'Give me five.'

'You sure?'

'Already started.'

He cuts the call.

She looks at the phone. Why do all techies have to speak in downtown New York accents like they're extras in *Taxi Driver*? She wants to throw the old thing at the wall, but it's all she's got, so she doesn't. Instead, she flops down on the sofa and cries again. God, her wrist hurts.

Ten minutes later, as she's finished wolfing down the food her mother has made, he phones back.

'Done, sister, but there's good news and bad.'

'Bad first.'

'Your machine cost ten K. You had one of only three we bought last month and if he's managed to get in, it could compromise the whole force, unless you were super vigilant.'

She shakes her head. It can't get any worse.

'Good news?' he says.

She grunts.

'Chances are he's dumped it straight away. Nothing since early this morning, round about nine o'clock.'

'That's when he left with it.'

'Have you checked in the vicinity? You're at home, yeah?'

'Yes.'

'Go look. If he has, that's a result, apart from the ten K of course. But your dad can stop that from your pocket money, so it's cool.'

'Fuck off,' she says, but he's gone.

And there's her mother standing in the doorway with her pursed lips.

Magda ignores her, finds a torch, and goes out to check the bins. Nothing there. And then she sees the water butt.

One sopping wet laptop. Is that saveable?

She rings Frank again.

'Is it closed?' he asks.

'Yes.'

'You may be the luckiest girl ever, especially as you've got me to save your pretty arse. Dry it gently. Put it somewhere warm. I'll come and get it. Fingers crossed. Stay safe.'

She sighs.

Normally she'd curse his misogynist mouth, but if he can save it, she might… No, that's too horrible.'

She looks at her mother. Goes and puts her arms around her. Takes her back up to the house. Has a cocoa and a large glass of her father's best whisky.

It's only then she realises. Tomorrow is lockdown.

Did that man count on that? And he's had all day to get away.

She goes back to her bed and crashes out. Her last thoughts are of her holding the bastard's head down in the water butt until he stops struggling.

LOCKDOWN MONDAY MARCH 23

CHAPTER 11

Tomasz Steil is the worst person in the world to put up with a lockdown. 'Restless' is hardly the word. More like a recently caught and caged wild animal.

He's also the last person to know for sure that today is the day it begins.

Fortunately, riding a horse demands at least two metres' distance at the best of times, so he's gone for a gallop on the next beach down, which is the other side of the headland. Nina might have liked to accompany him, but her last horse, Dido, passed away last year and she hasn't had the heart to replace her. Or the money, for that matter.

So he's out when the phone call comes.

'Hello. Can I speak to Tomasz Steil, please?' says the man's voice.

She hesitates. It's not his sister and it sounds too young to be his father, but she replies.

'Not at the moment, I'm afraid,' she says. 'He's gone out.'

'Ah…' says the voice. 'When do expect him back?'

'Can't say,' she replies. 'Who are you?'

There's a short pause.

'It's a private matter,' the man says, 'to do with his job.'

Again, something seems a bit odd, although Tommy is strange himself. Maybe he is not telling her the full story.

'Can I say who's called?' she asks.

This time a cough.

'No, it's fine. Tell him it's "good news".'

She puts the phone down.

Strange? No. More than that. Worrying.

She walks into the conservatory and looks out towards the headland. No sign of him yet, but that's not surprising. The other beach is nearly a mile long, and the cliff passage to and from it is narrow and difficult on a horse.

She stands thinking about the conversation. Was there something wrong with it?

Was that a Lancashire accent? She's from Stockport herself, and has always had trouble telling a Bolton from a Bury accent or somewhere else north of Manchester. So how could that be work? Can a non-Scot even join up to the Scots Guards?

She watches the old guy with the young retriever on the beach. He hasn't a clue about training a dog.

'Hang on a minute,' she says out loud. 'How does he know this number? Bloody man.'

She stomps back into the kitchen, picks up the phone and checks the number. Withheld. Is that a good sign or not?

'Bloody hell,' she shouts at the cooker.

**

So, once again, Ziggy has disappeared.

No note. Breakfast debris all over the kitchen.

Looks like he's set out for a long day.

His boots and rucksack are gone.

'So don't expect me back till dark,' seems to be the message.

I clear up while my breakfast is cooking. I'm still wondering about the person across the valley. What was he up to? Whatever it is he may not be back again. Why did he change cars? After sleeping on it I've told myself it couldn't possibly be 'Sparrow'.

When something mysterious happens like this, and with Ziggy it seems to be all the time, you can't help thinking it's something fishy.

I told him about what I saw, but he looked at me like I was crazy, and now maybe he's gone over there this morning to investigate. Without me.

Without a car, I know it's a long walk to the nearest bridge and then back along the other side. I checked on the map, over three miles. There are bikes in the cottage outhouse, but they're the new-fangled, off-road things, with hundreds of gears. I'd only fall off one like that.

So all I can do is hike back up the hill with my binoculars.

But, given the amount of washing up and other bits of tidying that my erstwhile 'not-mother' drilled into me that I had to do before anything, from being a babe in arms, it's well after ten o'clock before I set off.

It's a good hour to the ruined castle.

I settle down in the warm sunshine and get out the bins.

Not a soul in sight.

The big mansion sits there like a monolithic doll's house, the noonday sun bouncing off all the downstairs windows. It's at this point I realise that the upper floor windows are all shuttered. That floor is not being used, presumably.

I focus on the little cottage. Again there is no one in sight. But there is smoke today.

I check back at the big house. Yes, there's smoke there as well.

So everyone is sticking to the rules. That would not be difficult up there in the middle of nowhere, and I suspect that plenty of provisions have been laid in.

As I remember the strange behaviour of the mystery man yesterday, I pan across to the forestry car park. Sure enough, there's the black Audi. Does that mean he's coming back?

I put the bins down and sit there, puzzling.

Up here, I've no signal, meaning I can't start any other investigations, so I decide to forget about it all for the moment and find another route to follow.

On looking to my left I can see a track curling around the slope above the treeline that will bring me out above the cottage, and then maybe I can find another way down and back. Nothing like a contour path to raise your spirits.

I check it out on the map and see that I can get down to some cottages near the road. It's about four miles back to the cottage. Back in time for tea.

I set off.

Still not a soul in sight.

Just how I like it.

***

Louisa is standing at the door of the study, listening to Fletcher telling tales.

It makes her smile. She can't be doing with the sad face, and hopes that poor Laura doesn't last much longer. Then he can mourn properly.

She makes her way back to the conservatory and picks up the phone. She always gives Helena a ring the morning after bridge, especially if the old bastard has heavily lost the evening before. Terrible man. Her father hated him. They used to even resort to fisticuffs.

She waits patiently, knowing Helena might not hear or is some way from the phone in that ghastly monstrosity. She's about to give up when there's a wavering voice asking,

'Who's calling?'

'It's Louisa, darling,' she says.

'Oh, hello,' says Helena.

'You made it back safely then, last night?'

'Well, yes, but we've had a terrible shock, Louisa.'

'Oh, no. Are you all right?'

'Not us. Poor Magda.'

Louisa is thinking,

'What is she doing there, and who would take her on? Isn't she a karate black belt or something?' She asks,

'What's happened?'

'Well, I went down last night when we returned home. Magda's staying in the gillie's cottage for now, because of the medication she takes. Working from home, of course.'

Louisa remembers that Magda, who is as fit as a fiddle, has some weird condition, but doesn't know what drugs she takes. And now she can hear Helena trying to choke back an angry sob. She waits.

'Anyway she's all right. I spoke to our doctor and he says she should recover if there are no serious injuries.'

Louisa can't imagine what's happened, but knows she can't rush Helena or she'll get confused. She can hear her taking a deep breath before continuing.

'She'd been attacked by a strange man who left her tied up. He took her mobile and dumped her laptop in the water butt.'

'Oh, no,' Louisa exclaims.

'She's fine. More angry than upset. She was so abrupt on the phone to her young sergeant, poor man.'

'So what was the man after? Maybe he was a thief.'

There's another pause. Helena is blowing her nose and taking a deep breath. Louisa is thinking about Fletcher telling his tales in her study.

'I don't know. Magda tells me not to worry and that he's not likely to come back … and not to say anything to George.'

'Well, don't,' says Louisa. 'He'll only get into a rage.'

'Don't worry, I'm not going to. Silly old fool.'

Louisa asks a few more questions to be sure Helena is all right, but wants to go and talk to Fletcher.

She puts the phone down and stalks off through the house.

***

Nina stands at the window watching Tommy slowly riding his big horse along the tideline below. No hurry there. She wonders how he'll react to the mystery phone caller.

When he trots up the beach and out of sight, she goes to

make some food in the kitchen. He'll be hungry after such a long ride and doesn't seem to have taken anything with him.

Sure enough, he wolfs it all down.

'You've had a phone call,' she says.

He stops mid fork and stares at her.

'Who? My sister?'

'No, a man.'

'What did he want?'

'He wouldn't say, other than saying it was to do with your job.'

'My "job"?'

'That's what he said.'

That puzzles him.

'Did he give you a name?'

'No. He said you'd be pleased. That it was good news.'

Again, he looks puzzled. Not worried.

'Anyway, I was a bit put out that you've given him this number without asking me.'

He looks up at her again and frowns.

'I haven't. I've only phoned my sister. She wouldn't tell anybody else, especially not some stranger.'

This leaves them both puzzled.

'Shall I phone her?' he asks.

'If you like.'

She fetches him the phone. He knows the number and rings it. No reply.

'That's strange,' he says.

He stands there considering various possibilities. Has something happened to his parents? It's unusual for her to ring him, anyway. She is always on the go in her job.

He looks back at Nina, who is watching him suspiciously.

'Perhaps I ought to ring my mother. They're both getting on, but generally in good health. Well, the rude version for my father.'

She nods. He tries. No answer.

'Doesn't mean much,' he says. 'If they're out, only my mother has a mobile, which my sister has pressed upon her. But she doesn't like it. Often has it turned off.'

Nina has some sympathy with this, just like her father. Her mother died a long time ago.

They sit thinking about these things for some time and then the doorbell rings. They both frown at each other.

'Can't be for me,' he says.

Right now she's not so sure, but goes anyway, although she's aware that he's following her some of the way. She is not sure whether that's reassuring or not.

She opens the door.

A small, weaselly-looking man is there. Shorter than her.

'Yes, can I help you?' she asks.

He smiles and looks beyond her.

'I was hoping to speak to your friend, Captain Steil.'

Nina turns to look back at Tommy, who now makes his way to the doorway.

'Who are you?' he asks.

'Oh, we haven't met. And before you shut the door in my face, I'm not a reporter. I'm looking for someone like you to do a job for me.'

'Someone like me?' asked Tommy, with a sarcastic tone.

'Yes, someone of your calibre, as it were,' the man says, with a slight smile at his pun.

Nina is feeling more and more uncomfortable. She backs into the house.

'I don't want anything to do with this,' she says. 'I think you should take this man somewhere else, Tommy.'

He frowns at her, but then realises she's right.

'Yes, of course,' he says, turning to speak to the man. 'I'll meet you down at the beach in five minutes. Not here, OK?'

These last words were spoken in a menacing voice, which reminds her of his nightmare, and it seems to have the same effect on the man, who backs off and nods his agreement.

'Of course,' he says. 'I understand. I'll see you there.'

With that he walks away and disappears along the lane.

Tommy follows her back inside.

They go back to the front room. She goes to stand by the window with her back to him.

Tommy is both puzzled and annoyed.

'Look, Nina, I've no idea what this weirdo wants or is even talking about. I've never met him before. No idea who he is, but I'll go and put him straight. Send him on his way. Don't worry.'

She doesn't turn round.

He comes up to her. Doesn't touch her. Only comes to where he can see her face.

'Honestly, I don't know who he is or what he means about my "calibre".'

He reaches out to her with a grin on his face.

She manages a weak smile.

'I believe you. But it's scary, someone tracking you down like that.'

'I agree, but that's how it is these days. It's one of the reasons I don't have a phone. No idea how he's tracked me to here. I've told no one, not even my sister.'

She manages another smile. He reaches out to her and she allows him to hold her … close. They kiss.

He pulls away and looks for his jacket. He pulls it on and, with one last look, turns, and is out of the door.

She stands looking at the closed door, drops the latch, finds the key, and locks it, shivers, and goes back to the front room. Then goes to the window, not really wanting to, but knowing she must see how they meet.

Tommy is both angry and worried. Angry at the intrusion, yet worried about the ease with which a perfect stranger is able to track him down.

How has he found him? Who has given him such information?

He knows he has plenty of enemies in the army. People who resent his expertise. People in the higher ranks, who think he is literally a loose cannon, a weapon who they value highly, but they wish he'd just follow orders and not be so unmanageable.

He stomps down the lane and gets to the huts.

The man is down by the current tideline, walking slowly along, occasionally bending to pick up a shell or something, and looking like any innocent beachcomber.

Tommy decides he's not going to take any nonsense from this stranger. Perhaps he'll send him for an early bath. A cold salty bath.

He strides across the sand, knowing full well that Nina can see them, so perhaps a violent solution is not such a good idea where she can watch it. Maybe it would be better to take him inland a bit. Find a quiet corner to put him straight.

The man turns to look at him as he approaches.

Tommy walks up to him and tells him what they're going to do. The man agrees without any resistance and they set off back up the slope to the car park, where the man says he's parked his car.

But whatever he thought this man was going to ask him in no way prepares him for the proposal he's about to receive.

Nina watches this curtailed scenario and sighs in exasperation. Where are they going? Does Tommy know him? What should she do? And then there are two abandoned dogs sitting politely, wondering why they haven't been taken for this surprise second walk.

And his damn big horse in the paddock... Has he even fed it today?

***

Magda stands looking out over the valley holding a mug of coffee, which is rapidly cooling in the cold breeze.

There's smoke being wafted away from the chimney of Amelia's house. If only she could get on Sandy and go down for a morning chat.

She's waiting for Gatti to bring her a spare laptop, which he says he can get from Frank without telling anyone else, although she knows she can't put off telling Chief Superintendent Walters about what's happened for much longer. Frank has promised to get back to her by lunchtime. He came out to her in the middle of the night to get the drowned laptop, swearing profusely about people living in the back of beyond, and didn't think to bring a spare one with him. Not his fault, of course.

She can't go anywhere without a car, anyway, although her mother says she can borrow her father's. She doesn't want to do that because she'd have to tell him what had happened. She knows she could also borrow one of the cars from the farm, but again doesn't want people to know.

Frank also said he could find her car, via the satnav, but hasn't got back yet on that either.

It's all so frustrating.

There's a flash of light the other side of the valley. A reflection from something near the old castle? Someone watching her? That man?

She goes back in the cottage and finds her binoculars … well, they're Tommy's, but he won't mind.

Then she comes back out and focuses them on the ruin … in time to see a figure walking slowly along the track above the trees. Is that him? Why would he still be there? But now she can see Rico's car coming along the road below, so goes back inside in time to hear her mother's phone ringing.

It's Frank.

'You are one lucky girl,' he says.

'It's OK?'

'Only thanks to my superb expertise, ma'am.'

She sighs, overcome with relief.

'When can I have it back?'

'Best to leave it for twenty-four hours, to be sure. I've given your sidekick a replacement and a mobile. Should be with you by now. Can't do anything about all your boyfriends' texts and addresses unless you've got your own.'

'Thanks, Frank. I owe you big time.'

There is a wicked laugh.

'I'm working on that too,' he says, but she cuts him off before he can say any more, while thinking,

'What boyfriends?' And where is her other phone?

She goes back to the window and sees Rico's car slowly coming up the lane. Then goes to put the kettle on.

Rico hasn't been to her parents' house before, but she's told him how to get to the cottage.

He knocks on the door.

'It's open,' she shouts.

He appears in the front room as she's bringing through two mugs of coffee, knowing that he takes it strong and black.

His eyes are big.

'I know,' she says. 'Embarrassing, isn't it?'

'No,' he says. 'Amazing. Can't imagine how many rooms there must be.'

'Thirty-six,' she says.

He puts the laptop down on the table and backs away. He's wearing gloves. She picks it up and goes to plug it in.

'You've no idea how helpless it feels without one,' she says. 'Did you get a phone as well?'

He reaches inside his pocket and produces what looks like an exact replica of the one she's lost. Again on the table.

'Oh,' he adds, 'Frank's also found your car. It's only about half a mile away, in a forestry car park.'

'Ah, right,' she says. 'I know it.'

He smiles.

'Seems like he planned it,' he says.

'Yeah, and he must have walked round the back of the house, because he came over the wall behind here.'

'I'd drive you down, but...' he says.

She shakes her head, thinks of telling him about the snooper across the valley, but for some reason thinks she won't.

They sit in silence for a while.

'Any news on the old lady?' she asks.

He shakes his head again.

'No. Jamie still reckons she's in the river and, with there being hardly any rain for ages, she's unlikely to reappear until after there is a substantial downpour.'

Magda shakes her head.

There is another silence. She's wondering if their relationship has been affected by this situation.

'Sorry, to drag you into this, Rico,' she says quietly.

He shakes his head.

'Not your fault. I'm only glad you aren't hurt.'

She nods, not really wanting to think about that.

'I've not told the chief super yet, but I will be doing later this morning.'

He nods. Straight face.

'Thank goodness for Frank,' she says, 'even if he is a sexist bastard.'

He smiles and gulps down the coffee.

'Do you need anything else?'

'No, I'm fine. Gavin at the farm has organised food deliveries for us all, so we're good.'

He smiles again and she sees him out, at a distance, thinking she's completely forgotten all about that.

It's only as she's getting her coat on to go and find her car that she remembers that's where she's probably left her own phone. Will he have taken that as well?

Fingers crossed, she sets off down the field.

CHAPTER 12

The contour walk is delightful, but the descent is horribly muddy and gets worse the further down I go. As I said,

'Bloody cyclists.'

I even have to stand aside for three guys toiling up the steep hillside. They all nod at me through their wraparound shades and I try hard not to scowl at them. Should they be doing that in the lockdown? But then the slope eases off and I find myself back down by the river again. However, I can now see there's a route into the town. Walkerburn, it says on the map. No point in that, though, is there? It'll be all closed up.

So I set off on the path by the river.

As I can see that there is another pack of cyclists coming along towards me I decide to sit on the convenient Tweed viewing bench and let them pass me by.

I stare resolutely at the river. It's sluggish, but there are a few ducks fiddling about over the other side. While looking upstream towards the bridge I spot a heron, and am so focused on him that I don't realise the cyclists have stopped rather than going past me.

I turn to look. To find three faces staring at me. And a small dog snuffling my boots.

Two I recognise immediately. Becket and her friend John. What the hell are they doing here? But who's that other woman? Have I seen her somewhere before?

'What are you doing here?' asks Becket.

'Going for a walk. Trying to avoid bloody cyclists,' I say.

'We can see that, but how did you get here? In fact, why are you here? Is it that bloody mad bugger Ziggy's idea?' she says.

My expression gives me away, so I nod.

'Aye, but I hardly see him. Goes off on mystery tours before I even get up.'

The three of them have now climbed off their bikes and leant them against the fence. Although they're not keeping their distance from each other, they stay away from me.

'Are you staying somewhere around here?'

'Aye,' says Becket, reverting to her own accent. 'John found us a friend's woodcutter's hut up there,' she says pointing towards a wooded valley climbing up the hillside. 'Where are you staying?'

'Along the river from here,' I say, nodding downstream.

It's then that I recognise the other woman.

'You're James Sparrow's wife,' I announce, standing up.

The woman stares at me.

Becket looks at her and then back at me.

'What?'

The woman is looking away.

'Who?' she asks quietly.

I stare back at her.

'You went missing, and he was suspected of doing away with you. The police were harassing him. He came to us – Ziggy, that is – to try and find you.'

Now all three of them are staring at me.

I look away.

The penny drops.

It was all a fabrication. The bloody 'sad little guy' was a fraud. No wonder the police were so annoyed with us.

I sit back down again. My head is whirling.

I ask what they're doing here.

They look at each other awkwardly. John and 'the woman' look at Becket.

She sighs.

'How about a brew? I'll tell you when we get to the hut,' she says.

How can I resist?

Keeping our distance, we all walk back to their friend's hut, which is set back from the track surrounded by beech trees that are not fully in leaf yet but still block the view from the road.

We sit outside while John goes to make us all the promised brew. There's a table and some planks to sit on. I go to one end and they sit at the other.

'We've been together since well before the lockdown, so we think we're OK,' says Becket.

I nod my understanding.

'I think we're OK as well. Ziggy had it all planned, as usual.'

I look again at the woman.

'So you're not called Fiona or Paula or Joyce, then?'

She manages a slow smile.

'No … Freya.'

Becket makes a face.

'So she says.'

The two women look at each other, but they're both grinning.

I shrug.

'So what did you call him?' I ask.

'Jimmy,' she says. 'Jimmy Kemball.'

I stare at her but she doesn't waver. Her green eyes stay steady.

Silence descends.

John comes out with the coffees.

We sit there in the afternoon sunshine. A slight breeze occasionally makes me realise I might need my coat on in a bit.

'So where has Ziggy got you holed up?' asks Becket.

I take out my map and pass it over. I've circled it.

'White Cottage. God knows how long he's booked it for. Hardly talks to me. Disappears every morning, comes back after dark. Eats whatever I put in front of him. Little small talk or none at all. Straight back on his laptop. I watch the telly, which is dreadful. Go to bed. That's it.'

'What on earth is he doing?' she asks.

'Dunno … he did say there was some amazing history round here, but that's about it.'

'It's the Borders,' says John.

We all turn to look at him sitting on the bench by the hut.

'My family were originally from up here. "It's all blood and treachery," my mother used to say.'

We wait to see if he has any more, but he just shrugs his shoulders.

'Well,' I say, 'there is an old ruined castle on the hillside above us, but it's only a load of old stones now. Can't find anything about it, although there are plenty of books in the cottage, so maybe I'll find the story there.'

Something tells me they're none of them history buffs, so I tell them something maybe more interesting.

'The house across the valley from us is intriguing, though. Huge mansion on the top of the hill. Goodness knows how they got all the materials up there. People living there still.'

'That'll be the laird,' says John. 'George Steil. He owns all the land round here. My mate works for him now and again. This hut probably belongs to him, I suppose. Maybe your cottage as well.'

I stare at him.

'All the land?'

John nods.

'The ones who were the most successfully treacherous, I suppose.'

We all think about this.

'Must be bloody rich, then,' mutters Becket.

We talk for some time about rich bastards and then move on to the stupid rich bastards supposedly running the country at the moment and 'organising' the Covid-19 response. Universal derision is the group agreement.

We have some more coffee and then I say I'd better get back.

They say they'll come my way tomorrow and call in.

It's a good three miles and the sun's gone down over our side of the river by the time I get there. No Ziggy in sight, so I start to sort the evening meal, but can't stop thinking about what John said about the people up on the hill opposite.

It's only as I finally sit down with a glass of wine, that I think neither Becket nor the woman, who isn't Fiona Sparrow, told me who she was, except that her name is Freya. Maybe.

Why is my life so complicated?

No, that's not true. It's only been complicated since my 'not-mother' died and I found out I wasn't Rachel Henderson, but Ursula White, daughter of the infamous serial killer Fern Robinson, whose body has never been found. She's probably still out there like a ghost, waiting to come and find me again...

Which reminds me that her friend Anna told me about how they used to come up to the Borders every winter to that house, the one where she eventually went to live. With Fern. Further east from here near the sea. I wonder whether she's still alive. Still there?

I find the local phone book. There she is. Kerr, A. Edin's Hall Cottage. I look at the number.

Dare I?

***

Louisa corrals Fletcher in the conservatory.

He's looking worried. What has he done?

'Right,' she says, as she comes to sit down after shutting the door firmly, which will indicate 'No admittance' to the young man as clearly as putting a large sign on the door.

He frowns.

But Louisa puts up her hand.

'You've not done anything to upset me,' she says, with a slight smile. 'So there's no need to look so worried.'

He laughs nervously.

'Last night, when Helena and George got home, Helena went down to the cottage to see Magda.'

Fletcher is frowning.

'She's a detective inspector, based in Galashiels,' explains Louisa, which immediately worries Fletcher.

'Really?' he asks.

'Yes. Not what the public school was for, of course, but she's a strong-willed lass, as far as I can remember.'

Fletcher frowns again. It's beginning to sound like the sort of involvement he promised the 'three witches' he'd never engage in again … and here was one of them seemingly about to ask him to break that promise.

As if she could read his thoughts, which isn't that hard for her, she shakes her head.

'This is different. Just listen.'

He listens.

She tells him the story.

He waits to see if she's finished.

'So what do you think?' she asks.

'Well, if it were me, I'd be making myself scarce till I could do something about it.'

Louisa laughs.

'I know that, but she can hardly do that at the moment, can she?'

Fletcher gives the problem some thought.

'Why would the man want to contact her brother?'

Louisa looks thoughtful.

'To be honest, the only thing I can think about is what I told you last night.'

Fletcher stares at her.

'You mean … he wants to hire a gunman, an assassin.'

He shakes his head.

'You've been watching too many films,' he says. 'Like whatshisname in the *Bourne* films.'

She snorts.

'Don't be silly, Michael. I don't watch trash like that.'

He shrugs.

'Tell me another reason.'

She stares at him, then gets up, walks to the conservatory door and looks out at the cold sunlight. The wind is buffeting the trees.

He watches her, his mind wandering back to that man. What was his name? He was a sniper. Northern Ireland? He was decommissioned, given a false identity, and ended up being that rich woman's manservant. The woman who was horribly killed by one of those racist thugs.

Louisa sighs and comes back to sit down.

'Come on, then. I can hear the cogs whirring.'

'Almond,' he says.

She frowns.

'Not his real name, and he's dead anyway.'

She glares at him.

He shakes his head.

'My last case. Also the last resurrection of the Snow White Killer.'

She waits.

'Diane Winterburn's man. The woman who was killed by that Brexit nutter. We knew him as Almond, but he was an army sniper. Teamed up with Fern Robinson, who went on another rampage together with him, killing people who'd upset her, but men rather than women.'

Louisa nods to indicate she is following him.

'But, as I said, he's dead.'

She sighs again.

'I can't imagine Tomasz doing that,' she says. 'The only time I ever heard him saying anything about what he did was in here, as it happens. He was drunk, hardly conscious, burbling on about something like heads not being like melons. Crying

217

like a baby. Fell on the floor. I left him there. Couldn't lift him, but managed to get him on his side.'

Fletcher nods.

'Right as rain the next morning. Didn't seem to remember any of it.'

They sit staring out at the whirling trees. There is nothing they can do, as far as either of them can see.

'So who would be on your list?'

She turns to look at him.

'Maybe not the same as yours, but there are some pretty obvious ones.'

She stands up and makes her way to the door.

'Maybe you should tell William that story, while it's still fresh.'

He nods but doesn't move, so she leaves him there.

***

The man drives to St Abbs and pulls into the top car park. It's empty. The cafe is shut, obviously. There is no one in sight.

They sit looking at the wind chasing plastic bags round the empty spaces.

'What's it like?' he murmurs.

Tommy looks at him.

'What d'you mean?'

'Killing people?'

Tommy shakes his head and then grunts.

'Strange,' he says. 'No one else has ever asked me that before. The way you're taught dehumanises them. They become targets, "kills". Like potting balls on a snooker table, darts in the bull.'

'I mean, from so far away?' adds the man.

'You think it makes a difference … compared to stabbing someone in the guts?'

The man looks at him to see if he's serious. But he's not smiling, so he waits.

'Well, now I think about that I've no idea how many other people I've killed in close combat … probably not that many … five or six at the most.'

There is another long pause.

'But, yes it is different and I don't keep the score. It's documented by some scroat at HQ.'

The man stares at him, but Tommy is looking into a place way beyond the windscreen.

There is an even longer pause. The only sound is the slight buffeting of the wind.

'I've got terminal cancer,' says the man. 'Six to twelve weeks, if I'm lucky.'

Tommy looks at him.

'So you want to take some bastards with you? Is that it?'

The man nods.

'Why not?'

'That's your choice, but why involve me?'

The man looks straight ahead.

'Because I can't even swat a fly.'

Tommy laughs.

'You're mad.'

They sit there like an old married couple out for the day, unable to walk about because of the arthritis or whatever, perhaps wanting to be out of the house … reliving past pleasures. The wind comes and goes, whirling some leaves into the mix, then dropping them in heaps in sudden sunny corners.

Eventually the man puts his hand in his jacket pocket and brings out a piece of paper. Out of an exercise book, probably. Was the man a teacher? He unfolds it and passes it to Tommy, who reads the list and then nods his head.

'Not bad. Even predictable.'

The man smiles.

'Are they in order?'

He nods.

Tommy shakes his head.

'I'd not put him first. He's a busted flush now.'

The man shakes his head again.

'Don't be too sure. The virus may be top at the moment, but the negotiations are still going on.'

Tommy shrugs.

'The English deserve what they get. Maybe us Scots might not leave, anyway.'

Again they sit in this strange silence. The sun keeps coming and going behind the fleeting clouds.

'It's not easy, you know, acquiring the sort of rifle I use. It's not as if they let me bring one home.'

'But you could get one, couldn't you?'

'I've already said, that it's not easy. And how much do you think they cost? Not officially. Black market prices.'

The man reaches over to the footwell behind Tommy and pulls out a rucksack and hands it to him.

Tommy frowns at him, undoes the straps and peers inside.

He takes a breath.

'How much?'

The man mutters a response.

Tommy shakes his head.

'Where did you get this from?'

'The lottery.'

Tommy snorts.

'Are you for real?'

The man indicates the side pocket.

Tommy pulls out an envelope. He opens it and reads the letter inside then shakes his head.

'Why don't you have a massive party or something?'

'How many real friends do you think I might have?'

Tommy pulls a face. He has a point. How many does he

have? Plenty of people who'd turn up for a party, but he wouldn't want to be there.

He looks out of the window.

'Anyway, I couldn't do prison,' he says. 'I'm not Steve McQueen. No way could I go back every time and bounce my ball off the wall.'

'I've thought of that. It's why I chose you. You'd be so far away that they wouldn't know where you were or get there in time to find you.'

Tommy laughs.

'Of course they would know where I was. Any police weapons expert would be able to figure out the gun from the bullet and the distance and the trajectory. I'd get away at first, but they could work all that out and have strong ideas about who could have done it. There aren't many of us in the world, you know. Less than a few thousand, I guess.'

They sit there. The one waiting for the other.

'Your sister, Magda, right?'

Tommy looks at him.

'What about her?'

'Good-looking woman. Feisty, I expect.'

'So ... what are you getting at?' says Tommy, turning in the seat to look at the little runt.

'Not as clever as she thought, right now, though, is she?'

Tommy leans over to him and grabs his jacket collar.

'What are you saying?'

The man wriggles to get free, but Tommy is too strong.

'Her laptop. Police issue,' he manages to gurgle.

Tommy lessens his grip.

'What have you done with it?'

'Put it in the water butt. It'll be useless by now.'

'So how is that a problem?'

'I downloaded the data.'

'What data?'

'Police stuff. I know some people who'll make a lot of money selling it on, or using it, so it'll be a big problem for the police. They'll have to rejig everything.'

'So what?'

'So what will happen to your sister, d'you think? The laird's daughter? Your parents?'

'But what if you have a little accident right now?' growls Tommy, squashing the man's face against the window.

'I've already sent it on. All they need is the code to access the files. They're bidding against each other. The Glasgow gangs are in the lead.'

'As I said, how can you do that if you're incapable?'

'The message is timed to go in about an hour. It goes to the highest bidder at that moment. Only I can stop it.'

Tommy bangs his head against the window.

'You're lying. You don't know how to do all that. You're making it up.'

He bangs the little bastard's head again. Blood is now streaming down the man's face and smearing over the window.

Tommy lets him go.

He slumps forward, holding his head and whimpering.

Eventually the whimpering stops. He risks a glance at Tommy. He's staring sightlessly through the windscreen. A woman is crossing the other side of the car park with her dog. She gives them a wave. Doesn't get a response, frowns, and calls the dog back.

The man fumbles for his handkerchief, pulls it out and mops his forehead. The bleeding has stopped. He doesn't think the woman could see him. Maybe she was nonplussed by the lack of response. It might get a mention on the Skype call to her family later.

He sits up and glances again at Tommy, who is still staring out of the window.

He waits, trying to steady his breathing. His chest hurts. He needs to take some painkillers.

The sun comes out from behind the clouds, which are still rushing across a muddled sky.

Tommy shifts in his seat.

'OK, you're on,' he says, quietly.

The man stares at him, but doesn't dare speak. Does he mean it?

There is a long silence.

Two men sitting in a car.

'Two problems,' mutters Tommy.

The man coughs, but doesn't speak.

'One I can deal with. The weapon. Although your money might not be enough.'

Again, the man doesn't interject.

'But the other is yours. The target.'

Now he turns to stare at the man.

'I don't care who it is, but you need to get a schedule, a venue. They're all in lockdown like the rest of us, but getting about more than most. Better if it's someone not in London. Too crowded. Too much protection. Too few long-distance opportunities. It's not Afghanistan with its huge vistas of arid desert and mountains. It's your call. I'll be ready within a week. I'll contact you.'

The man looks at him. His heart is thumping again. Is this really happening? His thoughts are racing. He starts the car, but doesn't drive away immediately because he's still trying to take it in.

Another dog walker comes into sight. They watch him as he crosses to the opposite side.

'You know what,' says Tommy, 'I'll take this car. You find another.'

He puts the bag back behind his seat and turns to look at the man, who is frowning.

'I assume you know how to acquire another one. Most of them are not going anywhere right now,' he says, and opens the door.

The man reluctantly gets out of his side and stands watching as Tommy gets into the driving seat. He starts it up and winds down the window.

'See you in hell,' he sneers and sets off in a tyre-screeching roar.

James Kemball stands there as the leaves whirl and tumble about until eventually silence descends.

Is this really happening?

***

Forensics are all over Magda's car and the cottage. She doesn't expect much – her attacker was wearing gloves all the time – but at least he didn't find her phone. She had trouble finding it herself. Eventually she came across it down the side of the passenger seat, underneath a chocolate wrapper.

She's ignored the calls from the chief super. She needs something to reduce the disaster. Can't bear the idea of repeating her apologies over and over again.

She's asked Rico to come over, but they haven't really had a conversation yet. What can she say?

Eventually Forester, the taciturn forensics lead, comes to see her. Normally she'd be harrying him. He isn't smiling, which is normal.

She mouths,

'Anything?'

He shakes his head.

'Clean as a whistle. Expert job. Got to hand it to the guy.'

'I effing don't,' she says, her eyes blazing.

Forester shrugs and stands looking at her.

'You OK?'

She nods.

'Yes, thanks. Sorry.'

He gives her a rueful smile and goes.

Rico replaces him, wary and knowing he needs to keep schtum.

Magda stands looking across the valley. Was that someone with binoculars up by the ruin? An accomplice? Clutching at straws? Where is Tomasz?'

'Have you tried the number of the house near Berwick, ma'am?' he asks tentatively.

She stares at him. What?

She slaps her forehead. Hard.

'Stupid. What's the matter with me?' she cries, and looks for her phone. She looks at Rico, who is ready with the number. He offers her his phone. She calls.

A woman answers.

'Hello,' she says. A quiet voice. Nervous.

'Hello, this is Galashiels Police, madam,' she says, trying to sound official.

The woman doesn't speak.

'Can I speak to Tomasz Steil, please.'

There's another pause.

'He's not here.'

'Can you tell me when he'll be back?'

Again an uncertain silence.

'No, I can't. He didn't say when he'd be back.'

This time Magda is silent as she tries to picture the woman. Should she try another approach?

'I'm his sister. Are you expecting him to come back?'

Another pause. Is there someone else there? How does Tomasz know this woman?

'I'm not sure,' she says, hesitantly, 'but he's left his dog and the horse here.'

'Oh … but you don't know where he's gone?'

An even longer gap. What is wrong with this woman?

'Are you there?' Magda asks.

'Yes, look, I really don't know where they've gone. A man called wanting to speak to him, although I don't think Tommy knows who he is. He was angry with him. He told him to meet him down on the beach, but then they went away. No idea where or for how long, or whether he'll even come back.'

Now Magda realises the woman is nearly crying and is really scared. She changes tack again.

'Look, I don't know what my brother's up to, but I'll get someone to come and see that you're all right. OK?'

The woman agrees and Magda cuts the call.

'Fuck.'

Rico stares at her.

She paces round the room.

'Fucking fuck,' she yells, and then calms herself down.

'OK, who do we know in Berwick?'

Rico gives her a look.

'DI Wright?' he offers.

'Number?' she says, nodding her remembering of him.

Rico scrolls down and presses call. Hands it over when he gets a reply.

Magda quickly explains the nature of the request and does a lot of nodding and thank yous.

'OK,' she says to Rico, as she grabs her coat. 'He's sending a squad car right now. They'll wait with the woman till we get there. You drive.'

***

Jeanie ends up inevitably at Scott's view.

The sun's already going down behind a bank of grumpy-looking clouds.

She gets out and goes to sit on one of the benches like some visitor, but stares at Ballantyne House rather than the fairy hills.

What's wrong with her?

Isn't this what she suspected might be what he gets up to?

But he's been nothing like that with her. Charming, yes, but not lecherous or overly physical.

Maybe she's not his type.

She laughs and mouths,

'I wish.'

Is that true? Would she?

She shakes her head. No way.

She gets up, determined to go back and get stuck in. She drives herself back and marches in through the kitchen back door.

Doesn't see any Dees or Dums, and finds the kitchen as she left it. Ah, no, the kettle is still hot. And there are crumbs on the table. Afternoon tea for two?

She goes out into the hall and listens.

Voices are murmuring in the lounge. She steps lightly over and listens at the door.

His voice, a laugh and another voice. Female?

She knocks, waits and then goes in.

It's the woman she met on the lane. She's still wearing the strange half-mask on her face, which is all Jeanie can see until she turns to look at her. And she has the same smile. Knowing.

'Ah, Jeanie, there you are. I thought you'd abandoned me,' says Randolph, getting to his feet. 'As you can see we have a visitor: Ms Morgan.'

The woman smiles again.

'We've already met, Randolph, on the lane earlier and, please, call me Carole. We don't need to be formal, do we?'

Randolph looks from one to the other in cheerful surprise.

'Why no, of course not. Wonderful.'

He claps his hands like some posh boy, which after all he is.

'I've invited Carole for dinner, Jeanie. What do you suggest? That pork and apples the other evening was scrumptious.'

Carole is smiling, but shaking her head.

'I'm sure it was, but I've been a lifelong vegetarian, I'm afraid.'

Randolph's face falls.

'Oh, sorry. Er … help, please, Jeanie.'

'No problem, sir. I'm sure I can come up with something.'

'I'll help,' says Carole, getting up.

This is too much for Randolph.

'Oh, no, I can't have that,' he flusters.

'Not at all,' says Carole. 'It'll give me chance to find out about the real Ballantyne clan and their misdemeanours.'

Neither Randolph nor Jeanie find this easy to deal with, but Carole insists and tells him to go and change for dinner.

'Something wicked,' she suggests, and the two women set off to the kitchen, leaving him staring in disbelief.

Jeanie is surprised how easy it is to work with Carole, who obviously knows how to cook.

The two of them chat food for a bit and then Jeanie is encouraged to talk about local history, which inevitably leads to the fairies.

'I do have more than a passing interest in the supernatural myself,' says Carole. 'I used to own a business selling Goth outfits and paraphernalia.'

Jeanie is quick to deny any overlap there, especially as her only contact with the Goth phenomenon was her sister's daughter, who went through that phase at college, but who now works in Specsavers.

She recites the story of Thomas the Rhymer, which she's been relating since she was in primary school.

'So where is the entrance supposed to be?' asks Carole.

'Ah, that's the secret,' she says. 'I was always told that you'd never find it if you didn't really believe in fairies.'

She looks across at Carole, who has her back to her at that moment because she is filling a pan with water.

There's a slight pause as she turns the tap off and then she turns to face Jeanie.

'Oh, but I do,' she says in a soft voice.

Jeanie can't stop a shiver, but then laughs.

Carole laughs as well. But there's a gleam in her dead eye which shouldn't be there, Jeanie reflects much later.

Despite this odd moment the two of them enjoy each other's company, and this continues on into the dining room when they go through to have an aperitif with Randolph.

He's decided on muted dinner apparel, and has reverted to a dark velvet jacket and matching bow tie. Definitely not wicked. Merely embarrassingly sweet and old-fashioned.

The dinner passes amid laughter and a couple of his well-rehearsed ghost stories.

It's nearly ten o'clock when Jeanie suddenly feels she might be inhibiting a potential shift in the couple's relationship and so, despite their entreaties, she bids them goodnight and scuttles off to her own room, where she finds she is inordinately tired and is quickly in bed and fast asleep, so blissfully unaware of what might happen next.

CHAPTER 13

The rushed journey last night was too late.

In the time between the phone call and the squad car arriving, Tommy had returned and then almost immediately left as soon as Nina had told him what she'd done.

She said he wasn't angry, and just stood looking out of the window.

She'd gone to the freezer in the garage to get some milk, but by the time she returned he'd disappeared, leaving only a note asking her to take care of his horse and the dog and to call his sister about them.

The police constable said she seemed to be in shock and couldn't stop crying.

Magda can barely cope herself.

'What have I done?' she says to Rico, as they sit in the car afterwards.

Rico thinks of saying,

'It's not your fault,' but thinks better of it.

They've left a policewoman, who has been tested for the virus, to deal with the distressed woman. Given the situation, that's the best they can do. The woman hasn't relatives nearby, but they wouldn't have been allowed to come in person anyway.

The next morning Rico is back at Magda's cottage. They're barely managing any social distancing for now, but washing their hands a lot. Rico's even found a couple of masks but they decide not to bother wearing them, as neither of them seem to have any symptoms.

Magda is standing at the window looking out at the intermittent drizzle. In normal circumstances, as a keen gardener, she'd be happy to see the hard, undug vegetable patch getting a much-needed wetting, but she doesn't even perceive it.

'So where the hell has he gone?' she murmurs.

Rico, wondering more about the how than the where, stares at her back.

As if she's in his head, she turns round.

'And how?'

Rico shrugs.

'No message about stolen cars yet, ma'am,' he offers, to show he's on the case.

'Yeah, but people aren't using their cars, are they? He'll have gone down the nearest car park and taken one.'

'Good at that, is he?' asks Rico, without thinking it through.

She nearly laughs.

'You bet he is. Since he was only thirteen. He was sent home from school for doing that, and that wasn't the only bad thing he did.'

'That doesn't help,' thinks Rico. 'Pub brawler, and now a car thief. Not the sort of brother I'd want,' but he doesn't say any of that.

They're both silent for a while. He is looking at his phone and she is looking back out of the window, unable to stop feeling wistful as she sees the smoke from Amelia's cottage struggling up against the buffeting wind. What she'd give to be there now.

'Well...' he says. 'How about if we ask the Berwick station to get someone round there to check all the number plates in the nearest car park and knock on all the doors to see if they can find the missing car?'

She turns round.

'OK, but I expect you're wanting me to push my luck, feminine charm – whatever – to ask for that, then?'

He blushes.

She laughs and picks up the phone.

It works. Probably because they've bugger all else to do, she thinks.

It doesn't take long. Less than an hour.

'Typical,' she says, after she's ended the call.

Rico frowns.

'What now?' he thinks.

'My brother, even with the terrible trouble he's already in, chooses to steal a top-of-the-range Merc rather than anything else.'

Rico frowns.

'How the hell could he do that?' he asks.

She shrugs.

'How the hell do I know?'

The car is found the next day in a multistorey car park in Newcastle. No other alternative wheels have been reported as stolen so far, but by then the chase is cold. Whatever he's doing, they can't keep up with him.

'Whatever *is* he doing?' mutters Magda to herself.

***

Jeanie wakes up suddenly.

The sun is streaming through the gap in the curtains and motes are cavorting in the light.

Where is she?

It takes her some time to remember.

Ballantyne House.

Last night. The meal. That strange woman. What's her name? Carole? With or without an *e*? She bets it's with.

She snuggles down in the warm bed. Not her bed. She wanders about her little house. Should she have left the heating on?

She stares at the pictures on the wall.

One is of a church. But green. The background is grey and white smudges. A tree?

The other one is really weird. The horizon is skewed to the left. A house at an unreal angle. Two figures. The one on the ground has a horse's head. A white horse. He's wearing clown's trousers. The other guy is falling away, holding a red bottle to his lips. And in the bottom right-hand corner is a rabbit. It ought to be disturbing, but somehow it isn't. It's like a frozen moment.

She gets up, puts on her dressing gown and goes downstairs to the kitchen.

Makes some tea.

Randolph has a Teasmade, so she doesn't need to do anything about that, but he does normally have breakfast in the breakfast room, which is on the ground floor. The usual thing is for him to arrive down about eight thirty, but when she glances at the clock on the wall, she sees that she has over an hour to worry about that.

Has Carole stayed overnight?

How can she find out? She knows that she came in her car from her cottage to get here, but has no idea whether she slept here. With him or in another bedroom? There are plenty of them.

Was she wearing a coat?

She goes out into the hall and checks the cloakroom. No strange coat. It was distinctive. Long and black.

Jeanie returns to the kitchen. Well, she can put out the usual cereals and rack of toast, but he normally has a full breakfast: porridge, egg and bacon, local black pudding and fried bread, mushrooms when they're in season, which they're not, so she can cope with all that. She'll make it for two, and then if the strange woman isn't there she can eat her portion.

She puts her coat on and goes out to the chicken coop, where she gets four eggs and gives them some food. There's lots of excited clucking, but they're easily dealt with, thankfully. She doesn't like the smelly things and remembers her grandfather wringing their necks. Even worse, seeing one dangling from the washing line one morning, still wriggling about, spraying its bright red blood all over the ground. She shudders at the memory of it and hurries back indoors.

She begins preparing two meals. Turns on the radio more for the company than the music. She misses Terry Wogan. Zoe Whatsit isn't half as funny and is such a scatterbrain.

She's staring out of the window, half-watching the bacon, when something tells her someone's there behind her.

She turns round.

It's Carole.

Standing there smiling.

Didn't hear her come in.

Perfume? Is it that patchouli stuff? She didn't notice it last night.

She tries not to look too startled, but her heart is banging like a drum.

'Oh, hello. Good morning,' she stammers. 'Frightened the life out of me.'

Carole smiles.

'Thought I'd pop in to see if I can help,' she says.

'Pop in' isn't the right phrase.

'More like "slinked in",' thinks Jeanie.

'No, that's fine. I can manage, thank you,' she says.

They stand looking at each other for just a few too many seconds. Flustered by this, Jeanie turns back to the frying pan.

'Don't forget I'm a veggie,' says Carole, quietly coming up alongside.

Jeanie stares at the bacon.

'Oh, God. Sorry, I forgot.'

'No worries. I'm sure you've got some cereal and I could murder a piece of toast right now,' says Carole, going over to the toaster.

Jeanie is torn, wanting her to just go, but knowing she can't say that.

'Is himself up and about?' she asks instead.

'Not likely,' laughs Carole. 'Sleeping like a baby, or the dead.'

Jeanie shivers, the words carrying more meaning than she expected.

'I hope not,' she says, 'I haven't had a penny out of him yet.'

They both laugh, but it's still awkward.

Neither of them speaks for a while.

Jeanie tutties the bacon, while Carole stands waiting for the toast.

'That has happened to me,' she says quietly.

Jeanie looks across at her. Their eyes meet, but she can't sustain it.

Carole doesn't offer anything further.

Jeanie tries to stop the shivering.

'It happens quite often in the home,' she stutters.

Carole frowns.

'The home?'

'Aye, my previous job. At the care home the other side of the river.'

'Ah, I see,' says Carole.

'Mind you, they are generally in their own bed.'

'Um,' Carole says. 'Not nice.'

Jeanie checks to see what that means.

'Messy, I assume,' she says.

Jeanie nods.

'You get used to it, but not the smell.'

They're both quiet. Not a great topic of conversation.

'Did you have anything to do with the missing old lady?'

Jeanie stares at her.

'Randolph told me.'

Jeanie nods.

'I was on duty when she went missing.'

Carole waits.

'It was difficult. The police were … suspicious.'

'Well, it is a bit odd. Someone that frail getting over the wall, as it were.'

Jeanie frowns.

'She didn't – wouldn't have been able – to do that, so it's difficult to know how she did get away.'

'And where she went … or even why?' says Carole softly.

Jeanie realises she's about to cry, so she busies herself putting the bacon into the hot oven.

'No one knows,' she eventually manages to say. 'The police think she's in the river, so we'll have to wait until it rains again.'

Carole doesn't say anything to that, doesn't even nod. Jeanie wants her to go away, but she's now standing looking out of the window.

Jeanie checks the time. She needs to get a move on. She finds the tray and starts to put the cutlery on it.

'He said he knew her.'

Jeanie stops.

'I know,' she says. 'So did I.'

Carole stares at her.

'I mean when I was younger, long before I became a care worker.'

Carole nods.

'She was always a bit strange. People thought she was away with the fairies, as we say round here.'

Carole smiles, but it is somehow a cold smile.

'So I hear,' she says.

Jeanie frowns at her.

'I need to set the table,' she says, and takes the tray out into the hall and across to the breakfast room.

The room is heated, but Jeanie feels cold.

She bustles about laying the table and then goes back to the kitchen, telling herself she'll not be intimidated by some witchy woman.

She finds the room empty.

She shakes herself and puts the porridge on. Pulls the sash to wake up the gentleman and stares out of the window.

Where has the woman gone?

She goes and opens the back door. Looks both ways. There's no one in sight. She gives up and goes back to the porridge. He's generally surprisingly punctual, even when he has had a guest. She goes back out into the hall, and there he is coming down the stairs. Fully dressed, with a slight smile on his face.

'Good morning, Jeanie,' he says.

'Good morning to you, sir,' she says, and stops herself from curtseying, which he's insisted she mustn't do.

She follows him into the dining room and goes to pour him a coffee.

He's standing by the window.

'Any sign of the young lady?' he asks.

'Er, she was here,' says Jeanie, 'but now she seems to have disappeared.'

'Um,' he says.

Jeanie goes back to the kitchen. No sign of her there.

She makes up his plate and pops it back into the warming cupboard, glances outside once more and goes through to the dining room.

He's still alone.

They frown at each other.

'Maybe she's gone back to the toilet,' she suggests.

He nods, but he's looking a bit worried.

She puts his porridge on the table and, as he goes to sit down, goes back to the kitchen.

Where has she gone?

In the end, they both have to accept that for whatever reason she has disappeared. Her car is no longer there.

Randolph manages to eat his breakfast, as his mother

taught him to do, no matter whatever the day's traumas may hold. He goes out to look for her afterwards, but returns looking more worried.

He says she hasn't given him a phone number and that he's been to the cottage, but there's no sign of her there.

They both spend the rest of the morning finding things to do, but at lunchtime he picks up the phone and calls the police.

They aren't particularly helpful, but say they'll put out an alert, while reminding him to stay at home.

They're both trying not to think of the connections, which are clicking away in their heads. Jeanie is regretting she said,

'Away with the fairies,' to her and telling herself it was all childish nonsense.

***

Louisa is more than happy to be driving Fletcher to 'beyond Galashiels'. She's bullied him into thinking he might be of some help. Only someone with her contacts could have so quickly convinced Magda's superiors to tell her that she was going to get some help from a retired English detective, who has 'information' that might help her.

He doesn't think he has.

What can trying to find a professional marksman he can't remember from so many years ago – who is now dead, anyway – have to do with this particular case?

He's even more surprised when he gets a call from ex-DCI Violet Cranthorne. When is the woman ever going to stop?

He thought her gang of ne'er-do-wells, which mystifyingly included him, operated under the radar. He also though that they had been shelved since the virus took over the airwaves.

'But no', she says, 'we're still operational, eyes and ears cocked for the next move,' which she has decided is going to be now.

'If someone like Captain Tomasz Steil goes rogue then that is exceptionally scary,' she intoned on the phone that morning. 'Get yourself over there. We've squared it with the local brass.'

'So what "information"?' he asks again, out loud.

'Human nature,' says Louisa. 'Or rather, "the evil that *men* do" variety, in your case.'

He stares at her, trying to unpick that comment to see whether it is a compliment or a cynical view of the warped masculine psyche.

'I'm also reliably informed that a few of your erstwhile collaborators are already in the area and will be able to assist as well,' she announced.

'Erstwhile ... collaborators?' he asked, trying to think who that might be.

Louisa was accelerating along an empty bypass and frowning, so he pondered on a few 'possibles'.

DI Irene Garner died some time ago and he still misses her, and of course, there's the other sergeant he 'nurtured', Sadie Swift, who is now a retired ex-Met chief. But can't think of anyone else, other than people he's met since he supposedly retired, like DS Becket.

She would be good. Feisty and hard-eyed, but with a good nose. Last heard of being shot trying to stop that villain Ferris – wearing an old bulletproof vest, fortunately, but ending up with a badly bruised chest, no doubt. Not far from Louisa's, but the other direction. Why would she be up here? Again? He looked across at the hard-faced driver.

'There's your answer,' he thinks. Bloody women ... but he's learnt to say nowt, as they say in Todmorden, which makes him think of Laura, which makes him well up.

Louisa glances across at him, but doesn't say anything.

'Let him be,' she thinks. 'No, give him something to think about,' she counters to herself.

They're up and over a switchback lane, frightening a woman

feeding her horses, and then on a faster road. Speeding along by a large river.

'Back to the Tweed,' she confirms, but sees he's miles away. 'Hope he isn't going doolally as well,' she says to herself.

She's looking for the turning. It's some time since she's been up here. Nearly misses it, does a screeching fast turn across the oncoming traffic, gets beeped at, slows down through the clutch of houses and climbs the long sloping lane, where she catches a glimpse of the Georgian monstrosity though the trees and then turns into the drive and out into the sunlight.

She parks on the terrace in a tidal wave of gravel.

Fletcher comes out of his daydream and takes in his surroundings.

'Welcome to the Munster Mansion,' she says.

After stepping out he looks up at the roof festooned with redundant chimneys and the row of shuttered second-floor windows below it. A tall figure has appeared on the terrace and is now waiting for them to climb up the steps. Fletcher follows Louisa and greets Helena, although there's no sign of George, which is a blessing. After they refuse coffee, Helena points them down to the cottage, saying Magda is expecting them, and watches them as they descend.

Now they're all sitting, as far away from each other as they can, in the small front room, and DI Steil is grudgingly bringing them up to speed.

Fletcher has always been impatient with this process, as he prefers to ask the questions he's got in his head, but surprisingly he hasn't got many today … other than,

'Why am I here?'

He is, however, taken by the view, and doesn't realise he's being addressed until Louisa shakes his sleeve.

Magda glares at him and repeats what she's just said, while wondering why her superiors think this is such a good idea.

He stares back at her.

'So … this little guy, who stole your laptop, your phone, and your car, has now run off with your brother.'

Again, Magda glares at him, but she can't correct such a succinct appraisal. He's not quite the old fogey she thought she was being saddled with.

She laughs.

'That doesn't sound great, does it?'

He grins.

'I've been in worse pickles,' he says.

'I can vouch for that,' says Louisa.

'But, to be honest, I can't see what I can do to help,' he adds, looking meaningfully at her, 'although my "second coming" here is obliged by higher powers.'

'Second?' asks Magda, hoping that might mean some knowledge of the place, but he shakes his head.

'Sorry. Lifelong exile. I'm still a London boy at heart. Don't feel comfortable with all this space … the hills looming over you, all them trees hiding who knows what, and sheep. Sheep? What more can I say?'

They all laugh.

With the ice now broken they get down to details, and agree to do it Fletcher's way. He asks the questions. Many of them are predictable, but some not so. Magda has to admit that this clarifies everything, one thing on top of another, that has been happening. And yes, his first one-line summary does describe it to a tee, which brings back the misery.

'So what do we know about this little man?' he asks.

Magda and Rico share looks.

'Hardly anything. No name. Any description would be pretty vague. I'm the only one who has met him … apart from the woman near Berwick, but she says much the same. Small man, weaselly-looking. He must have a car, but no one has seen it – other than Tommy, possibly.'

They wait to see whether she'll say anything else.

'Well, you know, the crucial thing is… Why did he want to find Tommy?'

Magda and Rico share glances.

'Only one reason I can come up with, and it's scary,' she says.

Fletcher nods.

'Being good at being able to kill people, literally over a mile away, is some special reason,' he says.

They all contemplate this.

'But who would the little man want to have killed?' asks Magda.

'More importantly,' adds Fletcher, 'how could the little man persuade your brother to do that?'

Silence.

Magda's eyes fill up.

Louisa, surprisingly, puts her arm round her and offers her a perfectly white ironed handkerchief.

'To protect you?' asks Fletcher.

'Well, I've made a complete mess of it, haven't I?'

'He did have a gun,' says Rico.

'I do have a black belt,' she rasps harshly.

'No blame,' says Fletcher, making Louisa's eyes go big.

They all go quiet again. Lots of brains are squeaking but nothing is coming out.

'Well, I suppose he might think I'll lose my job if he doesn't do what the man wants.'

The others all check each other out on this.

The consensus is,

'Not really … would he?'

She shakes her head.

'He's always been embarrassingly protective of me and he can be frighteningly violent. I had trouble even getting boyfriends, never mind keeping them. The latest incident on the Greek island: five men down, two broken cheekbones, one ruptured spleen, one damaged eye socket... He's not only a long-distance killer, he's a violent, angry man.'

The others look at each other.

'OK, but that still doesn't tell us who the little man's target is, does it?'

They all stop and think some more. Rico goes to make some more coffee without being asked.

'Why would someone need a long-distance hitman to kill someone?' asks Louisa.

'Because the target is heavily protected, high-status, reclusive?' says Fletcher.

'Like a politician?'

They all look around again. There are some intakes of breath.

'My brother has no time for politics,' says Magda, 'which means he's not for one side or the other. He thinks they're all reptiles, only in it for the status and the money.'

'Sounds sane to me,' mutters Fletcher, which gets him a frown from Louisa.

There's another, longer pause.

'So are we saying it's possible that he has been persuaded to kill someone to protect your reputation?' he asks.

Magda looks horrified.

'But he wouldn't do that. He doesn't have much respect for the police. He wouldn't kill someone, to save my job, even my reputation ... and in any case I've been told that's not going to happen, that my superiors don't think I was incompetent or behaved improperly.'

'So why would he agree to do it, then?' asks Louisa.

No one could come up with an answer to that.

And it is all put to one side as Helena arrives and insists they all come up for some lunch.

***

Well, this is a surprise.

I get down this morning, quite late, with my old limbs telling me that a six-mile walk was a bit much yesterday.

And there he is. Well, he's in the front room, which the owners probably think of as a bijou dining room, but he's turned it into a hi-spec communications centre.

I say,

'Hi.'

He says,

'Doh.'

Not sure whether that's US cartoon talk or 'Sound of Muzak.'

I've learnt not to bother to ask whether he wants a coffee or not, and choose to take him one, but only when I feel like it.

I do this morning, so now I'm standing looking over his shoulder at one of his screens, which seems to be an official document of some kind. In fact, as I focus properly on it, I see it says MOD at the top. Even as I see this, it disappears. I'm not sure whether that was Ziggy's flickering fingers doing that or the machine itself.

I've also learnt not to ask him what he's doing. He either ignores the question or comes back at me with gibberish or something in Czech, or one of the other dozen languages he professes to speak. How would I know?

So I go back into the kitchen to have my breakfast.

It looks cold outside, but the sun is on the far hillside.

Ignoring the ghost at the machine, I put my coat on and take my second coffee out with me.

As I suspected, it is cold. The sun has not got over the hill behind us just yet.

I walk down to the river.

There's only the odd car or lorry going along the main road, but no walkers or runners in sight so far.

When I look up at the mystery house at the top of the hill opposite, I can see smoke coming from both the main building and the cottage below it. I remember seeing 'James Kemball' behaving strangely the other morning. And what did he do with that laptop?

I focus my binoculars on the house. There's no sign of anyone this morning, although both houses are already spouting smoke, so people are in residence.

I give that up and try spotting a heron downstream, where I saw one the other day. They stand so still, they're difficult to spot at the best of times. Sure enough, nothing in sight. I'm still scanning down the opposite bank when I hear a screech of tyres and a car horn blaring.

After dropping the bins back onto my chest I catch sight of the back of a car disappearing into the houses across the way. Two other cars are moving slowly eastwards.

I focus above the houses in time to see the car ascending the sloping lane, no doubt feeling chastised by whatever near accident the driver has just missed causing. It's a biggish car, but I'm hopeless at knowing one from another.

Sure enough, it disappears into the trees at the top and then reappears on the drive in front of the big house. A figure appears coming out onto the terrace. I think it's a woman.

Two people get out of the car and make their way up to 'her'? They stand and talk for a while, but then the two visitors descend to the cottage, where the door opens and they go in.

As far as I can tell, one of the couple is a woman. Tall, I think, wearing a hat. Does she look familiar? I can't see the man's face.

I watch for a while, but there's no more movement.

I check out the heron. Still can't see him.

I'm getting cold. Still no sun this side. I go back to the cottage.

Ziggy hasn't moved.

I get myself another coffee. And grudgingly take him another one, fully expecting to find he hasn't touched the previous one.

He hasn't. His fingers are flickering. Three screens. All gibberish.

I risk an intervention.

'Funny business going on at the big house top of the hill,' *I say.*

He ignores me.

'Nearly caused an accident turning off the main road … posh car,' *I add.*

Nothing.

'Did I tell you I met Becket and John and whatshername yesterday?'

Zero.

'You wouldn't believe it. They're only along the road. Staying in some shooting hut.'

'Nada.' *Learnt that from him.*

I give him one of my sighs. Watch the flickering screen for a bit and turn to go.

'She's called Freya,' *he says.*

I stop mid exit.

'The woman with Becket.'

I go back to stand behind him. He hasn't stopped flickering.

'How do you know that?'

He shrugs as if anyone would know. His usual response.

'So what do you think they are doing here?' *I ask, trying not to sound sarcastic.*

'Same as us.'

I consider this. How same?

'We're all congregating like starlings,' *he adds.*

Why does he have to always go gnomic? I ignore this. Except, why 'starlings'?

He swings round.

'Tell me about the nearly accident. What's the car?'

'Big, blue … posh?'

'A Daimler?'

'No idea.'

'How many people?

'Two.'

'One a woman, tall, blonde hair?'

'Tall, yes, wearing a hat, I think … vaguely familiar.'

'The other a man?'

'Yes.'

And they went to the cottage?'

'Yes, eventually, after talking to someone from the big house.'

'The gang's all here,' he murmurs

'The tall woman? Louisa Cunninghame? And the man?'

'Ex-DI Mick Fletcher,' comes the unbidden response.

I stand dumbfounded.

'But why?' I manage eventually.

'Written in the stars,' he says and then, totally bafflingly, 'Zoom … Zoom.'

CHAPTER 14

'Zoom … Zoom,' turns out to be real.

Well, it is if you call having a meeting of nine people online in any way real, but that's what is happening.

Him and me, with me perched on a kitchen stool. Becket and 'Freya', with John hovering behind them, and then the foursome up the hill. Louisa and Fletcher we know, but then we're introduced to the two local detectives. DI Steil and DS Gatti: Magda and Rico.

Magda tells us about her brother and his disappearance with the weaselly-looking man, who she confirms was the man who stole her laptop and put it in the water butt, although it's all right now. Really?

I'm still goggling at the split screen. How do they do that? So I'm not really following the conversation.

I'm looking at the array of characters here. Is the right word 'eclectic'?

Louisa is still managing to be both beautiful and elegant, even on screen. She also manages to combine both a still concentration and the occasional incisive comment.

Fletcher looks tired, and his face seems haunted. He's carrying the terrible burden of losing someone, but unable even to be with her. So it's amazing, really, when he makes such succinct observations.

The threesome from along the road is quiet but intent. 'Freya' hasn't contributed yet. Neither has John, standing at the back, but Becket has put in her pennyworth already: the usual stark, brutal truths she never shies away from. Like,

'How the hell can we trace anyone in the current situation?' I'm impressed that Ziggy doesn't say anything at this point.

The DI, Magda, is trying hard to tread the official line, but *she must realise she's in the presence of at least four wild cards. Her sergeant is another one of life's watchers.*

So, to repeat Becket's question, how does this work?

I tune in to hear Ziggy's first contribution.

'Well, one way is through traffic cameras,' he says, which gives him the opportunity to bring up another screen. It flashes through hundreds of camera views in a few seconds.

I can see from the expressions on the detectives' faces that they're a bit shocked by this.

'How ... can ... did you do that?' asks Magda, looking over her shoulder at Rico, who is doing a goldfish impression.

'Too difficult to explain quickly,' says Ziggy. 'Can we live with it?'

The police officers look at each other. Rico defers to his superior.

She makes a face at Ziggy.

'What else?' she asks, probably thinking,

'Let's get all the illegal stuff out in the open.'

'Good luck with that,' I think.

'There are lots of buildings that I can connect to as well, including some who people think I can't. Let's wait till we need to do that, shall we?' says Ziggy, quietly.

Magda shrugs and gives in. What else can she do?

But then it strikes me. What are we doing? Why are these two police officers allowing us, in fact condoning us – well, Ziggy – to do this? I blurt it out.

The screens all go silent.

We are all looking at each other and at other the people on screens. It's mind-boggling.

'Um,' says Magda. 'It's only us. Well, me,' she adds, glancing over her shoulder at her sergeant, who is looking a tad worried now.

'As far as the Berwick police are concerned it's only a

domestic, and my bosses are just relieved that I've got my laptop back and that police security hasn't been breached.'

I avoid pointing out that she's just witnessed Ziggy blatantly breaking into police camera searches and I'm sure he hasn't told her the half of it, given the amount of time he's spent locked in to his systems for weeks.

'So is this really about tracking your brother down?' I ask. She nods.

'Before he does something really bad.'

'Like what?' I ask, thinking I'm on a roll here. I'm quite enjoying a bit of Zoom time.

'Before anybody else can suggest anything,' a different voice interrupts.

'Like a high-status assassination?'

It takes me a few seconds to figure out who's speaking. But then I realise it's Freya.

'What?' I say.

'Who?' says Becket, turning to look at the woman sitting beside her.

Freya looks steadfastly into the screen.

'It's something the security service were tracking when they decided to lock me away.'

'How do you mean tracking?' asks Magda.

Freya frowns.

'Someone trying to find an assassin, but they couldn't figure out who was asking. Who the target was.'

Becket is staring at her in astonishment.

Ziggy is looking puzzled.

Becket recovers quickest.

'So that's why they wanted you hidden away?'

Freya shrugs. She looks slightly embarrassed.

'But why couldn't they find the person?'

Freya shakes her head.

'No idea, but they had their best people on it. Well, people

who don't have names, which generally means it's really top secret.'

Ziggy snorts.

I give him a stern look, but he merely shakes his head.

No one can think of what to say to this, me included.

'Can you tell us anything else?' asks Magda, eventually.

Freya frowns, but then shakes her head.

'Don't think so, but then I stopped getting those transcripts.'

'How long ago is that?' asks Ziggy.

'Must be over two months now,' says Freya, looking at Becket, who shrugs.

'Don't ask me. You were always on the laptop. I don't know what you were looking at.'

'I told you,' she says, almost pulling a pout, 'they were only images. I find it more restful.'

Becket nods her acceptance and reaches out to hold her hand.

'Well,' says Magda, 'that makes me even more worried.'

Ziggy suggests a timeout. They all agree. The screen goes blank, although there's another three still flickering away.

I think it's more that he gets bored in group situations than for any other reason.

I go to make some coffee, leaving him feverishly working at least two machines at once. Is he even human? Half-cyborg? Whatever that is.

I'm not sure that the two real police officers are comfortable with this at all. The sergeant particularly looks pretty worried about where this is going. Although it doesn't spoil his good looks. What lovely eyes he's got. Stop it.

So where is it going? How can anyone do anything in a lockdown?

I come back with the coffee.

Well, there's a first. No flickering fingers. Both screens not changing.

Just sitting there.

I put the mug down on the edge of his 'desk', which is the dining table.

For once he picks it up straight away. Should I be worried? He mutters something.

'What?' I ask.

'Quis custodiet ipsos custodes?'

'Meaning?'

'Who is watching the watchers?'

'Um,' I think. 'Indeed? Who knows?' I ask.

'Um, maybe,' he says, and predictably his fingers crawl across the keyboard.

As I've come to expect, he doesn't give me any further answers, but when we Zoom again, there's another new face in another screen. Someone I don't recognise.

Fletcher does the introduction.

'Ex-DCI Violet Cranthorne, never knowingly underinformed,' he announces.

The woman manages a smile, of sorts, but obviously this is not a frequent use of her facial muscles. She's old, but well preserved. Short grey hair. Piercing blue eyes. And you intuitively know that this is not someone to cross swords with.

'Thank you, Michael. I'm sure you can provide a succinct summary of my exploits if they are required, but we'll leave that for the moment. I need you to update your findings so far. Perhaps you can begin.'

Fletcher is succinct and brief.

Violet asks DI Steil if she's anything to add. She staunchly says that her superiors have agreed for her to lead the follow-up, as far as it affects their local involvement.

'Good,' says Violet. 'Unfortunately we've still no idea who might be the intended target or targets. Our "friends" in the big house are less than forthcoming and exceedingly twitchy at the moment. The politicians, however, are way beyond that, and

are bordering on psychotic displacement behaviour. Best to avoid them altogether.'

I've always found the way people like her talk to be impenetrable. They seem to always speak in a coded language that includes all sorts of half-meanings, which baffle me completely.

Fletcher merely nods and waits.

'You would think that with so little traffic on the roads it would be much easier to track vehicles, but this man is clever. We think he might have access to the traffic camera network, in order to avoid being tracked,' she adds.

Ziggy nods as though he already knows this.

'The other thing we're on to is this – and I'm sorry about this, Inspector – but there are whispers among the gun-selling community that someone has been enquiring about a certain type of weapon … a long-distance rifle.'

In a crowded meeting room it would have been difficult for all those people who knew about Tomasz Steil's reputation not to glance at Magda, but now she knows they are all looking at her.

And she knows she's blushing.

Violet stops, waiting to see if there any questions, but none are forthcoming.

What can Magda say?

I'm beginning to think that there's nothing any of us can do, me least of all, but then Violet nearly smiles.

'So here's what I want you to do, given that, apart from DI Steil and DS Gatti, the rest of you are all free agents, unencumbered by legal or, dare I say it, ethical restraints…'

I notice a wary uncomfortableness on all the other faces, which is presumably on mine as well.

'I'm assuming, DI Steil, that you can do a further drilling down into the disappearing car tricks. We've no evidence, for example, about who was in the car found in Newcastle. Secondly, and you can ask Sigismund to help you with this,

your laptop may be 'mended', but it may not be 'clean', if you get my meaning.'

Ziggy nods, but I can see that this has startled Magda. What does Violet mean by 'not clean'?

'Again, with Sigismund's help, Freya, you could do some drilling down yourself after I send you some other contacts and suggestions.'

Freya merely frowns and then nods.

'Finally, Becket, can you, and John, of course, continue providing the protection you've been so cleverly ensuring for Freya?'

Becket merely nods as well, but is wearing her hard bastard face, enough to scare anyone away.

'As for the rest of you, I hope you can continue to support whoever you're helping and try your best to keep strong. Thank you all.'

With that she is gone.

Ziggy suggests time out again and they all disappear. Blinketty blink.

'Whoa,' I think. 'What is going on here?' But, of course, I'm stuck with himself, and he's now flickering away like some demented moth.

I go to put the coffee on.

But I can't help wondering if her other name is Elizabeth, which makes me giggle, even though she's nothing like the Bott.

***

Magda is straight on to Frank.

'What do you think?' she asks, after she's explained what the Stork has suggested. She was impressed by her, nevertheless, and the geeky guy down at White Cottage seemed to agree with her suspicion.

As she expected, Frank is immediately dismissive and

downright touchy about it, but reluctantly agrees to give it another once-over.

So she and Gatti go over to Gala to give the laptop to him.

They then go to see the local traffic control, who grudgingly check again for the stolen Mercedes. The car park camera doesn't show that it's definitely Tommy, only a grey figure wearing a woolly hat briefly fiddling with the lock and then driving away. He is next picked up on the A1 passing the first petrol station. They confirm that this was tracked all the way to Newcastle, but again the grey figure is only seen getting out and walking away. Magda can't be certain it is her brother. He's not noted for his sartorial elegance and is more a fleece and jeans guy when he's not in uniform. And although they've been referring to the stranger as the little man, Tommy is only five feet nine himself.

They've nothing on the other car. No pictures including the little man at all.

How can he do that?

They go to the canteen to wait for Frank to give them a call.

Neither of them can think of much to say.

Rico has called to see if the old lady's body has been found, but there is no news there either.

Throughout all this Magda hasn't said a word about what Violet implied about her brother.

'What does Tommy do when he comes home on leave?' asks Rico, when he's carefully considered how he might broach this.

Magda makes a face.

'What he just did,' she groans. 'Rides the horses till they drop. Runs the dogs into the ground, which they all love. Finds some innocent woman to "shag and drop", as he so delightfully puts it, then goes to find his old drinking partners and gets into fights. Ends up in hospital and/or a drunken stupor. Does cold turkey. Goes round saying sorry to everyone he's upset, and visits them in hospital. Sometimes he even manages to get back with one of the women he's recently abused and tries to be nice, before going back to what he does so well. Killing people … from a long way away.'

Rico stares at her.

She bursts into tears. Curses obscenely. Wipes the tears away. Shakes herself.

'He needs help. When he's sober, he's wonderful. Funny, generous, kind … tells amazing stories, which aren't about killing people at all.'

She wipes her face again.

'It's the bloody army. It's them who have made him like he is and it's my father who made him join up.'

Rico doesn't know what to say.

Her mobile bleeps. It's Frank.

They go down to his workshop.

He's not smiling.

'Your bloody English lady was right. Annoyingly clever. A type of virus, ironically. Took some finding, though. I've transferred all your stuff onto this other machine and we're decommissioning yours permanently. I'm also calling in the laptops of anyone else you've been in contact with since the incident. Never seen that before, but as I say, clever. It's too difficult for me to explain, but I'll be writing a report, which will be sent to all police forces in the UK.'

Magda knows not to say anything about it and, after politely thanking him, walks away.

She contacts Ziggy, but he's already wiped her out of his machines and is keen to tell her he does have what might be a lead. He tells her he's sending her a piece of footage from a garage forecourt in Dunbar.

She opens it on her mobile.

It's of a man putting fuel into a small car.

For a few seconds, he looks to one side. Is that Tommy? Almost immediately she receives a blown-up version of the face. It is him. She shows it to Rico.

'That means, presumably, that the little man was in the other car found in Newcastle,' he says.

'But what's he doing in Dunbar?' she asks.

'Going to Edinburgh?' suggests Rico.

She nods.

'Makes sense, I suppose. He knows plenty of people there. Some of them are OK. He might just want to lie low.'

'Damn hard to find him there, though,' says Rico, who she knows has a low Borders opinion of the big city. Thinks it contains plenty of villains with guns.

Again they don't share their thoughts, which grates against their usual openness.

***

Tommy is indeed in Edinburgh.

Sebastian 'Tiny' Roper is a rogue, a card sharp, and a pimp, known for being able to find you a woman or a man or any other variation of human sexual proclivity pronto, as long as you can afford it. This inevitably includes some of the less wealthy and more innocent of his mainly student lodgers, who can be easily persuaded to pay a reduced rent in return for favours extended to his 'guests'.

Way back in the 1980s he had been canny enough to have befriended a gullible old faggot, who he probably helped on his way with copious amounts of sex, alcohol, drugs, and more drugs. Gordon Hardcastle was from old money, but was persuaded to leave his entire fortune to Roper, which, in a final ironic twist, turned out to be not so much as he had expected. This meant that the disappointed shyster had to let out two thirds of the grand house near Carlton Hill to the 'bloody students', while he descended to live in the warren of rooms in the basement, which would have previously been the kitchens in its Georgian heyday.

Tommy abandons the car in the out-of-town park-and-ride and walks the rest of the way, remembering the lanes and back alleys from his misspent youthful forays away from the dreary seminaries of St Andrews. This causes him some pain in his bad leg, which reminds him of Warrior. And Hengist. He hopes that woman is looking after them. Still, riding him through the back streets of auld Reekie would be a bit of a giveaway, although the thought of meeting the police in lockdown on horseback makes him laugh out loud.

He knows that knocking on the old bastard's door is a waste of time and hunts for the key, which is hidden under different plant pots and in various locations, depending on his whim, or in the other abandoned detritus in the shadows by the downstairs entrance. This takes longer than usual, and the key has to be reminded of its purpose in life with much finger-bending struggle.

Finally, he's inside, listening to the creaks and whispers of the old house.

Is that a voice? No, it's someone singing.

Grinning to himself in the gloomy corridor, he makes his way towards the music. Of course, it's Mozart. *Don Giovanni*. The old roué hasn't lost his taste for that miserable whinger.

At the end of the next corridor, he can see the light under the door and creeps slowly along. He listens at the door. He may be 'entertaining' or 'being the recipient'.

But there is no other sound than the miserable squawking.

He carefully opens the door … to find the grinning face of Roper staring at him, with the incongruously shiny muzzle of an old Luger pointing at him.

'It's me, you old flintlock,' says Tommy, carefully raising his hands in the air.

There's a squinting of rheumy eyes and then a frown of recognition.

'Oh, it's you, you little runt,' grumbles Roper, but he only slowly lowers the gun.

'Yup. Bad penny once again,' says Tommy, and lets his arms down as well, before creeping towards the nearest chair.

It takes a good half hour for the atmosphere to settle down, but soon they're recalling past bacchanalias and other lost souls.

Tommy has cannily chosen to arrive carrying a selection of bottles from the corner shop, which mystifyingly was still open. But eventually Roper's eyes narrow again and he asks the inevitable question.

'So what's thy trouble this time?'

Ignoring the disconnected spring digging into his thigh, Tommy settles back in his chair.

This room rarely changes, except for the occasional rearrangement of the paintings on the wall or additions to the teetering stacks of old books growing like giant toadstools on the floor. The sink in the corner is piled high with a clutter of crockery and pots, none of them matching, but many of them worth more than their current unwashed appearance belies. Has Roper's unbelievably loyal cleaning lady not been for while?

Tommy knows that the look of dereliction hides eye-wateringly expensive items peppered among the trash. That the drawer within reach at the side of Roper's armchair will be cluttered with diamond necklaces and gold rings and other jewellery worth thousands tumbled like sweeties among the worthless paste and gaudy plastic. Elsewhere in the warren will be dusty mountains of junk, cheek by jowl with Louis XV furniture of dubious provenance.

'Trouble? Me?' says Tommy, all innocent blue eyes.

Roper merely smiles.

'Come on, dear boy, tell an old man a couple of tales from the Orient. Like you did long ago.'

Roper makes a face.

'It's not that long ago, you old fart. I was here last summer.'

'Really?' murmurs the old man, shaking his head. 'Time's arrow, eh?'

They sit in silence for a few moments.

Roper takes a sip of his whisky, which is harsh enough to make him cough.

'I need a gun.'

The old man sighs.

'Will you fancy that? The highly acclaimed marksman needs a poor old man to find him a gun.'

Tommy smiles back.

'Not any old shooter. I need a TAC-50.'

Roper frowns.

'You're talking gibberish, young man.'

'I can pay,' says Tommy. 'Give you the prescription.'

'I should hope you can. They'll be more than a few groats.'

They sit there looking at each other.

'No desperate rush,' says Tommy. 'A couple of days?'

Roper laughs, which mutates into a death-rattling cough.

When he recovers, his eyes narrow into lascivious slits.

'So you'll be needing some entertainment while you're waiting, I suspect,' he drawls, wiping spittle from the edge of his mouth.

Tommy sighs. He knows where this is going.

'I wouldn't say no,' he agrees.

Roper's eyes are glistening now as he readjusts his crotch before picking up a venerable and grubby mobile from the table by his side.

'Why don't you rustle us up a bite to eat?' he asks, nodding in the direction of the door to his right.

Tommy has one more sip and then struggles out of the chair.

'Nothing too insipid, I hope,' he asks.

'To eat or to fuck?' comes the reply.

'Both,' says Tommy over his shoulder.

***

Back at Louisa's, Fletcher calls the hospice. He listens quietly, then puts the phone down. He has a little weep. And wipes his face and goes back to the conservatory where he left Louisa doing her crossword.

She looks up at him with a serious face.

'No change,' he says, 'but they wouldn't tell me anything on the phone, would they?'

Louisa bites her tongue on a tawdry piece of advice. She knows him well enough to know he can't abide trite words.

'You've had a letter,' she says, and indicates the white envelope on the table.

Puzzled, wondering who writes letters any more, he opens it and sits down to read it. It's not long. He sighs and places it back on the table.

Louisa looks up, but doesn't press him.

'It's from Cassie,' he says. 'She's been to see Laura.'

Louisa nods, recalling the enigmatic woman from Todmorden who seems to haunt Fletcher in a strangely comforting way. There aren't many women she envies at all, but she has always been intrigued by and respectful of Cassie's quiet yet sensuous presence.

'Remind me why that's even possible,' she asks.

Fletcher shrugs.

'Not sure. I never am with her.'

Louisa waits, but he's staring out the window.

'So what has she to say?'

'The usual gnomic stuff.'

She gives him a look of exasperation.

'Well, go on, then.'

Instead he gets up and brings it to her.

'I'm going for a walk,' he says and stomps off.

She reads the letter, frowns, and sits there thinking.

What does Cassie mean?

She reads it again.

It's only a few words saying that Laura seems a bit more settled, but then ... and Louisa says it out loud to see if it makes any more sense.

"In the end we must go where the flowers take us. The path into the hills. The halls await the final tremulous footsteps which we must tread. Be not afeared. All will dance."

At the river's edge he stands. Can't remember how he got there. Just had to come.

He stares at the limpid water as it folds and trundles past him, hardly making a sound. It hasn't rained much for nearly a month now, so all its muscular urgency has gone. Two ducks are earnestly heading upstream against the flow, undeterred by the effort needed for such a mysteriously necessary journey.

What did Cassie mean by *All will dance*?

He laughs. The sound is ignored by the birds and the fish and the sheep.

He remembers dancing with Ellie, Grace's eldest.

She should be going to Uni this year.

He's never felt so alone.

The tears come again.

An old man standing by a huge indifferent river.

That's all he is.

Why bother?

***

Since they've come back to the hut, Freya has been quiet. In fact, when Becket thinks about it, she's hardly spoken since the comments she made about the assassin.

When she looks round she realises she's not in the room.

Where has she gone?

John's outside chopping wood. There's plenty inside and a huge stack against the hut wall anyway, but she knows it stops him from going crazy.

She rushes to the door.

'Where's Freya?' she yells.

He doesn't hear her at first, but then realises she's shouting at him. He stops.

'What?' he asks.

'Freya?'

He stares at her, looks round.

'I thought she was with you.'

Becket shakes her head, thinking all the worst scenarios.

'Stop. Think,' she tells herself.

She looks towards the river. Then she screams at John, pelts off across the lane, vaults the fence and hurtles across the field.

John drops his axe and gets into the Land Rover, revs up and turns it round in a spray of mud and roars off towards the bridge.

Becket gets to the river looks left and right. A nightmare Ophelia scenario is screaming in her head.

She can see John stop on the bridge and get out.

She waves to him. He waves back and yells, but she can't hear him.

She looks where he's pointing.

Freya is crouching on a small beach twenty yards away ... feeding some ducks.

Becket tries to calm the beating of her heart. Not a bloody song.

She doesn't shout, tries to go quietly, but the ducks maybe

263

sense her jagged movements and paddle strongly away into the river.

Freya turns to see what's disturbed them and stares at Becket who is trying to march towards her.

'Hey, Freya,' she manages to say. 'You frightened me, going off like that.'

Freya glances at John getting back into the Land Rover and reversing along the bridge. She looks back at the ducks, who have now lost interest and are searching the weed on the other bank.

'Just talking to the ducks,' she murmurs.

Becket sits on a nearby stump.

'Aye, well,' she says. 'Tell me next time.'

Neither of them speaks for a few moments. Freya's watching the ducks search the far bank before they let the flow take them downstream. Becket gets her breath back and pulls at the long grasses and throws them into the current. Is she playing Poohsticks?

Her father's gruffness coming to mind. She knows that's where she gets her own from.

'Sorry,' she says, 'I wish we knew what was going on. Trying to keep you safe.'

Freya looks back at her and gives her a weak smile.

'I'm sorry you have to look after me, like I'm some lost child … but I can't forget what I've read. I wish I could.'

Becket nods and comes to stand next to her.

'Shame you're not like a computer. You could just delete.'

Freya shakes her head.

They stay together like this for some time. Becket reckons John is sensitive enough to know to let them be.

'I feel sorry for Jimmy Kemball, you know,' she says. 'Us meeting and getting together wasn't my idea. I was told I had to do it to "improve my security", although that didn't work out well for him, did it?'

Becket nods, but knows there's more.

'He was kind, but not used to being with someone else, especially a woman. I don't think he'd had much sex in his life. Amazing, really.'

Becket can't stop rolling her eyes at the thought of that.

Freya looks away, rubs her eyes.

'But the worst thing is that I think he knew he was dying.'

Becket frowns.

'Why d'you say that?'

'He'd been to the doctors a couple of times, saying he had a pain in his stomach.'

Becket waits, thinking of her father. Grumpy old bastard left it too late, as any beer-swilling, fag-smoking Geordie bloke would.

'Then the last time he said that the doctor had told him he was OK, and had given him some pills.'

Becket shrugs.

'But then I saw a booklet he'd shoved in a drawer.'

She turns away and stifles a sob.

Becket waits for a moment and then puts her arm round her.

She shudders, stifles another sob, and pulls herself together.

Becket waits.

'Effing bastards probably knew that all along,' Freya mutters.

Becket can only sigh at that.

They sit there not making eye contact until Becket can't bear it any longer and hugs her more determinedly.

Eventually Freya stops sobbing and they get up, which startles the flotilla of ducks, who hurriedly paddle out into midstream.

They stand watching them for a few moments and then Freya shakes her head.

'There is something else that's been nagging at me. Wasn't sure where I saw or heard it when we were being storked.'

She looks at Becket, who smiles back at her.

'Hey, I'm as scared of her as everyone else.'

They both giggle like schoolgirls, but then Freya goes still again.

'There was this mobile transcript. I don't think I was supposed to see it.'

Becket waits, knowing not to interrupt the remembering.

'It was stuck between two reports. A meeting between people who were only indicated by single letters. C, G and M. I don't think they're the actual initials of the people concerned. They don't do that. Public schoolboys all have nicknames, you know.'

Again she grins at Becket, who shrugs at this. Typical.

She can see that Freya's struggling really hard with this. She's closed her eyes and her forehead is deeply furrowed.

Her lips are moving.

Her eyes open.

'They weren't typed,' she says, frowning.

'What?'

'I don't know why, and my specialist doesn't either, but my photographic memory works best with typed words, books, and papers. But it's not so good with handwriting, or advertising, for some reason.'

Becket stares at her.

'So what did you see?'

'Three words. Two of them were crossed out, so not so easy to read. The clear one was 'adec'. I think the others were 'the fag' and 'hugger', but they weren't clear at all.'

Becket purses her lips.

'Search me,' she says.

They both stare at the ducks again. They are not sure whether they were the same ones coming back or another gang.

'And you've not told anyone else about this?'

Freya shakes her head.

'I wasn't supposed to have seen it. By the time I'd finished working with those papers it had disappeared anyway.'

They both stared back at the river.

'We'd better tell Violet,' says Becket quietly. 'It might mean something to her.'

Freya nods and wipes her eye.

'It could be nothing.'

They eventually walk back to the hut and Becket sends Violet a message.

There is no immediate response. She wonders whether she should send it to Ziggy as well, but decides not to.

The rest of the evening passes quietly. They eat John's stew for a third time. Freya goes to bed early. John reads a solemn Becket correctly and settles for a chaste goodnight kiss, but he knows she's not gone to sleep before he drops off. Chopping wood does that to you.

***

Tommy has to credit the old bastard.

No mention of a gun for hire yet, but the other activity is swiftly organised.

Tommy has only just finished devouring a dubious and illegal takeaway from Roper's local restaurant when there's another knock at the door.

The old man gestures to him with a look of sheer lechery.

Tommy makes his way down the darkened corridor, knowing that the light bulb not working there is deliberate.

Standing outside are a couple. The guy is standing at the top of the steps, looking away to his left. His face is in shadow. The woman is leaning against the wall.

Tommy's thinking,

'This is so unsafe,' but weakens when the woman smirks at him.

'You must be the soldier guy, the killer,' she says, her voice hoarse. The side of her head towards him is shaved to a dark stubble, with a wave of thick blonde hair combed back over the other side. Her face is thin, with pinched cheeks, dark lips, and dark eyes. The hand holding the cigarette is festooned with whirling tattoos and peacock eyes. She is straight out of *Blade Runner.*

She pushes him aside and insinuates herself into the darkness behind him. The man, an almost identical mirror image of her, follows. He has the same hairstyle, but in gleaming black, and the same dead eyes, the same etiolated body. Tommy imagines he's been invaded by a couple of replicants. It is definitely not safe.

He follows them back to Roper's room.

But to his surprise the table is now in the middle of the room with three unmatched chairs set out facing the old lech, who is still in his own chair, grinning like a Cheshire Buddha.

'You still play, I assume?' he smiles at Tommy.

'Depends what it is,' he says, feeling trapped.

'The only game in town.'

Tommy groans. Canasta. The most lethal game in the world. Highest death rate in Brazil, where it's a religion, only behind sex and tango.

The woman has now divested herself of the flimsy cobweb she was wearing for outside, to reveal even more of her tattooed body. If some of those creatures are fairies, they're not the child-friendly, fairy-tale versions.

The man is twitchy, obviously high on something, but his eyes are hard. He's not out of it yet.

'May I introduce Imelda and Yakov?' says Roper, although Tommy's sure that's not their real names. 'Yakov doesn't speak much English, so you'll have to forgive us if we lapse into Italian. Not that that's his first language, either.'

Tommy is aware that the woman, 'Imelda', is still staring at him.

268

He makes a face.

'Is it true?' she asks. 'Two hundred and thirty-three?'

Tommy glances at Roper and mouths,

'Twat,' at him.

'You wanted the hardware. This lady is in the business. Probably one of the best.'

Tommy looks back at the woman, who is still staring at him.

'I don't keep count, but it's in the records.'

She glimmers at him through half-closed eyes. He's beginning to think she might have a forked tongue.

'OK, let's play cards,' she rasps.

They play for two hours. The woman wins, as Tommy expected she would. He can only smile. Fortunately they weren't playing for proper money.

The guy says he must go to the loo. Tommy doubts that's for a pee.

The woman stands up and takes Tommy by the hand.

'Let's play a different game,' she quotes.

They go into another room. She pulls the blankets off the bed onto the floor.

'We don't want to hide from the audience, do we?' she grins.

The sex is violent. From both players.

Tommy reflects afterwards how long it's been. He has chosen to dismiss the relatively ordinary couplings with the lady by the sea.

Afterwards she replaces her flimsy clothing and kisses the burn marks on his chest and thighs.

'I'll let you know,' she hisses.

He stares at her. He didn't think he'd get a score out of ten.

'I mean when I've found you a weapon. I don't count any more than you do. One fuck is as good as another to me. I rarely repeat the experience.'

Tommy smiles.

She stares back at him for a few more seconds and then slithers out of the room.

By the time Tommy gets back into Roper's room the pair have gone. Roper is lying back in his chair with his eyes closed. His flies are open and there's a stain on his shirt. A computer screen flickers away across the room. The screen saver is nothing like what he's being recently watching. Tommy reaches for the half-empty bottle of tequila, not the first, and reminds himself why he doesn't drink it.

As there's no sign of Roper wishing to compare notes or anything else, he goes off to find a bed. But not the one where he feels he's just been mauled and savaged by a jaguar.

It's some time before he goes to sleep. His head is full of scary images and premonitions.

The house settles into its nightly miasma.

If the walls could talk…

***

Jeanie decides that she's going to go up to the cottage to see if Carole is there, more to satisfy her own curiosity than because she's worrying about her.

The sun has come out, but it's still cold. The wind is always here on this side of the hills.

She walks steadily along the track she's walked a thousand times. When she was younger there was a thriving farm here. A large family, the Cranstons. She'd played with Catriona, gone to school with her and they were still friends, although, of course, she doesn't live here any longer. Her father died young, in a tractor accident. Her mother never got over it. Her brother was not interested in farming so went off to university and became a vet, somewhere up near Aberdeen now, she thinks. Cat got married to a plumber and they now live in Gala with their three grown-up kids. The farm was sold and became another holiday home … strangers wandering the hills.

Now of course it's lying empty, but the fields are teeming with sheep and lambs, ugly flat-faced creatures. She can't remember their name.

She reaches the top of the rise, with the farm on the right and the two cottages at the end of the lane.

She thinks the adjoining cottage might be occupied as well, but that Carole has rented the nearer one.

She stops to watch some blackbirds and then, hearing a skylark, shades her eyes until she spots him. Spring is well and truly here.

No sign of the black VW, so she can't tell whether Carole's in or not. There's no smoke, anyway.

She gets to the door and knocks.

No answer.

She stands looking at the view … the whole of the Cheviots making its distinctive vast panorama.

She turns to watch the sparrows feeding their brood, who are currently residing in the martin's nest in the crux of the roof. The noise increases every time the parent flies out, urgently seeking for more.

The curtains are open so she goes to peer through the window.

The room is relatively bare. She thinks the furniture is what the owners have provided. There is little sign of the occupant's belongings.

She goes round the back. The garden is becoming overgrown with the spring flowers and weeds raising their heads. The kitchen is tidy. Only a few foodstuffs are in view. Some crockery is resting on the drying frame on the side of the sink and there's a kettle and an unwashed mug.

There's nothing to see in the side room. The curtains are shut.

Over the back wall is a rather unkempt wood. She sees thin

fir trees, nettles and the odd elderflower, not flowering yet, but bursting bright green against the dark interior, which makes her shudder.

She goes back round the front and stands looking out over the farmland. She knows some of the families, but not all of them.

It's quiet up here, although she's noticed one other person striding along the farm track. There will be no need to worry about social distancing. It's over three yards wide.

By walking to the other side she can look up at the Eildons. She's facing the central dip, where she knows the St Cuthbert trail rises to give access to both the peaks. She fancies she'll walk a bit further to go and see the beech avenue. There won't be much greenery yet as they're the last to leaf, apart from the ash.

Even as she's standing there she shivers, feeling as if someone is watching her. She glances quickly up at the upstairs window, but there's no face ducking back.

So she backtracks and goes along the other side of the hedge and on to the wood, through the stretch she knows where there will be brambles in the autumn. She used to come here with her Aunt Maggie to collect them.

As she enters the wood she wonders if people have been weaving the beech striplings together like they used to when she was young, pretending they were fairy gates, which she never dared to pass through. It's here as well that there was the fairy bridge, a venerable beech tree that had fallen across the stream. Sure enough, they're all still there.

And then she's out onto the beech avenue.

Its beauty rests in its straightness. There's a slight rise and fall, which means you can't see the other end until you're at the highest point, but already the beech trees are greening, while the primroses and violets are happily clothing the banksides.

She knows if she stands quietly and doesn't move that the birds will start chirping again and flashing from one branch to another. She spots a whitethroat. Small and delicate. And a robin giving her the once-over.

She reaches the centre point and sits on a tump.

Apart from the birds, there's not a sound. No wind.

And then the birds stop. Utter silence gathers like a thickening cloak.

She looks both ways, out onto the farm track and up the hillside. She senses there's something there. Someone.

But there's no one in sight. No footfalls. No twig snaps.

She shivers again. Gets up and starts to retrace her steps. But it's not until she reaches the far end again that the usual sounds start up again.

Disconcerted, she hurries back to the cottage.

There's a figure in the distance, walking away. Too far away to tell. But definitely wearing black. She walks quickly, but by the time she's back down into the wood the figure has disappeared.

She continues back to the big house. Goes in through the kitchen and out into the hall. Not a sound. Is he out?

She goes into the downstairs sitting room. There's this morning's *Telegraph*, which he's having delivered, open on the table, the crossword half-completed. But no Randolph.

She hurries up the stairs and knocks on his door. No answer. She goes in. He's not there. The bedclothes are pulled back and the pyjamas are neatly folded.

Back downstairs she goes into the kitchen.

She makes a pot of tea, but finds herself sitting alone at the kitchen table.

Where is he?

What's happened to Carole?

It's over an hour since she last saw a living soul … apart from that figure in the distance walking quickly away. Wearing black.

***

I still find it difficult to believe that Steil agreed to the plan.

I don't doubt he's capable of finding a gun, but now my problem is setting up the target.

It's not as if it's easy to get their address or phone number, and most of them have security handlers following them around like pet dogs.

However, I do have one useful ally.

Don Bishop is a reporter. A freelancer, because none of the big papers would admit to employing him. He's spent quite a few stretches inside, but this has only hardened his heart and soul.

He also went to the right sort of school and knows many of the people on my list. Knows where they live, their sexual proclivities and other weaknesses, which enables him to wheedle all sorts of information they'd rather not see in the public domain.

I send him the list with a reminder of a certain exploit he also would prefer to be kept between us and the gentleman concerned.

As usual the first response is a lengthy, but erudite, exposition of how I might die, before saying he'll see what he can do.

I'm back home in Saltburn now.

Never thought I'd end up back here.

It's not the same as it was when I was a child.

It's all spruced up for the visitors who haven't come this year yet, but they will. They always have.

I go for a walk along the top promenade. The sea is quite rough today. The wind is herding litter, while the few people I meet are surly and cold. All of them are managing to look both guilty and critical of anyone else.

Eventually I end up in the valley gardens.

I go down to my childhood hiding place.

THE LIES WILL HAUNT US

And sit watching the beck quietly going about its business heading towards the sea.

Where I first met Carole Morgan.

I'd long given up being surprised at the way she always seemed to follow me around, since we were children together, running wild in the woods.

The cottage I'd found in the Borders was as remote as can be, but still she managed to turn up next door.

We didn't actually meet, because I saw her arriving just as I was going to collect my stuff after making the deal with Steil.

It was dusk.

A hillside. Long shadows. A couple of estate cottages. No lights on in the windows. No cars.

The birds have stopped singing.

A small herd of cattle is resolutely mowing its way to the left.

There is the sound of a car approaching.

It appears from behind a line of trees to the right, slowly navigates the rough track, halts, reverses into the side of the house and stops.

A woman gets out.

She stands and looks at the remains of the sunset.

There's a flash of light from her face. Glasses or jewellery?

One or two of the cattle look her way for a few moments.

She turns, opens the back door, pulls out a suitcase and walks to the front door.

Without knocking, she places the suitcase on the front step and hesitates, but doesn't immediately try the door or knock on it.

Within minutes the sun has gone, dropping behind the beech trees over to the left.

In that brief moment she's opened the door and gone inside.

Silence reasserts itself.
Darkness falls.

I've only come back to collect a few things. Nothing important.
Maybe it's better to forget them. I don't want anyone who knows me to know I was here. Particularly not someone like her. Someone who delights in knowing other people's secrets.

Makes me think of Janet.
We left a lot of belongings behind in our last move. Not enough room in the ark. Well, the van was smaller than promised and there was only one helper. We left all the garden things behind, as if we weren't going to garden any more.
Gardens?
When did we become gardeners?
Neither of us grew up in houses with gardens.
Me at the bakers, her in the mill town.
We didn't plan it really, and when we did have our first garden a man on a digger said he'd dig it all up while we were away. So we moved.
Again.
And again.
And again.

But we did make gardens.
One had been a tennis court. The disintegrating tarmac crumbling from my spade became flower beds and ponds dotted about, with the grey rabbit murderer treading softly away towards the battlefield in the distance.

Another was a sheep field, out under the clinging ceanothus that grew up to the sea view. Criss-crossing paths led from a pond to a polytunnel, while the schoolchildren ran screaming and tumbling on the other side of the wall.

Another was a French field beneath the gigantic fir trees. The cat detective watching from his spyhole as the wary birds peckled at the newly broken soil high above the sleek Taurion, surging through its emerald-clothed valleys.

Another was the jewel. A rose bower leading to the budding monkey puzzle tree and the lone Virginian, hiding the laughter and the imaginary worlds of the gang of naked *kinder*. The cat detective sedately quartered in his final demesne, searching for the cool shadows to sleep, perchance to dream-chatter. The musky cherry dropped its overloaded treasure for wasps and bees to gorge on, while a 'verandah' assembled itself on drunkenly laid support towers.

All gone.

Memories of dawns and dusks.

Time slipping endlessly, ignoring our endeavour, our gathering expertise, our knowledge gradually assembled and now slipping effortlessly away.

For what?

To call ourselves gardeners.

No, to put off what plants know better than us. The seasons come and go. Death follows life. Nothing lives for ever. We can only procreate and die. We carry a few lessons from one generation to another, but we have only a scrabbling existence, a smear on the thin surface of a dot in the vastness of forever.

The darkness gives way to a cold dawn.

Frost lingers on the roof.

A couple of black-and-white cats appear. There are a few half-hearted feints and some arching of backs before they continue their search for alternative pickings, as the humans, neglecting their servant status, haven't stirred.

The sun rises, stately moving its view as it traverses the two sturdy dwellings, sleepily recalling their previous inhabitants.

Carole Morgan.

Her little shop in Whitby, selling Goth stuff, all that black sort of gear.

I thought she was dead. It was in the papers.

With that other woman.

Fern Robinson.

The Snow White Killer.

'Are you alright,' says a voice.

I turn to look at the speaker. A woman eyeing me suspiciously, holding back a growling dog.

'No I'm fine,' I manage to stutter, realising I'm cold, sat here on this bench.

She shakes her head and continues her brisk afternoon walk.

I go back to my flat.

The front door isn't locked. I felt sure I did lock it.

I stand listening.

Is someone there?

I go carefully along the corridor and into the kitchen.

A young woman is standing by the window looking out at the sea. Short blonde hair. Do I know her?

She turns to stare at me with a smile on her face.

'I'm sorry,' I say, but she merely nods ... although not at me. I turn to my left. A man ... with a gun...

CHAPTER 15

Becket comes awake with a start.

Her heart is pounding. She is being chased by two guys in a car. Fighting with them. There is the crunch of a broken bone as one goes down. A gunshot. All in a whirl.

She lies still.

She's not in Jávea. Those guys are all dead. She's miles from that azure sea.

A hand appears on her shoulder. Who's that? It's John. His brown eyes are staring at her. His face is serious.

'Are you OK?' he whispers.

She nods, turns into his embrace … which turns into a fierce, urgent fuck.

An hour later she's sitting at the kitchen table, while John makes his version of a full Scottish. She looks across at him, standing there staring into the frying pan with hair sticking up. His jumper barely reaches his naked thighs. He's wearing an apron to protect his equipment, as he calls it, which she knows must be sore after what it's recently been through.

She smirks to herself.

'Suits you,' she laughs.

He mouths,

'Fuck you,' at her.

She grins again and opens his shirt, which she's wearing, to expose her tits. He shakes his head and concentrates on the bacon and eggs, but has to adjust the equipment.

She grins again.

'Yer not half bad, ya knars,' she says.

Any further smutty talk is cut short by the arrival of a badly sleep-deprived Freya.

She walks slowly to the table and sits down.

'You two,' she says.

The 'two' can't stop grinning, but Freya continues to affect her 'disgruntled of Chorley' persona.

'How's a Christian body meant to get some sleep, when she's caged up with a couple of mating baboons?'

The couple affect astonishment and denial, but soon they're all laughing.

John has to change tack for Freya. She doesn't do bacon or eggs, or black pudding, so she has to settle for mushrooms, fried tomatoes and toast.

Afterwards, Becket is doing the washing up and Freya is standing next to her with the tea towel.

'The thing is,' she says, 'you two probably never listened to him on the radio, but Wogan used to do this ongoing silly monologue about a couple called Janet and John, which made me laugh till I cried.'

The current couple frown at each other.

Freya shakes her head.

'It was based on a series of Ladybird Books, in the 1950s, I think, when he was at primary school, presumably. They were very proper and serious, but his parodies, were like you two … utter filth.'

This made them all laugh.

Afterwards, over a strong cup of coffee, they return to pondering their current situation.

'Could be worse,' says John.

The two women look at him.

'Well,' he says, 'here I am stuck with two lovely ladies, only having to chop up wood and do the cooking and the—'

Becket flaps him with a wet tea towel.

'Hush yer mouth, yer dirty woolly-back.'

They all smile and shake their heads. But then they're quiet.

Freya gets up and goes to the room she's been sleeping in and returns with a sketch pad she's found on a shelf.

She puts it down on the table and opens it at a page with some writing on it. She turns it round so that they can see the three words circled on the blank sheet.

'The fag,' 'adec,' and 'hugger,' she reads out loud.

They all stare at them.

'Go on then,' she says. 'What do they mean?'

Becket and John look at each other.

Soon they've covered three sheets with words and ideas, encouraged by Freya to think both inside and outside the box. They stare at the array of possibilities.

Becket shakes her head.

'Impossible,' she mutters. 'Even if the answers were there we wouldn't realise which were right.'

It's at this point that Freya's laptop tells them Ziggy is calling.

They gather round to see him appear on the screen.

'Hi, guys,' he smiles. 'Have you heard?'

'What?' asks Becket.

'Johnson's definitely got the virus.'

'There is a God,' she says.

Ziggy affects to look appalled, but can't hold it for more than a few seconds.

'OK, so what's new with you?'

Becket holds up the papers for him to see.

He laughs.

'Done that,' he grins. 'So what do you think?'

'*Nada*,' says Becket.

'*Neni tak*,' says Ziggy. 'Not so. You've got to think public school euphemisms,' he says.

'What?' says Becket.

'Well, you Geordies use "gadgie", "hinny" and the like.'

'You mean like a foreign language,' says John, knowing he'll get a kick, and he does.

'No,' laughs Ziggy, 'not foreign. Geordie is a local accent, whereas what you're looking at there is a class thing. Words the upper classes use to cement their tribal secretiveness. Excluding the likes of us.'

Becket is nodding now.

'Right, so "fag" is a public schoolboy term meaning a younger boy running errands, et cetera.'

'Yeah, but unpleasantly it has sexual connotations as well,' he adds.

The others are quiet, but nod their understanding.

'So you're saying one of these targets is someone who's regarded as an errand boy.'

Ziggy nods again.

'Who?' asks John.

'Bit difficult when most of them probably were fags at some point in their younger schooldays.'

'And "adec" doesn't make any sense at all. Google says, "dental equipment",' mutters Freya, with a wry smile.

Ziggy nods. Becket looks at her, realising she's ahead in this game.

'Hugger?' he asks.

'Well, apart from the obvious, it's again got to be some sort of veiled insult or a clue.'

They're all silent. Becket's wondering if Ursula's a party to this, as she does think differently than other people.

'So where does that get us?' she asks.

'We need a mole,' he says. 'Someone from public school or, better still, a Tory boy.'

'Aren't they the same?' sneers Becket.

'Yeah. Huge overlap, obviously, but unfortunately I don't have many contacts among them.'

'We do,' says Becket. 'Louisa and the Stork, surely.'

'Um,' says Ziggy. 'I think you've forgotten they're girls.'
Becket snorts again.
'Hard to imagine that. But they'll know, surely.'
'Well, ask them.'
Ziggy pauses.
'I thought you'd be better at that.'
She frowns. That doesn't immediately make sense.
'All right. Who first?'
'Louisa.'

So it's agreed that Becket should contact her straight away.
She makes the call.
No answer.
Leaves a message.
What is she doing?

***

Talking to the Edinburgh police is like trying to interview Gala estate residents about someone's missing car or husband.

Basically, Magda gets bugger all in the way of help or answers. This all packaged in the superior, begrudging tone of those who are having a 'really' hard time, unlike people policing in a 'ghost town, full of biddies and auld lags'.

Being pretty certain that Tommy has got there doesn't help. Requests for some camera footage don't even get a reply. Asking who might be able to provide a long-distance rifle is greeted with barely suppressed sniggers.

Although he's her brother and she does think they're close in many ways, what he does or did in the big city are closed books … in fact, they have never been seen.

Given the lockdown, they can't even justify going to look themselves.

So Magda gets permission to go back to see the recently

abandoned woman at the coast, while sending Rico to follow up the missing old lady saga.

It's a fine sunny morning as she crosses the border and heads for the sea. She's taking the horsebox as the woman says she can no longer be responsible for such a big, unhappy horse. Magda knows Warrior well and understands her reticence. She has a scar on her arm to remind her of his temper. She's also agreed to bring Hengist back, although she's sure he'll have had more run-outs than her parents normally provide for him.

An hour later she pulls up outside the house and realises that Warrior has heard the rattle and banging of his box. She goes to the field gate and gives his nose a good stroke, before he gallops away to work off some of his excitement.

Inside the woman offers her a coffee, but Magda declines, saying she needs to get back. To be honest, she can't bear the woman's sad face. Bloody men.

So within half an hour she's back on the road. She's never seen Warrior so keen to get into the box and has to shout at Hengist to sit down on the back seat. He sulks all the way home.

The two animals celebrate their return by running exuberantly around their different territories, although Hengist is at a loss to find Tommy anywhere and only eventually lies down on the top step after he's exhausted every nook and cranny.

She's only just finished stowing the horsebox away when her mobile bleeps at her.

'Hi, Rico. *Que passa?*'

He always ignores her hopeless attempts to speak his father's beautiful language, but sounds even more downbeat.

'No one there,' he says.

'No one?'

'Well, the two gardeners are, but they don't speak more

than one word at a time or say, "Ah dunna ken," and shake their heads.'

'Have you tried the woman's home?'

'She's not been seen there for over a week.'

'Out for a walk?'

There's a sigh.

'Ma'am, it's on the slopes of the Eildons…'

She sighs back.

'Well, OK, keep in touch.'

She stands looking out across the valley. Amelia's smoke is taunting her yet again. Could she?

Well, yes she could.

She goes and saddles up Sandy, who is no dancing queen, only a gentle-natured being, a perfect antidote to all this sound and fury.

Soon the slow rhythm of her walk begins to relax Magda's pent-up frustration, which gives way to taking in the budding nature of all the plants and birds around her.

***

The reason Louisa doesn't respond to either Becket or Magda's calls is because she's trying to reason with Fletcher. A hard task at the best of times … and this is the 'worst of times'.

The home where Laura is being looked after has numerous inmates who have contracted the virus. Laura hasn't yet, but the manager says she thought he ought to know.

Fletcher is all for going down and rescuing her, but Louisa tries to explain that won't be possible. This sets him off on a rant against, well, everybody and everything. He storms out of the house and sets off down the drive, rather than taking his usual route to the river.

She waits for nearly an hour, but then sets off in her car to find him. She drives this way and that, but there's no sign of him. She's beginning to think she needs to call for help when she figures out where he might have gone.

Sure enough, he's sitting in the front pew of the little kirk above the bridge. Obviously this is not a normal activity for him, but she remembers how he was intrigued and slightly amused by its strange history, particularly how it ended up being a prison.

She coughs quietly.

He doesn't turn round.

'I knew you'd figure it out eventually,' he murmurs.

She goes and sits in the pew behind him.

They sit there in the ancient stillness. The walls are so thick that the buffeting wind, the calls of birds or the bleating lambs are all silenced. No snuffling mice or scuttling cockroaches. Only the sound of ancient dust settling.

Neither of them speaks for what seems an awfully long time. As a solitary person Louisa doesn't find this hard, but she worries for the man in front of her. He's a creature of bustle, scrabbling about in the undergrowth searching for answers, clues, anything to keep his mind roving.

Eventually he rubs his cheek. An errant tear, she thinks. He coughs. Not a real cough, more a disguised cry of anguish. She considers putting her hand on his shoulder, but doesn't … so she waits.

'Do you know what Ellie's last words to me were?' he says, his voice hoarse.

She dreads to think what that strange young woman might foresee, given her past utterances, and so can do nothing but wait.

'When the black horse comes, you must take the reins … and not look back.'

Louisa fights back her tears.

They're both still again. They both know that direct eye to eye contact will reduce them to weeping.

'She only went to see Laura the once and said she wouldn't

go again, because, "My gran is no longer there." He stifles a sob. 'I thought at the time that was so selfish, but now it's forced on me I can see what she meant.'

'Why is it that platitudes come so easily at such times?' thinks Louisa, so she dismisses them all. Just waits.

Eventually they're back outside. The wind has dropped. Some lambs the other side of the fence stare at them like they might be aliens, but then a call from a nearby ewe galvanises them into action and they stampede away.

They walk back to the car, her arm linked through his, like they're walking away from a wedding or a funeral. Or a christening, she thinks, bizarrely.

She drives them slowly back to the huge house she knows is ridiculous, but can't escape from.

There's no young man to take their coats. She's sent him home. It's good that Fletcher is an accomplished cook, because otherwise she would have starved. But today they've no appetite. She finds a fruit cake and some cheese.

They sit in the conservatory, its cavernous foliage humming with diligent bees.

At least there is an enormous cellar full of wines, many of them collected by her last husband, long dead now, but worthy of a toast.

No television or cards. No music played. No book even opened. Only twa auld yins sitting in the dark amidst a mock forest of stolen plants.

Nothing is real but impending mortality.

***

It's nearly seven o'clock when Magda gets the call from Rico.

'Ballantyne has been found, ma'am,' he says.

'Where?'

'Someone nearly ran him down on the bypass. He was standing in the middle of the road.'

'What?'

'At first they thought he was drunk but then he collapsed, so he ended up in the hospital.'

'What have they said?'

'Not a lot. Probably suffering from exposure. He was only wearing a shirt and trousers, no shoes. His feet are all cut up.'

'Can he speak?'

There's a pause.

'Well, yes, but he doesn't make much sense.'

Another pause.

'Well?' she demands, knowing there's more.

'He's talking as if he's away with the fairies, ma'am.'

She sighs.

'OK, I'll contact the hospital.'

She does. They don't have much more to tell her. They've put him in a side ward. They're not too worried about his physical injuries and suggest that he'll stop the gibbering when he's had a long, warm sleep.

She hopes that's true, but then remembers that woman from the care home has gone to be his housekeeper, so maybe they'll send him back to her.

Standing looking out at Amelia's lights makes her feel lonely again. It was good to see her and the kids this afternoon, even without any hugs, but then her husband came back and she thought it best to leave them to it. Never liked the man. Can't see what Amelia sees in him. Is she only putting up with him because of the kids? Nightmare.

Her final thoughts are about Tomasz.

Where is he?

What's he doing?

It's well after midnight before she falls asleep.

***

Tommy is on Imelda's bed.

He is not sure that this is her own flat, given the preponderance of the huge photographs of naked male bodies in various positions of sexual subjugation with other men.

She's sitting in a velvet-cloaked armchair in the corner smoking a spliff.

She's completely naked, if you can call a body covered in wicked fairies, peacocks and dragons naked.

The sex has continued to be violent, obscene, and excessive. She seems to be most turned on when inflicting pain, which he sort of gets, but is beginning to tire of it.

She has made the necessary calls and so they are now waiting for the responses.

He's only started to think about how he's going to pay the full amount for the weapon. He's plenty of money in his own account, but suspects that might not be a safe way of paying for it, so is pondering the possibility of contacting his mother. He knows she has money that she keeps hidden from his father. She learnt that rule long ago during her childhood in Communist Poland. Banks were not a good place to keep your money then, so he knew she had wads of notes stashed in various hidey-holes all over the ridiculously enormous building. When he was young he loved to disappear upstairs, playing hide-and-seek on his own, and he sometimes found another cache. Much of it was in old zloty, but still legal tender as far as he knows. He always left the money where he found it, suspecting that one day he might need it.

Which is now.

So at some point he needs to go back.

He glances across at Imelda.

She makes a face while turning a razor blade round and round in her fingers.

'You want some more, soldier?' she sneers.

He shakes his head.

'I need to get out of here,' he says.

She stares at him.

'Without the gun?'

'No, but as soon as it's sorted, I'm gone.'

She stares at him.

'Who you gonna kill?' she asks.

He smiles and shakes his head.

She opens her legs wide to reveal the giant dragon's mouth, its jaws dripping with blood.

'You tired of me?' she pouts.

'Not at all,' he replies. 'In fact, I think I might take you with me.'

She sneers at him and gently fondles herself.

'What makes you think I'd want to come with you?'

'Money. Sex. Horses.'

'Horses? You have horses?'

He nods.

'Oh, yes … and dogs.'

She begins to rub herself more fiercely.

'Where?'

'My family home. It's a mansion. Its huge. We could stay there and no one would know.'

She stops rubbing and sits up.

'Where?'

'About an hour from here. In the hills.'

'Are your family there?'

'Yeah, but they're old and they only live on the ground floor. We can get in without them even knowing.'

She gets up and comes onto the bed with him.

'Tell me about it,' she says.

He tells her. He knows every room. Every picture. Every hiding place.

She listens, while she strokes his body. The inevitable happens.

Later her mobile fizzes at her. She says little, none of it in English. The call finishes.

'They'll bring it wherever you want.'

'How much?'

She tells him.

He doesn't respond.

'You have that sort of money,' she asks. 'Not all of it,' he says. He tells her where to make the drop. She rings them back.

'They're not happy,' she says, putting her hand over the phone.

'He shrugs.

'Take it or leave it. I have other contacts,' he says.

She talks again, her harsh voice rasping off the device.

Ends the call.

'OK. Tonight. Eleven.'

He nods, looks at his watch.

'We'd better be going. Got to find some wheels.'

'That's not a problem,' she says. 'Time for some horse trials.'

He doesn't immediately understand what that might exactly mean, but he soon does.

Later they're waiting in the pub car park for the drop. Resting on the high ground above the headwaters of a surprising number of rivers, one flowing south to the Tweed, others to the Firth and one to the east, it's the only building for miles. The pub is shut, of course, but there are lights on upstairs. They're round the side behind a garage and a shed. The 'borrowed' car is back in a lay-by.

There's no moon, so it's pitch-black and cold. Imelda's wearing a huge fur coat, but still shivering.

'You should have stayed in the car,' he says.

She blows smoke into his eyes.

'Do you think I trust you?' she slurs.

He shrugs.

They wait. An owl hoots nearby. She shudders again.

'I hate the countryside,' she says. 'Fucking wild animals and birds.'

He smiles in the dark.

'There aren't any tigers or wolves,' he murmurs, thinking of hot nights in the jungle. And the freezing hills of Kurdistan.

He looks up at the stars. They're different here, obviously, but he remembers them from childhood. He points at the Pole Star and then at Orion's belt. His arms and legs.

She sniggers.

'Is that his cock?' she asks.

'No, his scabbard.'

She laughs again.

'Pity. It's fucking big. Bigger than yours.'

He grins to himself.

'It would choke your dragon, though.'

She pretends to swoon, but then stiffens.

He hears it too.

The gangsta Volvo cruises to a stop and douses its lights. The door opens and the regulation gorilla gets out. Imelda goes to him and they have a whispered conversation. The guy comes over to talk to Tommy. The deal is that he can take the piece now but minus the crucial component, which will be provided when the outstanding money is handed over. Within the twenty-four hours, as agreed. Otherwise they'll come to get it back. This is said in a voice which implies that this wouldn't be a good idea.

Tommy nods and they drive them back to the lay-by.

The gun is wrapped in a blanket.

Tommy examines it and demonstrates expertly how it should

work. Carefully handles and sniffs at the ammunition. Nods his approval, and then he and the smaller man in the back shake hands. All the conversation is in Russian, which has Imelda frowning, but eventually there are handshakes and the Volvo does a U-turn and sets off back towards the city.

Tommy gives a sigh as they sit in the darkness. He turns on the engine and sets off south.

They're soon down in the long valley and the night becomes darker. The lights of Edinburgh no longer illuminate the sky. Tommy says not a word until they turn off the main road and head for home.

It's a winding road six miles long from the edge of his father's estate to the house, but he knows every rock and wood and stream.

Imelda shrinks into her coat. She hates the dark, empty landscape and the huge expanse of glistening stars.

Eventually they come to the top of a rise. Tommy turns into the dark wood on the left and noses his way through the trees until they come out at the rear of the vast, hulking house that looms eyeless above them.

He turns off the engine and turns to look at her.

She shivers.

***

Away to the east, two bodies lie chastely apart on a bed.

The room is in darkness, apart from the occasional glint of starlight in the mirror opposite the window.

If you listened carefully you would be able to make out the sounds of their breathing, but neither of them is moving.

And also neither of them is asleep.

The cooling air is fraught with uncertainty.

The last words spoken were soft.

'Try to sleep,' and,

'You too.'

There's the tension of betrayal. Of despair. Of loneliness.

Two people who have known each other for most of their adult lives. Often tetchy, frequently sarcastic, and always combative. They've both been strong, difficult people, who other weaker mortals have feared or avoided.

Ploughed their own furrows, through trouble and strife.

Been blessed with caring but independent partners along the way, even though neither of them are naturally faithful nor always truthful.

Their lives have been intertwined by circumstance and serendipity, not intent.

Both are proud, yet knowing and protective of their own vulnerabilities.

If asked, they would have sneered at the very idea of this conjugal act ever happening.

But here they are. A few inches apart.

The man's face is streaked with tears, some dry, but others still flowing.

The woman's face is dry, but in her head she is weeping.

In the end, he turns and folds into her embrace.

They couldn't claim later, although no one would ever dare ask, even if they knew that it even happened, that this was chaste, but it was a genuine union of two lost souls in the dark.

They sleep.

The moon comes out and blesses them.

***

Tommy puts his fingers to his lips and tries to quietly open the car door.

Unfortunately it squeaks.

He stops and listens.

Imelda's eyes go huge.

He steps down onto the gravel and waits. Listens to the wind in the trees, which is making the stars flicker as the highest branches sway gently.

He walks carefully towards the metal staircase, which rises in two sections to the second floor. He beckons her to follow him, but she scrunches her heels into the stones.

A single gruff bark pierces the silence.

Tommy puts his hand up and she stops.

He steps softly to the corner.

There's a scrabble of gravel and a whine of delight.

He returns with a huge shadow at his side.

Imelda shrinks back against the metal, but the dog merely sniffs her leg before Tommy pulls him away.

The three of them climb the metal steps.

Tommy finds the key in its hidden niche and they're inside.

The corridor stretches the length of the building. More than ten windows, she guesses. She's only been in a house this size in Italy. A memory best forgotten.

'"Let sleeping dogs lie" is the English proverb,' she thinks.

Tommy leads her halfway along the corridor and then opens a door, which turns out to be a huge room the width of the building with a window looking out at the hills.

There's a gigantic bed and lots of tables and chairs. The walls are covered with old gilt-framed paintings.

He drops their bags on the floor and goes over to look out of the window, knowing he'll be able to see the Tweed winking its way through the valley below.

She has already flopped on the bed, still shivering, and pulled the cover over herself.

He comes back to her and they lie there together. Hengist lies on the floor and soon there are gentle snuffles and snores, but Tommy can't sleep. Is this a clever idea or is it stupid? Hiding right under his sister's nose. She'll surely notice that Hengist is behaving strangely.

He realises that they'll have to go, and has some ideas about where they might be safe. Not far away, but isolated. The food they bought coming down will keep them going for some time and the police will be thinking he'll be heading south, not realising that he's decided on a less predictable target. A counterintuitive decision. Obvious to someone whose life has depended on outwitting the cleverest of foxes. If you can out-think the twisted minds of the Taliban, the Western mindset is a piece of cake.

He can't remember the name of the old Uzbek chieftain who told him the mantra, but it roughly translates as,

'If you want the people to rise up, kill the one they love the most.'

Below them in separate rooms are the old couple.

The man, on his back, is snoring intermittently. Charts and dates overlap the grainy photographs in his dreams.

The woman lies awake. Anyone born and brought up in the forests of Mazovia would have learnt to fear the slightest movement in the darkness.

And recognise their firstborn's presence.

She smiles to herself.

She will let him think she doesn't know for as long as he needs, but she is already contemplating the meals she will make. She even senses he's not alone, but then frowns, reminding herself of all the unsuitable 'girls' he's brought there in the past.

She shrugs and tells herself not to be worried. Some day he will find the right woman and she will get to organise the most wonderful wedding celebration.

***

Ziggy's obsession with trying to find who the target might be is driving me mad.

He's turning out lists like an organ grinder on speed. Putting them up on long strips dangling from the washing lines he found in the kitchen cupboard.

He keeps pestering Becket and the others, who all seem to be obsessed with the same list-making disease. I even look it up. It's called glazomania. Don't know why. Other than it makes me glaze over.

So even though it's getting late I take myself off for a short walk along the lane.

There are not many houses this side of the river, but eventually I can see one in the distance. The road winds up a bit and I can look down at it. It's an old farmhouse, I think, with numerous outbuildings. Someone is living there, though. Smoke is coming out of the chimney.

There are horses in the fields, and although I'd not noticed it on the map there's also a footbridge, which goes over to the houses at the bottom of the lane up to Magda's house.

And there she is.

On horseback.

I watch as she comes though the houses and out onto the road, then cuts down the lane which leads to the footbridge.

As she reaches it, three small children come running out of the farmyard and chase each other to the bridge, then dash across to Magda.

She shoos them away and waits till they've gone running back to the farmhouse, where a woman has come out holding a babe in her arms.

Magda ties the horse to the fence the other side of the river, walks across and follows them up to the farm.

I can just hear whooping and laughter.

I stand and watch. Am I envious? Don't think so. The eldest of those kids could only be ten or so. That's some going. The woman must be bonkers.

I walk on a bit further and then turn back.

But when I get back I notice that Magda is already riding back up the slope. A big car is now in the drive. Was that the husband home from work? So that was only a short visit. The poor woman must have wanted some time off.

I go indoors and fight my way through the list forest and start on something to eat. I've forbidden him in the kitchen by telling him it's a fire hazard, which surprisingly he has accepted.

He's still at it when I go to bed.

Is there a cure for glazophobia?

***

In the wood above Magda's cottage a shadowy figure settles beneath a big oak tree.

He's taken the car back to a lay-by he spotted as they came over the hill from Stow.

Having attached the tracer back in Edinburgh he doesn't have to follow their car, but once on the move south he is pretty certain he knows where they were going.

Home to Mummy.

Which is perfect.

The target is quickly identified. Some obnoxious suit who lives down in the valley below. Apparently Steil has previous form with the woman and public spats with her husband, so it was easy to set up the backstory.

The distance is no problem. It's well within Steil's reach. And finding the man's own gun makes it cast-iron. It merely needed a forced entry to lift the weapon and then time to put the gun back. Nice and hot. Although you'd think people with so much money would have better security.

The target isn't furloughed yet – solicitors can work on their own, apparently – so he generally leaves about nine.

Time for a sleep.

He sets up his bivouac, has a bite to eat and then snuggles down.

The last thing he remembers before he goes to sleep is the look on Kemball's face.

Amazing how most people haven't the slightest idea of how much they are watched and how their 'secret' lives can be so easily manipulated.

The moment of death is only fleetingly recognised.

***

Ref/Tr/ /D*/03/29/20/15.37

'   '

'Yes.'

'Green light.'

'OK. So when?'

'   **on his way home now. So tomorrow, as we agreed.'**

'No problem. Everything is OK.'

'Well, take care. He's a screwed-up little bastard, but don't underestimate him.'

'Anything else?'

'   **we agreed.'**

CHAPTER 16

Tommy wakes in the gilded room.

An early sunbeam is fingering the frame on the first painting on the right. It's of some distant relative he ought to know. His father would wax lyrical about the inhabitants of this room … 'wax' being a good word for something that stuffs up your ears, endlessly clogging his younger head.

The old bastard has probably not been up here for years. The stairs are now an ascent beyond his arthritic hips. But he has prints to gloat over, all going back to the that infamous moment of their ancestor's ascendancy to the Thistle. The right choice at the crucial moment. Culloden. The bloodiest battle in Scottish history and the end of the Stuart cause. Not that the Steils had always been faithful to that dubious gang of cut-throats. They were after all, Borderers first, with an an even longer history full of many other false loyalties, betrayals and massacred enemies.

His childhood was stuffed with this 'history' and eventually he did the 'right thing', didn't he?

He dozes.

Comes awake a second time, this time from the heat and the ear-splitting barrage of shells.

Blood on his hands.

'Will they ne'er be clean?'

Except, of course, like Macbeth, his hands are clean. His victims are generally literally a mile away. Exploding heads in his scope, like smashed melons.

If he were to do this hit, it would have far more consequences than all the two hundred and whatever it is put together.

Civil war? A huge military lockdown, even harder than the current medical one. He'd be top of their list. They'd find him wherever he went. He'd never get out of prison. Probably be choked to death in some squalid toilet.

He finds himself at the window.

His naked, unmarked body, apart from the recent burn marks and thin cuts, exposed to the whole world.

His gaze falls from the azure sky to see the smoke climbing steeply from the farmhouse opposite.

Ah, the fragrant Amelia. Her beautiful lithe body now turned into a bloated milking machine. Shackled to that sly Donald Cameron: not a loyal bone in his elephantine body.

Perhaps he ought to have a pop at him instead. Piss-easy, downward trajectory, barely a kilometre, fat blob bursting like an overripened tomato.

Now there was a job he'd do for free.

He doesn't hear her coming until her fingers snake round his already tumescent member.

He closes his eyes and allows her to continue her lascivious intent, reaching up to hold the curtains at either side to steady himself.

Feels her lips and both the softness and the roughness of her hair on his back and his neck.

Her fingers fondle front and back. Enter him.

He is helpless and surrenders to the ecstasy of the eruption, which splatters up the fine Georgian glass.

She growls in his ear.

'You're such an exhibitionist.'

He laughs.

'Who is she?' she asks.

'A beauty long lost,' he murmurs.

She rakes her nails across his stomach and brings her knee hard up between his legs.

They stand like this for all the world to see until he goes limp and they sink to the floor.

But she can't last long in this cold room, so she scuttles back to the bed and snuggles down.

'What's for breakfast?' she demands.

He gets in the bed with her.

'Seconds,' he says and grabs her by the neck.

There's a fight. She loses. Gives in. Gets some of her own medicine.

They sleep again.

The sun rises until it's shining straight on to their 'slain bodies'. Motes are dancing, as they do, bringing a golden mist to cloud this scene of decadent oblivion.

***

Two floors below them, the old lady bustles around her kitchen.

She was up about the same time as her son.

Now she's getting bacon out of the freezer and ignoring the voice telling her not to count so many chickens, even if he might have come home to roost.

Of course, she knows nothing of what her daughter is involved in either, having always preferred not to know, and she knows even less about her son's activities.

Thinking of chickens, she scuttles out the side door to go and fetch some fresh eggs, and is both unsurprised and pleased to see the vehicle behind the sheds. It's not one she's seen before, but she's certain it's his, even though it's not the usual kind he prefers.

She returns to the kitchen and continues her preparations, while leaving the door open to let the morning sun creep in and offer an inviting gesture to anyone else who happens to pass by.

She's knows that Magda is up because she has been briefly seen standing in front of the open front door. Tells herself to stop planning family gatherings, but is unable to prevent them fermenting and growing.

Magda is up and dressed, but as yet has nowhere to go.

No morning calls from Ziggy to tell her the latest news. No calls from her chief to give her some more dreary paperwork to do. No calls from Rico to report on the hospitalised lord or the disappearing housekeeper.

She could contact any one of them, but thinks she needs a bit of a break.

The one call she is dreading, but thinks most unlikely she'll get, is from Tomasz. Is he really involved in this in some way?

She can't believe he'd even be tempted. He hasn't ever had the slightest interest or respect for politics or its practitioners ... which is ironic, because he's what they call a prime asset. Someone they'd order and expect to carry out the most violent of acts in their name. She doubted, for example, if the Stork would hesitate to do that.

So why did he agree to meet that man? What did he want, which has made them both disappear? How was the little man hiding his tracks so professionally?

Her phone bleeps.

It's DI Craig from Berwick. What does he want?

She answers his call.

'Hi,' she says.

'Hi. Listen ... we might have something on the little man.'

'Like what, a camera sighting?' she asks, all ears.

'No, but something nearly as good. The woman, Nina Kirby, is an artist, a professional portrait artist. We only realised when Danny, PC Roberts, the community officer, noticed the pictures on her wall and asked her who had done them. So we asked her to do a drawing of the guy.'

'Right,' says Magda, doubtfully.

'I'll send you a copy,' he says. 'She's good. Should be useful.'

She thanks him and goes to make a brew.

Her laptop calls her back and she prints out the picture.

Well, it is a good drawing, but the thick dark hair and the moustache aren't right. Are they a disguise? And who can she show it to? As far as she knows, Tomasz is the only person who has met him, apart from her.

Is there any point in sharing it?

May as well.

***

Tommy is down on the first floor, heading for the library.

The door is unlocked of course, but the room is in darkness. The heavy velvet curtains are keeping this whole battalion of words safe from the sun.

It takes him some time to wrench them open, and he's overwhelmed by the dust this makes. He has to go out on the corridor to get some fresh air, although even in there it isn't much better.

Eventually he manages to lever one of the long windows open and the cold morning air rushes eagerly in, weaving and eddying round all the forgotten stories and claims. His father would be appalled at this desecration, even though he's never ever likely to come up even one flight of stairs to see them again. There was a time when he employed a series of young, local gals to come and pretend to be librarians, researching the family's past exploits and honours, but a series of indiscretions on his part eventually made the applicants dry up, despite the increasing of the stipend.

Tomasz recalls the first time with Millie in here. A 'fumbling of ingénues' is how he later described it, but, given her eventual fecundity with the fat controller, he's now glad of that ineptitude.

'Anyway, I'm not here to court sad reminiscences,' he tells himself, as he peers out through the floor-length windows.

Fearing another lascivious assault, which might be noisy enough to awaken the old couple beneath, he checks behind him. But there's not a sound.

He reminds himself of the particular hiding place he's sure will still hold the biggest stash of Polish zloty and goes straight to the shelf to pull out the thick leather-backed book...

To find the cupboard is bare.

He stares in disbelief.

Pulls out the books on either side.

Not a note. Not even the dusty form of the box.

He shakes his head and stands back to look at the whole wall of books again.

This section is Polish history, volume after volume of dry misery. Many pages are festooned with his father's pompous underlining and specious commentary.

He pulls out some more.

Not a grosz.

He tries to remember where the other stashes are hidden. What was the little rhyme he'd made up?

But there is naught.

What the hell has she done with it all?

The thought of that huge Chechen gorilla crushing his ribs and pulling his heart out fill his head... There would be no hiding place.

It's clear he will have to confront her.

The thought of even speaking to his father, though, is beyond consideration.

So he needs a plan.

Introducing Imelda to his mother will be quite the conundrum, but first he must convince her to play the ingénue herself. The hair would be a problem, and so would the tattoos, the jewelled fingers, the Russian cigarettes and the piercings, although most of them wouldn't be on show ... which is a reminder that makes his sore appendage wince.

He takes one last look round the vast acreage of decaying paper and sighs.

He looks at his watch. The handover is eighteen hours away. Surely that's enough time. He tells himself to relax. His mother will save his bacon.

Again.

He shuts the wind out, but leaves the curtains open. He is unaware that one of windows has a loose pane, so doesn't hear it fall as he shuts the door and patters up the stairs. It falls soundlessly onto the bottom of the curtain and yet is so old and delicate that it crumbles into a myriad splinters, which play in the morning sunlight.

***

Magda is standing in the little front garden of the cottage, watching the resident swifts coming and going from their nest in the eaves. She's yet to put out more seed for the blue tits to continue their acrobatics on the feeders. So she doesn't hear the pinging on her phone, and then her laptop, as the messages arrive.

It's only when she returns and sees the blinking icons that she realises the deluge of missives is from Ziggy.

She picks up the mobile and responds.

She has to calm him down to understand what on earth he's so excited about and then stands open-mouthed as he manages to explain.

The little man is Freya's 'Jimmy Sparrow'.

Maybe it's not his real name anyway, and no, Ziggy has no other name to call him … yet. He's feeding the portrait into every portal he can think of, but has nothing so far.

However, as he says, no one can be invisible nowadays, and he will find him soon enough.

She suggests that they organise an online meeting for ten o'clock, which will give him time to continue his search. She tells him who she's sent the picture to and he agrees to widen that audience as much as he can.

Now she's standing at the doorway again.

She realises her stomach is hollow, and so the thought of her mother's full Scottish breakfast with new-laid eggs is suddenly irresistible.

She pops the cup on the window ledge and sets off up the path.

The man in the portrait has a moustache and isn't wearing a hat or glasses, unlike her attacker, but yes, it is definitely him. People are so easily fooled.

She puts the picture down.

What's driving this little man?

Why now?

You'd think he'd give it up, in the circumstances. Even someone as difficult to trace or recognise as him would be massively constrained by the lockdown. Unless... Maybe he has privileged access and clearance, for some reason. Like a police officer, for example? Or a health worker?

She texts Ziggy.

He replies,

'Been there. Done that. *Nada.*'

She wants to shout,

'Do it again,' but shakes her head instead.

'What you need is a good hearty breakfast, young lady,' she hears her mother's voice insistently calling, and retakes her steps back up to the house.

***

I haven't seen the portrait, but see the likeness straight away when Ziggy brings it up on the screen.

He's now powering away on his bank of machines like some demented copy editor, trying to meet an impossible deadline.

I assemble cereal, coffee and toast and take some to him,

which, as usual, he ignores, and also as usual I can't make head or tail of what's on his various multiple and fragmented screens. I don't know how anyone can do this. It gives me a headache just looking at them for only a few seconds.

So I decide to go for a morning stroll.

I had been intrigued by the sight of Magda's fleeting visit to the farmhouse along the way and, without thinking I'd go and visit or anything, I set off.

It's less than a mile away and so I'm soon looking down on the collection of buildings and outhouses.

The sun has come over the hill and is now bouncing off the white-painted walls. I can see there are horses in the field nearby, a couple of bigger ones and then a trio of ponies, presumably for the children I saw running to greet Magda yesterday.

I know nothing about horses, other than that I'm frightened of them, particularly the big ones like those two seem to be.

But as I watch I can tell there's something going on.

They're all gathered together by the fence nearest to the farmhouse, so I focus my binoculars and check them out. There's a bit of jostling and head-tossing going on. Is that normal? Do horses have breakfast?

I pan across to the outhouses. The car that arrived last night is still there.

Whoa. That's not right.

I fiddle with the focus. In and out? I manage the best I can do. The windscreen is definitely smashed. Is there someone inside? There seems to be a shape, but I can't focus any more clearly. The angle's all wrong.

I look without the bins.

The only door of the house I can see is shut.

What's going on?

The car wasn't damaged like that when I saw it arrive. The man getting out and going inside seemed normal to me. Just

308

someone coming home from work and going in to have a meal with his family.

So why is the windscreen smashed?

I go back to the horses. The ponies are still jostling at the gate, but the two bigger ones have given up and gone to find some grass to nibble.

I go back to the cottage.

A figure appears. A child. Quite tall. Probably the eldest of the ones I saw last night. She goes over to the ponies. But only stands there looking at them.

Then the woman comes out with the other two and the babe in her arms. She looks towards the eldest child and seems to be shouting at her. The girl ignores her. The woman gestures to her again, but then puts the baby on her hip and sets off towards the gate onto the road, with the two other children trailing after her.

As far as I can tell she ignores the car completely. Does she not have another one?

She reaches the road. Then she turns again and waves to the older child, who still ignores her and continues to stand with the ponies, who seem to be getting more agitated.

The woman sets off along the road towards me.

Something is very wrong here, so I set off to meet her.

I can hear the crying of the baby, but can't see them again until I round the turning by the stand of big fir trees.

By now they're only a hundred yards or so away.

The woman is still calling to the stubborn eldest child.

'Maria, please,' she calls, her voice a wail of anger and despair.

It's at this point that she sees me.

Not knowing why, I wave at her.

She stands transfixed like she's seen an alien.

I break into a stumbling run. Not my best physical activity.

She doesn't turn away, just stands staring at me, holding the baby close, while the two other children cower beside her.

I get to a couple of yards away from her.

Her eyes are red.

I put out my hand.

She sinks to the ground and hugs the baby, who is now crying fearfully as it looks at me, which I have to say is their usual response.

I don't know what to do.

The woman looks up.

'Help me,' she says.

I step towards her and put out my hand again.

She reaches out. I kneel down beside her. The two children cling to their mother. I try to embrace them all. The woman is crying uncontrollably now and the children are joining in.

I can't tell whether it's fear or relief.

I get out my mobile and press Ziggy's number. It stutters, but as usual the stubborn bastard doesn't respond.

I press Becket's number. She answers immediately.

She's incredibly calm and efficient.

'What? Where? Don't move. We'll be there. Five minutes.'

It seems longer than that, but is probably quicker.

To be honest, I don't know what I did other than try to hug the four of them. The woman and the two youngest are crying, while the other one stares at me with the blankest of eyes I've ever seen in a child. I begin to wonder about what on earth she might have witnessed.

John's Land Rover comes roaring along the lane.

Becket and Freya are out scooping up the whole lot of us as quickly as they can, but then we continue on to the house to look for the older child, who is thankfully still standing next to the horses.

Becket firmly persuades her to get in the Land Rover, although she won't go next to her mother so is put in the front seat. Freya is with the woman and the smaller kids in the back seat.

John meanwhile investigates the car and comes back with a stern face.

He mutters to Becket, and although she looks over at the car she doesn't go to have a look. Whispered words are exchanged. Becket's lips harden.

The mother is now silent, staring sightlessly, holding the grizzling baby to her chest. The other children are silent passengers, their eyes flitting from one to the other of these four strangers.

John quickly goes into the house.

We all wait for what seems like a long time, but is only a few moments.

He returns and shakes his head at Becket, who has been standing by the fence talking in rapid bursts into her phone.

She tells him to drive, and soon we're on their way back to their hut. Becket and I are clinging on in the open boot, zooming past White Cottage with its manic inhabitant who is no doubt still flickering his fingers hither and thither, but blissfully unaware of the drama unravelling outside his cocoon.

Back at the hut, we divide up the tasks between us. John in the kitchen making drinks and cooking a five-person breakfast. Freya and I are trying to coax the children and the mother into a comfortable state. Becket is barking orders on her mobile like she's a chief constable.

The other help arrives at the double.

The first one is a woman, who does an instant triage and then explains that the next bunch of people will all also be wearing masks and not to be frightened. She reckons that the half-cooked breakfast should be completed rather than taking everyone somewhere else for now.

She has an outside conversation with Becket, who then discreetly confirms to the rest of us that there was a body in the car. Probably the woman's husband, the children's father.

After some breakfast, the family are whisked away and we're left trying to comprehend the disaster that has unfolded before us.

It's only then that I remember last night when I saw the children running to meet Magda at the bridge. Becket nods and says she's been informed and that she and the woman have been friends since they were toddlers themselves.

And then my phone peeps.

It's Ziggy.

He doesn't know what's happened, but what I tell him for once leaves him speechless.

Is that a result?

***

Magda has only just kissed her mother on three cheeks when her mobile tribbles in her pocket.

She stands aghast, as Rico explains what he's been informed about the Cameron family across from them.

She finishes the conversation and stares at her mother, who, while concentrating on the cooking, looks back her.

'You'll have time to have your breakfast, won't you?' she asks.

Magda nods, still trying to take it in. She closes her eyes. Should she tell her?

'What is it?' asks Helena.

'Er … some sort of incident. I'm not sure whether it will involve me yet,' she says, not certain the chief will agree to that.

'How can there be an incident if people are not supposed to be going out?' asks Helena.

'Some people don't like rules, Mother,' she says.

Helena sighs, but doesn't mention her own son, who she knows is one of worst rule-breakers. Got that from his father, of course. Not his mother. But she has a brief memory of running along darkened streets with Zofia. She shakes it away.

She begins to serve up the breakfast, but can see that her daughter's mind is elsewhere.

'Speaking of unpredictable people, have you any idea where

your brother is?' she asks, and then looks astonished as she realises he's standing on the doorstep.

She drops the egg she was taking out of the pan.

It hits the floor and gently crumples.

She stares at it and then back at Tomasz, who quickly crosses the room and takes the pan from her hand.

He puts it back on the hob and folds his mother in his arms. She's shivering with the fright and then the excitement that he's there.

Magda quickly scoops up the mess and puts in the bin.

'Always wanting to make a fine entrance, Mash,' she growls.

He releases his mother, who fumbles for her handkerchief to wipe away her tears.

The next few exchanges are in rapid Polish, but gradually they both calm down.

Tomasz then puts his fingers on his lips and goes back outside.

Magda raises her eyebrows at her mother, whose face can't make up its mind whether to be fearful or excited.

The prodigal son reappears with a woman.

Fear and excitement are replaced by confusion and surprise.

This woman has only half her hair. Has she had an accident? Her poor face as well. Is that a snake?

Tomasz introduces her and explains that she's a tattooist, which goes some way to defuse Helena's concern, but also raises other issues, which she avoids by bustling around them all and feeding them like a mother hen should.

Magda has given him the evil eye and so it's some time before they can speak openly. Helena finally gives them the opportunity when Imelda admits her parents kept pigs, which means she has to be taken to meet the McDonald clan in their sty out the back.

'What on earth are you up to, you stupid bastard?' she rasps.

He shakes his head, but doesn't laugh.

'Only the usual mayhem and confusion,' he mutters, as he goes out onto the terrace.

She follows him and grabs his arm.

'Can you even begin to think how this is for me? You're not in those bloody mountains now. This is our home. My patch.'

He lowers his head.

'It's too difficult to explain,' he mumbles, 'but it'll work out OK. Trust me.'

Magda splutters.

'Trust? You?'

She can hardly speak.

He stands immobile at the wall.

'I don't know how much you've been offered or what crazy course you're set on, but it will end in misery. For you, you deserve whatever you reap, but for me, your mother … it will kill her.'

Now he turns to her, the old battle resumed.

'Your patch?' he sneers. 'If only you knew how precarious everything is right now. You've no idea what evil is creeping out of the shadows. Don't you think I know what's happening? I've seen things you couldn't even imagine.'

They stand facing each other. In the past she would always collapse into tears and run away to hide, but now he sees the Steil in her eyes. The peculiar mix of recklessness and hubris that they've both inherited.

He turns away and looks out over the valley.

The fire at Amelia's has died, but the flurry of police cars and vans tell a different story.

He points down to it.

'What's happening at the Camerons'?' he asks.

She comes to stand next to him.

'I don't know, but I doubt I'll be involved.'

Tomasz bites his tongue about reminding her of her patch.

They watch as the crowd of figures, many of them wearing

white suits, scuttle hither and thither. Much of the action is concentrated around Donald's car.

Magda goes back into the kitchen, and returns with her mother's powerful army binoculars.

She watches for a few moments and then passes them to her brother, who is squinting across the distance.

He refocuses them, puzzled at the difference in his sister's eyes.

He can make out a limp arm and a hand. The arm wears a suit sleeve, so it must be Donald.

He scans back at the house. No sign of Amelia or the girls.

He passes them back to Magda.

She takes another look.

'What do you think?' he asks.

She shrugs.

'Not a bed of roses,' she mutters.

'Worst-case scenario?' he asks.

She lowers the binoculars, but doesn't look at him.

'He's killed himself, after...'

The tears come. He puts his arm round her. She lets him. Her mobile peeps.

She listens, says a few yeses and gives the occasional slow shake of her head.

The call ends.

She says nothing for a few moments. He waits.

'Amelia and the girls aren't harmed, but he's dead. Two wounds.'

Again, Tomasz has to stop sharing his thoughts about that.

'Poor cow,' is all he manages to say.

Magda shakes her head.

'That's what he made her become,' she responds with a surge of anger.

She turns to him.

'Bloody men.'

He shrugs.

She turns to face her mother, who is chattering away to Imelda as they return from the excursion.

Magda shepherds them back inside. She'll wait until there's more to tell.

Tomasz frowns.

Does that mean Amelia has killed Donald?

That doesn't fit with his memory of her as far as guns are concerned. She hates them. Hates the grouse shooting. Would never go to the hunt ball. She was a vociferous animal rights activist, until the children took up all her time.

'Mind you,' he thinks again, 'it was an appropriate end for such a bloodthirsty bastard.'

Donald was well known for enjoying every blood sport known to man since childhood. He was the boy who was shooting rabbits and anything else that moved as soon as he got his hands on any kind of weapon, illegally of course, but his father was even worse.

He scents the patchouli wafting through the air and turns to find Imelda's frown.

'Do you know this woman?' she asks.

He nods.

Her gaze lengthens to include a further question, but he turns away. The memories accuse him.

She puts her hand on his arm and turns him round to fold him into an embrace. They stand there for a while until Magda coughs as she comes out with two cups of coffee.

'You're a hit with *Mamusia*,' she says to Imelda, but her eyes are hard.

Imelda conjures a gracious smile.

Magda's phone pulses in her pocket. She walks away and presses it to her ear. It's Rico. The words are quiet but urgent. Does he know Tomasz is there? She glances at him. He's staring down at the farm. The message ends, but she keeps it to her ear as she composes herself. What should she do? Rico can't know. Her head is racing with possibilities.

The couple in front of her are nuzzling like horses. Surely he couldn't be involved. But the policewoman in her needs to ask the questions.

'So when did you get here?'

Tomasz looks at her, his face puckering into a frown.

'Late. Midnight-ish? Why?'

She shrugs her shoulders.

'Too late to knock, so we … er … effected an entrance,' he says, and then winks and nods upstairs.

She rolls her eyes, but her brain fizzes with possibilities. Has he got a gun? From what she knows, it would be easy for him. She glances at the distance, but she knows anyway from her running routes. It's exactly eight hundred metres to Amelia's, even less in a direct air shot. She knows he's been deadly accurate at far further away than that.

But why?

Was Donald merely a practice shot? She thinks all this in an instant. What should she do?

This is all interrupted by the arrival of her father.

She is immediately drawn back into yet another re-enactment of the prodigal son saga, which of course, always ends in a horrendous row.

But before they reach that moment, Tommy excuses himself, and, abandoning Imelda, slips back upstairs. He saw that look in his sister's eyes and realised what she was thinking.

But his own gun is still in its hiding place. He takes it out and checks it over. And then freezes.

It's not exactly warm, but a man who has lived and breathed with guns for most of his adult life knows when a gun has been recently fired.

He smells it. He feels it. He knows. This is a set-up.

He needs to go. Right now.

The forensic guys down there won't take long to work out where it was fired from. Up here. Where there happens to be the errant marksman, brother of the investigating officer, who has not yet dobbed him in.

He puts the gun over his shoulder, grabs his and Imelda's clothes, rushes down to the car, and throws them all into the boot.

After making himself slow down, while trying to control his beating heart, he comes round the corner to find them all laughing. His father has managed to make some joke or other, perhaps, so the laughter is pretty forced.

'Hey, right ... We need to get off, don't we, 'Melda?' he says, his eyes boring into her. 'I promised her a proper castle, and the MacDuffs have phoned and they'd be delighted ... at a distance, of course.'

Despite all his mother's attempts and his father's injunctions, they manage to extract themselves and drive off. But he does note the stern look in his sister's eyes, which definitely includes suspicion. Perhaps she's already made a call.

Imelda, on the other hand, is much more clued up by the set of his eyes and doesn't slow him down.

He drives them away in a swirl of dust, then turns right at the top of the drive and heads for the drove road. It is often a treacherous muddy track in the rain and impassable in the snow, but is the quickest way to escape right now.

He needs to know what's going on. The one thing he's now certain of is that he's being set up as the fall guy. He can't ask his mother what she's done with the money. Maybe she's finally put it in a bank. His own gun won't do. It'll give him away.

So if he's going to do what he now thinks is his alternative solution, he still needs the missing part. And the only person he knows who can fix that is the Rocket Man.

CHAPTER 17

'Who are the MacDuffs?' asks Magda's father.

She shakes her head at him.

'I've no idea,' she says.

Helena looks worried and a little annoyed.

'I don't know about that woman he's stacked up with,' she says. 'She looked ill to me.'

'Oh, I thought you were getting on fine,' murmurs Magda, 'and it's "shacked", not "stacked".'

Helena frowns.

'Well, whatever she is I wouldn't want to trust anyone with half her hair missing and a snake round her neck.'

Magda shakes her head and taps on her phone.

It takes so long for Rico to respond that she starts to worry he's been forbidden to contact her.

But eventually he replies.

'What's happening down there?' she demands.

There's an ominous pause.

'Not sure, ma'am. I'm not really in the loop any more. The station's overrun with men in suits. English.'

She sighs. It's that bad.

'What are the forensics saying?'

'Nothing,' he says. 'Well, not to us, anyway.'

'What about Amelia and the kids?'

Again there's a pause. Is he thinking what he's been told to say, or not say?

'As far as I know she's still being questioned, but the kids have been taken away.'

She hesitates.

'OK. Take care. Don't let them push you around. Let me know if there are any developments.'

Again the hesitation. Are they listening in?

He says goodbye and cuts the call.

She stands looking out of the window. How much worse can this get?

***

Becket phones Ziggy.

'What do you know?' she demands.

'Which disaster in particular?'

'There's more than one?'

'You bet. There's a lot of traffic, although there's not much direction or control. More like panic.'

'Why?'

'Not sure. There's a lot of noise around the forensics results, then they're shut down. Conversations go onto more secure sites that even I can't access.'

Becket tries to puzzle that out.

'I thought it was a domestic,' she says.

'Yeah, I think they did as well. Then suddenly it all went quiet.'

'Which means something more sinister, yeah?'

'Yes, obviously.'

'Like what?' This is almost to herself.

'Can only be the forensics, I think.'

She gives this some thought.

'Hey, can you get onto traffic?' she asks.

'Ahead of you, hinny,' he mutters, and then goes quiet. Then he says,

'Uh-huh. As you suspected, the main road is blocked both ways and I got a squeak of some helicopter conversation before they capped that. Scramble from Glasgow, I think.'

'So they'll be here soon?'

'Ten minutes max, I'd say.'

She thinks again, but he's still listening.

'Have you tried that DI yet … Magda?'
'Nope. Do you want me to?'
'OK.'
'I'll get back to you.'

She puts the phone down and looks across at the other two, who have both been listening intently to her side of the conversation.
'They've blocked the main roads. A helicopter on its way.'
'So…' begins Freya.
'Ziggy says it's probably not a domestic.'
They both frown back at her, but she can't work it out.

***

I'm standing behind Ziggy while he talks to Becket and eventually realise he's not there any longer. All the way through he's kept on looking at lots of other screens, some of which have flickered and died now.

'So what's going on?' I ask.

He grunts.

'Something the police don't want us to know,' he mutters, but that doesn't seem to stop him trying to find out, I think.

If in doubt make a coffee.

When I come back and place it beside him, he's sitting back staring at a smaller number of screens than usual.

'Looks bad,' he says. 'Nearly as complete a blackout as I've ever seen.'

'Meaning?'

'Must be high-level security stuff. I mean national. Threat to public order, et cetera.'

I shake my head.

'Can't be a domestic, then?'

He shakes his head.

There's a crackle of static. An urgent voice saying,

'Go.'

Ziggy glances at me.
'Got to be a raid, I think.'

***

The first thing Magda sees is the helicopter coming along the valley.

When it stalls and comes round overhead, she knows what is about to happen.

She rushes back into the house.

Where's her mother?

Where's she gone?

She stands there terrified, thinking,

'Where on earth can she be?' Then she realises, so dashes through into the back corridor and hurtles up the main stairs.

At the first floor she hesitates, then hears a noise above. She takes the stairs two at a time and stands listening at the top. Where is she?

A muttering to her left. She calls out.

'Mamusia?'

'Hello,' comes the reply.

She tries not to run, gets to the doorway and walks in.

Her mother is struggling with a blanket. The room stinks of sex. She goes over to help her fold it up.

'Your brother's an animal,' her mother says in a peculiar tone, half disgust and half admiration.

Before Magda can say another word, the noise of the helicopter drowns out her voice.

Helena turns to look out the window to see the shadow go past.

Magda rushes to her.

'It's the police,' she says. 'They've come to find Tomasz.'

Her mother stares at her.

'They think he killed Donald Cameron.'

Her mother's eyes go very big.

'But—'

It only takes a few minutes.

The house is surrounded. Armed officers are around it like a swarm of oddly mute bees. She hears her father's outraged voice and its quick suppression. She holds her mother tight and waits till they come hurtling up the stairs. Big men in black with automatic weapons and visors arrive in twos, shuttling back and forth up the corners.

She and her mother are quickly apprehended and taken downstairs. Her mother's face is more angry than fearful – no doubt it's the horror of the *Ubeki* secret police surging back into her head – but she shakes the man's arm off and pulls Magda close.

Eventually everything goes calm, although they're well guarded after being herded into the kitchen. Magda knows throughout this ordeal that saying she's a DI would be pointless. They know anyway.

A man she doesn't recognise comes into the room. He is wearing a sharp suit and is full of determined authority.

'I'm Detective Chief Inspector Roberts. Please stay seated. I need to ask you a few questions. I know this has been frightening, but this is a murder case and we are searching for a man with a gun.'

Magda can see her father is about to start blustering, so she glares at him.

'I understand,' she says, trying to sound calm. 'I'm DI Magda Steil and these are my parents. My father has a heart condition and … my mother. Please be…' but she can't find the words. And in any case her mother doesn't look frightened at all. More like an avenging harpy.

The inspector winces and tries to smile.

'I'm sorry, DI Steil. I'll try to be brief.'

She nods her appreciation.

'Can you tell us where … your brother … is?'

She shakes her head.

'I've no idea. He left about an hour ago.'

The inspector nods and glances at one of the other non-uniformed officers, who gabbles quickly into his mobile as he turns away.

'Alone?' the man said.

Magda shakes her head.

'No, with a woman he brought with him. We'd never met her before. She's called Imelda.'

The inspector looks again at his fellow officer, who relays that as well.

He looks at her mother, who glares back at him.

'Look … sir,' Magda manages, 'I need to look after my father.'

The man frowns but allows her to get her father into the sitting room and seated on his chair. A WPC appears and comes to kneel beside him. He looks at her and then folds his arms.

Mugs of tea are made and distributed while the inspector waits impatiently to ask the next questions.

Magda leaves her father and goes to him.

'Do you know which vehicle he was driving?' he asks.

She frowns.

'No, I don't. He may have parked it round the back, but I never saw it.'

His eyes close.

'Any idea where he's going?'

Again she shakes her head.

'He said to the 'MacDuffs', but we don't know of any and I think he made it up.'

He looks round at his fellow officers, but they're all shaking their heads.

'Well, DI Steil, you'll understand we're very worried about what your brother might be planning to do.'

She nods.

'Any ideas?'

She grimaces.

'No'.

He gives her stern look.

'Does he have a gun?'

She shrugs.

'I didn't see him with one, but there are guns in the cupboard in the hall … although …' and at this point for the first time she looks across at her father, 'I'm not sure they're the sort he would take.'

With what she later thinks is amazing sangfroid, her father pulls the keys out of his jacket pocket and holds them up for the inspector to see.

'None of mine, I don't think, Officer,' he says with a sneer. 'Never let the little blighter ever have them.'

The inspector can only stare.

'So you've no idea where he might have gone?'

Magda can only shake her head. And then she bursts into tears.

They ask for a recent photo of Tomasz, but are not particularly impressed with the poor, distant shot that Helena eventually finds. And they have to settle for Magda's description of 'Imelda', although both they and she think that's not likely to be her real name.

So, an hour later, apart from a quartet of the men in black who have been selected to stay with the family – and Magda can see from their surly faces they think they're going to miss out on the action – the house settles down into its usual slumber.

'What a busy few hours,' its walls must be thinking.

Her mother is still muttering under her breath, so Magda suggests making a meal for the uninvited guests, which gives them something to do. Her father has gone back to his books after announcing he will be speaking to the 'authorities' about this. She can't imagine if any of the people he used to know are still anywhere near any authority nowadays. Most of them are dead or gaga, she suspects.

She tries contacting Rico again but only gets his recorded message. She manages to have a terse, few words with the chief inspector, but he merely tells her to be patient and to look after her parents.

So eventually she asks to go back to her cottage and is outraged to find her laptop has gone. Again. At least she still has her mobile, but of course every call will now be listened to and recorded.

She stands in the garden looking down at Amelia's house. There are still signs of continued investigations, although the car has gone. And there is no smoke there any longer.

She stands there thinking,

'The house phone will also be tapped. But then where is my mother's mobile?'

She didn't want it and has probably hardly ever used it independently, but it was only renewed a couple of months ago.

She goes back to the house. Helena gives her a blank look and shakes her head, but Magda hasn't got to be a detective inspector without learning where old ladies tend to hide their unwanted phones.

It turns up in the little room where she does her sewing. It's out of juice, of course, but fortunately the cable is still in its box. She finds an old bag and says she's only going to the loo to the two men, who are, surprisingly, having a conversation with her mother.

She copies some of the numbers on her own phone she'll need and then pauses.

Who best to contact first?

***

Fletcher is standing in the conservatory looking out at the rain. When did it last do that?

At least Louisa is happy to see the downpour, which lasts most of the night.

His mobile chirrups.

The Stork. Can he be bothered with all that?

He sighs and presses the button.

'There's been a development,' she says, before going on to succinctly report the goings-on at the Steils' house.

He shrugs.

What can any of them possibly do? A situation like that will have the worst sort of men in black crawling all over it. The worst set of uncommunicative, miserable bastards who he ever had the misfortune to 'work' with.

'They'll tell you nothing,' he says.

There's a tut and a pause.

'This is a case of national security,' she says, 'and we still need your help. Ask Louisa to get you in with the Zoom session in half an hour.'

With that she is gone.

Louisa has appeared during the course of the call and so he has to tell her. She beckons him along to the library, where her erstwhile young man has set everything up before he was furloughed.

'What a strange word on everyone's lips,' he thinks. It sounds like something to do with horses or daft runners.

Anyway, here he is, a coffee at his side, awaiting the call.

Louisa has gone back to reading the paper.

He stares at her, his mind whirling with guilt.

Did last night happen?

The culpability he has had to accept, but the visceral nature of the physical acts still keeps flashing through his head and his body.

She, as usual, seems to have taken it all in her stride. Is he merely the latest conquest? It almost makes him smile.

She glances over at him, aware of the intense inspection.

She smiles, briefly, before it mutates into her more familiar piercing stare.

He shakes his head, but a sly grin gives him away.

The laptop primly interrupts.

***

Becket is confused. This is not an unusual event, of course, but something is nagging at her. Something she's missed.

John is chopping wood, which she knows means he's thinking too.

Freya is sitting at the laptop Ziggy has given them. Becket is still mesmerised by the speed at which the woman uses the machine, like she's physically part of it ... an image that makes Becket shudder.

Something to do with the word 'assassin'.

And something connecting with that burning tower. She knows it's roughly north-west from where they are now, on the other side of Glasgow, over by the sea. Obviously, connecting back up with Fletcher and the weirdly omniscient Stork is worrying in itself. They always bring trouble with them like shadows.

She thinks about the woman whose husband has been shot. Is the policewoman's brother a suspect? Why would he do that? Why now? What does 'Freya' know? She's still not convinced it's her real name or that she's telling the whole truth, or if any of it is true.

As if she knows she's thinking of her, the green eyes turn her way. She frowns and then smiles.

What was that phrase that makes her shiver?

'Smile and smile and be a villain ... oh most pernicious woman.'

She can't help but smile to herself. She hated English literature at school. The teacher was a slimy villain who was eventually sacked, but long after she had left. Some people get away with murder for a long time.

'Ziggy says we're doing another Zoom in five,' says the 'pernicious woman'.

Becket nods at her and goes to find John.

As she steps out of the hut, she's struck by the silence. Where is he?

She finds him sitting on a log, gazing into the distance.

She goes over and strokes his shaven head.

He smiles up at her.

'Penny for them,' she says.

He shakes his head.

'Best not repeated,' he murmurs.

She frowns.

He gets to his feet.

'Soldier stuff,' he says.

She knows that's a closed door. Locked down. Do not attempt entry.

They go back indoors together holding hands.

It starts to rain again.

***

Of course, most of us are blissfully aware of what went on at the big house up the hillside this morning, but Magda has managed to bring Ziggy up to date. She can't be on the Zoom session because her mother's mobile isn't hooked up to such recent technology.

But the rest are there.

Between them Ziggy and Violet tell us what they know... which is that it seems that the police suspect that Magda's brother killed the man along the road, who's called Donald

Cameron. And the woman with the children who we rescued is his wife, Magda's childhood friend, Amelia.

The media lockdown implies that this is part of the political paranoia about the intentions of an assassin, who they seem to now believe is Tomasz Steil.

'But why would he kill this man along the road from his own family home?' asks Becket.

Violet shakes her head.

'Apparently, Tomasz and Amelia had an affair at some point. There's some indication that one of the children might be his. But we didn't get that from Magda, so let's keep it that way. OK?'

Lots of nodding heads.

'Jealousy?' suggests Louisa.

Fletcher, who is cramped beside her, frowns at this.

'Why now, if he's intent on some higher political target? Why risk being caught for something personal?'

The Zoom goes quiet, which is odd. The six faces all look perplexed.

'I think he's been set up,' says Violet quietly. 'The police are mounting a massive hunt, although it's all gone undercover. Helicopters were circling around earlier.'

They're all quiet for a few moments, although of course Ziggy's fingers are grobbling about on two or more other screens.

'So where do we think he might go? On the run? It's his own territory, mind you, and he's used to huddling about to avoid intense enemy observation,' says Violet.

'He'll need a change of vehicle,' says John, poking his face in beside Becket.

'We don't even know what vehicle he might be using. They could even be on foot,' says Ziggy.

'I doubt that,' says John, 'unless the woman is a trained soldier as well. He wouldn't risk carrying a passenger.'

Becket makes a face at this, but she knows he's right.

'They blocked the main road in both directions before they

went up to the house,' says Ziggy, 'and as far as I can tell there's only one minor road out as the only other route up north.'

'Not a problem,' says John, 'if he's in an off-road vehicle and knows the countryside well. Given his background and this locality, he'll have been on shoots all over the place. He'll know all the rough tracks and drove roads.'

'What we don't know is how long a start he had,' says Ziggy. 'I'll contact Magda now.'

Everyone watches as he calls her up. It's weird, I think, to see someone having to use older technology to be part of this. Mind you, it's still new to me.

The answer is,

'About an hour.'

Ziggy brings up a map in another screen, centred on the house up the hill, and quickly adds a wobbly line that indicates the driving distances in an hour from the house.

'To the east Berwick and the A1, north to Edinburgh, west to the M74, and south to the Kielder. He could be anywhere, and still moving as we speak.'

'We know, of course, that the police will have done this as well, and they may have a vehicle registration to follow,' says Violet.

'Not from what I've been able to pick up,' says Ziggy. 'They're in the dark.'

Everyone is quiet.

'So where would he go?' asks Violet.

'To someone he can trust,' says John.

Ziggy hesitates, then his fingers become a blur as he works on two or more screens at a time. Makes my eyes hurt.

'Where are you looking?' asks Violet.

Ziggy purses his lips.

'His service records. I found them yesterday. Scary. Losses among his troop were high. Lots of bad injuries. Men being sent home.'

We all wait, but eventually he sighs.

'Needle in a haystack. Need to give me some time.'

Violet decides it's best for us to close down and wait for what he can find. She's going to contact some other leads of her own, which implies they're not for common knowledge.

The Zoom disconnects and I go to make a coffee.

It all seems impossible to me. I've stared long enough at the local maps, and there are masses of upland areas without a building in sight. And only a few minor roads, which end in lonely farms. If you were going to choose somewhere to disappear, this would be a perfect place, especially if, like Tomasz Steil, you have known it so well, since childhood.

***

Becket is quiet.

But this is more to do with the behaviour of the two people she's shacked up with than her own concerns.

Freya has always puzzled her ever since she first met her.

What's that saying? 'An enigma wrapped up in...' She can't remember the rest.

Right now she's sitting at the table staring at the screen, but, unlike Ziggy, she's not touched it for some time. Becket is so intrigued that she wanders over to pick up her mug on the table beside the laptop. The screen is only the screen saver. It's John's laptop, so it's the Roman wall trundling along the ups and downs into a bloody sunset. Taken from above his house above Corbridge.

She goes to make some coffee.

John, on the other hand, has gone quiet. Again, this is indicated by the lack of chopping.

She goes out to find him.

He's at the outdoor table with the stack of maps that he's found in the hut.

They're all the local ones including some six-inch cycle

routes as well as all the OS Explorers. Her quick glance tells her he's looking west, beyond Peebles.

Why there?

She goes back to the coffee pot, pours the drinks, and takes them to the two silent shadows she seems to have inherited. She blames Ziggy.

She settles down opposite John, thinking he's less opaque than Freya and more likely to share his thoughts.

'What's up, Pussycat?' she asks.

He frowns at her and smiles.

'Not got you down as a Tom Jones fan.'

'There's a lot you don't know about me, John Shepherd, and a lot you are never likely to know either.'

'So cough up. What d'you think?'

His face is serious.

'OK, Detective, what do you know?'

She shrugs, thinking,

'Bugger all.'

John says,

'Steil was last spotted in Dunbar, filling up a car he presumably dumped when he got to the city.'

She nods.

'So he's there for three nights?'

She raises her eyebrows. He shakes his head at that.

'He acquires another car to drive south to his parents' house.'

She's thinking that the police will have already done this.

'I can't imagine that, no matter where he stayed in Edinburgh. The only sensible way to come would be the A7 to Stow and then along the lanes to the house.'

He shows her the route on two maps. She agrees.

'He'd leave from there and not go back to Edinburgh and I'd suggest he'd not go east either, where it's much more inhabited… That leaves south or west.'

She nods again.

'South takes him into the Kielder forest or the Cheviots, which is fine, except there are few settlements. You'd have to be really stocked up with fuel and food.'

She looks at the next of the maps he's unfolding on the table.

'So I'm betting west. It's slightly more populated, but it also has better escape routes, including Glasgow and beyond. I bet, for example, that he knows the Lomonds really well. Lots of training areas are out there, rather than the Cheviots, which are used by the English regiments.'

She's following all this, but is suspicious that he knows more than he's saying. After all, he's always been very reticent about his time in the field. Might he have been in Afghanistan at the same time as Steil?

'Well,' she says, 'this is all good, but presumably the police are going to be thinking the same.'

He nods, but then frowns.

'Yeah, but they have limited resources and must try to cover all the options.'

She nods. It always was the problem.

'Um, and we're dealing with a clever operator here, and someone with a plan. Someone who has been given a target. Almost certainly political. Not here. Down south.'

'So he's heading for the M74, M6, et cetera.'

He nods.

'And we know now he's got a long-range weapon. A kilometre or more.'

She frowns.

'They're saying that he shot the woman's husband from his own house.'

'Ah, right.'

It's only then they realise that Freya is standing behind them.

'Does either of you know who the Rocket Man is?' she asks.

The both stare at her.

'It's something I've been trying to recall. I saw it on a message. It was a transcript of a telephone recording that had been annotated, and they are always harder for me to remember.'

They both frown.

'I think the annotation said, "WTFH?"'

'What?' they both say.

***

One of the many advantages of being a good-looking guy in a uniform, especially one with Tommy's sexual appetite, is that there's invariably a port in any storm. Even when it's lockdown.

So here they are in the widow Crawford's house, in a nauseatingly ugly new estate outside Peebles. After her initial astonishment and look of alarm to find him at her door and the pathetic attempt to say he mustn't come in because of the situation, she falls for his ridiculous lies about being on some sort of secret undercover mission and needing a nice cup of tea, because all the cafes are shut.

Doreen obviously missed her latest hair appointment and must be well over fifty. She is wearing a dress that can only be called 'filled to the brim'. Red lipstick. White high heels. In the morning?

Imelda's sitting in the chintzy front room while he 'helps' Doreen with the coffee in the kitchen. She's not against a quick come and go herself, but listening to one offstage that sounds like someone pumping up a spare tyre with a strangled voice-over is excruciating.

But she has to admire his elan as they come back in with the cups, although the woman's hair sticking out in all directions and her smeared lipstick make her want to laugh out loud.

He goes over to window and looks out, as if he's checking to see if her dead husband is coming back from the pub.

'Anyway, Doreen, we can't stay. Got to be in Edinburgh by teatime.'

The woman gives 'the young lady' a glare.

'Are you sure, Geoffrey?' she says. 'I'm sure I could quickly rustle up a teatime treat for you and your secretary.'

'No thanks. And in any case Susan's on a diet, aren't you, sweetie?' he laughs, getting more and more camp by the second.

It couldn't come any sooner for Imelda, to be back out on the pavement walking away.

'Impressive,' she hisses as he gives a final goodbye and a flurry of air kisses.

Tommy's face changes.

'Needs must. Did you get the mobile?'

Imelda holds it up.

'And the clothes.' She points at the waterproof and the jacket on the back seat.

He stands watching as she pulls out the SIM card and throws it away, before dexterously replacing it with another one out of her bag.

Her old phone is now under the seat of Doreen's car, which hopefully she won't find for some time. She'll maybe report hers stolen, but the suspect she'll name doesn't exist. Thank goodness, thinks 'Imelda', who is of course used to people not being who they say they are.

'Where now?' she asks.

He gives her his wolfish grin.

'La Camargue.'

It isn't that far, it turns out. There is a beach, but there the resemblance ends.

They take an innocent turning off the small lane down into a wood. The road becomes a dirt track, savagely gouged by the rain and heavy vehicles. There's a steep final drop to the river, which she assumes must still be the Tweed, although it's going through a deep gorge at this point.

There's a glimpse of a castle high above on the other side, but then they turn away and it's hidden from view.

The trees here are densely packed firs and there's little sky or light until they're out into the evening sunshine, which they see glittering on the rushing water.

Their destination is a couple of well-hidden muddy fields running alongside the riverbank. There are some makeshift fences and five or six caravans, some on raised planking, up against the slope.

There's smoke from a bonfire next to a little jetty.

In the distance she can make out the looming line of a bridge high above it.

A few people, mainly children, are standing watching, staring at the newcomers.

Tommy stops the car and puts his hand on her arm.

'Stay here,' he says. 'You've got the wrong colour hair.'

She glares at him, but he only smirks and gets out of the car.

By now there are a few more adults appearing. All dark-skinned and dark-haired. She can see what he means.

Tommy walks purposefully towards them and puts out his hand to one of the men. They clasp each other and she can hear a few words, but they don't sound English.

The man laughs and pushes Tommy in the chest, but it's playful. Are they friends?

Now all the other people are gathering round him. There are lots of handshakes and kisses. Two for the women. Three for the children. No sign of social distancing here.

Until a small figure appears at one of the caravans.

Tommy strides over and goes up the steps. Two kisses, so another woman. Difficult to tell.

She watches as a few of the children creep over to the car.

One boy suddenly appears by her window, gapes at her, then runs away.

There's some excitement. The children group together in huddles, and then there is a succession of faces at the window. All excited dark, staring eyes.

She shakes her head and laughs. By the next time one appears she's taken off her scarf and loosened her shirt to reveal her snakes. The poor kid screams and runs away. They all gather in a huddle, whispering and staring back.

She later wonders how long this might have gone on, but then she sees Tommy coming back to the car.

'Come on,' he says. 'Hang on to your bag.'

She follows him to the caravan. The kids trail alongside them. She's pretty certain there are two or three touches, but she's got a strong hold of the strap.

Hengist is trying his best not to get into a fight. Lots of hackles and growling all round.

But then they're in the caravan.

It's as crowded as she is expecting.

Not with people but with piles of junk: a multicoloured assemblage of bric-a-brac and coloured materials … and, at the back, one old woman, sitting deep in a huge chair.

Later, having eaten what she hopes was mutton stew, she sits listening to the gabble of a language she can't recognise. It's sing-song, and yet with lots of harsh notes. Whether Tommy really knows what they're saying she's not sure. He doesn't say much, only nods and laughs, but occasionally he gives her an encouraging smile. Towards the end of the evening more men appear. They are more suspicious than the women and their voices are even more guttural and fast.

She can feel their eyes on her, like fingers in her hair. Not wanting to encourage them in any way, she tries not to smile at their glares.

It must be over an hour before he whispers to her that they need to go back to the car.

She follows him, still wary of the children, their dark eyes winking in the dark, who seem to have no intention of going to bed. Tommy whispers to her that they've been offered a bed, but they need to empty the car.

Later still they're huddled together on a mattress on the floor of another cluttered caravan. The children have stopped appearing at the windows, although she can still hear their voices and the occasional rocking of the caravan.

'What are we doing here?' she asks.

His eyes glint in the darkness.

'Change of vehicle,' he whispers. 'You did say you know how to ride, didn't you?'

She frowns at him.

'I do,' she says.

'I hope so. They're a bit wild.'

'Good,' she says.

He frowns, but she can't see that.

It's a long time before she goes to sleep. But Tommy, who unexpectedly doesn't want sex, is off the moment his head touches the pillow.

It's obvious that these people are gypsies, but she can't imagine how Tommy could have become their friend.

She wonders about the guns in the boot of the car. Is he giving them those as well? Where are they going to go on the horses? What will he do when he can't pay the remaining money? She's tried the mobile, but there's no signal down in this ravine.

Eventually she falls into a troubled sleep, still nervously gripping her bag to her chest.

CHAPTER 18

Magda can't sleep.

She's up in the middle of the night. Goes down to make a brew. Stands in the doorway looking up at the stars.

The moon is in Aquarius.

It's a clear sky again. Cold for this time of year and there hasn't been a drop of rain for ages, apart from last night. If Tomasz is sleeping rough, she hopes he's got his sleeping bag. As for that strange woman, she doubts she'll last the course. He's always bringing home women like her, just to infuriate his father.

She knows there are still at least three or four men outside, watching, no doubt feeling miffed, because nobody is thinking he'll come back there. Surely.

She goes back in when the shivering makes her spill the tea.

Unable to bear her mother's look when she said she was going back to the cottage, she's back in her old room. Although she knows she's a tough old bird. Anyone who's survived both the Gestapo and the Russians might fear the knock on the door, but they're inured to it in some way. They've learnt how to look at the floor and harden their hearts.

So where has he gone?

She's said she has no idea to the Special Branch guys, but thinks they don't trust her. They'd be right. Her brother is an arrogant bastard who thinks he's going to live forever, but underneath all that bravado she remembers his way with dogs and horses and other creatures, and this reminds her that Hengist has gone with him as well.

The other farm dogs miss him. She heard Jess calling for him last night. But she's curled up in the kitchen corner now, maybe dreaming of their joint exploits. Do dogs do that?

She can't believe he killed Donald Cameron. She knows he

held him in the deepest contempt and has shown that once, when he gave the man a thoroughly deserved good beating. But Amelia told him that only made it worse. So he'd settled for keeping out of her way since then.

Where will he have gone, carrying a woman like that?

Back to the big city would seem the obvious choice. Dump her, find a hideaway.

She sleeps.

But only for a couple of hours.

She gets up, has another brew, and goes to saddle up. If they try to stop her she'll tell them to follow her, if they like.

But there's no one in sight. Which means they're on to him somewhere else.

Her mother appears at the kitchen door as she walks Sandy down through the garden.

She waves and shouts, saying she's only going down to the river and back.

Her mother tries a smile, but it soon fades.

Magda grits her teeth and guides Sandy through the gate.

She doesn't look back until she's halfway down, and is relieved to see that her mother's gaunt figure is no longer standing at the kitchen door.

Soon she's down and across the road, and is surprised to find no one guarding the bridge the other side. She follows the track that skirts the Camerons' field and goes out onto the road. She wonders what's become of Amelia's horses. There is a van at the end of their drive and a figure gets out to watch her go, but she's not stopped. They've obviously decided that her brother is far away from here by now.

But are they aware of the strange couple staying in the cottage along the lane? And the others? She can't remember where they said exactly.

***

Tommy wakes Imelda before dawn. Well, before there's any sun in this wooded cleft.

A silent dark-eyed teenager takes them to the field beyond. One big mare for Tommy and a feisty-looking pony for Imelda. The young man has already fixed them up with saddles and helps them to mount. Tommy can immediately see that Imelda is as good as her word and is relieved that he doesn't have to abandon her.

The sun has only just nudged itself above the horizon when they come out onto an old railway bridge across a tumbling river. This turns into a well-maintained walking track and so they make good headway. Hengist is running this way and that, chasing the many animal scents and trails.

'It's only about four hours,' says Tommy, and as the wind has dropped since yesterday it's not so cold. Even so, she's glad he thought to take an old fleece and a pair of thick trousers for her from his parents' cloakroom. And a woollen hat he brought back from a trip to Peru. He hasn't told her where they're going, but she's enjoying the ride, and tries to put the thoughts about the big Chechen behind her.

The railway track turns out to be only a starter for ten, because within a mile or so they turn off and up into a wood with a few beech trees at the edge. But then it's a dark, straight tunnel through the firs where there's no end in sight. He slows to let her come alongside.

'They might figure out the sort of terrain I'd choose to follow, but as they don't know where or how far we're going the choices are endless. And they'll put most of the resources in the north.'

She pulls a face. He's probably right, although, knowing a thousand places she could hide, getting back to Edinburgh would be her choice. Preferably one with a shower. An unwashed fanny is not a good idea. She's already started to consider the pros and cons of a wilderness stream.

342

A coniferous plantation forest is quiet, with few birds and only the occasional startled deer.

She settles to the rhythm of her pony, and starts to pay attention to its flickering ears. Tommy is not hurrying these horses, but is letting them choose the pace. She gradually realises that they're gaining height as well.

They must have been going for an hour like this before there was an opening between two plantations. Tommy goaded his mare into a clumsy gallop and Imelda's pony went frisky with excitement. But it was all over in a few minutes and they were back in another dark tunnel.

There was once the droning of a helicopter, but they just waited among the nearest trees. It didn't even pass overhead.

The journey became so mind-numbing that she nearly fell asleep. She was jerked back in the saddle as the pony stumbled in a hidden rabbit hole.

'Is there anything more tedious than fir trees?' she thinks, and then remembers her one experience of golf, which makes her grin.

***

Ziggy has found something. It's easy to tell. Hi-fiving yourself looks a bit silly, but you have to smile.

He won't tell me, of course. Says he wants everyone to know at once.

So a Zoom is booked and he spends most of the time before it starts 'creating a presentation'.

We're nearly at Zoom time when there's knock at the door.

There's a haggard-looking detective standing there, with a white pony tied to the fence. I invite her in. She doesn't look like she's slept much, and she hasn't brushed her hair. I make her a strong coffee and tell her I'll make her some breakfast. I get a weak smile.

I know we shouldn't be doing this but I can't send her away, she looks so forlorn.

Ziggy explains that the Zoom call will begin in five minutes, but he's got to finish his show. He doesn't mention social distancing either, but then he thinks he's immortal.

The two of us are sitting there, at either end of the table, when his machines start to chime. It's a different sound from before. This one sounds like a clip from a film track, something I think I've heard but can't identify.

There's Becket looking stressed, and John looking determined. Louisa looking like she's just come back from the hairdresser's, as she always does. Fletcher looking strangely blank-eyed. Is he taking drugs? And the Stork, her pale eyes penetrating your soul, flanked this time by a woman I don't recognise, who is introduced as Bianca Kennedy. Scary eyes. Short dark hair, which looks like she's cropped it herself.

Ziggy's presentation is a collation of flashing images. Lots of jumbling faces and buildings and parties and school photos, which seem to coalesce into three distinct faces. Three boys. Then their three adult faces. Lots of photos. All smiling.

I recognise them and know why all three of them invite a varied press, as they're all arrogant weasels.

The final three photos are accompanied by the origins of the three noms de plume they've been given: 'the fag', 'adec' and the 'hugger'.

I think quite a few people would have guessed 'the fag', but now Ziggy's giving us chapter and verse. Equally, the 'adec' is exactly right when it's explained, but the 'hugger' is a surprise revelation of the man's family history, given the politics he espouses.

There's a reverent silence after the screen fades to the simple words,

'What do we do about it?'

If Ziggy was expecting a round of applause, he doesn't show any disappointment when there isn't one. I suppose we're all waiting for the Stork to pronounce, but she knows how to hold her audience.

'It's possible than many of you aren't surprised that it should be these three gentlemen, but think again.'

We all frown as if we are doing.

'You may find them detestable in their different ways, but that's not how the Tory faithful see them. These are the beacons of the Brexit mentality, the ones who voice their anger and their perceived sense of the betrayal of our historic English superiority.'

The frowns become nods. But there's still uncertainty, especially from me.

'But what Sigismund has uncovered is their real usefulness as expendable frontmen. The Guy Fawkeses who'll take one for the cause. They have been duped into thinking they'll get a chance at the top table. But they never will.'

'Why?' I ask, out loud, forgetting my humble position in this throng.

If we'd all been in the same room I think their heads would have all turned towards me, but they're already all looking.

Violet clears her throat, but it's Fletcher who speaks first, looking sideways at her with a grin.

'Bushy, Bagot and Green,' he says.

Violet smiles and nods.

Some private joke? Who are they?

'They're all outsiders,' he continues. 'Not part of the gang, not from the right background, the right families, the right schools, or the right sort of money.'

Violet nods and takes up the baton.

345

'They're what their monikers are: they're all "fags", "aides de camp" and "of foreign descent".'

'I accept that one of them did go to a public school, but it's not on the list,' says Ziggy.

I haven't even heard of the school the 'hugger' went to, so that's seems right.

We're all silent.

What does this mean?

All our heads are turning all the possible conclusions and suspicions and questions around in a Zoom brainstorming.

'It means,' says Violet, as if she can hear us all asking these questions, 'that they're expendable. They're the fall "Guys". Not only as sacrificial lambs but more than that… Their deaths, their "martyrdom", will enable vindication, revenge, "a threat to our democratic liberty".'

There are now a lot of frowns.

'Any one of these three being killed would enable a different sort of lockdown. Limitation of rights, meetings, opposition, marches … fighting in the streets, water cannons, stun guns. A police state. You think the Americans have problems? The far right always thrives in such situations. Hitler and Goebbels were masters of repeating the 'big lies', although they claimed they learnt it from the English.'

She allows this to sink in.

'As my recently deceased friend Anthony declared in his last few words, "Every thread will be torn." Society will fall apart.'

We're all silent now. Our minds are racing, no doubt, but I can't really imagine what it would be like.

'Imagine what the different effects the opposition targets would have,' continues Violet. 'Some similar confusion. Maybe riots. But, if anything, it would be twisted the same way. But not as effectively. I can imagine the press statements:

'"Terrible, not acceptable," but then there would be the caveats. "He did ask for it. She did go walkabout. He didn't take *the warnings seriously. She upset a lot of people, et cetera, et cetera".'*

This doesn't help. Not me anyway.

'So how are we're got to stop him?' says a voice.

I can't figure out who it is until I realise it's not on the screen. It's behind me in the room. Magda is sitting by the door.

The others on screen are all squinting. They can't figure out who it is, or what was said.

I look at Ziggy. He shrugs and turns towards her.

'Do you want to be seen?' he mouths.

She shakes her head. He nods his understanding. Hands me a pair of earphones with a mouthpiece. I lob it across to Magda. It doesn't have a wire, but Ziggy presses a couple of buttons and she's on. He puts his finger to his mouth and then his fingers patter away. Satisfied, he nods and whispers to her,

'You're scrambled.' She nods her understanding.

The others have waited patiently while this is going on, but now we can hear her voice.

'I've really no idea where he's gone,' she says.

Everyone waits again.

'He's with a woman. She says she's called Imelda, but I doubt that's true. She's pretty easy to identify. Blonde hair, left side of her head shaved, dragon tattoos on her neck and hands, no doubt the rest of her body as well. She was dressed in bits of floating black silk and taffeta, so she'd need some decent outdoor gear to survive out there. They arrived on foot, but they must have a car, although Tomasz has roamed these hills since he could walk. My bet is he will have ditched the car for a horse. He knows lots of people who wouldn't hesitate to lend him one. Don't know whether she can ride, but if she can't he'll ditch her as well.'

Everyone is listening intently to this, but no one says anything yet.

'Assuming they get some horses, he'll stick to the forests and plantations, avoid all the settlements, but he can also rely *on any number of people for food and shelter ... even if there's an all-points bulletin out for him, which I doubt is happening straight away. The officers who came here aren't local. They're not even Scottish. They're the men in black: ruthless, highly trained, and will shoot to kill if that's the order.'*

Again, no one speaks, asks questions or makes a move.

'So I can't help you much. I'm shielding, and regarded with suspicion anyway. They probably know I'm here.'

There's a long silence after this. A lot of brains are straining to come up with some response, but really they are all waiting for some leadership.

Which eventually comes from Violet.

'I need to talk to people,' she says. 'Give me a couple of hours.'

Everyone agrees.

The connections go down.

Our little cottage is still.

For once Ziggy has nothing to say. He is not even fingering his pads. I do what I always do. Make some tea.

When I come back they go silent. They've been talking. I could hear their mumbled conversation.

Magda stands up, downs the tea, nods at me, and sidles out of the room.

I'm left with himself, looking glum for once.

'What ails thee?' I ask.

He shrugs.

'Nada. Tutto.'

Even I know what these words mean.

***

Becket wonders why Freya didn't say anything in the Zoom session.

But as soon as it's finished the strange woman is back on her own laptop.

The only thing Becket can come up with about Rocket Man is Elton John's song. Her mother had it in her record collection, used to play it occasionally. But then there was also the film that was made more recently.

She checks out the lyrics, but can't see anything relevant.

But then she remembers there was another Rocket Man, a few years ago. It was one of David Bowie's last releases. She looks at it. It's entitled 'Like a Rocket Man', but it's about a junkie woman.

She goes to find John, who's sitting on the woodpile, rather than adding to it.

'Penny for them?' she says.

He shakes his head.

'Tell me the words of the song.'

She stares at him.

'I wasn't even born, but my mum used to play it.'

'Can you tell me the lyrics?' he asks.

She goes back into the hut and brings out the laptop, plays him 'Rocket Man' and then 'Like a Rocket Man'.

He shakes his head.

'It's not there.'

She frowns at him.

'What's not there?'

'His name.'

'Whose name?'

'The Rocket Man's name.'

'It's Major Tom,' says a voice behind them.

They turn to look at Freya.

It's not in Elton John's 'Rocket Man'. It's in Bowie's 'Space Oddity'.

John slaps his forehead.

'Of course. "This is Major Tom to Ground Control,"' he sings out loud.

Becket is looking from one to the other. Are they both going stir-crazy?

'So?' she asks.

John is on his feet.

'When Freya asked who the Rocket Man was, I knew it meant something. The original song was way back – we weren't even born – but in Afghanistan there was this guy, an old soldier. He should have been discharged years ago, but he was so good at repairing stuff, particularly guns, I mean out in the field, that they kept keeping him on.'

Both Becket and Freya are staring at him now. They're both thinking that John's lost it.

'The thing is, he was called Major Tom. He wasn't a major – don't think he even made it beyond sergeant – but he loved the song, would sing it whenever we got in a hole. Bloody annoying, actually. Anyway, he was booted out eventually. Way past his sell-by date. I think he became something of a mascot.'

The two women are still waiting to see where this Ancient Mariner's story is going.

'So? asks Becket, who is rather shorter of the patience gene than most people.

'Well,' he says, trying to squash the grin coming into his cheeks, 'he's a Scot and I think he lives not far from here.'

'So?' says Becket. 'I think if Tomasz shot the man along the road, he must already have a gun good enough to shoot eight hundred metres or so.'

'Yeah, but Tomasz Steil would regard that as a toy. He uses things like Maxims.'

'Why? what's so special about them?''

Now John's face is serious again.

'Because with one of them he can kill people over a mile away.'

Both the women frown.

'That's not possible,' blusters Becket.

John speaks quietly.

'Check it out. I did a few days ago. He's one of the top ten marksmen in the world. Held the record for a few months a couple of years ago. Not quite a mile and a half.'

Freya nods her head.

'He's right.'

Becket looks from one to the other.

'Does Ziggy know this?'

'Probably, but not about "Major Tom", or he would have said.'

They're all quiet.

'I need to make a call,' says John.

Becket frowns.

'Wait a minute,' she says, and she gets up and goes back into the hut.

Freya sits down at the bench and stares into the woods.

Becket comes back with a mobile.

'Ziggy gave it me. It's untraceable, he says.'

John grimaces.

'I hope so. I don't want any of my friends on someone's list.'

But he goes to find his own phone and is inside for some time.

The two women can't think of anything to say. The afternoon sun is waning and about to fall below the hill.

Eventually he reappears. His face is stern. He shakes his head.

'I can't get into army records. Don't know where he is, but I do remember him talking about this place where he said he was going to retire to, which was somewhere "back of beyond", something "cleuch", which isn't much help. There are thousands of them. It means a gully in the Borders.'

The other two look at each other.

Becket is thinking,

'Do you mean there are places more back of beyond than here?'

***

Magda rides back over the river and up the hill.

She's deep in thought as she walks Sandy up through the gate and into the yard. She gives her some hay and goes back into the house.

Afterwards she told herself she should have realised. But the shock of seeing her mother sitting in the kitchen chair with a towel tied around her mouth stops her dead in her tracks.

A small man appears at the doorway to the hall. He's pointing a gun at her.

He grins. A Dickensian leer.

She senses someone behind her.

Another man. A giant. He fills the doorway. He has enormous hands. A full-length black leather coat. A shaved head. And he sports a long, deep scar on the side of his face.

Her mother's eyes are staring at her.

The first man steps into the room. The gun is now dangling arrogantly from his fingers.

He motions her to sit on the other chair.

She does as she's told.

'Your old man's OK,' says the man, 'for now. He's gone to bed early.'

She glances behind, but can only make out the huge shadow blocking the light from outside.

She frowns.

He reads her mind again.

'Don't think much of the protection,' he says. 'It's OK. One of them has a headache. The other needs to go to hospital, but he'll live.'

She realises the accent is Russian, but then can't stop wondering why there were only two of them.

'I don't know where he is,' she says.

The man leans forward. His eyes have gone hard. She can see the barbed-wire tattoo on his neck.

'Try again.'

She shakes her head.

'I'm out of the loop, shielding. They're not telling me anything. Not even giving my family decent protection.'

The man stares at her. His eyes are red-ringed.

She can sense the size of the man behind her. He smells of … bad meat?

Then he's grabbed her by her hair, pulled her head back, and there's a cold blade at her neck.

The sitting man shakes his head.

The man behind pushes her back to the chair with a grunt.

The man in front gets to his feet.

'We're going to take your *Mamusia* for a little ride. You'd better find where he's gone. We'll be in touch.'

Her mother's eyes go even bigger, but she doesn't cry.

They're gone.

She rushes upstairs and finds her father. He's wheezing and in shock but otherwise not harmed, as far as she can tell. She quickly unties him and rubs his red wrists.

She explains what's happened to her mother. He wavers between anger and despair. Then gives in to the latter and weeps pathetically. She holds him close and realises he's hardly any flesh on him. She can feel his bones through his jumper.

She thinks of Rico but then remembers Ziggy has given her a phone, so she rings him. He hesitates, but then says he'll call the local police.

She thanks him. Feels numb. Thinks of the look in her mother's eyes.

Rico arrives in less than half an hour, accompanied by an ambulance crew and quite a lot of other people she doesn't recognise.

She doesn't even see the two guys who've been disarmed by the gangsters.

Rico is terse. He has obviously been told to watch what he says. The ambulance crew want to take her father to the hospital, but neither he nor she want to do that. So after checking him out they relent, and leave her with a few pills.

She's told the armed protection is being beefed up and they've got some leads, but other than that it's all over in less than an hour.

She goes through the motions of giving her father something to eat and then puts him to bed. When she looks in ten minutes later, he's still awake staring at the wall. He's been there before.

Worrying for him, she sits down on the bed and holds him in her arms. He whimpers like a dog, but eventually the medication overtakes him and he drops off to sleep.

She stays with him for a long time, until his breathing is regular.

It's only then that her anger at Tomasz begins to ferment, but she's no idea where he is or how to contact him.

Selfish bastard.

But then starts to think about the security men. Only two? There are more now, she's been assured, but can't help thinking,

'Stable door.'

She tries not to think about her mother, but then bursts into tears.

***

Tomasz thinks it's best to wait an hour or so, as the last few miles are out over the open moorland. They shelter at the edge of the last plantation.

He can see the slight rise of the oddly named Macbeth's Castle, which has nothing to do with either the old king or Shakespeare's twisted version. From up there you can make out a lot of the ancient fields and see the stone piles from abandoned crofts and medieval buildings.

And the towers.

He can see already the courtyard and tower where Major Tom is holed up. He is inclined to think that he spends more time in the outhouses than the house.

Soon they're making their way down in the dusk and find an old track heading the right way.

It's dark when they trot through the gateway and onto the cobbles.

There are no lights on in the house or the tower. But, as he suspected, there's an outside light burning in the corner of the courtyard and smoke billowing from the chimney.

He gets down from the mare and ties her to a nearby rail. It looks like Tom's turned into a proper blacksmith because there are lots of old horseshoes nailed to the wall. Imelda does the same. He puts his fingers to his lips and makes his way to the door in the corner, but he only gets halfway, before there's a strangely high-pitched voice telling him to stay where he is.

Tomasz does as he's told.

A figure appears at another doorway over to his left.

'What do ye want?' comes the voice.

Tomasz turns and holds out his arms.

'I expect you've been watching us since we came out of the trees … Major.'

There's an intake of breath. A gravelly laugh.

'Whit are ye doing here, ye Polack bastard?' rasps the voice.

'Whit d' ye think? I need a gun.'

The figure comes out from the shadows.

He's smaller than Imelda was expecting, almost a dwarf, and only comes up to her shoulder. He has a thick thatch of white hair falling over a bulbous, pitted nose and deep-set piggy eyes.

There's a peculiar stand-off for a few more seconds. Then there are some more exclamations and then Tomasz is picking the little guy up in a bear hug.

Imelda is introduced, the horses are put into the field out at the back, and bales of hay are handed out before they all go into the one-storey house on the north side of the courtyard.

The fire in the grate is resuscitated and drinks are poured. Tomasz is put in charge of renovating a stew on the hob, while Imelda is told to open some wine. Hengist has sniffed everywhere, but, disappointed not to find a friend, settles down to act as a fender, until he's so hot he has to retreat to the corridor.

It's not until after the meal, and they're all draped across the two old tapestry-covered settees, that Tomasz gets down to the reason for the visit.

The old guy listens attentively. His eyes going big at the mention of the proposed possible targets.

'Are you sure?' he mutters. 'Ah mean, all three of them deserve much slower deeths than that.'

Imelda is quiet.

Tomasz looks at her. Her green eyes are hard and her dragon neck is flickering in the firelight.

'You never told me that,' she says.

Tomasz shrugs.

'You never asked.'

She shrugs back, not sure whether to be more scared or more intrigued.

'Why?' she asks.

He looks into the fire.

'Why not?'

They're all quiet for a while.

'I can't guarantee to fix your gun,' says the little guy. 'I've got lots of equipment, but if it's the latest model I might not even have the specs.'

Tomasz shakes his head.

'It's not the latest. It's maybe ten years old.'

Again, there's a long silence.

'Well, we'd better take a look at it, then.'

Tomasz goes and fetches the bag.

They get it out on the polished dining table.

Imelda watches as the two of them expertly reassemble the weapon. Each click and clunk is met by a shake of the head from the small man.

'Needs a good clean, but the piece that's missing is hard to make.'

Tomasz sighs.

But then the old guy chuckles.

'So it's lucky for you that I have one similar.'

Tomasz frowns.

'Really?'

'This is Mission Control,' he croaks, his little eyes sparkling like little glass beads.

CHAPTER 19

Imelda eventually tires of the reminiscing about the army and sets off to find a bed.

Major Tom gives her directions, but then appears with some towels and shows her into a surprisingly ornate bathroom.

'It's not the one I use,' he laughs. 'It was like this when I arrived.'

He's already told them that this was his uncle's house and although they never got on, he inherited it as the only surviving relative.

He shows her the guest bedroom as well, which is a wood-panelled room bigger than her entire flat in Edinburgh, with a four-poster bed and lots of wardrobes full of women's clothes.

'His wife's, I assume,' he says. 'She was quite the lady in her time. I meant to give them all away, but never got round to it.'

Imelda knows she could make a fortune with some of this stuff on the Grassmarket, if and when the lockdown ends.

She lies a long time in the enormous bath, soothing her aching limbs.

The two men's voices drone on and on, interspersed with cackling and whooping laughter.

She comes awake in the cooling water and gets out and dries herself, and looks at her thin body in the floor-length mirror. What is she doing here? Is it time to split in the morning? She's spotted a little van parked in the corner.

She walks naked back to the bedroom and is soon snuggling down under a cool duvet. She shivers and then lies listening.

It's all gone quiet. What are they doing?

She dozes off.

She comes awake with a start.

A shadow moves in the dark.

She tenses.

But then the moonlight catches the side of his face. It's Tomasz.

He's takes off his clothes and gets in beside her.

They embrace.

He stinks of whisky.

But they kiss and begin to explore each other's bodies. She's half-asleep, but he wants more. She gives it to him, but not in the way he was expecting. She's stronger than he expects and he's drunk. She punishes him for all the trouble he's causing her.

Lying satiated, she's happy to hear him snore.

Maybe once more in the morning and then she'll be gone.

***

The big black Volvo is parked in a hidden lay-by north of Stow.

Helena is lying on the back row of seats of the seven-seater.

Her hands are still tied with what feels like a piece of washing line, but they've put a blanket over her.

She's not said a word to them and knows they've decided she's too scared to try and get away.

She waits till she can hear one of them snoring. It's the smaller man, who seems to be in charge. She takes a peep over the middle seat. He's lying across the car, covered with his coat. There's no sign of his gun.

Making sure she can't be seen in the mirror, she checks out the big man. He's sitting in the passenger seat at the front. Not moving, so he could be asleep. She ducks down again.

She starts to work on the washing line.

It's plastic, so when licked it gets slippery. What these two thugs don't know is that she's been tied up before, when she was a teenager in Soviet bloc Poland. She was out with a street gang when the local *Ubeki* were doing a round-up and ended up in the cells for a couple of weeks. She was abused and threatened with worse, but then released.

'Think of it as a lesson,' they said. She was a good learner. She and her friend Zozo had practised hard by climbing walls, sloshing around in the underground drains, scaling up the sides of buildings and opening locked windows from the outside.

And figuring out how to get out of handcuffs and ropes.

She was good at it. It's just a matter of patience and the flexibility of your fingers and thumbs. Even though she's sixty-eight this year, a lifetime working with horses and cattle has kept her fit. She grits her teeth, closes her eyes and makes her breathing steady.

Gradually the knot begins to loosen. A few more twists and she's free. She rubs her thumb. Feels something cold by her shin. Reaches down. It's a wheel wrench. One of those heavy ones, covered in grease.

She pulls it out.

What is she going to do?

She can't reach the back of the big man's head even if she tries and it's the sleeping man who had the gun. Where has he put it? She doesn't think she can open the boot door from the inside. So what?

She uses the cloth to wipe away a lot of the grease off the handle, so she can get a good grip of it.

The car rocks.

The big man is opening his door. Cold air rushes in. The car leans over as he gets out into the dark. She waits while he shuts the door and she can't hear him before she peeps out of the window.

He's standing about five yards away with his back to her and his legs wide apart.

While he's out she stuffs the wrench inside her coat and wraps the rope round her wrists. She waits till he opens the door and clambers back in.

'I need to go too,' she says in her best feeble old lady voice.

He turns to look at her, grins and shakes his head.

'OK, *dama*,' he says, and gets back out again.

He comes round to the back door and opens it up.

She struggles to get out holding the wrench to her chest inside her coat with her hands apparently tied.

He doesn't offer to help, just grins as she struggles.

She staggers a few yards and turns her head to look at him.

'Are you going to watch?' she asks.

He sniggers again, but turns away.

She checks that he's not looking, takes three steps towards him, pulls out the wrench and wallops him hard on the back of his head.

He collapses like a bullock in the butcher's shed.

A couple of twitches and then still.

'If he's dead', he's not my first,' she reminds herself with a shudder. She turns back to check the other man is still asleep. He has not stirred. She considers repeating the strike, but her courage wanes.

Instead she goes over to the big man's body and checks his pockets. The knife feels cold and is surprisingly heavy. The thought of what she has done makes her shiver again.

The blood on the back of his head has stopped flowing.

She goes back to the car and opens the side door.

Inside the man's head is half-covered by the coat. The cold air wafts over him. He stirs. And opens his eyes, which then go wide.

He can feel the cold blade of the knife on his cheek. The coat is pushed aside. The point of the knife digs into his cheek. He winces and his hand comes up.

'If you move I'll have your eye out,' says a hoarse voice, in Russian.

He stares at her face upside down.

She grabs the collar of his jacket and pulls him half out of the car. He's still lying on his back. His hands come up. She slashes at one of them. He yells. The gun, which he's put in his jacket pocket, falls out onto the ground. She bends down and snatches it up. He's yelling in pain and lunges at her. She jumps back and points the gun at him.

Despite the cut on his arm, he manages a laugh.

'You're not gonna do that, old lady.'

The shot is astonishingly loud.

They both stare at each other.

Somehow or other she's missed him.

But now she's got both hands on the gun and is pointing it firmly at him again. So now he changes his tune and starts wheedling.

She backs away and points the gun at one of the back windows and fires again. The glass shatters and splinters shower all over him.

By now he's a huddling wreck. His hands are over his head.

She waves the gun at him. He scrambles to get out and gets on to his knees.

She points the gun at him. It's wavering, but that makes it worse.

He stares at her.

'Run,' she says, her voice taking on an evil menace.

He frowns.

'I said, "Run,"' she shouts.

He staggers to his feet, backs away and runs.

Into the darkness.

She waits until his footsteps recede, then quickly gets into the car. The keys are in the ignition. She fumbles at it and it stalls. Tries again. It starts. She realises it's automatic, like hers, and sighs with relief. She sets off.

Twenty yards down the road she sees him staggering along, holding his arm.

Something snaps inside her head. She swerves the car.

There's a jolt and she struggles with the wheel. A white, staring face is down on the ground beside the window.

She carries on.

It's only then that she is aware of the racing of her heart.

She puts her foot down and speeds into the darkness.

***

Despite the drink and the beating he took last night, Tomasz is up and out before Imelda the next morning.

'No chance of a last goodbye,' she thinks.

She drops off again, only coming round a second time when she hears the sound of gunshots.

She gets dressed quickly and goes down to the kitchen, which is empty, although the kettle is still warm.

Outside she listens to the echoing sound rippling off the hills.

'Not a surprise to hear that sort of noise around here,' she supposes.

They're round the back. Tomasz is kneeling with a huge gun resting on a tripod aiming into the distance. As she gets close she can't see a target. But he fires again.

The old man is standing next to him with a pair of binoculars.

'Two feet out,' he mutters.

Both the men turn to look at her.

'Breakfast?' she asks.

They look at each other and grin.

'Are you offering, young lady?' says the older man.

Tomasz laughs.

'Don't look a gift horse, Tom. It'll be a first for me as well.'

She pulls a face and turns her back on them as she walks away.

'It'll be on the table in twenty so you'd better be there,' she calls as she disappears round the corner.

Tommy hands over the gun and the older man twiddles the sight with his tool.

They try another three times, but they're still not happy.

The major decides to take it back to the workshop, but agrees to postpone that and do as they've been told.

**

The first thing Magda hears is the dogs barking.

She sits up. Can't figure where she is, but then realises she's on a mattress on the floor.

Not two yards away she sees a pair of eyes staring at her.

It's her father.

She remembers. Tears come. She brushes them aside and gets to her feet. She goes to him and kneels. He stares at her. Is he OK? His hands are freezing, but now he focuses on her and manages a thin smile.

But the dogs are still barking. And there are some yelps as well.

She gets up and pulls on her big jumper and, after telling her father to stay where he is, sets off downstairs.

But by the time she gets down, still worrying what the dogs are getting so excited about, she realises that it doesn't sound like how they bark when they think there's an intruder. It's more like someone they know.

It's still dark.

The kitchen clock says three thirty.

She puts the kitchen light on.

Is that someone at the door?

She goes over to unlock it, but now she can see the thin figure through the glass panes.

Unbelievably, it's her mother.

She fumbles with the key, eventually manages to turn it the

right way, and wrenches the door open. Helena falls into her arms. She's weeping with exhaustion.

Magda helps her to a chair. Helena's freezing. Her hair is wild. Her eyes are even wilder. She's shivering. Gibbering. Can't speak.

Magda grabs the big dressing gown off the back of the door and wraps her in it. Holds her tight. Can't think what to say. How can this be? How has she escaped?

Her father comes stumbling into the room. She helps the two of them to embrace. They're all weeping with relief.

It takes a long time for them all to calm down.

Magda goes and gets blankets and gets the stove going again. She makes some tea and puts bread in the toaster, all the time wanting to know what has happened.

Eventually the crying and shivering calm down.

Magda and her father sit staring at Helena, who's finally managed to be calm and manages to speak.

'I think … I think … maybe … I've killed them.'

The daughter and husband stare at her.

Magda can only manage a,

'But—'

Helena shivers again and then nods, before bursting into tears again.

Eventually Magda gets her to tell them what happened.

She remembers the stories that come tumbling out when her mother and her best friend Zofia meet up. The tours round Krakow to the 'important' sites, not the tourist ones, but where the much more significant teenage 'adventures' occurred.

They always seemed so unreal, like they were making it all up. As she got older Magda got irritated by these 'imaginary histories' and would say things like,

'Yadda, yadda, yadda,' or, 'For heaven's sake, Mother,' to shut her up.

But now?

What are they going to do?

After all, she is a police officer.

She ought to be on the phone. Except of course she hasn't got one, apart from her mother's. The gangsters took it away, as well as ripping the landline's cable and socket out of the wall. And of course she can't remember any numbers. No one can nowadays, can they? There's never been a line at the cottage. Old Jamie never wanted 'the blethering thing'.

Helena is now holding her weeping husband, who's still recovering from shock. He needs to be safe. What should she do?

She thinks of Amelia, but then remembers she's gone to stay with her mother in Melrose.

What about Ziggy and Ursula? But she knows the cottage is too small.

Where can they go?

Then it hits her like a bolt out of the dark.

She decides not to tell her mother, who is giving her a puzzled look. Best to just get on with it.

She rushes around collecting important stuff, which turns out to be clothing and toiletries, her dad's meds and a few of his books. Nothing of the houseful of treasures and memories.

Her mother's frown has changed into the realisation that they're fleeing. She knows about fleeing. She disappears and returns with a small battered case, as if she's always been prepared for this.

Magda doesn't ask. Just grins and nods her head. Helena gives her a stern look, but then it becomes a malicious sparkle in her eyes.

Helena bundles her husband into the passenger seat of the Land Rover and gets in the back. Magda shouts at the three dogs over in the boot to calm down, which only makes then howl and yap louder.

They've locked the house up and they now set off.

An adventure. How long ago did they last have one?

They get out to the gate and Magda realises she's forgotten all about the protection.

How did her mother get past them?

The men are confused.

'Where are you going?' they ask. She tells them.

They talk to their superiors. They try to persuade them to stay. But Magda is savage in pointing out their previous inability to protect them and, revving her engine, scatters them out of the way. There is the sight of a few white faces staring at them as she spins in the gravel and accelerates through the gateway yelling,

'Geronimo.'

It's only as she's speeding down the long lane to the main road that she thinks of Tomasz.

Wherever the hell he is, she knows he'd be laughing and hooting at this, demanding to know who the worst-behaved family in the Borders is right now.

Once on the main road she hurries to the big roundabout before turning off on to a minor road, which will take them most of the way to their destination. What it will be like she's no idea, but she can only hope the old aristocratic bonds will still be strong and they'll be received with welcoming arms.

***

Tomasz is watching Imelda.

Not her usual persona.

The little wifie getting her men's breakfast on the table?

He grins at her. She pouts back.

His back is sore.

Does he want more beatings like that? It was not exactly unpleasant, in fact quite arousing, but…

He looks out of the window.

Another cold, dry day. The sun is already high in the east.

Does he really want to carry on with this?

The gun's a problem, but it's more what he's going to do with it that is bothering him. He's no cold-hearted James Fox or a sick killer like Bruce Willis. He knows that his prowess is nearer to sharpshooting at plastic ducks in a funfair booth than being a political weapon.

He now understands the contradictory sly thinking of the selection of such targets. People he has no sympathy for at all. His father might espouse similar politics, but is far more wrapped up in the past.

His sister has a naive belief in the rule of law. He knows the false hope in that.

So what if he turns it on its head? Shoots one of the real villains? Bojo or his *éminence grise*?

Surely that would produce the same result. After all, he's only a frontman. A Jolly Roger on the mast. Along with the other Jolly Rogers, flying the flags of lies and illusions. Telling them only 'bigly' lies. The English superiority. Ruling the waves. All that jingoistic tosh.

No, they are, pathetically, only the motley crew.

The real villains hide in the sunshine on treasure islands, already whining about the loss of their hyperinflated profits. Already posturing about the 'damage to the economic model', which is strangling the nation's abilities to look after their slaves.

He sighs.

Who is he to complain about or solve these conundrums?

Imelda bangs the plate down in front of him.

His temper flares and dies. But she sees it. Instantly fears it. Turns away.

He tries and misses to catch her arm, whispers,
'Sorry,' so softly that she doesn't hear it.

It's late morning when the major declares that the gun is ready
and he's found some extra ammunition.

Tomasz take a few more practice shots, but he doesn't need
any more convincing. It's serviceable.

He goes to find Imelda. She's sitting on a wall smoking a
joint.

She offers him a blow. He shakes his head.

They sit there together, not touching.

The sun is high in the sky. Not a cloud in sight.

'I'll only slow you down,' she eventually says quietly.

He smiles.

What else can he say?

An hour later, at the crest of the hill, he turns to look back
down at the house.

She's still sitting there on the ground by the wall.

He waves.

She waves back.

He turns and sets off into the woods. There are real trees
here all the way to the road.

***

Ziggy has found a few possible places fitting the 'back of
beyond' place with the cleuch credentials.

John has found the relevant map in the hut.

There are not only a few cleuches, there's a whole tribe of
them up in the hills south of Peebles. He points them out in the
long valley, which ends in a fan-shaped clutch of them.

'A clutch of cleuches,' says Becket, laughing at her own
joke.

The most likely place Ziggy suggests that fits the bill is an
old steading, which was a blacksmith's back in the day.

'So we're going to the even further back of beyond?' sighs Becket.

'I guess so,' he replies. 'What's not to like? Have you got anything else to do? Going online to buy some summer dresses ... nice pair of high heels?'

She pulls a face. Doesn't grace that with a reply.

Freya goes to fetch their coats.

He follows the back roads almost all the way into Peebles, but then takes a turning through a new housing estate and heads off up an increasingly bumpy lane into the hills.

It takes about two hours before they pull up in front of the red stone courtyard.

The gate is open and they walk onto the stone flags. There's some thick black smoke coming from a chimney over one of the outhouses in one corner. They can hear the occasional clang of a hammer on metal, confirming the expectation that this is probably the sort of place you could fabricate weapons, both old and new.

There are horses grazing in the field though another gateway to the far side. A shaggy pony gallops restlessly about, stopping only to look their way.

A woman comes out from a doorway in the corner.

She's not an old lady. Quite the opposite.

She's dressed in black overalls and a high-necked woollen jumper losing some of its threads and wearing a big pair of old Doc Martens. Her blue-black fringe bob cut looks a bit too shiny to be found up there in this wilderness.

She stops and gives them a glare.

'Can I help you?' she asks.

'We're looking for a couple of people,' says Becket.

The woman stares. The big jumper's not hers. Her fists are gripping the sleeves from inside.

'One... Is the person we think owns this place called Major Tom?'

'And you are?' the woman asks, with a sneer.

Becket sighs and produces one of her old police identity cards.

The woman holds out her hand, which is covered in a selection of old rings, winking silver and gold.

Becket steps forward and offers it to her.

She merely glances at it.

'Way out of yer jurisdiction, fella,' she smirks, while Becket is still trying to place the accent.

Becket shrugs and takes out her mobile.

'I can call in the locals for support if you want.'

'That won't be necessary,' says a voice from their right.

They all turn to see an old guy with a hammer in his right hand and blackened arms up to his elbows. He's wearing a leather apron over a greasy overall.

He wipes his hand with a slightly cleaner cloth and offers it up with a grin.

'You'll have to forgive Miriam. She's had too many unhappy dealings with officers of the law.'

Becket manages a forgiving smile, but also a questioning look.

'I'm Major Tom,' he says.

Becket nods and produces the photo of Tomasz in uniform, which Ziggy has printed off for her.

The old man cleans his glasses on a cleaner cloth he takes from his pocket.

'Maybe,' he says. 'It's some time ago. My memory's not as good as it was.'

'Let me give you some help,' says Becket. 'He's called Tomasz Steil. Captain. Currently temporarily discharged, pending investigation into unsavoury activities while on leave.'

The old man laughs.

'Well, that's not a first.'

Becket waits, stony-faced.

'I'm afraid that's what he's like, although he's also one of the best marksmen I've ever known.'

Becket nods.

'That's why we think he might have come to see you.'

The old man grins.

'Don't be daft. What for?'

'He's been offered a job.'

'So, as I said, why come here?'

'Because you could provide him with the weapon.'

He stares at the three people and then laughs.

'Well, you'd better take a look,' he says and waves his arm towards the forge.

They do take a look, but as expected there's nothing to see. No guns, not even some bits. It's all horseshoes, bespoke kitchen and garden equipment and other trinkets intended for the good denizens of Peebles, no doubt.

He offers them a cup of tea, which they accept because it will allow them to take a further look round. There's no sign of Tomasz Steil. Maybe they would be able to find something if they got forensics up here, but then Becket reminds herself that she's no longer got that sort of authority.

Eventually they give up and drive away. Further up the valley first, until the road peters out. They get out and scan the hillsides, but there's no horseman in sight.

Disheartened and beaten, they drive back down the lane, with Becket wondering who the strange young woman might be. She doesn't exactly fit the description Magda gave them, even though that jumper could have hidden a load of snakes befitting a real Indiana Jones.

Later that afternoon, back at the forge, the young woman, who is now calling herself Miriam, is pondering the future.

The old man is lying asleep on the bed. He's exhausted,

poor bastard. Won't take much more of that sort of exercise. She scratches the fuzz of her shorn head. Fingers the strands on the wig – a good buy, in the circumstances. And now she's worn it for a few hours she's thinking when her hair grows back she'll have it like this.

She's already missing the taut muscle of Tommy's hard body... But, hey, she can hole up here for a bit. There are plenty of young farmers around for entertainment. And, if the bad guys do turn up, she has their gun, with the spare part attached.

***

Fletcher sits in Louisa's car, staring out at the Sainsbury's car park.

Maybe he isn't focusing on the people patiently standing in line in the spring sunshine, most of them wrapped up warm against the biting north-easterly wind.

It's this normal behaviour that depresses him most.

People getting the shopping. Having a chat from two metres away with a friend. Laughing. Sharing stories from 'the front'.

It will be the same in Todmorden, he reckons. Yorkshire folk making do.

But he can't stop thinking about her. Lying in her bed complaining or sitting sullenly in a brightly lit communal room. Refusing all offers of food or drink or anything to read. Her back to the television. Not joining in with the games or the Tod banter.

Would he be any better?

'Not a chance,' he mutters out loud.

He feels such a traitor. No matter what anyone says. He should have never let them take her away. If he'd only known they'd not let him go visiting.

But then, no one knew what was coming.

He watches as a couple come slowly across the car park, stopping whenever a car comes along. The old guy has a stick and can hardly walk more than five yards before he has to stop for a breather. His wife is younger, more mobile, but patiently waiting at each stop.

They're dressed in that Borders way. A bit of tartan somewhere. His scarf, her skirt. Ordinary folk.

He glances in the mirror. His hair's still there. Only a touch of grey. His eyes their usual bizarre configuration. One green. One blue.

As a young child he didn't really get it at first when other kids stared at him, and there were a few scuffles before they knew not to make fun. Or pretend to be scared of the 'alien'.

As a teenager he used it on the girls, but then as a copper they came in handy for disconcerting people. It's not that he practised glaring in the mirror, but just knowing what the first effect would be was quite useful.

'And nowhere as scary as Ellie's stare,' he whispers to the windscreen.

He thinks of his first 'granddaughter'. Those strange pale green eyes. Her haughty presence, which often crumbles into a giggling naughtiness. Always on the brink. Expecting to do well in her A levels, and not entirely reassured by the promise of a university place without actually achieving the estimated grades.

And what else would such a person choose but psychology? Although having weird visions and second sight might prove a bit of a challenge for her lecturers. He grins. There's no blood of his in her veins, but he likes to think she's imbibed some of his awkwardness and desire for the truth.

Louisa appears, pushing her trolley.

He still finds the image unbelievable and disconcerting, although she dismisses his sniggering, saying she enjoys the role and how it allows her to meet her friends.

Friends who previously wouldn't be seen dead in such places, let alone pushing the trolley themselves.

But, as she comes nearer, he sees her face.

Is something wrong?

He gets out of the car and goes to help.

She doesn't make eye contact, but allows him to empty the trolley and put it away.

It's only when he gets back in that she turns to look at him.

The blue eyes are hard.

But then she shakes her head and a tear runs down her cheek.

He knows.

CHAPTER 20

Jeanie shakes herself.

What's going on here?

One minute it's like a scenario of the end of the world, where she's the last person alive. The next thing the house is full of people.

Some she knows or thought she knew. Other's she's met before, and then there's a gang of strangers.

Any sense of social distancing goes out of the window.

Apart from anything else, going from two people to a houseful is scary for her. Coming here was her plan to stay safe.

First there's the homecoming of Randolph Ballantyne.

The doctors at the BGH have decided he'll be safer at home, especially when they found out that Jeanie was shacked up there. He's come with a stack of pills and limited advice, probably thinking she'll know very well how to deal with him.

Now he's standing there in the drawing room looking out of the windows at the hills … singing.

Children's songs.

One after the other.

Some she knows, but has forgotten she knew them. Others, in Scots-Romani, she thinks might be what her mother used to sing.

She tries talking to him, but he ignores her.

She brings him cups of tea, but he doesn't touch them. Offers him food. Chocolate? Oh, aye, he's up for that.

It's only when she thinks that she'll have to call the health centre again that she realises he's stopped singing.

She goes back to the room. He's gone. She searches downstairs, goes upstairs, and finds him lying on the floor in his bedroom, shivering and muttering to himself. She gives up trying to communicate with him and covers him with a blanket. Goes to the phone and rings the health centre.

They're not much help, but point out that he has a private doctor, which she didn't know. They can't be sure which one, but make a few suggestions and offer a couple of numbers.

It's the third call before she finds the right one. He says he'll come as soon as he can, but meanwhile she's to leave him on the floor and keep him warm.

She does that and then hears some knocking downstairs so goes running down.

To see faces at the door.

She opens up.

It's the detective inspector whose name she can't remember, but with an elderly couple. Some dogs are whining and barking in the back of a Land Rover out on the drive.

Magda reintroduces herself and her parents and asks to speak to Randolph.

Jeanie tries to explain and Magda goes up to see him.

Jeanie invites the older couple into the kitchen, makes them some tea, and asks if they want anything to eat. The detective's mother, Helena, says she's starving and offers to help. The father, George, looks as lost as many of the men in the care home.

Magda comes back downstairs looking worried.

'When did he start behaving like that?' she asks.

Jeanie explains what's happened.

Magda shakes her head and then tells her what's happened to them.

Jeanie can't believe it.

Magda asks,

'Can we stay?'

Jeanie doesn't know what to say.

'Well, I suppose so,' she manages, but then explains her worry. How she stopped going to the home because of her condition.

Magda listens and then says she doesn't think there's much chance that she or her parents have had any chance of contracting the virus.

Jeanie gives in, just as she remembers she's lying.

The doctor comes wearing a face mask and gloves.

He can't explain the condition, but he gives Randolph some pills and they calm him down.

He asks when it began and Jeanie tells him of his disappearance and brief hospitalisation.

The doctor shakes his head and phones the hospital. Come back with a worried face.

'They think he must have had a fright, I think,' he mutters. 'Some kind of shock. Without knowing what's happened, it's difficult to know what to do. They recommend letting him sleep. Maybe he'll come round.'

He asks who everyone else is and frowns at the unbelievable tale the policewoman tells him. He goes back out to the car and returns with a box of gloves and face masks. Suggests they ring 111.

Jeanie shows the three visitors the bedrooms and gets some linen. Not from the store upstairs, though. She's found a smaller stash in the second bedroom.

She and Helena begin to prepare a meal.

Soon they're chatting like old friends, talking about people they both know, although most of them are from Jeanie's mother's generation. There's also a couple of these ladies who are now in the home where Jeanie works … worked.

George is watching some history programme on the TV in the living room.

Magda asks if she can use the phone and then asks for the password for the computer connection. Jeanie has no idea, but they find it on Randolph's desk.

She contacts Ziggy and tells him what's happened. He says he'll keep in touch and arrange for food and stuff.

He says he's heard nothing about the two thugs – there's nothing on the police chatter yet – but he does tell her what happened when Becket and the other two went to find the man who mends the rifles and their suspicions about him.

After all this she finds herself sitting staring at the screen.

Where are her brother and that woman?

What's happened to the two thugs?

She goes to find her mother.

She's in the kitchen with Jeanie, who's taking a good look at her wrists. Magda feels awful when she sees the livid bruises.

'Why didn't you tell me?' she demands.

Helena shrugs.

'Where did you say they took you?' she asks.

Realising she's blocked it from her mind, Helena frowns. She shudders. Magda feels awful and puts her arms round her.

The shuddering gradually stops.

'Somewhere beyond Stow,' she mutters, 'in a lay-by not far from Eleanor and Kenneth's house, I think.'

Magda hesitates. Who best to tell?

She tries Rico's number. It's engaged. She wonders about asking Ziggy, but what would she say?

'Hi, Zigs. Can you send in the medics? My mum's just taken out a couple of Russian gangsters. They're probably both dead.'

Maybe not.

She goes back to the kitchen.

To find a strange woman standing by the back door.

The woman has long dyed black hair, weirdly streaked with

blue stripes, black clothes and boots, but, most astonishingly, is wearing a half-face mask that is glinting in the light.

Jeanie introduces her, thinking this is getting beyond real. Now there are four extra people. And three dogs.

Carole goes upstairs with Magda to see Randolph, but he's sleeping so they leave him alone.

***

When she was younger Magda used to say her brother had a woman in every port.

As she got older, she came to think this was neither true nor a good thing.

But it's not far off the truth.

Tomasz Steil is a womaniser, although he would say that he just prefers the company of women.

He's always adored his mother and was the one who wanted to hear her tales of derring-do. The running through the streets with men in black leather coats chasing them with dogs. The hiding in coal bunkers and bread ovens. And the stealing eggs and cabbages from the allotments and milking the cows in their sheds.

All this was amazing, although cabbage stew is never going to be his favourite dish.

So he became a soldier, not because of his father's stories of the desert and the Rhine crossings, but because he was inspired by his mother's backstreet running.

He's met dark-skinned kids who are still doing that, their dark eyes brimming with excitement and raw courage. Depending which side they chose to be on at that moment they would ask for food or want to cut your throat in your sleep.

Now he's decided to lie low and avoid the manhunt, to wait for a future opportunity to take out a few of the real villains. He knows where they live.

He needs another woman, of course.

Fortunately she's nearby.

Literally over the hill and not far away.

Somewhere he can hide in plain sight … well not exactly 'plain' sight, more 'hiding under her skirts'.

The ride is stiff uphill, but the mare is strong.

At the top you can see the change in the trees. All the other plantations around are for spruce and industrial wood-growing.

But beneath him, lying like a great green shawl, is a much richer and varied forest. Beech and tall sequoias, non-native species from all over the world. Japanese maples next to Canadian pines, and he knows further down there's a valley full of other strange plants … exotic rhododendrons and azaleas. Some of them will be flowering right now.

He takes one last glance back at the old man's inherited resting place. He can't stop a smile. How appropriate and how right for him to be gifted such a spot.

He doubts whether Imelda will stay there for long. No doubt the lure of the drugs and the underground scene will call her back to the big city, but he doesn't fear for her safety. She's got a wicked streak and that will keep her alive.

He nudges the mare gently and urges her downhill.

The woman he's going to is not expecting him, and he knows the returning soldier will be given a rough ride.

'So what's not to like?' he mutters to himself, and gives the mare her head down the slope.

Hengist follows joyfully, picking his own way.

It takes a good couple of hours before he's down by the river. The same river that flows past the Romany camp and the same one that flows beneath his parents' house.

He lets the mare Caro drink her fill. Hengist follows suit.

The pool is a serene oasis midst the beech-covered banks. New saplings are springing up all around. Violets are winking and primroses are grinning at him. There's a fallen tree lying across the beck as it bustles on down to the bigger river.

As he gathers his breath the soft silence thickens the air before birds start to rustle and fly again. Quick calls and glancing slivers of colour.

Victoria's house is downstream. The road travels along the other side of the valley. He can hear the occasional car rumbling past, but that's not his route.

He follows a half-hidden track on this side of the river, which the horse picks her way along with care. He urges her gently but lets her choose her pace over the slippery rocks.

The old house, when it appears through the trees, which are mainly holly and old ash here, is blurred among the branches and the rocky cliffside. It's been here a long time, three hundred years or more.

The horse deftly picks the narrow path above the waterfalls and across broken screes, while Hengist stumbles and lunges a more adventurous route, until eventually the ground slopes away to a grassy bank.

He lets the horse stop and snuffle at the rich green turf. Calls softly to Hengist to come by as he sets off, following a criss-cross of trails. He's not best pleased, but stands and waits.

Tomasz knows there will be at least one other horse and two or three dogs.

He listens.

The wood settles on his shoulders, gradually releasing their tension.

The sun has gone from this ravine, but he knows the house gardens begin a few yards around the bend.

He steps down onto the turf and calls Hengist. With his ears cocked and his eyes flickering this way and that, the dog comes reluctantly.

He strokes the horse's damp neck and fondles her ears. She flicks his hand away. She too, is wary. Many unknown scents are wafting her way.

He leaves her there and walks with Hengist to heel.
The barking and baying begins the second they come out into the last rays of the sun coming over the roof and chimneys of the house.

He waits while the dogs come tumbling towards him. Four of them. Two deerhounds, a collie, and a little Jack Russell.

He stands still, talking quietly to Hengist, who is bristling and growling.

It's probably only a few moments, but it feels like one of those shootouts in a western with the clock ticking down.

Then there's a loud, stern voice.

'Bala.'

One of deerhound's ears flicker and then its head jerks to look back.

A large figure comes through the bushes.

The dog looks back at the intruders and snarls.

'Oh, it's you, you crazy bastard,' the woman growls.

The two them stand looking at each other.

He's hoping she's forgiven him for whatever he did the last time he was here. She's looking like she's making a long list.

'Victoria, darling,' he tries. 'Any chance of a brew?'

She laughs.

All her dogs look her way.

'Haway, yer daft hounds. 'Tis jest a banshee cam to haunt us.'

He smiles.

Her dogs trundle about in disappointment, until eventually there's some bum-sniffing from them and tummy exposing from Hengist, while the two humans manage a gruff hug.

Ten minutes later, Victoria – her name is never shortened in any way if you wanted to stay her friend – is stirring some broth on her Aga.

Caro has been brought through into the big meadow and is snuffling with her new companions, while the dogs have tired of the rough and tumble and are now lying dotted in various spots about the yard and the hall.

Victoria's kitchen is one of those old-style high-ceilinged baronial caverns with a flagged floor, which in bygone days would be busy with servants. But now it's just the two of them, eyeing each other up before the inevitable battle of wills.

'So, Maister Breck, which army is pursuing ye the now?'

Tomasz ignores the cod Stevenson allusion.

'I'm afraid it's the real polis,' he says, 'and maybe a clutch of Russkies as well.'

She gives him a slit-eyed stare.

'Well, I'm not sure I want to know,' she says. 'How far behind?'

Tomasz sighs.

'I've no idea. And, as it happens, I'm not guilty this time.'

She pulls a face and shakes her head.

'That's one thing you're never going to be, so tell me what they think you've done.'

'Killed Donald Cameron,' he murmurs.

She looks to see if he's kidding her, but sees the hard face.

'Um, not sure that's a crime or worthy of another medal.'

He nods.

'So do you know who did kill him? Amelia?'

He smiles.

'No. It might have been a man called Kemball.'

She frowns.

He shakes his head.

She brings over the soup and places it before him, grabs two glasses and a bottle of wine from the fridge, and sits down opposite him.

'So why? Other than that the bastard deserved it?'

He took a couple of gulps of the soup.

'To frame me.'

'Why for?'

'It's a long story.'

She pours the wine.

'Now, why is it I'm not surprised about that?'

Later, the big door is shut and bolted.

The horses have been fed and put into the barn. The dogs are arranged in various postures like satiated old Roman diners, while the two humans are by the fire in the grand salon, which is one of those big Georgian monsters with an old grate and a stack of logs cut from the trees on the estate. Shadows are dancing on the old teak and beech furniture.

Tomasz is slumped on one of the ancient brocaded settees doing his best laudanum- overdosed impression of his namesake Chatterton, while Victoria's sitting on the carpet with her back to the big armchair. They've not put the lights on, but are watching each other in the flickering light of the fire, which has stopped spitting and roaring and has now settled down to some serious heat manufacture.

'So ...' she says with a sigh, 'let me attempt to summarise your recent exploits.'

He closes his eyes.

'You're on leave, possibly about to be decommissioned – again – and then you are approached by this man Kemball who asks you to bump off some English Tory twerps ... but then he compromises your chances by ridding the world of a snivelling bully, so that now you have to keep moving from one shag stop to another to avoid the termination of your womanising life.'

He opens his eyes.

'Being able to reduce any story to one sentence... That's a great example of the importance of a good private education.'

'I don't think spending eleven years of my life being beaten and sexually abused by evil, lecherous nuns was a 'good' experience, but pain clarifies a lot of things.'

He stares at her.

'So that's where you learnt how to hurt people?'

She grins like a Cheshire cat.

'Oh, yes, both emotional and physical distress.'

His answering smirk slowly softens to a frown.

'Do you like Leonard Cohen?'

She stares at him.

'You mean that dreary old Jewish moaner?'

Tomasz grins.

'Yeah, him.'

She shakes her head at him.

He's quiet for a few moments.

'I met this old woman on Hydra.'

'You mean the island?'

'Yeah. Have you been?'

She shakes her head again.

'Well, she met him, knew him when he lived there.'

'Too old for you, then?' she laughs.

'Actually … no…'

She stared at him.

'You mean…?'

'Uh-huh.'

He gets up and gets another drink for them both.

'She knows all his songs. That's how we met. She was doing her set one night in a bar.'

Again Victoria can't think where this is going.

He goes to sit opposite to her.

'You've heard the song called "Dance Me to the End of Love"?'

She nods.

There's this line that goes, "Dance me to your burning violin".'

She nods again.

'It's about what happened at the Nazi death camps. Some of the prisoners were allowed to play classical music while their fellow prisoners were being killed and burnt.'

She stares back at him.

But he's looking through her.

The air thickens. Even the fire seems to be holding its breath.

'Every thread is torn...' he says, in a curious hoarse voice.

She thinks he's going to weep, but he doesn't. His eyes harden.

He focuses on her, then smiles. But it's false somehow.

She can't think what to say.

They're both silent and still for a moment. Their eyes are locked in a curious knot.

He shakes his head and struggles up to an upright position.

'Have you got a mobile?'

She frowns back.

'What's happened to yours?'

He shakes his head.

'Don't have one. Can't abide the little buggers, people always knowing where you are.'

'So why do you want one now?'

'Got to phone *Mamusia*.'

She continues to stare, thinking that after all, he's only a lost boy.

'But then they'll be able to trace you to here, to me.'

He frowns.

'Yeah, you're right.'

They both go silent.

'How about you call her, worrying if they're all right in the lockdown?'

Victoria gives this some thought,

'Um, I suppose I could do that.'

Again there's a long pause while she stares at him.

But eventually she gets up and goes back into the kitchen, retrieves her old mobile and comes back.

She flicks through her contacts and presses a button.

'OK, what am I saying?' she asks.

'Just checking how they are. Don't mention me,' he suggests.

She puts the phone to her ear, but then frowns.

'Unobtainable,' she says.

'How do you mean?'

'The line is dead,' she mutters. 'Have your parents got mobiles?'

He shakes his head, thinks of Magda, but has no idea what her number might be. But then he thinks of Gavin, whose number he knows off by heart.

Victoria taps it in and calls.

It's answered eventually and Tomasz has to listen to her end of the conversation, which is a series of her saying 'Yes,' and 'No,' and 'Really?'

She finishes the call and shakes her head at Tommy, whose frown has been getting harder all through the one-sided exchanges.

'What?' he demands.

'Well, they're OK. Gone to stay with old Randy Ballantyne. Trouble with their connection and he's not well, apparently.'

'Who's not well?'

'Randy.'

This doesn't help Tomasz at all.

'My mother hates the old goat.'

Victoria pulls a face.

'I don't know, and Gavin wasn't too impressed either, but that's what's happened.'

Tomasz frowns.

'Doesn't seem likely to me … except I think Magda's been

up there recently. Some old biddy disappeared from the care home down near the bridge.'

They're both quiet.

One of her dogs gets up and turns round before settling again with a sigh.

The silence expands. Neither of them is trying to make eye contact. They know what usually happens next. Both of them are a bit disconcerted after hearing the strange news about his parents.

Eventually he looks across at her.

She's already looking at him.

The fire is starting to die down, so the light is fading to a red glow.

He stares at her.

She hasn't changed much since he first knew her back in their teenage years. They've had a few feisty encounters along the way. More banter than sex. He can't remember the last time. Some years ago.

The firelight picks out highlights in her golden red hair. She's never gone in for different hairstyles, so it still a mass of tumbling curls, and has probably not been brushed since she got up this morning. Her freckled cheeks are sunburnt even now. Does she winter abroad? Her forearms are freckled as well and her hands are somewhat raw. She's bigger than the average bear, he's reminded. Taller than him by more than a couple of inches. More heavily built, and with the ample chest of a farmer's wife.

But it's her eyes that hold his gaze.

'The emerald eyes of a true Highland lassie,' He grins.

She frowns... and gets to her feet. Hesitates and then goes to fetch the bottle of Highland Park, which he's pleased to see is still her preferred tipple.

Nothing is said as they take a dram, her standing, him still on the settee, but then she puts down her glass and gives him a haughty sneer.

'Well, I guess we've already totally failed at the social distancing palaver, so we may as well go the whole hog, don't you think?'

He grins and gets up.

'Only if you promise to be gentle with me.'

She stares at him.

'Whenever do you think I'd do that?'

***

Later, while their two bodies lie cooling in the grand bed, in that other valley over the hill another body is already cold.

Old Major Tom had survived more tours than most squaddies. He'd picked up a couple of long service medals, which lie abandoned in a drawer somewhere.

He'd mended a shedload of guns and other broken equipment, and bedded not a few lassies.

Now he's come home to live out his days mending farm equipment and tools, the odd restoration and a few new bits and pieces.

He's happy to have inherited his uncle's old place, which he's already brought back from the wreck the miserable old bugger had died in.

And just now young Captain Steil had brought him a fine filly, although she might be the death of him.

But death doesn't come when you want or how. Sometimes he comes as a whisper. A few coughs and you're gone. Sometimes you might not even hear the whisper. He's seen men die in the middle of a laugh. And others taking days in agony, before giving up the fight with a dreadful rattle.

The girl was out on her horse.

He turned to see the figure in the doorway, blocking out most of the light.

Death was polite.

Even when he was screaming in agony. The blindness at least saved the terrible knowing what might come next.

But he told him nothing. Didn't know where the captain had gone. Never knew. He always came and went like the desert wind.

Now old Tom's lying on the kitchen floor, oblivious to the cold gradually settling into his old bones, gathering him in like the sea.

The man was gone. He has taken one of the horses and is now halfway up the slope. He looks back, wondering where the woman might be, but nothing moves other than the sheep and horses and the windblown birds.

Imelda watches from the copse at the edge of the road.

She realises something is wrong as she comes back down the cleuch. There was no smoke climbing into the wind from the smithy. The old man never lets it out until dusk.

Now she can see the murderer slowly making his way up the hill, roughly following the route Tomasz went this morning. What can she do? He's not told her where he was going. He never does.

She waits until the man disappears and then half an hour more, by which time it's dark.

She goes down to the darkened building, finds the old feller's broken and crumpled body, and sees the black holes where the old rheumy eyes had wept.

She finds the keys for the van, takes an hour or so to stuff it full of the old lady's clothes and trinkets.

With a last look round the empty kitchen she retreats, closes the door, and goes to find a different horse. One to take her back to another old man, who'll maybe be better at keeping her alive.

She takes one last look up the hill and wishes Tommy good luck.

He'll need it.

***

In another darkened room, way over towards the sea, sits yet another old man.

He's finished with the endless phone calls, the messages of condolence, awkward silences on awkward Skypes, which he hates at the best of times.

And this is the worst of times.

Laura is dead.

Even the three words don't make sense.

How is it possible?

Why isn't he there?

'They' have all stopped him going to her. To be with her.

But then no one was there. Not Grace. Not Ellie. She died alone.

He knows that's not true, that there would have been nurses. They'd organised one last Skype with her, which Ellie, of course, refused to do.

She died while he was skulking in another woman's house. Sleeping in her bed. Feeling her warmth beside him, while Laura went cold.

People said she didn't know him or anyone else any more. Her eyes frowned at him the last time he went to see her. He told her he loved her. She looked away. Stared at the television.

Now he is truly alone.

MAY

CHAPTER 21

I was still in bed when Ziggy must have got the call.

Dreaming about that tower going up in fire and smoke.

That one glimpse of my mother's face. Pale, short hair.

I come awake with a shudder, telling myself it's only a dream.

I go for a pee and then realise Ziggy's already up and at the screens.

I take him a mug of tea.

He's on some police site. I can see the logo. Think it's Manchester.

He nods at the screen.

'They've found James Kemball,' he says. 'In our office.'

'Our office?' I'm thinking, 'It wouldn't look like that if I had any say in it.'

What's that on the floor? A bag of some sort?

'He's been there for some time, apparently. Probably a couple of weeks.'

A couple of weeks.

'They're going to have to fumigate it when they've finished. It stinks. It's only because the guy in the shop downstairs came to check on it, as he's been closed since lockdown, that he noticed the smell. Otherwise he wouldn't have been found yet.'

I can't believe it.

Why would he end up there?

'Trying to implicate us, I suppose. They say he must have been killed elsewhere and brought there in the body bag.'

I'm thinking this through.

'So how did they know it was him?' I ask.

'They had photos of him on their files and there was a wallet and other stuff.'

I'm still trying to take this in.

'Anyway, they've checked us out and realised we were up here at the time of death, but they're still sending someone to ask us a few questions.'

Ziggy turns back to his screens with a frown on his face. Is something else troubling him?

I go to make some breakfast.

When I take him a bacon sarnie and another mug of tea, he's sitting staring the screen.

No photos. Only a timeline, dates, and photos.

'What you thinking?' I ask.

'Um,' he says. 'Well, there's one thing that Magda won't like. If the police are right, Kemball can't have shot Cameron because he was already dead.'

I stare at the screen.

'So that puts her brother back in the frame?'

He nods.

'I'm afraid so.'

He picks up one of his phones and makes a call.

It's Magda he's calling.

The conversation is brief.

He says he's still heard nothing about the 'men up the road'.

'What men up the road?' I ask.

He tells me.

I stare at him.

'You mean Magda's mum?'

He nods.

'But … how old is she?

'Sixty something, I imagine.'

I shake my head.

I can see the little wheels going round. He whizzes about on a couple of screens, showing black-and-white pictures. War zones. The Berlin Wall coming down.

Red and white flags. The Solidarity movement. Poland was the first eastern bloc state to come out from under Russian domination. In 1989.

'She'd have been in her late teens, early twenties, when Solidarity began,' he says.

I'm puzzled by this. What's that got do with anything?

'If she was there, she might have been involved. Teenagers and twenty-somethings created a lot of spirited and violent disruption. She would have seen all sorts of things. Maybe she knows how to use a gun.'

I can't take this in. I've not met the woman, but old ladies in their mid sixties don't go round killing Russian thugs, do they?

***

The irony of Tomasz Steil's reputation as a troublemaker is that although he causes a lot of trouble, he rarely gets involved in sort of the mayhem that happened on the island of Hydra. He may be able to kill people one and half miles away, but close-up physical violence is not really his thing at all.

In the latest ruckus in that Greek taverna he spent most of the time under a table with the waitress who, it has to be said, caused the trouble in the first place by being overfamiliar with the profligate British soldiers.

But Henry Ballard doesn't know this.

So when the trail ends in a narrow gorge downstream from the botanical garden centre, he stops and looks at his map. Not many possibilities. There are maybe ten houses in the near vicinity. Most of them are small cottages. If his target is true to form he's more likely to know the people in his own class, the ones with big houses.

He dismisses the huge rambling buildings associated with the health spa the other side of the road and spies the large property with the long drive and the ruins of a historic site in its grounds, which looks like it belongs to really old money.

He leaves the horse to its own devices and sets off through a narrow defile.

Although he might be reluctant to proceed with a horse, he soon spots the recent evidence of his target's advance.

He stops and considers his approach.

He knows the man has a dog and it's likely that the owner of this grand property will have them as well. Probably big dogs. Although night-time might be good in some ways, it's also the most likely time to arouse sleeping dogs. Better to wait. Go back and gain some height. Neither he nor his paymasters are fussy about how the man dies, and there would be a certain synchronicity in him being killed from a distance. Maybe he can't emulate the man's extreme ability, but a few hundred metres won't be a problem. After all, the most recent target was more than a thousand metres. One shot.

He retreats, remounts the horse, and sets off back up the hill.

***

Sex with Victoria has always been a challenge.

Big women who prefer to be on top are dangerous for your pelvis, your spine, your thighs, and most of your internal organs.

So when the first bout is over, he's glad to be still alive.

They lie there like two hippos wallowing in their own sweat.

Eventually he manages to heave himself into a sitting position and looks down on her still pulsating body.

'And when was the last time you were serviced, madam?'

She flaps a lazy flipper at him and drowsily opens her eyes.

'Impossible to get the proper *traitement* round here. They're all too damn thin. Even the ones who come to give away wads of cash to the leeches across the road are generally too feeble to last the course.'

He grins and reaches for the bottle on the floor, takes a swig and then lies back down to look at the ceiling.

'I expect it's closed for now,' he murmurs.

She nods.

'Of course. Why? Do you want a workout?'

He snorts.

'Don't be daft ... when I can come to you.'

This time her arm has more intent.

But then they are quiet for a while.

The house settles around them. There's no wind outside, so it's not resorting to its usual groans and sighs.

The darkness unthickens and a blowsy moon appears at the window.

Staring like loons, they both watch it floating among its minions of stars.

A dog reassembles its limbs at the foot of the bed.

'Penny for them,' he says.

She looks at him with the moonlight flickering in her eyes and then lies back.

He waits.

'He is patient as she tries to arrest time
suspend now for ever
to feel the intensity of the only vivid existence

then he breaks it with a look ... a smile ... and it's over
they go their separate journeys ...
but he carries her mark ...
fading but indelible ...

only the lies will haunt us.'

He waits, her eyes are open, but they're staring elsewhere.

'Who's that?' he asks quietly, not recognising the author at all.

'Me,' she says.

Later, after a gentler exchange, he falls into a dead sleep.

She listens to his breathing.

How can a man be a cold-blooded killer and such a gentle lover?

***

A few hundred feet above the house, Ballard finds an old shaft, which not only has a covered entrance but a handy rock to steady his aim.

He can make out the entrance gates and the Land Rover to the right. Outhouses and gardens stretch away down to the river. He can't see it, but in the silence of the windless night he can hear the distant tumbling of the water.

He settles down and waits for the dawn, although the moonlight is bright enough to see what he needs to know.

He checks the time and sets an alarm, although he doubts they'll be up that early, given the man's insatiable appetite.

He's disabled the landline and Internet. If his mobile is anything to go by the coverage there is non-existent.

He thinks of his own wife. No doubt she's snuggled up with that bastard from the gym. Well, little do they know. Their sordid lives have only been put on hold...

Which reminds of his own latest little sordid encounter. The trackers had finally figured out Steil's escape route, which led him to the phone under the woman's car. And he'd enjoyed her pathetic neediness to tell him all, until her struggling resistance petered out. In any case they'd figured out where he was heading for, although to be honest the old feller was a much tougher nut to crack. Not a word. Just one glance up the hillside to give him a clue.

He thinks of James Kemball. Poor bastard. All that effort for a 'noble' cause. Like that's gonna happen. Mind you, his little list was a bit of shock to the big yins. They hadn't contemplated such an ambitious clear-out. Interestingly, 'the fag' was the only one on their false list as well. Shame, really, the nasty little two-faced bastard that he is.

***

In another ancestral home thirty miles downstream, Magda can't sleep.

Her mind is racing, hopping from one problem to another.

What's going to happen to her mother? Did she really kill those two thugs? Does it mean that all her tall stories of murder and mayhem in Krakow were true?

What's going on with her father? He's seems suddenly to have deteriorated. Should she have got him out more instead of leaving him buried in his genealogical maze? Hunting for what? A glorious past?

And what's happening to Randolph? He's not her favourite man, but he's lost as well.

And who is that weird woman insinuating her way into his life, his house? Is she a gold-digger? How would she get her hands on his money? And where are his ex-wife and the daughter nowadays?

And where's Edith MacDonald? There's only been a couple of days' rain for a month at most. A trapped body all that time under water?

How's Rico getting on with all those men in black crawling all over the place? What or who are they looking for, apart from Tomasz? And where is he?

And what's going to happen with Amelia? And her children?

And who are all those people in the houses across the river? Are they still here? Who is the man with Louisa Cunninghame? What was his name again?

***

Eventually it's been agreed that Fletcher and Louisa can travel back for the funeral, but that there can only be two other people present, who are likely to be Grace and Ellie. This the work of Louisa pulling strings he couldn't bear to think about.

In the car Fletcher hasn't spoken since they set off.

Louisa doesn't mind driving in the dark, and in any case the roads are eerily empty. They are stopped twice. Louisa murmurs a few names, calls are made, and then they're waved on, but with stony faces.

Even so, it doesn't take as long as usual and it's just getting dawn as she turns up the hill.

Laura's wish was that she should be buried in the cemetery next to their house,

'So that I can continue to keep an eye on you.'

He can see the old pub, their home, with its white-painted walls mocking the sullen indifference of the blackened church that blocks the view of the hills across the valley … while from the cemetery you can see the slope all the way up to the Pike.

Fletcher stands looking out over the valley as Louisa waits by the car.

'I never thought she'd go before me,' he says quietly.

Louisa comes to stand by him.

'None of us choose, you know,' she says.

He nods and allows her to put his arm through his.

They stand there until the sun tries to rise up over the moors, but then the clouds come down.

The funeral is at ten o'clock.

It's raining. Drizzle moving steadily up to deluge.

Only the four of them are there.

He's numb when Grace puts her arms round him and kisses his tear-stained face.

But he can't meet Ellie's eyes. Can't hold her. Can't even look at her, knowing the green-eyed look will destroy him.

The ceremony is mercifully short.

Grace delivers a brief, heart-breaking speech.

Ellie reads 'Wind' by Ted Hughes.

'This house has been far out at sea all night ...'

They all weep.

The cars trundle up the steep hill back to the cemetery. The church and the pub and the rain.

One of the bearers stumbles on the slippery little steps, but the coffin doesn't fall.

There a few other people all standing apart. Trying hard to hang on to umbrellas in the blustery wind and the nithering rain.

Fletcher can't see them, can't acknowledge their presence.

The coffin is lowered into the hole.

Ellie says a few more words.

He can't hear them.

The rain is dripping down his face.

And then they leave him standing there alone.

Until another figure comes close.

It's Cassie, her hair more white than blue and black these days, hanging wet and limp like a mermaid.

She puts her hand on his arm.

He shudders, but manages to look at her, thank her for going to see Laura in the hospice.

She smiles and then opens her gloved fist to give him something. It's a crumpled playing card. Folded in four. He opens it. The two of hearts. The letters F and L are drawn crookedly in spidery handwriting, but the hand is still recognisably Laura's.

He stares at Cassie.

'A nurse found it in her pocket after she died.'

He doesn't remember much more of that day and falls asleep in the car going back up north.

It's not quite dark when they get back and so he insists on

going for a walk to the river, where he stands staring sightlessly at the water.

The rain has stopped.

'No tears for us,' he mutters again, and then for some reason remembers what Adversane had quoted.

For a fleeting moment he wonders if the old villain really is dead. . . after all he was always a bit of ghostly presence.

Eventually Louisa comes and persuades him back to the house.

He doesn't remember anything at all after that.

***

Although dawn is before six this time of year, the sun doesn't reach the windows of Victoria's bedroom until well past eight o'clock.

The two bodies don't stir until the light starts to slide across the man's face. He blinks and rubs his eyes, gradually remembering where he is. Victoria's hair is like a waterfall of gold across the pillow.

He stares at the motes he's disturbed that are now swirling about in the sunbeam.

A slurry voice murmurs from underneath the duvet,

'Black, two sugars.'

He sniggers.

'Yes, your highness, I'm on my way.'

The hair disappears in a flurry of movement. The motes go crazy.

He finds an old dressing gown on the back of the door and makes his way downstairs via the loo.

In the kitchen he's greeted by a pack of hounds, all his best friend.

He opens the door and lets the morning air swirl round, which makes him shiver.

The dogs are in two minds about something, but, seeing he seems to have no immediate interest in them, they decide to empty their bladders instead.

He finds the coffee and sets up the pot. The Aga's still warm. A couple of logs and it's flaring again, so he's time to feed the 'wolves'.

Afterwards, waiting for the coffee, he stands at the open door, watching the birds quartering the huge courtyard competing with the chickens among the dust and the gravel. Flowers are sprouting in all the borders although most are not yet flowering, so are difficult to identify. Some vivid red poppies and a lively gaggle of lavender are the only two he knows for sure.

'You live well, don't you?' he quotes, from some film he can't remember.

He reflects that he was also brought up in another beautiful place, but not like this. Here the trees are mainly deciduous. Beech and ash and couple of huge sequoia, no doubt filched from the nearby botanical gardens. A couple of maples and some of those trees with black-and-white bark whose name he can't remember.

The coffee pot burbles to call him back inside.

He fills the mugs and grabs some biscuits from a glass jug.

After returning upstairs he shakes the dormant form into life and slips back under the covers to get warm again.

But after one sip she snuggles back down. Leaving him contemplating sunbeams again.

So what now? Where now? Stay put or run?

He wonders what's going on back at the ranch. How Magda is dealing with the fallout from Cameron's shooting. That look on his mother's face. The little man's list was fairly predictable, although he'd omitted the leading players, maybe thinking they'd be too well protected.

He frowns at this.

The Bullingdon boy and his thin controller have already

cleared out any vaguely coherent or more nuanced voices, getting rid of the people who prefer ambiguity and blurring of their intentions, and replacing them with some of the outright racist and far-right people who are on the list he was given.

And so now he's the fall guy? The latest distraction?

Which means they'll be still trying to find him.

No, that wouldn't do. What if he blabbed?

No, the Cameron shooting was setting him up so that he can be hunted down. His own weapon will be used as the evidence and then the little man's list will suddenly be found.

So the guy who killed Cameron is now after him, which almost certainly means that the little man is already dead.

He gets out of the bed.

Victoria grunts and wriggles into the shapes he leaves behind in the bed.

He goes downstairs and scuttles out to the barn, keeping close to the walls. Finds his gun where he hid it behind some bales, picks up the bag and goes back to the house.

If the guy has followed him from Major Tom's he'll be coming from behind the house, up the hillside. Maybe he's already in place. He's good enough at eight hundred metres, maybe better.

He goes into the main room and rekindles the fire, then goes back into the kitchen to find a dopey-looking Victoria making another pot of coffee. She sees his face and the gun and frowns.

'What's going on?' she asks, now more awake.

'I'm sorry, but I think someone's on my tail and they're not going to offer me any variable terms.'

She growls.

'You bastard. Why involve me?'

'I've only this minute worked it out. Too complicated to explain. I'm sorry.'

She stares at him.

'I'm going to get dressed and go and find him. You stay here.'

'And become collateral damage? No thanks, I'm ringing the police.'

'Too late, I suspect,' he says, and sets off back upstairs.

She curses and goes to the phone, picks it up, only to hear the dismal drone off the disconnected line. Then she looks for her mobile, finds it, and sees the no signal sign. It isn't much good at the best of times.

She looks down at her dressing gown and curses again.

Tomasz returns in his clothes, gun in hand.

'Have you got a gun?' he asks.

She nods.

'Of course. My father's.'

'Can you use it? Have you fired it recently?'

She makes a face.

'Two weeks ago.'

'OK,' he says. 'Get dressed, go up to the attic and wait. I'm going out to find him.'

'And what if you don't?'

He shrugs.

'I don't suppose your father left you his gun without teaching you how to use it.'

She glares at him, but he turns and is gone.

She does as he told her to do, but not without a lot of cursing and saying what she'll do to him afterwards.

Outside the side door, which is well hidden under the overhanging rock, Tomasz Steil reverts to his hunter role.

He runs back up under the cliffs along the riverbank the way he came down. He sees the spoors of the horse that isn't his and spots the returning tracks.

Running fast, bringing the terrain back into his mind's eye, he quickly clambers further along the gully, where there isn't a track, and on towards the botanical gardens. He heads uphill and back round above, needing to get well above the contours at five hundred feet, where he figures his hunter will have chosen to take up the best kill position.

Part of him knows the adrenaline will get him up the hill, but then he needs to stop and calm down, to revert to the hunter's colder regime.

Back at the big house, Victoria is following the instructions as she curses and swears what she'll do to the instructor.

She checks and loads her father's gun.

Then takes up a position at the top of the stairs with a view down below of the courtyard.

High above on the hillside the man sees only one suggestion of these manoeuvres, when earlier on he sees Steil go round to the barn and back. It's not clear enough for a shot, but he can wait.

It's only when nothing else happens that he starts to get twitchy.

Of course, there's no reason why they should come out now. Knowing his target's habits, he hasn't expected to see him so early.

There's no hurry.

Eventually he'll reappear. Going to the Land Rover on the far side of the courtyard is the best set-up. A clear shot. Less than six hundred feet away.

Then perhaps some fun with the lady friend. Muddy the waters afterwards.

Unlike his target, he's not used to the signs. The silence of the lambs, Tomasz has christened it. That moment when even the slowest-witted should realise that it's all gone quiet. No birds sing. The hunter has become the hunted.

Ballard frowns, then turns to look above and behind.

Nothing.

Merely a slight breeze up there.

He's not above the treeline, but there are not as many trees as lower down. A few scrubby bushes. He'd see anyone moving, or hear them, for sure.

He looks back at the house.

There's smoke now coming from the chimney.

They're probably having their breakfast.

But the thought of bacon and egg is his last, as his head blossoms like a bloody exploding melon.

SEPTEMBER

CHAPTER 22

We've been back home for nearly two weeks now.

We have had to suffer hours and hours of police interrogation.

Most of Ziggy's equipment has been confiscated, but he grins and says,

'Good luck,' to the hard-faced goons who search every nook and cranny of both our houses and the office.

So I'm surprised when I get a visitation one late afternoon.

Of course he's acquired new equipment, but what he's got to show me is all on one little stick.

At first I can't figure out what I'm looking at, but then realise it's a catalogue of newspaper headlines and the first few lines of reports. They are from different papers or online news sources.

Lancashire Evening Post
BODY FOUND AT PRIVATE INVESTIGATOR'S OFFICE

A man whose last known address was a cottage near Melrose, in the Scottish Borders, was found dead at a private investigator's office. He has been identified as James Kemball, who went missing from his home in Teesside over a month ago. Police are now satisfied that the owner and his associates are not involved and are continuing a murder investigation.

Border Telegraph
LOCAL WOMAN STILL MISSING

The body of Edith MacDonald is still missing, although it is assumed she must have been swept away in the Tweed after being reported missing from her care home.

The owners of the care home are adamant that all their procedures were followed to the letter and cannot explain as to how she could have left the grounds.

Southern Reporter

DISAPPEARANCE OF LOCAL LANDOWNER

Sir Randolph Ballantyne was last seen walking uphill in his garden towards the top gate, accompanied by a Ms Carole Morgan, who had only recently taken up residence in an estate cottage a mile away.

Sir Randolph was well known for his writings and research into Thomas the Rhymer and his stories about the Fairy Queen in her underground world beneath the Eildon Hills, which are above his house and estate.

Peeblesshire News

BODY FOUND NEAR STOBO

The body of a man was found in an old mining shaft above Stobo village. Although his remains were badly decomposed and disturbed by wildlife, forensic experts were able to identify him as Henry Ballard, former sergeant in the Royal Marines, reported missing by his wife at the beginning of May. As far as she knew, he had never been to Scotland in his life and could think of no reason for him to go there.

Scottish Daily Mail

TWO MEN FOUND DEAD NEAR STOW

Two men have been found shot dead in a lay-by north of Stow.

They have been identified as immigrants from Russia. Both men were known to the police as having connections with drug and prostitution gangs in Edinburgh.

Peeblesshire News

WOMAN FOUND RAPED AND MURDERED IN HER OWN HOME

Concerned neighbours alerted police to the disappearance of Doreen Naismith. Her body was found in the bedroom. She had been raped and strangled.

Daily Telegraph
MISSING SOLDIER
Police are continuing their search both here and abroad for the missing soldier, Captain Tomasz Steil, son of George and Helena Steil, who disappeared from his home while on leave from active service in Afghanistan. Captain Steil is a highly decorated soldier and member of an elite corps with a sniper record of over 200 kills.

Selkirk News
MAN FOUND MURDERED
The body of an ex-soldier, Ian McArthur, known affectionately by his comrades as 'Major Tom', was found dead in his workshop south of Peebles. Police have not yet released the cause of death.

Sunday Times
MURDER IN PARADISE
The financier and philanthropist Sir Henry Wyatt was found dead this morning at his house in Jamaica. It appears that he was shot. He was a well-known supporter and financial backer of the Conservative Party, who have expressed their shock and dismay.

He leaves a wife and six children.

I look up from the list to find Ziggy looking a tad bored.

'So … quite a roll call,' I offer.

He makes a sad face.

'Yes, but who else is making these connections?'

I'm still trying to take the list in.

'And how come Becket and her soldier guy, who happens to know where Major Tom lives, turned up three miles from White Cottage, with a woman desperately wanted by the secret service because she has a photographic memory, which isn't

true … and all this conveniently across the valley from one of the top long-range marksmen in the world?'

I can only shake my head and go for the kettle.

As I stand looking out at my overgrown garden, thinking I'll have to do something about it, he continues in an unusually passionate voice.

'The whole thing: a woman who can't forget things, the list of targets, the plots, Kemball . . . they're all part of the distractions to cover up what is really going on.'

I turn round. He's looking beyond me.

'Which is?'

He shrugs. It's only now that I realise his eyes are redder than usual. Far too much screen time, even for him.

'It's what Violet said. There is an obvious template. Germany 1930. A rabble rouser and his puppeteer, feeding people's prejudices, spreading lies and fabrications.'

What can I say?

He sighs and goes to the door, but then turns to look at me with a stern face.

'And … does anyone still believe in fairies?' he asks.

I can only manage a suspicious frown.

'And you were brought up in a religious family . . . am I right?'

So . . ?' I manage, images flickering uncontrollably though my mind.

'You'll remember the story about the Tower of Babel, then?' he added.

I allow him a cursory nod.

'But do you remember why they built it?'

'To save themselves from a second one,' I murmur.

'A Second Great Flood?' he asks with a smile.

Where is he going with this?

'So maybe 'there are more things in heaven and earth, Horatio, than are dreamt of in your philosophy.'

I actually know where this quote comes from, as I did it for A level, but I'm no Horatio and he's too sneaky to be Hamlet.

And of course he's gone before I can say any of that, though 'the rest is silence' is unlikely to happen with him.

It's only later that the penny drops.

Who was it who booked White Cottage in the middle of nowhere, who swears he's never been there before?

***

Magda looks out of the kitchen window.

Amelia's three older girls are running up and down the terraces.

Her mother is standing at the top watching with a big smile on her face, no doubt.

Amelia comes in after putting Hamish to bed.

She comes over and puts her arm round Magda's neck and kisses her on her cheek.

'I think the little bugger's gone,' she says.

They embrace.

Helena has surprised them by not being at all critical of this new relationship.

In fact, a couple of nights ago she regaled them again with stories about her and Zofia, back in the terrible days of their youth, which left them with little doubt about their feelings for each other.

She's only just come back from visiting George, who is finding it harder and harder to be too grumpy, now he's been allowed to have a lot of his books in the large room at the eye-wateringly expensive care home in Peebles.

She's also has survived the immediate aftermath of her kidnapping, including her interrogations by the Edinburgh police, which resulted in her being cleared of any criminal offence, given that the two men died from shots to the head, which they regard as evidence of gangland retribution … and two days ago she declared she didn't want to talk about it any longer, so that was that.

Magda knows that the local police are still not entirely convinced of her brother's innocence regarding the murder of Donald Cameron, but he's completely disappeared anyway.

She's had a few conversations with Jeanie Tait, who is still trying to come to terms with the windfall she's received from Randolph Ballantyne's will, although without a body yet and his daughter contesting it, she can't be sure what the outcome will be.

She remembers the last time she saw him. Walking like a much older man, supported by that strange woman with the mask on her face.

She did have one last contact with all those people on Zoom, but Violet says everyone's been gagged. *Omertà* is the only word on everyone's lips, without the least sense of irony.

***

It's getting late in the Edinburgh Grassmarket.

Lots of stallholders have already packed up and gone.

It's good that the market's open again.

Miriam comes back from the van to collect the last few boxes of clothes. As she begins to take down the last few racks, a voice calls from behind her.

'Nice-looking dresses you've got there.'

'Yeah,' she says, thinking perhaps it's a guy needing a 'Sorry I'm late' present.

She turns.

Sun-bleached hair.

Tanned face to die for.

Tomasz?

Bastard.

In case the reader can't remember the volume of lies and evasions told by the UK government during the course of this book's timeline, here is a list of some of the most 'memorable'.

1. 'We pay £350 million a week to the EU.' Brexit bus
2. 'The free trade agreement that we will have to do with the European Union should be one of the easiest in human history!' Liam Fox
3. "We've got a deal, oven-ready, by which we can leave the EU in just a few weeks." Boris Johnson
4. "The UK economy is performing strongly," said Kwasi Kwarteng, Conservative Business Minister, "much more strongly than the doom-mongers and naysayers have suggested."
5. 'There will be no forms, no checks, no barriers of any kind between Northern Ireland and the rest of the UK.' Boris Johnson
6. 'I think most of the work has already been done. We already start from a position where the EU and the UK is aligned, we're agreed on all the key principles.' Sajid Javid
7. 'The government's approach to tackling COVID.19 has the benefit of creating 'herd immunity' across the UK.' Sir Patrick Vallance Chief Scientific Officer. 13 March
8. 'I want herd immunity' Boris Johnson to the Italian Prime Minister. 13 March. At the time, up to 500,000 thousand deaths were being forecast in the UK.
9. 'The government initiated a speedy lockdown.' Even though at the first Coronavirus COBRA meeting Johnson attended on March he was told there were already 11,000 infections in the UK and that Imperial College modelling indicated

that 250,000 could die without a severe lockdown. The government ignored the call for another THREE weeks.

10. In the week before lockdown, large events such as the Cheltenham racing Festival – attended by 250,000 people over four days - went ahead, even though Imperial College and Oxford University modelling indicates that infections soared to 1.5 million before social distancing measures were introduced.

11. On 18 March, Johnson was still prevaricating. When asked when the virus' epicentre would be shut down, he said: 'We've always said that we are going to do the right measures at the right time.'

12. 2 April, Matt Hancock said that the government would conduct 100,000 COVID 19 tests a day by the end of August.

13. 'We have joined the EU's procurement scheme for ventilators and personal protection equipment.' Matt Hancock.

14. The Government said it was not a part of the PPE scheme, because 'we're no longer part of the EU.

15. The Government claimed it had miraculously reached its target of 100,000 tests. However 40,000 of the tests included in its figures had been sent to people's homes and not yet taken. Soon after, official testing figures dropped below 100,000.

16. Covid-19 Death statistics are accurate and transparent. For the first month of the pandemic, daily death reports from DHSC & NHS England only recorded hospitalised COVID-19. Care homes were not included until 16 April.

17. For seven weeks, the Government publicised comparing UK death tolls with other countries. These were dropped on 12 May when they showed that Britain had the highest death toll in Europe and the second highest in the world.

18. Due to limited COVID-19 testing, initially confined to hospitals, the UK has an estimated 65,700 'excess deaths - 49% above the historical norm, one of the highest in developed

countries. Britain has the highest case fatality in the world according to a study by John Hopkins University.

19. In late February Public Health England said it was 'very unlikely' care homes would become infected. The guidance was not withdrawn until six weeks later on 12 march.

20. By then, many untested patients had been discharged form hospital into care homes and the sector was at breaking point because of the number of infections and the lack of PPE for staff.

21. Speaking to reporters outside his home, Mr Cummings said: "I behaved reasonably and legally." When a reporter suggests his actions did not look good, he replies: "Who cares about good looks? It's a question of doing the right thing. It's not about what you guys think."

22. 'Too many care homes didn't really follow the procedures in the way that they could have,' Boris Johnson.

23. In his Downing Street rose garden press conference, Cummings told reporters: "Last year I wrote about the possible threat of coronaviruses and the urgent need for planning." The only problem was that this was added to his blog just after he broke lockdown on 18 April 2020. This rare case of 'retro-superforecasting' was spotted by Jens Wiechers, a data scientist, using the internet archives 'Wayback Machine.''

24. The Government promised to 'follow the science' at every turn. But the Scientific Advisory Group for Emergencies it relied upon had a shocking lack of relevant expertise with no molecular virologists, immunologists, intensive care experts, and (more importantly) public health experts. A former WHO director Anthony Costello said that "this could have cost thousands of lives."

Lightning Source UK Ltd.
Milton Keynes UK
UKHW011940251120
373986UK00010B/261